THORNBROOK PARK

SHERRI BROWNING

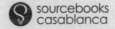
sourcebooks
casablanca

Published by Sourcebooks Casablanca, an imprint of Sourcebooks, Inc.
P.O. Box 4410, Naperville, Illinois 60567-4410
(630) 961-3900
Fax: (630) 961-2168
www.sourcebooks.com

Printed and bound in the United States of America.
QW 10 9 8 7 6 5 4 3 2 1

One

September 1906

MISTY FOG DRAPED LONDON LIKE A BRIDAL VEIL, obscuring Eve Kendal's first view of her homeland in six long years. She was left to imagine the tower, the bridge, and the clusters of chimney tops merrily puffing out smoke. A dusk arrival hindered sight of the skyline, fog or no. Better to employ her time in making plans for disembarking rather than idling on deck where a fetid stench rolled off the water. Colonel Adams, who had accompanied her from India, approached her, apparently in the same frame of mind.

"I've arranged for a hansom cab, and I would be pleased to deliver you to your friend's address. No need to tempt the ruffians, a lovely young woman alone. It will be dark before we're finally off the ship."

"Thank you, Colonel. You're very kind." *Too kind*. Colonel Adams and his wife, a doting older couple, had done little else but fret over Eve's welfare in the year and a half since the colonel had delivered the news of her husband Captain Benjamin Kendal's unfortunate demise.

Six years earlier, when she'd eloped with Ben to India against her parents' wishes, making her own way in the world was something that had never crossed her mind. Now that she was on her own, she craved a chance to manage her own affairs. She'd only accepted the colonel's offer to accompany her because he had matters to attend that coincided with her return and it seemed wise to make the passage with a companion.

Her finances necessitated a return to England. Her widow's pension would only stretch so far, and she couldn't find out what had happened to their savings. Ben had spoken of investing them. Her fervent hope was that her late husband's solicitor in London would know where their money was.

That her family had disowned her for marrying Ben, an army captain instead of the earl her mother had hoped for, seemed an unhappy turn, but no crucial setback at the time. They had each other, and together they would conquer all, even life in a strange, new country. But they hadn't accounted for natural disaster. When an earthquake rocked the Kangra Valley in India, where Ben had been sent on a special mission for the magistrate, he was killed in a shower of falling rocks.

Eve had stayed in the safety of Raipur, where they'd made their home among a small community of expatriates. They'd once talked of a quiet retirement in the English countryside, their many children all around them. In six years of marriage, Eve hadn't yet conceived and she'd begun to fear that she couldn't. With Ben—and their savings—gone, it was probably for the best that she didn't have children to support.

Still, how she would have loved a child with Ben's eyes and laugh to be her constant companion. Her memories were all that remained, memories she wouldn't trade for anything, not even to win back her parents' support. Over a year later, she was out of mourning and on to a new life, the dreams she'd shared with Ben behind her.

Her parents and brother never answered her letters. Besides Colonel Adams and his wife, Adela, Eve had one friend in the world, her girlhood companion, Sophia.

All through her absence, Eve and Sophia had kept up correspondence. When Eve had written Sophia about Ben's death, she'd been touched to receive her friend's offer of the Dower House on the grounds of her estate. She was grateful to Sophia for throwing her a lifeline when she needed one most.

Standing next to her on the deck, Colonel Adams suddenly placed his hand over hers on the rail, interrupting her thoughts.

"Time heals all wounds, my dear, as they say. Or someone said. I don't recall who…"

"I believe it was the Greek philosopher Menander, as echoed by Chaucer in *Troilus and Criseyde*."

"Ah." He stroked his silver mustache. "Very clever, but perhaps best not to demonstrate that so readily. A number of suitors would be discouraged from pursuit of a bookish woman."

"Suitors, Colonel?" Eve suppressed a smile and shook her head. "Even if I wanted one, I wouldn't accept a man who shied from intelligence. You know me better than that."

"I do." He nodded dismissively. "What I mean to say is that time heals, perhaps, but it works all the faster when you're in familiar territory. As much as Adela and I will miss you, I believe being back in England will be restorative for you. A fresh start in—where is this place you go, again?"

"Thornbrook Park, the Earl of Averford's estate in West Yorkshire."

"Thornbrook Park, indeed. Nothing like the clean air of the English countryside to restore good health and spirits."

"Yes. A night at Averford House, my friend's house in town, and then the train straight to Thornbrook tomorrow morning."

"They know you at Averford House?" A bushy brow arched over inquisitive green eyes.

"No, but Sophia, Lady Averford, sent a letter ahead to the butler informing him to expect me. I don't anticipate any problems."

"Good. I'm in town for a fortnight, don't forget, at the Langham, should you need me."

"So you've told me. Three times now." Eve smiled. It was probably more like ten times. "You've no need to worry. As much as I love your company, I hope I won't need to look you up. Lady Averford's brother-in-law, an army captain, currently resides at Averford House. You might know him, Captain Marcus Thorne?"

"I don't know the name." The colonel shook his head, though his eyes brightened at the news that there was a man in charge at Averford House, an army man.

"I'm sure I will be quite safe. Give my love to Adela when you get home."

"We will start looking for your novel as soon as I get back."

She laughed. "I have to write it first. I'm not sure when I'll find time. And then, I'll need a publisher. You won't have to start looking for at least a year, and I'll send plenty of letters in the meantime."

"We have faith in you, my dear."

"Thank you, Colonel." She wished she had as much faith. As she noticed activity picking up around them on the deck, she removed her hand from under the colonel's and reached for her bag. "I believe it's time to disembark."

⁓

Captain Marcus Thorne, his hands in his pockets, shouldered his way through the rough crowd gathered in the street outside the Hog and Hound.

"A fighter!" one of the lads said, gesturing to him. The boy was too young to be out late in such a neighborhood. Marcus stifled the urge to reprimand the boy, but kept his head down and kept walking.

"No, 'e's a gentleman," said a toothless old hen. "Come to watch and wager like the rest of 'em."

No one could accuse him of dressing impeccably, but he supposed his clothes stood out as fine, more befitting a gentleman than a fighter: dark frock coat concealing broad shoulders, black trousers, and black hat low over his eyes covering wheat blond hair, close cropped to be suitable for fighting, nothing for an opponent to grab. *Onward. No sense in correcting her.*

The black rage was upon him, taking him over, becoming more impossible to control by the minute.

After the war, he suffered many black rages, pounding at the back of his brain like a time bomb ticking toward explosion. And when it went off, God help those around him. The only thing he'd discovered that could dismantle the rage, as he had disabled box mines in South Africa, was to hit something, someone, anyone.

During the war, he'd had steady hands, a sharp mind, and nerves of steel. Now, his nerves were shot to hell, and the rest of him was on the way there, too.

After he'd spent too many nights to count in holding cells for starting brawls, a friend had suggested Marcus put his fists to better, or at least more profitable, use and take up prizefighting. He spied the friend, Thomas Reilly, a private detective, at the bar as he entered the room.

The dim lighting and haze of smoke in the air could not disguise that the pub had seen better days. Perhaps the worn state only served to make him, and all the other miscreants, feel more at home, though the gentlemen among them seemed equally undaunted by the divots in the wood-paneled walls between prints of racehorses and pugilists, or the occasional dots of rodent droppings on the sanded floor.

Marcus acknowledged Tom with a nod and kept walking to a table in back occupied by a slim young man in a suit cut two sizes too large, perhaps to add the impression of size. Without a word, Marcus placed a note stating his intentions on the table and waited for a response.

The man did not answer, but raised his brows in surprise, jumped up, and ran through the faded red velvet curtains to the ring in back.

"Gentlemen." Marcus could hear the man, his voice sturdier than his build. "We have a newcomer waiting. He demands a fight to the finish with the best man in the room."

The announcement was followed by silence and then hoots of laughter. The champions of all weight classes had undoubtedly been decided and declared by the time of Marcus's arrival. A challenge to take on the best, without specification of age or weight class, would be considered either a fool's mission or an outright joke.

Marcus had served in the Second Boer War, the biggest fool's mission of them all in his mind, and there could be no more ridiculous joke than sending him, a gentleman's son, off to war. Commissioned officers weren't often sent to war, and being directly involved in bloodshed hadn't been what he'd expected when he'd purchased his commission. He'd only meant to impress his father and show his brother that he, the bookish one, could pursue an active life of adventure, while his brother, the sportsman, was destined to a custodial life in charge of a house, grand though it was. Perhaps the real joke was that he had returned when so many had not; that he, a pampered mother's favorite, had faced every challenge thrown his way and survived.

He was not the same man upon his return. Memories haunted him, his conscience nagged him, and the black rages took him over on occasion, but no longer as frequently as they had when he'd got back, before he'd first stepped into the ring.

Tonight's rage had been initiated by the carriage

driver who swerved and nearly killed the little urchin selling flowers at the roadside before continuing on his way without pause. *Tick*. And the lady in the bird-ornamented bonnet walking right on by, stepping over the child without a moment's hesitation to ask if she were hurt. *Tick*. And when Marcus stopped to help the girl up and gather her flowers, he could see that her eyes had the same gray-green hue as another child he'd known. His mind flew back to the South African concentration camps and a mother and daughter separated from the rest of their family by force and held against their will.

"For your own safety," Marcus had been instructed to reassure them. "Wouldn't want innocents to get caught up in the fighting." For the safety of the troops, Marcus knew. Wouldn't want opposition to grow and spread like wildfire among the civilians.

Tick. The rage had fallen upon him, ready to blow, pounding behind his eyes, throbbing in his ears, and he'd dropped his evening plans and come straight to the Hog and Hound to have a go.

Win or lose, it didn't matter as long as he got to pummel something hard and fast, someone there with the full intention of being hit and of hitting back in return. It wasn't the safest of diversions, but the money was good when he won, and even better when he had the sense to stay out of the ring and wager on the right fighters. When the rage took over, though, there was no help for it.

The slim young man returned, taking a good look at Marcus as if sizing him up. He shook his head, a gesture Marcus interpreted to mean that he'd be fighting a heavyweight, probably the biggest of them all. Marcus, six feet of solid muscle, was a match for anyone under sixteen stone, but over that he had to be fast on his feet and dodge all blows. "Come with me."

Marcus followed, any sense of impending doom deadened by the incessant throbbing at the base of his brain. Instinctively, his hands curled into fists. Without a thought to the throng of gentlemen and commoners alike assembled around the ring, Marcus forged through the crowd, climbed up, stepped into the ropes, found his corner, and began to strip down. He felt all eyes on him and let them look. If his size and the shrapnel scars dotting his muscle-bound chest made him any more intimidating, so much the better.

"Seconds?" a craggy old man with cauliflower ears, known to Marcus simply as Jameson, called from the ringside.

"Here." Tom Reilly appeared, the crowd parting to allow him to make his way to the ring, where he hopped up and took his place beside Marcus. Tom looked like a fighter in his own right. He stood only an inch shorter than Marcus's six feet, all of him lean muscle. His hair was short and brown with a natural curl that he couldn't seem to tame. His Irish blue eyes had an occasional twinkle that lent him an air of joviality, but they could just as often turn dark and threatening like clouds rolling in for a storm.

"Here." Another man waved from across the ring. He was as short as he was wide and swarthy enough to resemble a storybook troll. Augustus Hantz. Which meant that Marcus's opponent was none other than Smithy Harris, a formidable giant to whom Hantz might have been physically attached since they were so often together.

Harris appeared in the ring seconds later. He came by his nickname honestly, as he'd been a blacksmith by profession. His arms—thick like sides of beef from wielding his heavy hammer—bore the hallmarks of the trade, and he stood half a foot taller than Marcus, if not more. Some men might think this spelled trouble for Marcus, and no doubt the betting was fast and furious against him. But Marcus had watched Smithy Harris before and knew that his size, though unnerving, was a hindrance to easy movement and that he could tire the giant out in minutes as long as he kept bobbing and weaving around the ring.

Once stripped to the waist, Marcus followed Tom to the center where they shook hands with his opponent and the second. The blackness had taken over to the point where he couldn't think to lock his gaze on Harris, and he'd lost all awareness of the boisterous throng in the room. He did hear the whip cracking down to discourage spectators from crowding too close, and when Jameson started reading rules, he found his voice.

"American rules," he growled, and stalked off to his corner of the ring. Bare knuckles, his preference.

"Queensbury," Jameson countered, and Tom stayed center ring for some minutes arguing Marcus's case.

In the end, Tom returned to Marcus's corner and handed him his gloves. "Queensbury rules."

Marcus answered between gritted teeth, "Queensbury it is."

The time for argument had passed. He was desperate to hit something, fists gloved or no.

As soon as the bell sounded, he rushed in for Harris's head, missed him, and received a sharp body blow in return, leaving an angry mark above his ribs. He danced around, much lighter on his feet than Harris, and managed to herd him into a corner against the ropes, where he rained punches into Harris's steel-like chest and iron abdomen before landing one square to his jaw.

Unflinching, Harris returned a sound jab to the side of Marcus's head. Marcus reeled but managed to stay on his feet. His ears rang. Fortunately, so did the bell for the end of the first round.

"What's the matter with you?" Tom sponged him down and handed him a towel. "The object is to tire him out, remember? He's capable of beating you to a pulp."

Marcus grunted. His body, coated in a fine sheen of perspiration, glistened under the gas lamps. The bell rang for the start of the second round. This time, he managed to duck and weave, avoiding all blows until the bell rang again. What he didn't do was land any hits of his own, which added to his frustration. It didn't matter if he got pummeled. He needed to hit, and hit hard.

The third round delivered the satisfaction he craved. The half-minute break hadn't allowed his opponent sufficient time to catch his breath, and Harris's huge, hairy chest rose and fell while he blew air through wide nostrils like a spent old workhorse ready to be put out to pasture. Marcus didn't intend to let him recover. He sprang at him with unimpaired energy, punching, weaving, ducking, and punching again—left, right, left, left, jaw, nose, ribs, jaw, jaw. The giant staggered back and looked as if he would fall. The black had begun to fade from Marcus's mind, and his instincts of survival came back to him.

He landed one last dig to Harris's chin, and Harris recoiled and spun in a slow circle. It was all but over. Marcus's gaze swept the mob to gauge the reactions of all who had bet against him. And that's when he saw him, shaggy brown hair over soulful brown eyes wide with wonder, the very image of his buddy Cooper who had died in his arms during the war.

"Coop?" he said, but he knew it wasn't Coop. It was Cooper's son, Brandon. Brandon, fourteen years old and in need of guidance and approval, who now looked up to Marcus like the father he'd lost. Brandon, Anna, Emily, and Finn. And Prudence Cooper, widow of Lieutenant William Cooper, the best friend and best man Marcus Thorne had ever known.

"Coop!" Marcus said it again, not to Brandon, but a summons to his dead friend, as if William Cooper could come flying out of heaven to deliver his errant son safely home. The pub was no place for a boy, especially not during a boxing match, and Marcus was powerless to defend him, should something go amiss. The Coopers were Marcus's responsibility now. He'd promised his friend as Cooper lay dying, his gut ripped open from one of the box bombs they'd been sent to dismantle. "I'll look after them, Coop. Find your peace."

The last of Marcus's rage melted away, replaced by a growing sense of urgency to see the boy from the pub and home to safety. And in those few seconds of inattention, Marcus lost sight of the glove speeding toward his face until it was too late. The slam struck with such force that Marcus staggered and lost his balance, followed swiftly by his awareness. The black returned, but this time with the deadly silence of nothingness instead of a roaring rage.

When he woke, his friend Coop stood over him. Marcus recognized him through a gauzy haze.

"Coop, brother," he said, "I'm sorry I've let you down."

"You can't win every match, hey?" A higher voice than Coop's velvet baritone answered him. "But well done!"

Marcus's vision cleared. He hadn't died and met up with his departed friend after all.

"Brandon Cooper." Marcus found his best paternal voice. "What are you doing in a pub late at night? Your mother must be sick with worry."

"She thinks I'm at the millinery. I had a feeling you would come tonight. I didn't want to miss it."

"At the millinery?" Marcus shook his head to clear it and managed to sit up. The crowd was leaving, the match over in a mere three humiliating rounds. The few who remained were collecting their winnings from wagers placed against him, insult added to injury. "Whatever would you be doing at the millinery?"

"Trimming bonnets. I've taken up some work to help Mum."

"And your mum approved?" What had Prudence been thinking? He would have to speak with her. Their lot must be harder than she had let on. How had he not realized? How could he have been so lax in his duty to his friend? He would have to be more attentive. Brandon was at a tender age, too eager to grow up but not ready to face heavy issues. Left on his own, he could easily turn to unhealthy habits, fall prey to bad advice.

"I didn't give her much say in the matter. I am the man of the house now."

Marcus sighed. "Man? You're not a man until your whiskers come in. Now come on, no more talk of the millinery. I've got to dress and get you home."

"I have whiskers." Brandon stroked his soft, young chin. "And we're not leaving until I collect my winnings." He offered a hand to help Marcus to his feet.

"Your winnings? You wagered against me?"

Brandon had the decency to blush, at least. "Did you get a look at your opponent? Smithy Harris is enormous."

"I'm fast on my feet."

"Not fast enough." Brandon chuckled, his lip curling up at the corner like his father's used to do. His brown hair, in need of a trim, nearly hid his eyes but couldn't block the golden spark of mischief shining from them.

At least someone had made money for the Coopers tonight. Marcus watched Brandon run off to collect his winnings and bid good night to Tom.

Two

After arriving at Averford House, Eve settled into the bath that the maid, Lettie, had drawn for her. Mr. Sutton, the butler, had welcomed Eve, shown her to a room, informed her that he was having supper prepared, and then left her in Lettie's capable hands. At Eve's request, the supper was being sent up. She eased back into the hot water and savored the release of tension from every muscle.

Captain Thorne hadn't been at home to greet her, which was just as well. It was late and she didn't feel up to being social. Tomorrow morning, after a good night's rest, perhaps she would make his acquaintance at breakfast before she left to catch the train.

"Are you all right, ma'am?" The maid knocked at the door and peeked in. "Your supper's arrived. It's not fancy fare as you might be accustomed to, just a simple stew. Cook wasn't prepared for guests so late in the evening. Should I keep it covered for now?"

"Covered, yes." Eve wasn't ready to get out. She closed her eyes and inhaled the steam fragrant with lavender. "Stew sounds delightful. I'll be out shortly."

"Shortly" turned out to be nearly half an hour later and her stew was cold, with pasty potatoes, but Eve was famished enough to enjoy every tasteless bite of it. Clean, dry, and with a full stomach, she wanted nothing more than her bed. She settled in and fell right to sleep.

Sometime later, a noise awakened her, a crashing sound followed by some cursing and scrambling.

"Blast it, lemme go, Sutton," a big, deep voice said. "I'm perflecty well."

"Sir, if you please, sir. I only want to open the door for you. There. Now—" Another boom. "Oh, not again."

What the devil was going on? Eve got out of bed, reached for her wrapper, and peeked out her door.

A man was sprawled in the middle of the corridor, Sutton leaning over him.

"I apologize for disturbing you, Mrs. Kendal." Sutton, in slippers and a robe over his nightclothes, stood and delivered a curt bow. "I have everything under control. Please go back to bed."

"Captain Thorne, I presume?" Eve stepped out. Sutton's eyes went round with alarm. "Do not worry, Mr. Sutton, I've seen plenty of snozzled men in my time, officers serving with my husband in India. I'm not at all shocked. Let me help you."

Sutton looked positively mortified. He paused, as if considering which was worse: allowing a female guest to help him remove the Earl of Averford's intoxicated brother from the entryway, or being incapable of doing it himself. Captain Thorne was six feet of solid muscle, by the look of him. The man had removed his jacket and undone his shirt nearly to the waist of his trousers, exposing a taut, rippled abdomen and the solid planes of his chest rising and falling with each breath. Eve's gaze lingered on that chest.

"Just give me a hand getting him to bed, then," Sutton said, clearly against his better judgment, snapping Eve to attention. "The others are all asleep and I hate to disturb them." Eve suspected that what he would actually hate was for another member of the staff to witness his inability to handle the situation on his own. Though it was highly improper, Eve was already awake and might as well assist him.

"His face is bruised," she noticed, leaning over Thorne. "Did he run into the doorjamb?"

"No. I believe he was fighting."

"Fighting?"

"In the ring. Since his return from the war, he has taken to occasional participation in prizefights."

"A prizefighter?" Eve, unfazed at his state of inebriation, expressed some surprise now. "I've never met a prizefighter. Fascinating."

Thorne, apparently more aware than they knew, cracked one eye open, propped himself up on an elbow, and offered a hand. "Catpin Marcus Thorne, at your service."

"Oh, indeed." Eve couldn't stifle her laugh at his attempt at a proper introduction. Still, she took his hand. "Mrs. Eve Kendal, at *your* service, *Captain*. Shall we try to stand up? Come on, then."

She leaned in to wedge herself under his arm in an attempt to lend him some leverage to push up from the floor. Sutton came around to the other side of him, and they got Captain Thorne back on his feet and headed toward his own room. Once they got him settled on the bed, Eve took a longer look at him.

He didn't have the bloated appearance of a habitual drinker, she noted. His jaw was defined, practically chiseled, and dotted with golden stubble. She took note of shrapnel scars marking his solid chest. He'd seen some action in his time.

"Fetch him some bread and broth, Sutton," Eve commanded, taking charge. "Something to absorb the alcohol and help him recover more quickly. I'll stay with him until you get back."

Sutton appeared equally unhappy to leave a woman unattended with an inebriated man who was not her husband, but short of bodily removing her, there was little he could do. "If...you think it best," Sutton said reluctantly, leaving the room with a skeptical tilt to his bushy eyebrows.

Almost as soon as Sutton left them, Thorne fell asleep sitting up in bed, leaning against the head-board, head lolled back, and snoring loudly. She took a seat next to him and tried to make him more comfortable, reaching for a pillow to slide under his head and shoulders.

As soon as she touched him, he startled. Both eyes, clear and brown as the whiskey that likely accounted for his state, shot open. The area around his left eye was swollen and bruised, preventing him from open-ing it all the way and lending an air of danger to his appearance. She really hadn't considered what kind of man Captain Thorne might be before sending Sutton away.

"There, love," he said, as he curled an arm around her waist and urged her up against him. "Not tonight. I'm in my cups."

"Ha." Unable to shake free of his hold, she plucked at his thick fingers one at a time until he stretched his hand, allowing for her release. She scrambled off the bed. When he reached to pull her back, he found the pillow she held out to take her place. He pulled it to him in a tight embrace, like a child with a stuffed bear.

Sutton returned with a tray.

"Set it on the table, Mr. Sutton. We may not need it after all."

Sutton did as instructed, then came to stand at Eve's side by the bed. They hovered over their charge. "Shall I attempt to undress him?"

Eve sighed. "No, Mr. Sutton. I think it's best to leave him alone to sleep it off."

"Do you think it safe to leave him, then? Or should I sit with him?"

"I doubt he will be aware of anyone's presence in his room tonight," Eve said. "I believe it's safe to go back to bed. No doubt he will need you in the morning. Leave his door open, perhaps? I'm right across the hall, should he require anything."

"Oh, but ma'am—"

She took the butler's arm. "I'm aware that it's not exactly proper, but I'm a widow, Mr. Sutton. Men hold little mystery for me. Besides, he's fully clothed. Mostly clothed. I can handle any little emergencies that may come up without compromising myself, I believe. Please, go on and get some rest."

Sutton hesitated, but the bags under his eyes spoke

for his exhaustion. "All right. But do ring the bell if you have need of me. I can be back in an instant."

"Yes. If I need you, I will ring for you at once."

Seemingly reassured, Sutton bid Eve good night and escorted her back to her door before ambling off down the hall. No sooner had Eve gotten back into bed than she heard Captain Thorne call out, a strident wail. She darted from her room to his side. He thrashed in his bed, occasionally groaning, seemingly in the grips of a nightmare.

She placed a cool hand on his warm brow. "There, Captain Thorne. It's only a dream."

He stirred, opened his eyes, and grabbed her hand, his eyes finding her but seeming to look right through her.

"Please," he said, barely a whisper.

Just the one word. He gripped her hand, but he might have been gripping her heart. In that one second, she felt for him so completely. *Please.* She had no idea what he wanted, but he looked so terribly lost and overwhelmed that she couldn't bear to leave him.

"Yes," Eve answered. "I'm here. It's all right now."

He exhaled sharply, as if he'd been holding his breath, and suddenly seemed to relax again. He released his grip, closed his eyes, and eased into the mattress, falling back asleep. But what if the nightmare returned? She took the risk of removing his shoes, one at a time. That done, she spread a blanket over him, moved the chair from his desk over to his bedside, and sat watching over him as he slept on.

Occasionally, he shifted fitfully, but the nightmare didn't return. Sitting by his bed, stroking his hair to soothe his fidgeting, gave Eve a sense of satisfaction she hadn't felt in some time. Perhaps it was the intimacy of the situation. How long had it been since she had touched a man in a meaningful way? Or it was how deeply she felt needed, as if Marcus Thorne wouldn't make it through the night without her.

Of course he would. A grown man, he had probably been deep in his cups more than once. But to be the one sitting by his bed, drawing up the covers when he shivered, stroking his brow when he seemed to be on the verge of another nightmare, allowed her to feel she was providing a very necessary comfort. She stayed by his bed until the very last second she could manage, when her own eyes started to close, and only then did she reluctantly leave him to slip away back to her room.

His head throbbed as if he'd fallen on the track and a train was rolling over him, *chug-a-chug, chug-chug*. But he wasn't on a train, he knew before opening his eyes, or under a train, thank the gods, not that he had a precise memory of where he was or how he'd arrived. His last memory was of stopping at a tavern after escorting young Brandon back home, his head and his pride aching from his fall to Smithy Harris.

When he became brave enough to crack open one eye, he saw that he was in his own room at Averford House, viewing the pale green walls, his childhood watercolors of various plants and flowers still hanging over his desk, and the forest-green spread draped over him on the bed. He'd fallen asleep in his clothes, some of them anyway. His memory returned in bits and pieces as he began to recollect his misadventures: Sutton helping him up the stairs, falling down in the hallway, and a pair of eyes, the startling blue of a gas-lamp flame, burning through his haze. Those eyes were extraordinary. If only he could recall more of the woman around them.

There had been a woman, he knew more certainly, sitting up. She'd sat on the chair at the side of his bed. The chair remained, but no woman was in sight. It hadn't been Lettie, Sylvie, Cook, or any of the other maids at Averford House, the ones with names he never recalled.

A new set of clothes was neatly arranged on the valet stand. Paulson, the footman acting as his valet while Marcus made his home at Averford House, must have been in to check on him. He started to get up when Sutton entered the room bearing a tray.

"Ah, Captain Thorne. How are you this morning, sir?"

"Recovering, I suppose."

"Yes, sir, I imagine so." He set the tray down on the table next to the desk.

"The darnedest thing, Sutton. Last night, I seem to remember a woman tending me. Blue eyes. Startling blue. What was her name?"

"Her name, sir?" Sutton fidgeted as if uncomfortable. "A woman, you say?"

"Soft creatures, like men, but with longer hair, notable differences in the, er, chest area…"

"Yes, sir, I am familiar with women." If Sutton felt any inclination to smile, he held it back well. "But there was no woman here. Unless one of the maids checked on you when I was not aware?"

"Not one of the maids. This one was unfamiliar to me, fair hair, bright blue eyes? Unless we've hired a new maid whom I've yet to meet."

"Perhaps you dreamed her. You were quite out of sorts, though I hate to point it out." Sutton cleared his throat and went to fetch the tray. "Sit up now. I suggest you eat something."

He set the tray down in front of Marcus.

"Sutton, you remembered," Marcus declared after a look at the tray's contents. Black coffee, strong, not tea. Dry toast. Runny eggs. Marcus's favorite hangover breakfast, which had also been his father's. "I daresay I'll be feeling better soon."

"I'm counting on it, sir."

"You're sure there wasn't a woman?"

"How are your eggs, sir?" Sutton did not wait for an answer. "A good breakfast might help to clear your mind. I have duties to attend. Shall I send Paulson up?"

"Not right away. I'll call for him when I'm ready."

"Very good, sir."

Sutton turned on his heel and left before Marcus could ask about the woman again. Dreamed her? Possibly. He'd had a vivid nightmare that he was back in the field, bombs exploding everywhere, nothing he could do to stop them. There was no time. The panic nearly overwhelmed him, and then two blue eyes, like beacons, appeared to lead him through the smoke and ash. By Jove, perhaps Sutton told the truth. He'd dreamed up an angel, right when he needed one most.

In that case, he wished his subconscious had brought her forth a little sooner, perhaps in time to warn him of Smithy Harris's left hook. He rubbed the side of his face. That was going to hurt for at least a week, and the bruising would last even longer, a suitable reminder to keep his wits about him at all times.

Three

WHEN EVE KENDAL STEPPED OFF THE TRAIN FROM London, she failed to notice Lady Averford's driver waiting by the hackneys and horse-drawn carriages to take her to Thornbrook Park. The young fellow in the gray livery had to step forward and call her name from off to the side of the station, where he'd parked the motor car. She'd never thought to look for an automobile. But of course, Sophia, Lady Averford, had all the modern conveniences.

"Mrs. Kendal," he said, with a nod and a sweep of his just-removed cap.

Eve had never ridden in a car. There were few of them in India, most in military use and not intended for civilian pleasure jaunts.

"I am Mrs. Kendal." Eve stepped forward and extended her hand. "And you are?"

He looked at her gloved hand, as if a little taken aback by the gesture.

"Dale. The chauffeur. Let me see to your bags." He reached for her hand at last, a light touch before he brushed away and ran off to the porter.

"Just the brown leather case, Mr. Dale," she called after him. Her trunk had been shipped ahead, cargo class, but likely wouldn't arrive for another week.

Dale returned out of breath to help her into the car. The motor, once he started it up, purred like a hungry jungle cat from the wilds of Rajasthan. Other than the motor sounds and a faint petrol smell, the ride wasn't much different than a ride in a horse-drawn carriage—slightly bumpy and not as fast as she'd hoped. But she could say she'd ridden in a car now, and that was something.

They trundled through quintessential English pastoral scenes that cheered her, past white sheep grazing in green fields, broken intermittently by stretches of yellow rapeseed. The leaves had barely begun to turn, dots of gold and orange here and there scattered in the green. Home. How she had missed it all!

In India, there was dust. Sand. Brown earth, water like clay. The people added color, though, wrapped in their hand-dyed silks and cottons, the same colorful fabrics that made up the tents of the bazaars. She already missed the spices, having been treated to last night's bland English dinner. She'd finally acquired the skill to cook a long-simmering curry, rich and hot on the tongue, not that she would do much cooking now. It wasn't proper for an Englishwoman to fuss in a kitchen with the help. On her own, though, she could break with convention—if the Dower House were far enough from the main house, and the staff could be trusted to keep secrets.

Finally, they passed through the village, a quaint little square of shops, a tavern, and cobbled streets bustling with activity.

"Thornbrook," Dale said, with an edge of pride that suggested he might be a native.

At the edge of the square, they passed a church and a manor house behind a low gate before pulling into a long, winding tree-lined drive.

"The Dower House," Dale tipped his head back in the direction of the manor house. Eve straightened up to get a better look, but they had already passed. "That's the great house, up ahead."

All she could see were trees and a great stretch of green before they crested the hill and the rows of enormous gray chimneys came into view. Five, six, seven. She couldn't count them all as the rest of the house gradually appeared, a veritable wonder of rose stone, standing in the middle of a hundred acres of good, green land. There would be farms not far off, surrounded by woods, and lakes well-stocked for hunting and fishing.

A good old English country estate, Thornbrook Park, larger than she'd imagined but just as imposing. She should have felt at home, having grown up in such places, being doted upon and handed everything she could ever want. Everything except love, which she had found with Ben and lost again. Running off with him had been like escaping the pages of one book for another, a traditional fairy tale for a romantic adventure. Turn the page, and she was back in the traditional story, just like that, but it was hardly a fairy tale now.

Her clothes weren't up to princess quality, to be sure. She hadn't shopped in ages. A number of her dresses were simple and black, dyed for mourning, and the rest were out of date. The old Eve, the girl, might have been mortified at not keeping up appearances. The new Eve, the woman, found she did not care. She would write a brand-new story of her own, a new beginning.

The chauffeur came around to open the door and Eve stepped out, adjusted the coat over her black traveling dress, and inhaled deeply of the country air, a dank, earthy aroma she had never forgotten but missed more than she knew until now. Similarly, her heart surged when she caught sight of Sophia making her way down the steps to stand at the head of the few servants lined up along the drive.

Sophia might be Lady Averford now, a countess, but she was still Lady Sophia, the graceful girl with the loping gait, as she crossed the drive to greet Eve, her once dearest friend. The old, familiar feelings came back to Eve: warmth, love, and the pang of inadequacy she felt standing next to her friend. *Some things would never change.*

Eve wasn't plain by most standards. Some had even called her pretty—golden-haired, rosy-cheeked, petite-framed. But Sophia was one of those rare breathtaking beauties, a glorious star shining bright enough to cast shadows over anyone in her proximity. The afternoon sun paused at the perfect juncture to frame Sophia in a halo of light as she stepped away from the house. The pale sky set off Sophia's lustrous jet black curls, falling artfully from their chignon and not drooping like Eve's own hair, which refused to stay put after hours of travel.

Eve's breath caught as she remembered the last

time she'd seen Sophia, and the differences that had parted them.

"Think of everything you're giving up. Your family. Your friends." Sophia had given Eve's hand a tight squeeze. "For an army captain?"

"For *love*, Sophia." Eve had pulled her hand away. "True love. He's the air I breathe. I can't live without him. You, of all people, should understand."

Sophia hadn't understood. She had already given up on their youthful "true love or die" pact, made over their dog-eared copy of *Jane Eyre*, when she consented to marry the Earl of Averford for fortune and position over love.

"Eve Sinclair." There was no sign of any lingering tension to cloud Sophia's blue eyes as they exchanged cheek kisses and she stepped back to survey her friend. "You haven't changed a bit."

"Eve *Kendal*." Eve studied Sophia's elegant ensemble: a high-necked blouse tucked into a purple sash nipping in her tiny waist, and a long skirt of violet satin striped with orchid velvet, the height of fashion. "Lady Averford."

"Oh, my." Sophia laughed and embraced Eve again. "Sophia, please. Let's go inside. You've had a long journey. You'll need some tea. And rest."

The butler greeted them as they neared the front door.

"Welcome to Thornbrook Park, Mrs. Kendal."

"Mr. Finch, our butler." Sophia gestured to him and walked on by, as if she were pointing out a hat stand or a new chair.

Eve reached for his hand, apparently startling him. His gray eyebrows rose an inch, looking like the fuzzy caterpillars she used to hunt in the woods with her brother. She dropped her hand, realizing that she'd blundered in extending such courtesy to the butler, but she couldn't muster any remorse. "Lovely to meet you, Mr. Finch."

He was only slightly taller than Eve's five feet two inches, with a few wisps remaining of his hair, a double chin, and kind eyes. "And you, Mrs. Kendal."

Eve had to run to catch up to Sophia, who hadn't stopped. They walked down a short hall, over polished wood floors and oriental carpets, past a grand staircase, and through a wide double doorway into the drawing room, probably twice as large as the entire first floor of Eve's house in Raipur.

The tea cart was set up in one corner of the room, which had soft peach-colored walls, mauve velvet drapes, and an enormous window overlooking the gardens. There were two fireplaces and three separate seating areas including a grand piano in the far corner of the room. With heavy wood accents, columns, large carved mahogany mantels, oriental carpets over wood floors, pastel-striped and floral upholstered furnishings, and fresh flower arrangements all around, the room was pleasing to both masculine and feminine sensibilities.

"Your mother-in-law?" Eve paused at the portrait over the central fireplace. "The Dowager Countess of Averford?"

Sophia turned, a flush on her cheeks. "How I would like to take it down and replace it with one of my own. But you know men and their mothers."

"No, I'm afraid that I don't. Ben's parents had passed away before we met. Is the earl devoted to her?"

Sophia laughed. "Not exactly, but he feels the need to keep her portrait there. Perhaps he's a little in awe of her."

"She looks harmless enough," Eve said, trying to be friendly. "Sweet smile, gentle eyes. And that figure? Enviable for a woman her age."

"It was painted some twenty years ago. And clearly, you haven't met her. The woman is a dragon, but I should keep my voice down. Some of the staff remain devoted to her. Let's just say I'm pleased that she's enjoying a prolonged stay in Italy." She waved a hand dismissively and took a seat near the tea cart.

Eve sighed and took a seat beside her friend. "You'll laugh when I tell you that I envy you the mother-in-law, no matter how monstrous. I wish I had someone to love or despise, a connection. It's better than being all alone."

Sophia patted Eve's hand. "Easy to say when you're safely removed from the situation. Strong or weak?"

"I could do with a good strong cup today." Anything to help rouse her. She'd barely slept last night, but it wouldn't do to mention that Sophia's brother-in-law had kept her up. She blushed at the very recollection. "With lemon."

"I still take mine the same." Sophia poured. "Creature of habit. Splash of milk, two lumps."

Eve took the offered delicate porcelain cup. "And you used to spill some milk into a saucer for your aunt's cat. You spoiled that cat when you thought no one was looking."

"Too true. No cats around here. Well, maybe in the barn. But Aunt Agatha is with me. And Alice."

Sophia nibbled her lip, as she always did when she was holding something back. Creature of habit, indeed.

"Agatha and Alice, what a treat. I will get to see them soon, I hope."

"Soon enough." Sophia twisted her fingers in her long strand of aquamarine beads. "They're at the Dower House."

"The Dower House?" About to sip, Eve looked over the edge of her cup, then set it down. "Oh. I'll have company. Is it large enough for the three of us to share comfortably?"

Sophia met her gaze. "Eve, I'm so sorry. I offered you the Dower House, but then Alice and Agatha came along. I'm hoping to see Alice married, and of course, Aunt Agatha never had any proper place to be, having never married, so it seemed perfectly ideal to take her on as a sort of guardian for young Alice and—"

"You set them up in the Dower House. Of course. They're family. You're saying there's no room for me, then? I understand." Her mind raced. Without the Dower House, what was she to do for accommodations? How much further could she stretch her dwindling widow's pension?

Sophia sat straighter, gaining height as she gained confidence. She placed her hand over Eve's. "I don't mean to turn you out, Eve. My goodness. What did you think?"

"I don't want to be a nuisance. I'll find other arrangements." It was just like Sophia to make promises she couldn't keep and think nothing of the inconvenience to others. Eve shouldn't have been so trusting, but she'd been in such a bind.

"You'll stay here, of course. In the house with me. It will be like old times. We'll have adventures."

Adventures were often short-lived. If only she could have stayed at the Dower House, as they'd planned. She wouldn't feel so in the way. "Young Alice, you said. Alice is one-and-twenty, is she not? We're not speaking of a child. She doesn't need constant supervision, one might hope."

Eve took a sip of tea and hoped she didn't sound too judgmental. After all these years, Sophia apparently still treated her younger sister as if she were a babe and not a mere four years their junior.

"One might." Sophia shrugged. "But you know Alice. She never acts in her own best interests. To be honest, I had to take Agatha off Mother's hands. Agatha has been having more of her spells. Father was threatening an exorcism. Bringing her here, with Alice, seemed to make the most sense."

"Agatha's spells, yes. She's still channeling the spirits?" Even as Eve put down her cup, she couldn't help but wonder what Agatha might read in the tea leaves. Sophia's eccentric aunt claimed to be in communication with the dearly departed as well as having a touch of the second sight. In fact, she had predicted that Sophia's father would take a late-night tumble down the stairs, breaking his foot—and he had, keeping the family at home for most of the season, to Sophia's relief. Sophia hated London. Agatha had also foreseen great tragedy in Eve's life, though Eve and Sophia had laughed it off at the time.

Agatha had been a great source of amusement and wonder to the two of them as girls. As they

matured, though, the wonder faded and only amusement remained. The worst kind of amusement, Eve
remembered with some regret. They'd been unkind to
poor Agatha more than a few times. Eve felt all resent-
ment dissipate. The obligation to protect Agatha from
Sophia's cantankerous father should take precedence
over accommodating an old friend, even if that friend
was Eve.

"You know, I've come to admire Aunt Agatha,"
Eve said. "Never married, she does what she likes, no
concern for fashion or public opinion. We should all
be more like Agatha, perhaps."

Eve meant to be. Why should she care what others
thought or said about her? Except for the people
who mattered, and Eve had precious few of those.
Fortunately, she did have Sophia, who might raise
an eyebrow at the state of Eve's wardrobe but would
never judge her for it. Not too harshly, anyway.

Sophia leaned across the table and touched Eve's
leg-of-mutton sleeve. "She's more insistent than ever
that the dead speak through her. She held a séance
with the servants. The table shook. A dish flew and
crashed into a wall. The dogs in the kennel clear across
the field started howling so loudly that you couldn't
hear yourself think. My maid quit on the spot and
refused even to stay through the night."

"What fun!" Eve clapped. "Who needs a horrid old
maid, afraid of a few ghosts? Good riddance. You do
have a new maid?"

"Mrs. Jenks." Sophia nodded, pouring out more
tea. "She's not as meticulous as Bowles, but she's
skilled with a needle and thread. I'd hired her for

Alice but ended up keeping her for myself and sending one of the housemaids over to tend the ladies of
the Dower House. Speaking of Alice, I have a plan.
It involves you."

"Aha. So we come to the heart of it, at last." It
wasn't friendly generosity alone that had inclined
Sophia to invite Eve to come and stay. Sophia needed
her. The news actually soothed Eve a bit. It was better
to be needed than to be tolerated.

"Your letters from India were beautiful. I've never
wanted to go there, but you made me dream of bazaars,
spices, and men in turbans." Sophia sighed. "The
romance of it all. You were painting with words."

"I'm afraid I used rather broad strokes." Eve
shrugged. She hadn't mentioned the fleas, the rats, the
sandstorms, the riots, the Indians who were not at all
pleased to have the British in their midst.

Caught up in her plan, Sophia paid no attention. "I
need you to write a letter to Lord Averford's brother.
I think he would be perfect for Alice, if only I could
get him to visit. I've written a few times and he never
answers. You might succeed where I have failed.
Captain Thorne is an army man, like your Ben."
Sophia didn't say more, but Eve detected the rest of the
thought. *Like your Ben, only from a noble family.* "Oh,
but you were at Averford House. Did you meet him?"

Eve hesitated. What could she say? If he did come,
and she said that they'd met but he didn't know
her, one or both of them would look a fool. But if
he remembered her? She suddenly felt weak, out of
breath. She inhaled deeply to try and steady her nerves.

"No, I didn't have the opportunity. He got in quite

late, and I was up and out so early. Our paths never crossed." There. Perhaps that would serve. She prayed he had no recollection of her.

"What a shame," Sophia said.

"Yes. A shame." Eve wondered what it might have been like to meet Captain Thorne properly, perhaps over the breakfast table. She would ask if he wanted any butter for his toast, and he would look at her with those amber eyes and say please, before accidently brushing her hand when he reached for it. "Why don't you tell me what you know of Captain Thorne? To help formulate this letter."

"Oh, you will do it then? I knew you would. Thank you, Eve. How I've missed you!" Sophia clapped, excited. "Come, to the writing desk."

∽

The night air was chill and dank, and the reek of the Thames lingered thick in his nostrils well after his return to Mayfair from Bloomsbury and the Strand. Tonight, free of any sign of a black rage, he had only wagered on the fights instead of taking part, a good thing because his ribs were still sore from Harris's hammering blows. He had done well, too. The Coopers would be set for the month, maybe two, on his winnings from the last match alone.

He had set Prue's mind at ease and ensured that her son wouldn't have to return to work at the millinery, for now. But how long could he keep Brandon from falling in with a bad crowd, from growing up too fast on the streets of London? And after Brandon, what of Finn and the girls? The responsibility weighed on him.

He'd never had to worry about anyone other than himself until he'd gone to war. Now, after the war, he had a whole family to consider and not even a wife of his own. Not that he wanted another obligation.

He settled by the fireplace in his favorite chair and considered the matter. Perhaps he should send Brandon to school. However, he doubted that Prudence was ready to part with a son after having lost her husband. Brandon didn't strike Marcus as much of a scholar, though the youngest, Finn, seemed studious enough.

Marcus remembered Coop mentioning that his father, long deceased along with Cooper's mother, had been a farmer. He could see a farmer in Brandon, the rugged build and large, capable hands. It might suit Brandon, if only Marcus could buy the Coopers a farm. Marcus's annuity, inherited from his grandfather, was enough to support himself in comfortable style, but he wasn't sure how far it would go toward buying and running a farm, even with his pension, despite his esteemed family name.

That name looked up at him, scrawled in looping cursive across an envelope that Sutton had placed on the end table, leaning against a decanter of whiskey where Marcus was sure not to miss it. He filled a glass now if only for the sweet fragrance of the liquor to replace the stench of the Thames.

He picked up the crystal goblet, swirled it under his nose, and held it to the candle's flame to admire the amber hue before putting it down without taking a sip. He had no desire to repeat his misadventure of last week, when he'd ended up in bed with no recollection of how he'd gotten there, only a lingering memory of a blue-eyed woman who apparently was a figment of his own addled mind. Since he'd tracked down Cooper's widow and gotten to know Prudence and the children, he'd begun to actually flirt with the idea of finding respectability. *Respectability*. Wouldn't his brother be surprised?

He supposed he wasn't quite ready for it as long as he kept succumbing to his rages and engaging in boxing matches. Blackened eyes were not in style among the posh. He picked up the envelope, smoothed it between his fingers, and thought of his brother's wife and her dogged insistence that he should return to Thornbrook Park for an extended visit. The woman was as determined as she was beautiful, and Marcus couldn't imagine why his brother remained without sons. A baby or two would distract Sophia suitably. Until then, it appeared that seeing Marcus reformed and married would be her pet project.

Captain Marcus Thorne
Averford House
Mayfair, London
18 September, 1906

Dear Marcus,

    Rest assured, my purpose in writing is not to attempt yet again to convince you to come home to Thornbrook Park. I can understand the appeal of London's bustling, merry crowds and endless entertainments. I merely thought to catch you up on some of the matters concerning the residents of a quiet country estate.

Autumn is not yet upon us for another few days, but you would not believe the abundance of apples in the orchard. Mrs. Mallows is in delights for now, baking sauces, pies, and tarts, and coming up with new ways to use apples in even savory dishes, chicken and apple patties, and squash apple soup. I've been enjoying my afternoon tea with apple tarts and Mrs. Dennehy's cheddar from Tilly Meadow Farm. Mrs. Dennehy struggles to keep up on her own now that Mr. Dennehy has passed on, but she still manages to make her renowned cheese.

I'm sorry for all you must have endured at war, Marcus. I hope your London society fulfills you in ways the country could not. The smells of baking apples, burning fields, the crisp night air—these are things I cannot imagine being without, just as you perhaps can't spare your clubs and entertainments. Everyone is more or less mad on one point, as Kipling says. Enjoy your autumn, and think of us, as we keep you in our hearts.

Sincerely,
Sophia

What he wouldn't do for the smell of baking apples at that very moment. How did she know? Once, he had eaten so many apples that he'd gotten sick to his stomach and lingered in bed for two days before waking and asking for more. There were apples in London, mealy little things that never matched the wondrous taste of the ones picked fresh off a tree. Thornbrook Park had lovely orchards.

But it was the line about Tilly Meadow Farm that stood out in his mind. He remembered it well, the wooden house, red barn, and green pastures. It was perfect, exactly what he had in mind for the Coopers. Mrs. Dennehy was struggling on her own, was she? Dennehy had been a tenant farmer. The land belonged to Thornbrook Park. Wouldn't Mrs. Dennehy be happier with a nice position in the house, something easy for an older woman, more of a retirement really? Of course, it would mean spending time with his arrogant ass of a brother. Marcus and Gabriel had never gotten along.

Growing up, Gabriel was his father's son, an avid outdoorsman, while Marcus was Mother's favorite. Gabriel would complain that Marcus was indulged, and Marcus would chide back that it wouldn't hurt for Gabriel to put down his guns and pick up a book once in awhile. But Gabriel's disapproval stung.

Marcus disliked the sort of sport that appealed to Gabriel and their father, hunting and fishing, but he'd wanted to prove he was no dandy. He'd labored with the groundskeeper to build a fence all along the border fields and couldn't wait to show his brother what he'd done. When he'd finally had the chance, Gabriel had dismissed him with a lecture that it was their responsibility to provide employment for the common folk, and he had no business taking away their work.

And when Marcus had announced that he'd bought a commission in the army, he'd expected Gabriel to be the first to congratulate him after their father. Instead, Marcus watched his brother's eyes darken as their ailing father had praised Marcus's choice and finally expressed pride in his younger son. Gabriel hadn't spoken more than a few polite words to him since that day, not even after their father's death right before Marcus was sent off to war. Sophia, then new to the family, had seemed particularly perturbed by their estrangement. She'd never had brothers of her own.

What had gotten into Sophia, anyway? A Kipling quote? Perhaps it was time he returned to Thornbrook Park for a short visit, long enough to have a look around Tilly Meadow Farm and make a few suggestions, even if it meant putting up with Gabriel's condescension.

Four

WITHIN A WEEK, EVE HAD SETTLED INTO A ROUTINE AT Thornbrook Park. She would get up and dress with the maid Lucy's help, and then join Sophia and her husband, the earl, in the breakfast room. On days when Sophia meant to sleep late, which were at least half the days of the week, Lucy arrived at Eve's bedside bearing a breakfast tray.

This morning, with no sign of Lucy or a tray, Eve got up before ten and managed her morning routine on her own, washing and choosing one of her few dresses that hadn't been dyed black, a lovely afternoon gown in cream with tulle sleeves, little rosebuds around the scooped collar, a ribbon sash, and an intricate pattern of satin trim at the hemline. A little dated, but serviceable, she thought, glancing in the mirror. She tried to do something with her hair, managing soft finger waves gathered into a chignon, and set off to see what Sophia had planned for the day. She assumed Lucy had been otherwise engaged or had simply forgotten her.

But when she got downstairs, she realized that the house was in an uproar. Maids hurried here and there, dusting, straightening, lighting lamps. Footmen laden with armloads of flowers rushed to fill every available vase.

She met Mrs. Hoyle, the housekeeper, in the drawing room, where she stood examining the central fireplace and running a hand over the mantel as if not quite satisfied the maids had done a proper job of it.

"Good morning, Mrs. Hoyle." Eve thought it best to make her presence known.

"Some might think so, Mrs. Kendal," the housekeeper said. "Captain Thorne is coming home to Thornbrook Park."

She hadn't thought of him much since her first day. "He must have answered our—Lady Averford's—letter."

"Not that I'm aware. Mr. Sutton telephoned Mr. Finch this morning that the captain had set out for the station determined to show up at our door before noon. Just like him, that one."

"Noon today? Full of surprises, is he?" Eve smiled, remembering the shock of finding him on the floor outside her chamber.

"Full of blatant disregard for common courtesy, more like. He might have made us aware of his intentions in time for us to arrange a suitable welcome. The lady is beside herself in handling preparations."

"I shall go see if I can be of assistance," Eve said, eager to get out of Hoyle's way. Guest or no, she wouldn't put it past the housekeeper to thrust a broom in her hand if she lingered too long.

Upon first acquaintance, Mrs. Hoyle had struck Eve as a hardworking, no-nonsense sort of woman. But upon witnessing Hoyle's interactions with the maids, Eve had decided the woman was a harridan who had come to Thornbrook Park straight from hell with the devil's own recommendation. Mrs. Hoyle paired her intimidating stature with a mix of shrewd suspicion and bitter disgust, wearing an expression that looked as if she were tasting month-old mutton and trying to decide if it were still fit for consumption. Her hair, apparently once dark but now liberally shot with gray, was pulled back in a tight bun that added to the severity of her appearance.

Eve took her leave and made her way back up to Sophia's bedchamber, where Sophia paced, leaving a trail in the plush pink rug.

"Extraordinary news—your letter worked! How did you hear? I hardly expected you to be up at this hour."

"It's not exactly early," Eve observed. "Lucy usually brings my tray at half past eight. No Lucy today, so I suspected something was amiss. Hoyle has filled me in."

"Ah, the ever-pleasant Mrs. Hoyle. I thought she would go apoplectic when she heard."

"She didn't seem all that pleased. She reminds me of Lady Tedford. Remember?" Eve asked.

"We called her Lady Tedious. Of course. How could I forget? She was always correcting our grammar. Remember when we put a frog in her soup? You had to catch the frog, of course." Sophia laughed. "How could our mothers have kept such a dreadful friend? Turn around. Let me look at you."

Eve spun. "Frogs aren't so bad. Better than dancing with Mr. Fellowes." They had both despised the dance master their mothers hired to improve their presentations. "I thought he was going to kiss you that first time you managed a perfect waltz."

"Thank goodness he didn't. You look lovely. But then, you always do. Even in last season's styles. Or several seasons ago? We need to get you some new things."

"In time." Eve shrugged. "We have more pressing concerns. What are you going to wear?"

Sophia gestured to the bed, where two gowns were laid out, a fussy pink concoction and a more stylish blue. "I'm torn."

"The blue, definitely. Cornflower brings out your eyes."

"I think you're right." She held up the blue sheath. "And I can wear the sapphires that Gabriel gave me on my birthday. Anything to improve his mood."

"He's not happy to hear of his brother's arrival?"

Sophia shook her head. "They've never gotten on well. Not as long as I've known them. You're sure it's not too matronly?" She pinched the sheath's lace overlay.

"Not at all." Eve didn't bother pointing out that they were getting on enough in years to suit more mature styles. At five-and-twenty, they weren't old, but they were hardly debutantes. "What really matters is what Alice wears, I suppose. You still intend to make a match?"

Lucky girl, Alice. Would Captain Thorne know Eve? Remember her staying by his bedside through the night? Perhaps it was better if he didn't, Eve thought with a surprising feeling of regret.

"Absolutely. They're perfect for each other. Marcus can marry Alice and keep her settled close to me. I've sent Lucy over to help turn her out properly."

Eve chose not to add that the situation seemed perfect for Sophia, without much consideration for Alice or her brother-in-law. "Ah, so that's what became of Lucy. I wondered when she didn't turn up for me."

They were interrupted by a knock, but Lord Averford entered before his wife could answer.

Eve stood back at the edge of Sophia's sitting room, a little in awe of the earl, who seemed slightly out of his element in Sophia's delicate, feminine environs. In a plaid coat and with baize trousers tucked into brown boots, he looked more ready to lead a wild expedition than to greet a guest. Despite his sporting apparel, he looked to be a man more fitted for drawing rooms or parlors.

"I'm headed out," he informed Sophia, taking no notice of Eve's presence. He pursed his lush lips, an Adonis displeased with his Aphrodite. As fair as his wife was dark, Averford was her perfect foil.

"You aren't even going to stay to greet your brother?"

"You're the one who invited him." Lord Averford practically growled his words. "I don't see why you expect me to give up my afternoon."

"It's raining," Sophia observed, seemingly calm as she placed her dress back on the bed. "He'll arrive within the hour, just enough time to exchange your hunting clothes for more proper attire."

"Dammit, Soph, I need to shoot—something." Lord Averford sighed loudly. "I'm going. Marcus doesn't want to see me any more than I want to see him. For whatever reason, he's here to see you."

"But darling." Sophia pouted prettily, turning to

face him, her fingers toying with his rough collar. "Please. You're brothers."

"I'll be back in time for dinner." He dropped a kiss on her forehead and made for the door. "Mrs. Kendal, don't let her be the center of attention. I won't have my brother coveting my prize."

Ah, so he was aware of Eve after all. Frozen in place, she responded with a wave toward the door after he was gone.

Sophia's cheeks colored, and Eve couldn't tell if her friend was flushed with anger or blushing from embarrassment. "I wish he would stay."

"Perhaps he knows best. They will have a chance to become reacquainted later, after Captain Thorne is more comfortably settled." Eve had half a mind to run out with the earl. What if Captain Thorne spotted her and knew her at once? "Maybe I should take a walk to the Dower House to see how Alice and Agatha are getting on."

And if she happened to be away when Captain Thorne arrived, so much the better. Nerves made her stomach tighten. Another knock on the door and Alice swept in before Sophia could answer. Did no one wait for permission to enter at Thornbrook Park?

"Ah, here she is now. No need," Sophia said, addressing Eve before turning to frown at her sister. "Alice, what's this strange getup? That's not what I instructed Lucy to set out for you."

"To hang with Lucy," Alice scoffed. She wore a severe blouse buttoned all the way up to her throat, paired with a mannish necktie and tucked into a narrow, drab skirt. Given the circumstances, Eve was certain Alice found no fault with Lucy but really meant to say, *To hang with you, dear sister.* "I chose what made me comfortable."

Sophia and Eve shared a glance.

"Comfortable? That tie is likely to choke you, but to each her own," Sophia said. "Where's Agatha?"

"In the drawing room. She had something urgent to reveal to Mrs. Hoyle."

"Lord." Sophia rolled her eyes. "Let me hurry and dress. As much as I am ever at odds with Hoyle, I can't afford to lose another servant just now, especially one so crucial to the running of the house."

"Why don't I go down?" Eve suggested. "I might be able to distract Agatha."

"Thank you, dearest." Sophia sighed with apparent relief. "As it is, I'm going to need to ring for Jenks to do something with my hair, and who knows how long it will be before I'm presentable."

Eve laughed to herself on her way down the stairs. Sophia was presentable in her dressing gown with her hair all mussed from sleep, but who was she to argue? She found Agatha staring at the family portraits in the hall at the bottom of the stairs.

"This one resembles the earl's brother, don't you think?" Agatha asked her, not looking up from the painting in question of a sweet-faced young clergyman, judging from the collar and robes.

"A little around the eyes, perhaps, but the mouth isn't right," Eve considered, drawing on the memory of Thorne's lush lips. "I think there's a bit of the devil in Captain Thorne, unlike in this particular ancestor. But how do you know him? He hasn't arrived."

"Most recently, I've seen him in a vision." Agatha turned, waving her hands as if to wipe away the memory. "But we met at the wedding, too, of course, not that I remember him from that, so many years ago."

"Ah, yes. Six years is a long time."

"But the better question is how do you know him, Mrs. Kendal?" Agatha smiled. She had the perpetual look of one who had been startled from a deep slumber, her green cat eyes occasionally widening and darting to and fro.

Eve nibbled her lip. What to reveal? For all she knew, Agatha's vision involved her settling a drunken Captain Thorne into his own bed.

Agatha might have started the day with her white hair pulled back into a severe bun, but it had escaped to curl in wild, stray tendrils around her head. Oddly, Agatha remained a comforting presence despite her occasionally alarming revelations. She favored bright colors, today a peacock blue gown paired with a long, fringed shawl in chartreuse. To Agatha, wearing complementary colors or patterns never seemed to matter as much as making an impression, and that she did.

Once, as girls, Eve and Sophia had asked Agatha why she dressed in such vivid hues. Agatha had replied that it made it easier for the dearly departed to find her again when they returned.

"I see. No need to reveal your secrets, dear. We all have them." Agatha laughed and attempted to smooth her hair.

"It's no secret that I stopped at Averford House

when I first returned to London," Eve said. Better to offer something to Agatha than to keep her wondering.

"After losing your husband, poor dear." Agatha stepped forward to enfold Eve's hands in her own. She closed her eyes as if meditating. "Never fear. What is lost shall be found. Yes, I see it all. Here at Thornbrook Park you will find what you have lost. It's good that you've come."

"I suppose it is," Eve said to keep her mouth from gaping. Agatha's revelations always came on quickly and took her by surprise. For all Eve knew, the woman liked to spout nonsense to keep them all on their toes, but Eve never discounted Agatha's predictions entirely. More than occasionally, Agatha had been proven right. "But Captain Thorne will be arriving soon. We should go to the drawing room to be ready when the car pulls into the drive. Have you seen Mrs. Hoyle? I was about to ask her something."

Agatha shook her head. "Alas, no. I wanted to speak to her myself."

Eve was both relieved that she had intervened in time to stop Agatha from scaring Hoyle off with any cryptic revelations and curious as to what such revelations might be. Fortunately, Sophia and Alice came down to join them before Eve gave in to the temptation to ask. With Agatha, sometimes it was better not to know.

"Jenks said that a footman clearing brush from the eaves reported seeing the car turning into the lane," Sophia said. "Shall we go out?"

All in agreement, they stepped out the front door into the unseasonably warm sunshine, the remains of the rain evaporating in a steamy mist that curled around their ankles. Though Eve had spent more than an hour at Captain Thorne's side, mopping his brow and putting water to his lips, she waited with anticipation as the car wheeled around to come to a stop. Her throat clenched as she waited to see the captain step out. She knew intimate details of his body—that he had scars on his chest, a tiny mole on his neck, and freckled shoulders—and yet she didn't know the man at all. How odd.

One of the footmen opened the door for him. "Welcome home to Thornbrook Park, sir."

When Captain Thorne emerged, he took a quick glance over the lot of them and down the line of assembled servants. Instinctively, Eve drew back a little behind Alice. He wore a dark coat over a white shirt and a simple blue-patterned silk necktie, perfectly arranged. His eyes were bright and inquisitive, and when he swept off his hat, his close-cropped hair glistened like late summer wheat under the sun.

There was something rough about the captain, something rugged and wild in contrast to his brother's dignified demeanor. Although Thorne was not the more aesthetically pleasing brother, Eve found him more to her taste. Alice did not seem especially interested in him, though. She stood next to her sister but looked off into the distance as if distracted.

Captain Thorne's nose sat slightly crooked with a bit of a bump, as if he'd been injured in his youth. His jaw was square and defined. When he smiled at Sophia, he showed the same perfect white teeth as Lord Averford's, but with a bit more fullness to his lower lip, a lip that begged to be nibbled, Eve thought, and then wondered at how such a thing had even occurred to her.

"Marcus," Sophia greeted him familiarly, taking both of his hands rather than just the one he'd reached out. She leaned in for kisses, a quick buss on each cheek. "So good to see you. Not in uniform?"

"I'm embracing the civilian life. I'll probably sell my commission soon enough, and who wants to be reminded?" He shrugged but Eve thought she detected a grimace underneath it. A vein pulsed at the side of his neck just under his earlobe. "Gabriel couldn't be bothered, I see?"

"Gabriel can't sit at home when there are birds out there to shoot." Sophia gestured, holding hands aloft, as if helpless to have held her husband back.

Captain Thorne gave a sharp snort of a laugh. "I'll expect quail for dinner."

"For the remove, perhaps. Mrs. Mallows shares your expectations. She will be pressed to make alternative arrangements, should he fail to deliver." She led Marcus to where Alice stood patiently waiting. "You remember my aunt Agatha, and my sister, Lady Alice Emerson."

"You've suffered a loss." Agatha stepped forward, took Captain Thorne's hand, and closed it in both of hers, her eyes closing. "Recently. It weighs on you. Poor man. You must let it go, let go! Forgive yourself. Bathe in the powerful waters of forgiveness."

Placing her hand over the older woman's as if to break the spirit bond, Sophia gently interjected, "Now, Agatha, our guest has just arrived."

"A bath sounds like a fine idea." With amber eyes shining, Captain Thorne made light of it. "Perhaps after I'm settled."

Alice nudged herself between her aunt and the captain, no doubt instinctively trying to protect strangers from Agatha's eccentricities. "A pleasure to see you again, Captain Thorne."

"Likewise, Lady Alice." He bowed to her most attentively, and she blushed prettily.

Alice did not have her sister's overwhelming beauty but she did have a youthful radiance. Her hair was a pretty shade of auburn and her eyes were intriguing, a true hazel. The eyes marked her as unlucky, though, according to Aunt Agatha.

"Oh look," Agatha said. "He remembers Alice, though she was just a little girl when they met. Look how she's grown, Captain Thorne."

"I see." He flashed his white teeth in what Eve considered a wolfish grin. "Not a little girl any longer."

Alice would have been fourteen at Sophia's wedding, Eve recalled. Not quite a little girl on meeting Marcus. Captain Thorne humored them, perhaps. Or he really didn't remember.

Her heart hammered against her ribs when his gaze flitted over. Would he know her? But just as quickly, he stepped around to hand his hat to Mr. Finch. Sophia joined them, issuing some orders with regard to the luggage. Eve held her place, assuming an introduction of her own was to come, but instead Sophia and Captain Thorne followed Mr. Finch straight inside.

She should have been relieved, not out of sorts.

Disappointed? How could she be when she'd been hoping he wouldn't recognize her.

"You're to go in for tea." Mrs. Hoyle took Aunt Agatha by the elbow as if to hurry her along.

"Some of the maids seem to think he's really handsome," Eve said to Alice, catching some of their comments and giggles from across the drive as they dispersed.

"Captain Thorne? I suppose. He looks a lot like his brother, don't you think?" She wrinkled her nose.

"Many women find Lord Averford handsome, too. I remember how they were all so envious of your sister when she announced her engagement."

"Silly hens. What's to envy in a marriage? To be tied to one man, considered his property, bah."

"Don't you want to marry one day?" Eve truly hadn't considered that Alice wouldn't want a husband.

"Sophia would like that, wouldn't she? Then she can stop worrying over my welfare. Marriage is not for me, Eve. No, I shall never marry. I might be quite happy to remain here forever. Wouldn't that bother Sophia to no end?" She laughed loudly.

"Marriage is not all bad. With the right man," Eve said, her voice low.

Alice took her hand. "I'm sorry. I've been thoughtless. You were one of the lucky ones to have a love match. You must miss him dreadfully."

"All the time." But she wasn't thinking of Ben as much lately. Another man had occupied her thoughts, and now he was here and she was about to face him. "But we should go in now. Your sister expects us to join her for tea."

Alice rolled her eyes. "With Captain Thorne. She fancies a match between us. Don't deny it. I know when Sophia's up to something."

"It's not my place to confirm or deny."

Captain Thorne. The memory of him half naked stirred something deep inside her. Her knees shook so that she had to grip the rail to steady herself going up the stone steps. What if he knew her after all? It should be Alice's moment, Alice's chance to form a first impression. Worse, though, would be if he didn't know her when she felt such a connection to him, remembering him intimately, his hand curving around her waist or on her bottom—as if she had any right to such recollections. He'd been in his cups, she reminded herself. Unaware. She was being ridiculous, she knew, but she wasn't ready to face him.

"I have a bit of a headache," she said, bringing her hand to her temple. "Please make my apologies, Alice."

"Goodness. I hope you feel better." Alice reached out to Eve. "Let me help you to your room."

"Thank you, but no need to deprive Sophia of two companions. I'll manage. I just need a moment's rest."

She stepped back to let Mrs. Hoyle lead Agatha and Alice through the hall to the drawing room, where Sophia was already entertaining Captain Thorne.

Five

MARCUS SAT IN THE OVERSTUFFED ARMCHAIR BY THE fire and listened to Sophia prattle on about how much his brother was looking forward to seeing him. Bollocks. Gabriel hated him. They both knew it. Thinking of the lengths his brother would have gone to in order to avoid greeting him almost brought on the haze that often signaled a rage about to emerge.

Fortunately, the footman brought out the tea cart, a suitable distraction, and a good thing. If he needed to regain control of his temper while he was at Thornbrook Park, who would he hit? A smile tugged at the corner of his lips as he imagined himself smashing a fist into Gabriel's smug jaw.

"Ah, I see you've noticed the apple tarts." Sophia mistook the source of his grin, but no matter. "I had Mrs. Mallows make them just for you."

"Delightful. I will have one as soon as I've had some—"

"Coffee, sir? Black. Mr. Finch said it would be your preference." The footman returned with a pot and poured a cup for him.

"Bless Mr. Finch. How I've missed him."

"So you *have* missed our humble abode. At least some parts of it?" In her enthusiasm, Sophia stirred her tea so vigorously that she spilled some into her saucer.

"Nothing about Thornbrook Park is humble, dear sister. But I've missed it a little perhaps."

"The Dower House," Alice said, entering and crossing the room to take a seat on the sofa next to her sister. "It's humble, and it's part of the estate. So there. Oh, Mrs. Kendal sends her apologies, Sophia. She has a sudden headache."

"What a shame," Sophia said. "We'll have to carry on without her."

Alice looked at Marcus, triumph shining in greenish-brown eyes that were quite unlike her sister's deep blue. Not the gas-flame blue eyes that had haunted his thoughts since his drink-fueled nightmare weeks past, but still he could appreciate another woman's fine eyes, along with other things. He studied Alice's figure but couldn't discern much of her shape under the high-necked blouse and man's necktie, a purpose-fully chosen deterrent for his attentions if he'd ever seen one.

Over his cup, he flashed Alice his most charming grin. "I've been put in my place. I don't think I've been in the Dower House since Grandmother's time. Mother kept her usual rooms the last time I was in residence at Thornbrook Park. I can't imag-ine anything humble in the Dower House if Mother had a hand in the decorating. Perhaps you could show me around."

Sophia sat up straighter. This was exactly what she

wanted to hear, apparently. "Perfect! What a lovely idea. Tomorrow, maybe."

"I knew it," Agatha said, taking a seat next to Alice after having a wander about the room. "I've felt her spirit. Your grandmother died there in the house, at the table in the corner of the kitchen, right in the middle of breakfast."

Marcus laughed. "Not quite. Mother found her— well, it's not for polite company, but she was most certainly not found dead in the *kitchen*."

Agatha shook her head. "That can't be right. I'm sure I felt a force in the kitchen. A powerful force."

"Grandmother did have a favorite cat, Miss Puss. I believe Miss Puss might have passed away at table after getting into Granny's digestives."

Alice clapped her hands, delighted. "Miss Puss. Aunt Agatha, really! You've been in communication with the spirit of a *cat*."

Her aunt shrugged. "Not surprising. They're very intelligent creatures. Miss Puss was no doubt an observant soul. She has shared many secrets."

Agatha stared meaningfully at Marcus, long enough for him to notice she had the same sharp green eyes as Miss Puss. No wonder they'd hit it off.

"No doubt she has revealed my boyhood transgressions," he said. "I used to hide Grandmother's spectacles and steal her apples, then replace them with onions."

"Naughty boy." Alice raised a thin, brown eyebrow. "I'm sure that's not all Miss Puss might reveal."

"No," Agatha said, pointing an accusatory finger. "He also put his grandmother in a basket and floated her down the river. You knew how she hated water. How could you?"

Marcus tried to hide his surprise. Perhaps Aunt Agatha was more in touch with the spirits than anyone had credited.

"I did put something in a basket and float it down the river, but it wasn't Grandmother. It was Miss Puss. I was a budding scientist, experimenting with water currents."

"Miss Puss." Agatha shook her head. "All this time, I could have sworn it was the Dowager Countess."

"They were truly two of a kind." Marcus wished to reassure her. "But Grandmother would have been a lot harder to stuff into a basket."

Sophia, who'd had the fortune of knowing Grandmother, not a diminutive woman by any stretch, joined Alice in laughing at the idea.

"Your grandmother was a"—Sophia struggled to find the right word—"a thoughtful woman."

"She certainly had a lot of thoughts," Marcus said. "And she shared every last one of them."

"That she did," Sophia agreed.

"You have an aura about you, Captain Thorne," Agatha decided as she munched on one of the sandwiches. "A deep red aura. You're grounded in reality, with strong willpower and a sense of survival. No doubt it protected you while you were away."

"Being surrounded by skilled and brave men is what protected me. I'm afraid auras don't stop bullets or bombs."

"You would be surprised." Agatha nodded over her tea. "The personal qualities your aura reveals will continue to serve you well. But a man of your intensity might need some guidance from the spirits to avoid misdirecting your passion."

Marcus shared a glance with Alice, who again had raised a brow. He began to think he might find his time at Thornbrook Park amusing after all.

∽

Instead of heading up to her room, Eve joined the maids—Nan, Lucy, and Ginny—in the servants' hall, where they took turns peeking out a door to get a better look at the handsome newcomer in the drawing room.

"He's all right," Lucy said, backing off to give way to Nan. "Not quite as good-looking as Lord Averford."

"I see the resemblance," Nan said, taking her look and ducking back in. "He's not as polished as the earl, perhaps, but there's something about him, isn't there?"

Ginny, a cool blonde who seemed very aware of her own aesthetic appeal, pulled Nan out of the way to take her look. "Something, I'll say. He's rougher around the edges, a little dangerous, the way I like them." She licked her lips.

"Tell you one thing," Nan said. "If I could be out there, I wouldn't be hiding back here. I don't understand you, Mrs. Kendal."

Eve waved Nan off, took another peek at Captain Thorne, and barely managed to contain her sigh. There was something about him, yes. She couldn't deny it. He smiled at Alice, but there was a hint of volatility simmering just beneath the surface, perhaps the danger that Ginny had recognized.

"Not hiding," Eve said, stepping away. "I'm giving Lady Alice her chance to shine. I wouldn't want to manipulate the conversation."

"The conversation could use a little manipulation. Dead cats and grandmas?" Ginny snorted. "If that's Lady Alice's shining moment, she'll remain a spinster for certain. His hair's so short. I would like to see it a little longer, something to grab hold of…"

"He's a prizefighter," Eve said without thinking. "Short hair probably keeps him cooler when he's working up a sweat."

Conversation paused as they all looked at her.

"A prizefighter?" Lucy said. "How do you know?"

"I think I heard Lady Averford say something about it." Eve shrugged. "Perhaps I heard wrong."

Eve prayed *that* bit of gossip wouldn't work its way around the house with any speed, but she had her doubts.

"I barely noticed his hair," Nan said. "I was too busy studying his strong physique."

Ginny and Lucy both reached for the door to risk another look, but Mrs. Hoyle happened along to put an end to their fun.

"I believe the table linens need pressing. And the laundry needs sorting. Off with you." With a wave of her hand, Hoyle scattered the maids back to their duties. "And you, Mrs. Kendal? Is there something I can do for you?"

"I came in search of a cool cloth for my head," Eve lied quickly. "Headache. I mean to lie down for a while."

Hoyle peeked through the door to check what

had kept her maids occupied and caught an off-center view of Captain Thorne. "I see," she said, backing away. "Cool cloth indeed. Come along to the kitchen, Mrs. Kendal. Mary will fetch what you need."

Six

EVE STIFLED A SIGH OF ENVY AS SHE FASTENED THE necklace at Sophia's throat in her preparation to go down to dinner. Strands of gold beaded with onyx and pearls dripped down Sophia's décolletage, the perfect complement to the cranberry velvet gown. Eve once had a necklace like it, only lovelier. She'd sold it, among other jewels, to settle her accounts in India and make passage. To go with her simple black evening gown, Eve had chosen one of her few remaining necklaces, a simple chain of clear crystals bearing a single, round melo pearl.

"I should have had Alice dress here so we could supervise her wardrobe," Sophia said, smoothing her hand over the waves Mrs. Jenks had artfully arranged in her hair. "I can't fathom what drove her to choose that masculine necktie this afternoon."

"Really? You can't fathom?" Eve couldn't tell if Sophia meant what she said. "You don't realize that she wore the tie to spite your matchmaking efforts?"

Sophia looked up, stunned. "You really think she did it on purpose?"

"Of course. Alice hasn't quite come around to the idea that she needs a husband."

"Needs?" Sophia scoffed. "Of course one needs a husband. What on earth can she be thinking?"

Eve shrugged. "She's young. Maybe she fancies spending her inheritance on her own."

Sophia's grandmother Emerson had left both girls quite enough money so that a marriage of convenience could be avoided in favor of one for love. Eve still wasn't certain which Sophia had ended up in. Had she fallen for Gabriel in their years together, or was it still merely his title that appealed?

"On her own?" Sophia gasped. "She has no idea. You could tell her, I suppose. You know what it's like to be alone now. I'm sorry. Once I said that out loud, I realized how insensitive it sounds."

"No, but it's true. I do know what it is to feel quite alone. When I married Ben, I lost my family. Now I'm on my own again, or I would be without you." Eve smiled to show that she had taken no offense.

"But you still miss your parents? You never speak of them."

"Of course I miss them. If I had been able to marry Ben and keep my family in my life, I would have. You were right when you said it would be difficult to be without them. I've never stopped wishing that I could talk to my brother again."

"Maybe he will come around one day."

"One day," Eve agreed. "I have no regrets. But I would give anything to truly belong somewhere again." There was nothing she wanted more fiercely.

Her heart gave a twinge with the memory of having

been everything to Ben, and he to her. The way he used to look at her, his brown eyes—no, blue. His eyes had been blue. Oddly, she was picturing a different pair of eyes in her mind, clear whiskey-brown eyes tinged with gold. Captain Thorne's eyes.

"Are we ready to go down? The gentlemen might already be waiting in the drawing room." She might as well get introductions over with once and for all.

"I doubt it." Sophia laughed. "I think we would hear the sound of fisticuffs if Marcus and Gabriel ended up alone. I'm not quite ready. Why don't you go? Make sure they don't come to blows if they do find themselves together."

"I'll see you shortly, I hope?"

"Within minutes. I'm just going to call Jenks and see if she can find my onyx earrings."

Eve braced herself. No sense putting off the inevitable. It was time to see if Captain Thorne had a good memory.

&

Marcus paused outside Sophia's room on his way down. He knew Sophia's voice well enough, but the other seemed oddly familiar. It wasn't Alice. Sophia's maid? Or perhaps that friend of hers who had gone to bed with a headache? They hadn't been introduced upon his arrival, he realized. He'd been too caught up in choking down his annoyance at Gabriel.

Tonight, Marcus would sit at the table, have a good meal, make pleasant conversation with Sophia, try to avoid Gabriel's pointed barbs, dodge Agatha's attempts to read his aura, and maybe flirt with Alice. God help him if Sophia had called in a throng of neighbors to celebrate and adore him. He didn't have the patience to make nice with strangers or, worse, to endure the curious questions of people he used to know.

Yes, I fought in a war. Of course it was brutal. No, I wasn't injured…much. I felt more stupid than brave. How could I not be a changed man?

Perhaps Sophia's maid was in her room sharing conversation. They seemed to be friends. He found it refreshing that his sister-in-law would be so forward-thinking. First Kipling, now relaxing class distinction. *Bravo, Sophia.* He picked up some of the conversation. The woman with the oddly familiar voice remarked on missing her family and wishing she belonged somewhere. Marcus could keenly empathize.

His thoughts flew back to South Africa, to the families he'd had a hand in separating—women and children herded into camps, separated from their men. Had they found each other again? He knew he should be proud to have fought for his country. And yet, he felt a good deal of sadness and regret, a sense of loss that could never be restored. Good men were lost from both sides. Loss of life was never cause for celebration. And William Cooper had been such a fine man, a husband and father who would never come home to his own. Marcus had to remember how much he needed his brother if he wanted Tilly Meadow Farm for the Coopers.

Just then, he heard the women speak about Alice. Ah, so it was Alice that Sophia planned to throw into his path? No wonder she hadn't given up easily on luring him home. Perhaps he shouldn't encourage her. He needed to help the Coopers, not to be saddled with a wife. But just as he turned, about to go down to the drawing room, the door opened behind him and curiosity made him turn back.

He stood face to face with a petite blonde, the friend of Sophia's. He'd barely noticed her earlier, but now his immediate attention was drawn to her bosom, showcased with a melo pearl hanging provocatively down past her décolletage. Regretfully, staring at a woman's breasts was generally considered impolite. He forced his gaze up. His regret faded when he realized she had quite a pretty face, too. Heart-shaped, perfect little nose, high cheekbones, and a lush mouth, pink lips opened to a startled gasp.

"Captain Thorne. We haven't met." She kept her eyes lowered at first. Then something seemed to strike boldness in her, and she lifted her gaze to meet his. "I'm Lady Averford's friend, Mrs. Kendal."

"Of course," he answered absently before he met her eyes and froze. Gas-flame blue. *My bedside angel.* She stood right in front of him. But how? How had she been at Averford House on that unfortunate night? And now, to turn up here? Brazening out a lie that they hadn't met? Did she really think he wouldn't remember eyes like hers? "Mrs. Kendal."

"Yes." She seemed to relax, as if relieved she hadn't been found out.

"And how do you happen to be here?"

She blinked, perhaps becoming more uncertain. "By invitation, of course. I've come from India. My husband and I made our home there until he passed away."

"In India? How fascinating. You've recently arrived?" *Her husband had passed away?* She looked so young to be a widow.

She inhaled sharply. "Somewhat."

"Were you headed down?" He offered his arm. "I would be happy to escort you. We can get to know each other better."

"Thank you." She hesitated. Sophia was still in her room, leaving Eve little choice but to accept the offer or cut him coldly. She placed her dainty gloved hand in the crook of his elbow. "She 'travels fastest who travels alone,' but it is kind of you to offer. I accept."

"Kipling." He tried to hide his surprise. Yet another Kipling quote? He'd suspected Alice of writing for her sister, but now he'd found the truth. "Are you a great reader?"

"I do enjoy a good book. I have mixed feelings about Kipling, however."

"As do I. I'm sorry."

"Don't be." She laughed, a pleasant tinkling. "I'm sure Kipling has his share of detractors."

"No, about your husband. It must have been quite unnerving to end up a widow in India."

"It was. He was an army captain, too, killed in an earthquake in May of last year."

He couldn't hide his cringe. "Terrible way to go."

"They say it was instant, no suffering. He was a wonderful man. India was quite an adventure for us, but I'm glad to be back among friends now that I'm on my own. Lady Averford has been such a dear."

"That she is, inviting you here, and Averford House? You must have stopped in London, then, after disembarking." He stopped and faced her. "You didn't think I would remember you?"

She bit her pretty, pink lip and looked down. "I'm sorry. I don't know what you mean."

Yet unwilling to give up the game? He slipped a finger under her chin and urged her to lift her face until she met his gaze. For more than a few seconds, they remained as if frozen, looking into each other's eyes. Hers held a wealth of secrets, he imagined, and he suddenly wished he could uncover them all.

"Sweet mercy, woman, I couldn't forget you. You stayed with me, a stranger, at my bedside the whole night."

"Not quite the whole night. It was foolish of me, I know, but you seemed so frantic and—"

"Foolish? It was the kindest thing anyone's ever done for me. Embarrassed as I am that you've seen me at my worst, I'm relieved to have the chance to thank you. Sutton denied you'd even been there. I'd begun to think I'd dreamed you up."

"I asked Sutton not to mention my presence, just in case our paths ever crossed again. Though, I truly didn't think they would so soon. I had no idea you would come here, and then Sophia, well…" Her lips curved into a smile that lit her whole face, making the gas-flame blue eyes flare all the brighter. "You're welcome. Now let's put it behind us, shall we? Probably best if we never think of it again."

"But you wrote the letter? Kipling? Not exactly Sophia's style."

"I wrote it," she confessed. "Sophia asked me for help. She told me most of what to say. I couldn't deny her request, though I had no idea that it would actually succeed in enticing you here."

"I was overdue for a visit. Now I find that I'm meant for Lady Alice. Don't deny it. I overheard you and Sophia."

Eve blushed. "She has high hopes for you and Alice."

"She's not used to being disappointed, is she?"

She shook her head. "She's determined to have her way in all things."

"Then you'll have to help me. Let's give her a little scare when I ignore Alice and flirt with you instead." He smiled conspiratorially. "Are you game?"

"For flirting?" She laughed. "Sophia won't like it at all. What kind of friend would I be?"

"Come on," he urged. "Let's have some fun with her. No harm done."

"I don't know." She tilted her head, a golden strand falling from her chignon to brush her cheek. He resisted the urge to sweep it aside. "What's the fun in flirting if you're guaranteed success?" she asked. "You'll just have to see what happens if you try."

She took her hand from the crook of his arm to continue on alone. He trailed after her. "Mrs. Kendal, you minx. I believe you've already started."

Seven

SHE COULD FEEL HIS GAZE ON HER, PRACTICALLY burning through her dress as she made her way down the stairs. Lord Averford stood in the center of the hall speaking with Agatha and Alice. Agatha wore subdued peach and blue for the evening. Apparently, Alice had decided to please her sister and wear the recommended emerald silk that suited her in its simplicity. It was a long-sleeved sheath with a high collar that accented her graceful neck.

On sight of Captain Thorne, the earl broke away from the ladies to greet his brother with a clap on the shoulder.

"Look what the cat dragged in. You've finally come home."

"After two years, it seemed about time to make an appearance." Hands in his pockets, Captain Thorne shrugged, his black tailcoat accentuating his broad shoulders.

Though dressed alike in their evening finery, the two men could not have appeared more different. Lord Averford wore his with proud ease, the picture of effortless elegance. But even dressed to the nines, Captain Thorne managed to bring more casual scenarios to mind, as if the clothes were an encumbrance to be torn off at his earliest convenience. Or perhaps Eve was simply getting carried away. She checked the urge to run her fingers through his close-cropped hair and give it the rumpling it seemed to deserve.

"Did I hear you speaking with Mrs. Kendal on the way down? You've met?" Lord Averford asked, playing the role of dutiful host.

"We've made our own way in getting to know one another." Captain Thorne smiled in Eve's direction, and she felt the acknowledgment in a tingle at the base of her spine. "No need for introductions."

"Oh, that's right," Lord Averford said. "You stopped at Averford House along the way, Mrs. Kendal. I hope my brother was a proper host."

"We somehow missed each other." Thorne arched a brow in Eve's direction, and she felt her pulse quicken in response. "I never had the pleasure of a conversation with Mrs. Kendal at Averford House."

"Mr. Sutton took quite good care of me. I was there and out again so fast that I barely had time for anything." Eve spoke up in defense of Captain Thorne before his brother could take issue with him. "I've been meaning to make my way back to London for a day of business."

"Ladies needn't bother with business." Lord Averford dismissed her. "I'll set you up a meeting with my solicitor. He can handle your affairs."

Eve didn't get carried away with the issue of women's rights, but the suggestion that a lady didn't have the head to manage business rankled. "Thank you, but I can handle my own affairs."

"Right you can," said Alice, ever ready to jump into a political discussion. "Gabriel, for goodness sake. Before you know it, women will have the right to vote."

"Ah, well, let's not get ahead of ourselves." Lord Averford laughed. "I was only trying to help."

"And I thank you for it." Eve didn't mean to start an argument. "It's possible I may still need your help, and I'm pleased to know I can count on you if it comes to that. I think I need to go into London myself to check on a few things first."

"I have affairs to attend to in London as well," Captain Thorne said. "I can take you to Town, if you don't mind company."

Eve's mouth went completely dry at the idea of traveling alone with the man. She couldn't speak.

"Go?" Sophia, glorious in her cranberry gown, swept down the stairs to join them at just that moment. "How can you speak of going, Marcus? You've only just arrived."

"Only for a day. I'll come right back. You see, Brother, your wife misses me already."

"Wasting no time in wearing out your welcome, *Brother*." Lord Averford cast a heated glance in Captain Thorne's direction before he smiled to show that he was joking, or so he would have them all believe. Eve wasn't quite so sure. "Shall we go in, then?"

"Not yet, darling. We're expecting more guests."

"More guests?" Captain Thorne straightened his tie, and his full lips flattened to a grim line.

"It's not a proper homecoming without friends to welcome you home. Lord and Lady Holcomb are coming."

"And Lord Markham with his new wife," Alice piped in. "I can't wait to see her. They eloped. She's half his age."

"Maybe half." Sophia's eyes twinkled with the hint of scandal. "I believe she's more of an age with his son. But let's not speak of it."

"Let's not." Captain Thorne looked ready to bolt.

At the sound of Finch welcoming a new arrival, Eve closed the distance to stand at Captain Thorne's side. "I dread meeting new people—all the questions about my husband and how he died. Perhaps you can sit by me and help me steer the conversation when certain topics arise?"

His amber eyes lit up. "Of course. I'm happy to oblige."

"Thank you, Captain Thorne." What she really intended was to help him through any uncomfortable questions about the war. She only used her widow-hood as an excuse, and she knew he realized that when he found her hand and squeezed it gently in his own.

"Thank you, Mrs. Kendal. I begin to wonder if you really are an angel, after all."

Her heart raced. For the second time of the evening, she found herself at a complete loss for words. Fortunately, all parties had arrived and the commencement of introductions and going in to dine would give her plenty of time to regain command of her tongue.

～～

Of all the rooms at Thornbrook Park, the dining room had changed the most from what Marcus remembered. The walls had gone from green to a pale shade of violet. Sophia had replaced Mother's green glass chandelier with an elaborate crystal one. In addition, there were lit silver candelabras down the middle of the long rectangular table, and new lamps sat on all the side tables around the room next to elaborate flower arrangements. The paintings remained but had been rearranged, with a recent addition taking the center focal point between cabinets: a portrait of Gabriel posed like a red-coated Adonis on the hunt. Marcus rolled his eyes.

A portrait of Sophia on the opposite wall could have been a companion piece, except that she had chosen a staid interior rather than appearing as Artemis in the grand outdoors. She sat in a queenly white dress, surrounded by vases of flowers, her loyal subjects. It was a suitable likeness, but he would have advised her to embrace the wild theme, let her hair down, pose outdoors, perhaps bare a bosom. Well, perhaps the bare bosom would have been taking things a tad too far, but a loose Grecian gown wouldn't have been out of place. He imagined Mrs. Kendal in a loose gown, blond hair flowing.

Except for the pretty face of Mrs. Kendal at his side keeping his imagination occupied, dinner had been a dull affair. Conversation meandered along, a tedious trek through the usual mundane topics: the weather, the stock of game, and war. Everyone wanted to make Marcus out to be a hero, but he was just a man.

Fortunately, Mrs. Kendal changed the subject to ask if Marcus had ever met a few of her compatriots in India, especially a Colonel Adams who had served briefly in South Africa before ending up in Raipur. Marcus remarked that he hadn't had the pleasure, but Eve's question was enough to turn talk to India and away from his own time in service.

"Was it dreadfully hot? I think I might die from heat if I ever have to go to India," Lady Markham remarked as the first course, a glazed quail, was served.

Mrs. Kendal took it in stride. "The heat kept the flies from becoming too active. They get lazy, you know, when it's hot."

Marcus flashed Mrs. Kendal a look, and she winked at him. He knew she was having them all on. The heat would have brought the flies in droves.

"Oh, flies! Dreadful." Lady Holcomb recoiled. "Thank goodness you're back in England."

"Thank goodness for me," Sophia said. "I missed her. And I've missed Captain Thorne as well. Now I simply have to find a way to keep all my favorites here at Thornbrook Park. Alice, you must help me. How can we entice Captain Thorne to stay on?"

"Ha. I'll work to keep Eve on, perhaps. I haven't made up my mind about Captain Thorne yet."

"I'll have to convince you, but not too aggressively. I'm not set on staying for long," Marcus said. Though Mrs. Kendal, if not Alice, made him consider the possibilities. Eve, a fitting name. Like the biblical Eve, she put thoughts of sin in his mind, original or otherwise. The combination of those eyes with that figure was too much for any man to resist. He was just about to steal another glance at her when Aunt Agatha made a pronouncement.

"We have a new visitor in the room. Lady Markham has joined us."

"I've been here the whole time." Lady Markham laughed and reached for her near-empty claret glass.

"No, my apologies. I mean the first Lady Markham. She considers herself the only Lady Markham," Agatha added in a loudly whispered aside.

"Well, how about that?" Lady Markham humphed and reached again for her glass, barely waiting for the footman to finish filling it.

"She does not approve." Agatha shook her head sorrowfully. "Please take no offense, Lady Markham, or I should call you by your given name to avoid provoking her. Do not take it personally. The dead often don't approve of their replacements."

Lord Markham smiled. "That was my Sarabeth, always finding fault."

"Your ghost wife passes judgment on me, and that's all you can say in my defense?" The new Lady Markham pursed her lips, clearly not at all pleased with the conversation.

"We're talking to a chair." Lord Markham gestured. Unsatisfied, his young wife crossed her arms and turned slightly away from him. He shook his head, defeated, and readdressed the chair. "Very well. Now, Sarabeth, darling, you left me and what was I to do? You know I could never manage on my own."

Lady Markham rose in a huff. "You never call *me* darling."

"Oh!" Agatha exclaimed. "That did it. She's gone."

"What did it?" Sophia asked, drawn in to the scene. "Lord Markham's confession?"

"No, the new Lady Markham's indignant reaction. The former Lady Markham threw back her head, laughed, and disappeared. Sometimes the spirits just want to make trouble, don't they?"

"Mission accomplished." Gabriel rolled his eyes. "Now let's get back to more pertinent discussion."

The new Lady Markham, perhaps realizing she looked silly, settled back in her seat.

"Pray, what is more pertinent, Brother? 'Words are, of course, the most powerful drug used by mankind,' as Kipling says." He smiled at Eve. "So go ahead, Gabriel. Intoxicate us!"

Eve flashed him a look as if surprised he could even mention intoxication.

"Lady Markham knows all about such states, I believe," he whispered, delighted to see her blush in response. The spectacle with Agatha and the Markhams had interfered with his planned flirtation.

"If you want a good drunk, I've got plenty of excellent scotch." Gabriel missed his point, as usual.

"I want to be drunk on words, Gabriel. You mistake me. Sophia, dear sister, you like words well enough. Go on, speak! Let us drink our fill from your font of wisdom."

"I don't think anyone has ever accused Sophia of wisdom," Alice said with a laugh.

"Now, now," Marcus defended. "In the letter that lured me here, the lovely Sophia quoted Kipling."

"Kipling?" Alice laughed. "I doubt Sophia has ever read Kipling. Have you, dear?"

Sophia's cornflower eyes darted between Marcus and Alice, as if she couldn't decide if she was pleased that they were interacting, even if it were at her expense. Or maybe she was trying to figure out if it was indeed at her expense.

Sophia shook her head. "I can't say that I have. I prefer Brontë."

"Brontë? 'Better to be without logic than without feeling,' as Charlotte said. I applaud your choice." Marcus raised his glass.

"You know Brontë, Captain Thorne?" Eve asked, surprised.

"Charlotte? Perhaps she meant Emily. Or Anne," Alice suggested.

"I've read some Brontë, I must confess." He met Eve's gaze warmly. "I wouldn't sneer at a book simply because it was written by a woman, as some of my fellow men might do."

"'Terror made me cruel,'" Eve said, trying to hide that she was most favorably impressed with his answer. "Do you know that one, Captain Thorne?"

"Was it Lockwood who said so? *Wuthering Heights*?" Marcus knew it was. Test him, would she? "Tell me, Alice, are you ever cruel, and is it terror that makes you so?"

"I'm not sure I've ever been terrified," Alice said, after a moment's consideration.

"Oh? I'm certain you've been cruel." Marcus flashed a smile.

"Why would you think so?" Sophia asked.

"A beautiful woman such as our Alice, not yet wed? She's no doubt disappointed any number of suitors. Haven't you, Alice?"

"A woman can't be expected to say, Captain

Thorne. You scoundrel." Sophia tried to admonish him, although she couldn't help but smile in her obvious delight at the flirting going on in front of her. "Don't answer him, Alice."

"Alice has met her soul's equal, but she didn't know it at the time," Agatha said, closing her eyes and rubbing her temples. "He's a shadowy figure. I see him digging in the dirt with bare hands. What could it mean?"

"Perhaps he's burying treasure," Gabriel jested, probably for the chance to steer the conversation away from another spiritual reading by Agatha. "You're destined for a pirate, Alice. My brother doesn't like dirt. Do you, Marcus? He's never liked to make a mess, always his nose in a book. As you can see from the way he quotes to us. Kipling, Brontë, bah."

"I was a bookish lad. But then I put away childish things and went to war." He stared Gabriel down, aware of the hardness in his eyes even as he felt a rage edging in. "I learned to shoot. I don't think my brother has the guts to bring me out with him, lest he find himself bested. Isn't that why you haven't invited me to join you, Gabriel?"

Gabriel laughed and pushed the quail around his plate. "As it is, the fish are biting. I won't be shooting again until next Thursday at the earliest."

"There's a hunt!" Alice interrupted. "Isn't there, Lord Markham? On your lands, I believe. A fox hunt? In a fortnight? I hope to practice some so I can take part."

"There is indeed," Markham acknowledged. "But it's only a cub hunt."

"A cub hunt?" Alice wanted to hunt, who knew why, but she clearly hadn't mastered the terms.

"A cub hunt serves many purposes," Markham explained. "Some use it to cull the young foxes to make a more manageable skulk when the real hunt begins. I use a cub hunt to train my pups, so that they learn to go after foxes and not rabbits or squirrels. I have some fine hounds this season. I think they will learn well."

"Foxhounds?" Alice asked. "I love dogs."

"Foxhounds, yes. I also keep terriers. They're more likely to go right into the burrow."

Sophia fanned her hand in front of her face. "Oh, no. I think of the poor foxes and I feel faint."

"She's never been one for blood sports, have you, sweetheart?" Gabriel took his wife's hand most tenderly, and they shared a quick glance that made Marcus's own heart tighten in his chest. In some ways, he wished he had someone with whom to share private glances. In other ways, he might be better off alone.

The rage. He'd even forgotten about comely Eve Kendal seated at his side when it started to come over him. Fortunately, the darkness passed with the turning of the conversation, leaving as swiftly as it had arrived. But he wouldn't always be so fortunate. It might come upon him again, and what then? Perhaps he shouldn't have come. He might be headed back to London sooner than expected.

Eight

EVE'S CONSCIENCE NAGGED HER THAT SHE'D BEEN
avoiding her business in London by living leisurely
at Thornbrook Park. She needed to see to her affairs
before Lord Averford deemed her incapable, an infe-
rior female, and stepped in. Besides, she didn't want
to get in the way of a budding romance. Despite his
proclaimed intention to flirt with her, Captain Thorne
had turned his attention to Lady Alice before they'd
even passed through to the drawing room for cordials.

Sophia had been in delights. It was then that Eve
had formed her plans, made arrangements, and gone
off to bed early with the excuse of another headache.
She woke before daylight and donned her most practical traveling suit, black like most of her wardrobe.
She added a hat trimmed with pink ribbon for just a
touch of color and set off. As the sun began to rise, she
quietly left the house to find Dale waiting.

"Shall we go?" she asked softly, approaching him.

The chauffeur met her gaze only briefly before his
eyes shifted to focus on something behind her. "Good
morning, Captain Thorne. The car's ready."

She startled, barely resisting the urge to turn. Captain Thorne? Her heart gave a queer flutter and her mouth went dry as ash.

"Good morning, Dale. I see I'm fortunate to have company. Going to the train as well?"

Before she could steel her nerves, she found him standing at her side, the warmth from his amber eyes spreading through her veins like whiskey. Yet her knees shook as if she were chilled.

"I am." She checked her urge to pinch her cheeks or smooth her hair, though her tongue darted out to wet her lips before she gained control of herself. It could only be that she'd been deprived of male company for over a year, and Captain Thorne was of a type she found pleasing—solid, athletic, and overwhelmingly male. "But you've only just arrived. Leaving us so soon?"

"Unavoidable business." He, too, wore somber black, coat and trousers, white shirt, blue tie, and a dark Homburg hat, much like the one he'd arrived in.

She nodded. "Sophia suggested a night at Averford House in case my business goes late, as I expect it will."

She had no idea how long it would take to straighten out her affairs.

"We'll be a moment. I'm preparing the engine," Dale informed them. When Captain Thorne placed his hand on her waist to escort her to the side of the driveway, a jolt of heat seared straight through her. Imagined, of course. She tried to discount it.

"I'll be staying the night at Averford House as well. Perhaps we can dine together."

"Yes. I would like that." She hoped she didn't answer too quickly. "Won't Mr. Sutton be surprised?"

"Ha!" Captain Thorne had a loud, merry laugh. She worried he would wake the house before they set off. "Won't he, though? Perhaps I'll pretend not to know you."

"Or I can pretend to be a figment of your imagination." She smiled.

"If I imagined you, I would have made sure you remained in the drawing room after dinner last night. By the time we finished our cognac and passed through to join you, Sophia told me you'd gone up to bed. How are you feeling today?"

"Much better, thank you. It was just a headache. I'm better now. Perhaps I simply needed some time to adjust to a new environment."

"I know what that's like. Unfortunately, I adjusted with an awful lot of whiskey followed by time alone in a dark room. After the war."

"Before the prizefighting?" She saw his eyebrows shoot up. He didn't expect she knew. "Mr. Sutton had mentioned it to explain the bruises."

"The fighting did help me recover some, I think, yes. After I got in the ring for the first time, I started drinking less. Until that last time, when I obviously decided to let defeat encourage me to drink a bit more." Was that a glint of embarrassment in his eyes?

"And now you're here." She gestured around them. "I know Sophia's so glad you've returned. You do plan to come back?"

"I do," he said, after a moment's hesitation. "Probably tomorrow. But we're both unsuitable

houseguests. I made my excuses not long after you
left us."

"You're not a guest. You grew up here."

"That only means they place more expectations
upon me. I suppose we're ready, Dale," he said, noticing the poor chauffeur standing at attention, waiting
patiently for them to finish their conversation.

"Yes, Captain Thorne."

"Ladies first." Captain Thorne nodded in her direction as Dale came around to get her door.

"But Captain Thorne," she said, holding his amber
gaze and savoring the warmth that flooded her. "I'm
not a lady."

Instead of a reply, the scandalous man had the nerve
to flash her a crooked, wolfish grin as he waited for her
to get into the car.

∾

He'd had the opportunity to study her figure as he
approached the car, her nipped-in waist and the slight
curve of her bottom. She wasn't as willowy as Sophia,
but she stood barely tall enough to lean her head on his
shoulder or to press the curve of her breasts into his chest,
should he pull her close. She would be soft in his arms
and smell of ginger and oranges, a heady combination.

He'd caught the scent, exotic and unexpected,
wafting from her when he'd run into her in the hall
outside Sophia's chamber, and he could catch a hint
of it in the air intermittently as they rode along. Some
perfume her husband had bought her in India, no
doubt. He wondered if she wore it to remember the
husband or to bring India back to life in her mind.

As they pulled to a stop at the station, he didn't wait for Dale to come around. Waving the chauffeur off, he stepped out and around to open her door. He liked that she took his hand and allowed him to help her from the car instead of protesting, and he wasn't inclined to give the hand back even as they said their good-byes to the driver and walked away from the car. He tucked her hand into the crook of his arm, where it felt right.

She raised her face to him, a smile in her blue-silver eyes. "I've known men like you, Captain Thorne."

"Men like me?"

"Mmm." She nodded. "Confident, charming, ready to say and do all the right things."

"You mistake me. I'm perhaps only one of the three."

"You would say so. You want me to try to guess which one. It adds to your intrigue. But really, you prefer to believe there are no other men like you."

He laughed, taking her comments lightly. She fancied herself a judge of character, did she? "I want you to believe it as well."

She laughed, too, a delicate sound that reminded him of the bubbles in champagne, refreshing and sweet. "Perhaps it's best that I just smile and allow that I've been speaking out of turn."

"Speak freely, Mrs. Kendal. We can be friends, I hope. If you've known men like me, then you know I'm not like my brother."

They approached the ticket agent. He bought two fares without giving it a thought.

"Oh, but—I can pay my own fare, Captain Thorne. I don't believe we'll be seated together."

"We will." He waved the tickets. "Don't leave me alone with my thoughts for the entire ride into town. Please. I enjoy having company."

He enjoyed having conversation, a distraction from the dark thoughts that crept in any time he was alone in the quiet for too long.

She pursed her full lips, withdrew her hand from his arm, and reached into her pocket. "All right. But let me pay you for my share."

He took her hand back and put it in the crook of his arm. "We'll work it out later. For now, let's get settled."

The train was already at the station.

"The first-class car?" She hesitated.

"The first-class car, of course. What else?" To save on expenses, she probably hadn't taken it to come to Thornbrook, but she deserved the best and so she should have it.

He helped her inside and to their seats, his gaze drawn to her backside as she settled in. He hadn't thought of women in months, longer perhaps, but God help him, she brought every basic male instinct back to immediate attention. At that hour, the train remained empty enough for them to take seats facing each other so he could watch her as they conversed.

"Call me Marcus," he said, leaning forward, hands on his knees. "At least while we're away from Thornbrook Park."

She raised her thin, blond brows as if surprised but taking it under consideration. "You may call me Eve."

"I suppose we're in a unique enough situation to be less formal around each other, considering that we were in intimate conditions before even having met properly."

She laughed again. "That's not entirely true. You introduced yourself."

"Did I? I can't remember."

"*Catpin* Marcus Thorne, at your service." She mocked his deep voice and held out her hand.

"Ha! Sounds like me. Catpin? I'm sorry that I can't remember."

"Rest assured, Marcus, I did not take advantage of you in your unfortunate state."

It was his turn to laugh. "I'm sorry for that, too. Tell me, Eve, how is that you're not a lady? I think you could have married an earl or a viscount if you'd wanted. Your husband didn't have a title? He must have worked up the ranks the hard way."

"He did." She nodded. "He was a hard worker. Determined. He'd risen to captain before we'd even met. And after we'd met, I didn't want anyone else. Mother hoped I would end up a marchioness, or a countess at least. But I was in love. I didn't think they would be completely pleased, but I had no idea they would disown me. My father earned his money in trade. He purchased our estate. Apparently, Mother had hoped I would ease the censure by bringing a title into the family. Grandfather was an American."

"The horror." Marcus smiled so that she could see he was not serious. "Instead, you tarnished the family name further with an elopement."

"When Ben died…" She hesitated, emotion darkening her eyes. She blinked quickly and went on. "I was alone in India. My pension wasn't stretching as far as I'd hoped. I'm headed into London to meet with my husband's solicitor, a former associate of his father. I'm hoping he has some idea where our money was invested. It seems to have gone missing."

"I'm sorry. And your husband's parents?"

"They passed away before we were married."

"So you are quite alone in the world."

"I have Sophia. And sometimes, it feels like Ben is still with me."

"Agatha would know for certain. Shall we inquire?"

She laughed again. Fortunately, the effervescent giggle that delighted him. "I confess that I'm a little afraid to find what Agatha might reveal."

"She can be frightening, that one. I hope you find what you need in London."

"As do I." She nodded. "Perhaps I haven't known men quite like you after all. At first, you reminded me a bit of some of the dashing young officers who would visit us at home, bragging of their exploits. You're not one to boast, though, are you, Marcus?"

"I wouldn't say so, or I would be boasting." He shrugged.

"Hmm. It can't have been easy growing up a second son, always having Gabriel ahead of you."

"In everything." He rolled his eyes. "Everything sporting, at least. He wasn't one for books. I had him there."

"And you purchased your commission. To prove a point or fully intending to be sent off to war?"

He shrugged. "Honestly, I hadn't considered being sent off to war. I had to make a place for myself, and the army seemed a good start. I wasn't cut out for the clergy, much to my mother's dismay. We have that in common, I suppose. We've both disappointed our mothers."

"I'm sure she's very proud of you now. You went off to war, but you came back."

"I came back." Cooper didn't. Eve's husband didn't. It hardly felt like a worthy accomplishment.

"I imagine that Gabriel secretly envies you," Eve said. "He has been stuck at home all this time, and you've had extraordinary adventures."

"He has what he wants. He would never envy me."

"You might be surprised. You might enjoy some time with your brother after being away for so long. You might find that he, too, has changed. You still have a brother, Marcus. I can't tell you what it would mean to me to have a family again, a place to belong."

He didn't set her straight on the impossibility of dealing with Gabriel. "You miss them? Even though they let you go so easily?"

"I do. Please give Gabriel a chance. You're not boys anymore."

"I'll consider it if we can move on to brighter topics. Tell me about India."

Her face lit up. "It was a different world. But one I rather liked. I don't miss the heat, the sand, the unrest, but I do miss the people, the colors, the smells, and a good curry."

"Ah, curry."

"English food tastes bland to me now, though Mrs. Mallows is a wonderful cook."

"Only the best for my brother, the earl. But we're back to unpleasant topics."

"Is that why you're running off to London this morning? To get away from him?"

He didn't like the sound of it coming from her, that he had to resort to running away. Perhaps it was time he stopped running and faced all of his problems head on. After today.

"As I said, I have affairs to tend. But how lucky that we're both escaping on the same day. We can return together as well, tomorrow morning."

"I made the return trip from India. I'm certain I could handle a train trip from London." She straightened up, squaring her slender shoulders as if to prove her mettle.

He shook his head. "There are ruffians everywhere."

"I might be looking at one."

"You wound me." He held his hands to his heart. "I want nothing more than to look after a lone damsel. Plus, I've enjoyed our conversation. I'm pleased that we get to continue it over dinner."

"I'm pleased as well. I look forward to seeing you again tonight."

～

Leaving the station, Eve felt disoriented. Marcus had pointed her on the way, but nothing looked as she remembered it. She might have managed to navigate Mayfair, but Cheapside? Shops had closed, new ones opened. How was she to find her way to Edgar Strump's office?

She walked along, careful to lift her skirts to avoid the mud that occasionally splattered up from the road, where a mix of carriages and cars shared the way. She knew that she had to walk away from St. Mary-le-Bow, cross the road, and continue down to the right. Or was it left? Ben would never have asked for directions. Not if his life depended on it, she suddenly recalled with a smile. But she'd never shared his hesitance to request help when in a bind. The problem was getting someone to stop long enough to pay her any mind.

After the fifth person she stopped gave her the information she needed, she followed his instructions to the address, only a few blocks from where she'd started. She might have missed it except for the small sign over the doorbell that read "Marsh, Phillips, and Strump." She rang the bell to no avail, and eventually turned the knob and walked in.

She approached a man sitting at a desk not four feet from the door. "I'm Mrs. Kendal looking for Mr. Strump, please. We have business."

The sandy-haired man with spectacles trailing down his nose got to his feet. "I'm Gibbs, Mr. Strump's assistant. Do you have an appointment?"

"No." She'd been so eager to get on with the things that she'd never considered making one. "But please, ask him to make time for me. I've come from Yorkshire for the day."

Gibbs sighed as if she'd asked for the moon. "I'll do my best. Please have a seat. Mrs. Kendal, you say?"

"He would be more aware of my husband, Captain Benjamin Kendal."

"A moment, Mrs. Kendal."

She did not take the offered seat in a row of dusty chairs lined up down the hall by the door. She paced, studying the certificates and portraits that hung on stark white walls. When Mr. Gibbs returned, a stocky, brown-haired man walked with him.

"Mrs. Kendal. Mr. Edgar Strump, Esquire, at your service. Come along to my office and we'll talk."

Relief washed over Eve. "Thank you for seeing me." She followed him down the hall to a crowded little room so stuffed full with shelves of books and papers that there was barely room for a desk and two chairs. She eased around the far side of the desk and wedged her way into the seat he indicated for her.

"Now, Mrs. Kendal, what can I do for you?"

"My husband, Captain Kendal, passed away last year, as you may be aware. Earthquake. In India."

"Bad business, bad business. Yes, yes, of course. So sorry for your loss. So sorry."

"Thank you. I've come to inquire into his investments. I believe he made arrangements with you?"

"Arrangements, arrangements." Mr. Strump tented his fingers as if he was struggling to remember. "Yes, yes. We made arrangements. We did. We did."

She wondered if she would suffer through Strump repeating himself all afternoon. "You did? I would like to know what arrangements. Where did he invest our money, and is it possible to get any of it? Are there dividends, perhaps? Anything of note?"

"Oh." He flattened his hands on the desk. "It will take some time. It's all in my files. Some time, I say."

She followed his stare to a cabinet in the corner of the room. Papers leaked out of every drawer, the cabinet so crammed that the drawers couldn't completely close. She inhaled deeply, a futile effort to draw patience from thin air. "How long, Mr. Strump? Tomorrow? Next week?"

"Oh, tomorrow. Tomorrow, to be sure. Come back in the morning, and I'll have it all sorted out."

"Tomorrow, really?" Her mood brightened. It was more than she had hoped after seeing the state of Strump's office. "When you say sorted out, what exactly do you mean? Have you any idea where our money is? Is it simply a matter of tracking down the relevant accounts? Anything you can tell me now would be a help."

"Finding the accounts, yes. The relevant accounts. But memory, too." He tapped his forehead. "I remember Ben Kendal well, bless his soul. A good man. Most of your husband's money went into a diamond mine. Diamonds, good business. Strong investment. I introduced him to the owner of the mine right about the time I found a house for him in Raipur."

"A diamond mine?" Ben had handled all the arrangements for their move without her, not wishing to trouble her with business. How she wished she had insisted on being part of the planning.

"In Golkonda. I have notes on the transaction around here somewhere. There might be some delay in actually retrieving your funds, but I think you should be very pleased. Very pleased."

She remembered Ben taking a trip to Golkonda shortly after their arrival, but a diamond mine? A practical man, he would have had to be convinced of the security of such an investment. "Thank you. I will be back in the morning, then."

"In the morning," the solicitor parroted. "A new

day, Mrs. Kendal. A new day." He walked her to the front door.

"I certainly hope so, Mr. Strump. Until tomorrow, then." Filled with hope, she walked out into the cloudy afternoon. Her business concluded earlier than planned, she thought perhaps she would have some tea and do some shopping, maybe buy a new dress for her dinner with Captain Thorne.

Nine

MARCUS FELT VAGUELY UNSETTLED AS HE LEFT EVE Kendal to make his way to the Cooper flat. Without the soothing effects of her influence, the prickling under his skin had returned. Being back in London should have brightened his mood, but perhaps a visit with the Coopers would improve his state of mind.

They weren't expecting him. He hoped a visit wouldn't be an imposition. Prudence was far too good-natured to say so if it were. He stopped at a cart to buy some flowers on the way. With few windows, no electricity, and Prudence's thrift limiting even their use of candles, the little five-room flat that housed the Coopers could get dreary. Flowers would brighten it up a bit. He made a second stop for the tea cakes that Anna and little Emily adored. Deciding that wasn't enough, couldn't possibly be enough, he made a few more stops and arranged for a fat goose and some baskets of fresh fruit and vegetables to be delivered later in the day, too late for Prudence to attempt any refusal of his generosity.

Only then—armed with flowers, pastries, and the

knowledge that any meal she tried to feed him would be replaced in her pantry after his departure—did he walk up the three flights to knock on Prudence Cooper's door.

"Marcus! What a lovely surprise. Do come in. Never mind your boots." She stopped him when he stooped to remove his boots. "Children, come and see who is here."

He found her good cheer contagious. Such was her nature. She was a pleasant-looking woman with a round face and ready smile, the sort that made one feel at home.

Her green dress was clean, faded but not frayed. Her house was immaculate, making him wish he'd ignored her and removed his boots. Not a half minute after she closed the door behind him, the children came running to greet him. Emily and Anna, the two girls, and Finn, the youngest, who was now nearly as tall as Emily, trailing behind.

"Are those tea cakes?" Emily spied the brown-paper-wrapped parcel in his hands before he even had a chance to greet her properly.

"What, this here?" He held the parcel out by the string. "Cakes? No, just some old fish. Do you like old fish?"

Emily darted forth to give him the requisite hug, reaching for the cakes before her sister could get them.

"I get the almond ones," Anna declared, stepping forward. How much she had grown. At nearly thirteen, she was no longer a slip of a girl. She'd begun to develop her mother's curves. Before long, she would be courted and married, properly if he could arrange it. Once he got them to the farm, he might encourage Sophia to introduce the girl to a wider circle of acquaintances.

"They're all almond," he pronounced before the girls commenced fighting over them. He remembered which they'd favored last time.

"You're becoming wise to the ways of parenting, Captain Thorne."

"Too wise, perhaps." He shrugged out of his coat and ignored her reach for it to go to the corner and hang it himself. "Where's Brandon?"

She blushed. "Brandon's just gone off with some friends. Boys, you know."

"He hasn't come home," Finn offered proudly, perhaps not aware that he was causing his idol brother trouble in his haste to report any and all information. "After supper, it was his turn to clean up, but he called Mum a shrew and ran off."

"Is this true, Prudence?" Marcus turned to her, unable to mask the concern in his eyes. "Did he speak to you in such a manner? And he hasn't returned?"

"It's nothing, Marcus. He's at an age, no longer a boy but not yet a man. You must remember what it was like."

"I never disrespected my parents." Though, God knows, he had come close with his father at times. "You can't stand for this, Prue. I won't stand for it. I'm going out to bring him home."

"I have no idea where he might have gone." Prudence twisted her hand in the chain at her throat, the one that she never removed. It held a charm shaped like a key, from William. The key to William's heart. Marcus ached for her.

"I have an idea. I'll bring him home, Prudence. And I'll make sure he never disrespects you again."

Less than an hour later, Marcus had Brandon in his sights in an alley a few blocks from the Hog and Hound. Bent over dice, the little bounder remained ignorant of Marcus's presence until Marcus pulled him up by the collar. The other lads scattered to the alley corners, all except for one, who hauled himself to full height behind Brandon.

"We have a score to settle," Marcus informed Brandon from between clenched teeth as he turned the lad to face him. "Like men."

"Marcus." Brandon's brown eyes, so like his father's, widened in surprise. "When did you come to town?"

"This morning."

Brandon dusted himself off, leaned in, and said quietly, "You've been to see Mum?"

Marcus smiled ruefully. "What do you think?"

"He's got something to settle with me first." The foolhardy lad who remained close to Brandon stepped forward and held a hand out. "Pay up."

"Pay? Does Brandon Cooper owe you money?" Marcus stepped forward, nudging Brandon behind him.

"A bob." The rotter nodded. "'E's not going anywhere 'til I get paid, then, 'ey?"

Marcus laughed. "You don't say. And I suppose you won this money gambling with dice in the streets? Which is illegal."

"I'll get my money." The rotter was a bold one, moving into Marcus's personal space and waving his arms dangerously close to Marcus.

"You will, but it's the last you'll see of it from Brandon Cooper." Suspecting that Brandon didn't have means to pay the debt, Marcus tossed the little rotter a bob. "Off with you, then."

Once Brandon's associates moved along, Brandon turned to Marcus. "You've ruined everything. One more round and I'd have had him, double or nothing."

"And I can beat Smithy Harris with one hand behind my back."

Brandon laughed. "That'll be the day."

"Exactly." Marcus turned to the boy and looked him in the eye. "That's the trouble with gambling. You're leaving your fate to chance. One more round, and he might have realized you couldn't honor your wager and beaten you senseless. Don't worry. You're going to earn back every penny of the debt and more."

"Are you fighting tonight, then?" Brandon's eyes brightened at the prospect. "Smithy Harris? Last time, I earned a florin betting against you."

Marcus sighed. Was it his fault that Brandon had caught the gambling bug? The excitement of wagering on the fights? "I have a surefire way for you to repay me, and it doesn't involve making risky bets. You, Brandon Cooper, are about to learn the value of hard work."

"But Mum doesn't want me going back to the millinery."

"Not the millinery. I have a better idea, and I'm fairly certain your mum will approve. How do you feel about breathing some nice, clean country air?"

Brandon froze in his tracks. "You're shipping me off to the army?"

"Not the army. I'm talking about life on the farm."

"I don't know anything about farming."

Marcus rumpled the lad's hair. "And you're just at the right age to learn. You'll come with me when I go back to Thornbrook Park, and I'll put you to work for a friend of mine, Mrs. Dennehy, on Tilly Meadow Farm. She has sheep, cows. You can ride horses. I pitched in some myself there when I was your age in exchange for all the apples I could eat. It's good solid work and plenty of adventure for a young man off on his own."

"I don't know. Getting paid in apples for hard labor? I'm not all that keen on apples. I found a worm in one, once. Well, half a worm." He pulled a sick face and rubbed his stomach.

"I know you like cheese. You'll never taste any better than Mrs. Dennehy's cheddar. Besides, you don't have much choice. You owe me a bob."

"What did you mean, a young man on my own? Won't Mrs. Dennehy be looking after me?" He cocked a brow, so like William Cooper.

"She's a farmer, not a nursemaid. She'll put you to work in exchange for room, board, and wages." At least, Marcus hoped she would. He would have to bargain with Mrs. Dennehy to take young Cooper on. And after he established Brandon on the farm, perhaps he could convince Mrs. Dennehy of the merits of retirement in favor of letting the whole Cooper family take over at Tilly Meadow. It was a good start.

"Wages? I'll earn some money to send home to Mum?"

"If it all goes well." Marcus put his arm around him. "Come on, boy. It's time we made you a man."

∽∾

As she made her way to Averford House, Eve had an uneasy feeling that she was being followed. It had started with a queer tingling down her spine as she'd sipped her tea, staring out the window of Wilson's Tearoom at the crowds passing on the street. She'd noticed a man in a dark suit and black bowler hat who had passed the window and, after a time, had passed back again.

She walked faster now, suddenly very glad that she would soon be reunited with Marcus. It wasn't that she needed a man or was incapable of finding her way alone, but there was an added sense of safety in numbers.

Preoccupied as she turned a corner, she ran right into a man coming from the opposite direction. On instinct, her hand went up between them to cushion the blow and she nearly dropped her parcel.

"Fancy meeting you like this," he said, tipping his hat. "I hope I didn't hurt you."

His hand curled around her waist as if to steady her, but it stayed there. She felt the hard planes of his chest under her palms. She stepped back.

"Not at all." She smoothed her coat, as if to show that all was well. Hearing his voice instantly calmed her nerves. "I seem to keep bumping into you, Captain Thorne."

"As habits go, it's not a bad one to get into." He took her hand and tucked it into the crook of his arm, another habit that could become all too comfortable. They looked like a couple. If a man followed her for any reason, it would do well to appear as if she had a man looking after her. A large and capable man.

Instead of setting off as expected, Marcus paused and turned. Had he been followed, too?

"Marcus?" Eve asked. "Something amiss?"

"There you are, Brandon," he said, looking behind him. "Try to keep up. Averford House isn't much farther up the road."

Brandon? A young man with shaggy brown hair joined them.

"Mrs. Kendal, might I present my young charge, Brandon Cooper? He will be joining us for the evening and returning with us to Thornbrook Park tomorrow."

"Brandon." She tipped her head in greeting and turned her gaze back to Marcus. "Your young charge?" Was this what had kept Marcus in London and away from Thornbrook Park? He had a "young charge?" A ward? Or—

"Brandon's father and I were at war together," Marcus began, somewhat awkwardly.

"Father didn't make it home," Brandon interrupted.

"I'm very sorry for your loss," Eve offered, pieces falling into place. Marcus had served with Brandon's father and somehow had assumed responsibility for his friend's child. Wouldn't Gabriel be surprised to learn of his brother's philanthropy?

"I'm going to work on a farm," Brandon boasted with enthusiasm, avoiding further acknowledgment of her sympathetic words. She understood, having become tired of finding pity in the eyes of friends and strangers alike when they learned of her widowhood.

"Tilly Meadow, with Mrs. Dennehy," Marcus clarified. "If all goes according to plan."

If. He still had to clear it with Gabriel, she supposed,

and who knew how that would go? He must care a great deal about Brandon Cooper to put himself in a position to ask for something from his brother.

She stole a glance at him. "Oh my, you have a bruise. What happened?"

Marcus's inflamed cheek sported a purplish-black mark, and his lip seemed a tad fuller than usual. "Ah, yes. The marks of manhood, my dear. Nothing to fret over. Brandon and I did some sparring, blowing off steam after obtaining permission from his mother for his immediate departure."

She looked at Brandon, not a mark on him. Marcus had probably gone easy on the boy. "Congratulations, Brandon. You must have been the victor."

Brandon smiled, pride in his chocolate brown eyes.

"Hold on. I think, yes, Marcus, you're bleeding." She stopped, took out her handkerchief, and dabbed at the blood on his lip where it split ever so slightly.

Her knees shook. A rush of heat surged through her bloodstream and pooled between her thighs. The urge to kiss him was suddenly so overwhelming that it was all she could do not to cover his lush lips with her own. Nearly. She stepped back and tucked her kerchief away. It certainly wouldn't do when they had a child present. "There. All better."

She wanted him, she realized, biting her lip. She wanted Captain Marcus Thorne, a man meant for Sophia's sister, a man she couldn't have. Where had the sudden wave of longing come from? More importantly, how could she make it go away? A lump rose in her throat. Perhaps better that Brandon had joined them than that they found themselves alone. All night.

"Thank you, Eve. Sutton's a good sport most of the time, but blood at the dinner table might put him over the edge."

"We'll have time to change before dinner, I hope," she said, hugging her parcel to her chest. She'd found a glorious gown on the rack, half price, because some baroness had ordered it and had never come back for it. As luck would have it, it fit Eve perfectly. She hadn't even had to pay for alterations. She'd also bought a skirt in the new shortened style, perfect for the modern woman who made frequent use of trains. Stepping up to board would be much easier without the cumbersome length of her usual skirts.

"We'll make time. It's all up to us. Can I carry that for you?" he asked, as if just making note of her parcel.

"Oh no. Thank you. It's not heavy." She willed herself to move on, just keep walking, just keep making conversation, pretend to be completely unaffected by the man at her side who made her pulse race every time she stole a glance at him. "A new dress. Sophia keeps insisting I need some, but I haven't had time to bother. Must keep up appearances, she says. I used to think so, too, but I suppose India transformed my sensibilities. I no longer care about wearing the right clothes as much as wearing what I like."

Clothes. Her mind jumped to the image of Captain Thorne in no clothes. Not a stitch. She nearly covered her face with her hands as if seeing him before her very eyes. The wide chest, lean waist, his rippled abdomen, and lower.

"'Beware of all enterprises that require new clothes,'" he said. "Was it Mark Twain who said so?"

"I believe it was Thoreau." She remembered Colonel Adams's warning about discouraging suitors by showing her intelligence and almost held her tongue. Almost. Intrigued as she was by Captain Thorne, she refused to resort to artifice.

"Bah, American writers. I get them all confused." He laughed. "But here we are at Averford House. It's time to give Mr. Sutton a shock when we walk in together."

"Together with me," Brandon interjected, as if to remind them of his presence. "No doubt Mr. Sutton will be surprised to see me, too."

"Oh, no doubt at all." Marcus laughed. "You've grown so since your last visit that he won't even recognize you."

She didn't have the heart to inform Marcus that Sophia had telephoned a warning to expect them. He might have figured it out himself when Mr. Sutton opened the door, unflappable as always.

"Good afternoon, Captain Thorne, Mrs. Kendal." Sutton tipped his head to each of them. "And is that Master Cooper? My, how you've grown."

"He recognized me." Brandon shook his head. "There's no pulling one over on you, Mr. Sutton."

"No indeed." He smiled at the boy. "Mrs. Kendal, can I unburden you?"

She handed him her package and shrugged out of her coat.

"Oh, you see Mrs. Kendal, too?" Captain Thorne joked. "I thought she was my imaginary friend."

Sutton ignored the reference. "I've set you up in your usual rooms."

"Usual?" Eve was nearly overcome with a feeling of

acceptance. She'd been at Averford House only once, and she had a usual room as if she belonged there? God bless Mr. Sutton.

Sutton nodded. "Brandon, I admit you are a surprise, but Cook's preparing enough food to serve a whole battalion."

"Is there a battalion coming to dinner?" Brandon asked, eyes growing wide.

"No, young sir. But you ate enough to feed an army last time you visited."

"You can set him up in the blue guest room," Marcus instructed. "He's staying the night and returning with us to Thornbrook Park on the morrow."

"Thank you, Sutton," Eve said, preparing to take her leave. "I'll go right up to get settled."

"I believe I'll have some refreshment first. Eve, are you sure you won't join me?" Marcus asked.

"No." She kept her head down to hide the tears forming. How ridiculous that she should cry over something as simple as having a usual room. "Thank you. I'll be down in time for dinner."

Before he could protest, she fled up the stairs. She was halfway up when she heard footsteps behind her and Marcus calling out her name.

Before she turned, she wiped her eyes. "Yes, Captain Thorne?"

"Eve." He gripped her gently by the elbows, urging her closer. "I thought I saw you crying. Are you well?"

"Of course. It's silly, really. Please just let me go on up."

He didn't release her. "You can rely on me if there's something troubling you. I want to help."

"It's nothing. Lack of sleep, perhaps. Excitement kept me up all night, and then I woke early for the train. Ben's solicitor gave me reason to believe that my financial troubles may be at an end, though I dare not hope. And then…"

"And then?" He slipped a finger under her chin and tipped her face up to meet his gaze.

She took a breath and found that she was able to laugh off her fear. "Then, I thought someone was following me around London. I suppose I dare not allow myself even that brief glimpse of hope before my imagination rips it straightaway. Who would follow me? Ridiculous."

His amber eyes clouded over, glinting gold in the dim light of the stairway. "And yet you don't strike me as a hysterical female. You seem very level-headed to me. What did you see?"

"A man in a black coat and bowler hat behind me, and then passing again and again by the tearoom where I spent an hour or so. But don't half the men in London fit such a description? I convinced myself that I kept seeing the same one. On further consideration, it had to have been different men, many different men. As I said, lack of sleep."

"Hmm." He pursed his lips. "Perhaps. But I mean to stay by your side tomorrow, just in case."

"It's not necessary. I have another meeting with the solicitor."

"I have no pressing business. I'll go with you."

"All right." As much as she craved independence, she had to admit that she felt more comfortable having a companion, and spending more time at Captain Thorne's side definitely appealed. "Thank you."

Curse it if her eyes weren't welling up again.

"What now?" His voice sounded far more concerned than annoyed.

"I'm embarrassed by my weakness. I'd been so determined to handle my business all on my own, and now you think I need a bodyguard. Not that I mind having one, but I mean to stand on my own two feet, no need to be looked after like a fragile female. Exactly what I must appear to you when I resort to tears. I might not even be in such a spot if Ben had relied on me. He wanted to do everything for me, to look after me."

He placed a finger to her lips. "You can still be independent and rely on friends now and then. Do you know how remarkable you are? You stayed strong when other women left alone in India might have crumbled. You moved out of your house and back to England. Of course, you can take care of yourself, Eve. Who would doubt it?"

Did he really see her that way?

"I wish I had been more insistent with Ben. If only I had demanded to be aware of all of our business instead of letting him think he was protecting me from big decisions." She couldn't hide the surprise in her voice, and she met Marcus's gaze without thinking. "The entire time I was married, I wasn't quite myself. What can it mean? I loved him. I did. But I wasn't me."

"Love makes us do foolish things." He stroked her face and moved closer. "Foolish, foolish things."

Her eyes met his, seeing the sudden fire of determination in them, then strayed to his lush lips that he nibbled briefly before he said the one word that would set her over the edge.

"Please."

One word, and she was lost. All fight and sense went out of her. She wasn't sure if he had kissed her or she had kissed him, but their mouths were together, meeting hungrily. He slipped his tongue between her lips, and she drew on it, pulling him deeper. Somewhere, a service bell rang, an angry tinkling, but she was breathless in his arms, pressed up against the banister, his hands on her backside. What if Mr. Sutton came along? Or Brandon?

She pushed him away. "I must go. I must. I'm sorry."

Before she could be persuaded to stay, she ran up the stairs and left Marcus standing there alone.

⤞⤝

He had never meant to kiss her. It made everything so much more complicated and impossible. But the sudden sadness darkening her eyes and what she'd said indicated she'd had some sort of self-realization that had obviously shaken her. He'd only wanted to help. In the end, he was probably no better than her husband, so desperate to protect her from any pain or inconvenience that he failed to think about what she really needed.

But she'd loved her Ben. Despite his flaws.

He ran his hands through his hair, staring up the empty staircase after her. She was not for him. Never for him. He had a responsibility to the Coopers. She was the kind of woman who needed to stand on her own, to support herself. She had just told him as much, possibly only just realized it. How could he take that away from her? He couldn't. He wouldn't. He didn't dare. He wished he had her courage.

What if it was lust, plain and simple? He hadn't had a woman in years, couldn't fathom taking someone he didn't care for as a lover. She'd been a widow for over a year. No doubt she had quite a bit of pent-up longing. Lord knew, his senses were currently impaired. His mind was light and fuzzy around the edges, as if he'd been drugged. He could scarce manage to pull a thought together that didn't involve Eve's eyes, lips, or curves, or imagining her body in some state of undress.

And they would have been alone for dinner. Somehow, he couldn't manage to be put off by the idea, which made him all the more relieved that Brandon would be joining them. Otherwise, he feared he wouldn't be able to keep from making a move that they might both regret come morning.

Ten

THEY WAITED FOR AN HOUR IN THE DRAWING ROOM, and then another half hour in the dining room, before Marcus began to be concerned that his kiss had put her off. Perhaps she'd arranged for a meal to be sent up to her room?

"Sutton," he called out, "have you any word from Mrs. Kendal?"

Sutton peeked his head in from the hall, where he, too, seemingly waited. "Here she is now."

The double doors opened and she swept into the room, a vision in a figure-hugging white gown dripping with silver beads. Marcus stood, fortunately recovering his ability to speak.

"Eve. You look..." He felt his mouth drop open in search of the word. Maybe he hadn't quite recovered.

She blushed, or at least the pale gown contrasted with her rosy complexion. "Thank you. You're looking well, too."

He adjusted his tie. "I left some of my formal clothes behind, fortunately. I had a feeling that I should dress for dinner."

"Can we tuck in, then?" Across the table, Brandon fidgeted. He wasn't dressed for dinner and didn't seem to understand the need for fuss. He was simply a hungry, growing boy. "About time."

"Brandon, mind your manners," Marcus corrected him and stood to pull out a chair for Eve before Sutton, approaching, could get to it. He placed her to his right at the head of the table. Brandon, amused by the length of the table in the formal dining room, had claimed the chair at the opposite end from Marcus. Now that Eve had appeared in that dress, Marcus was especially grateful to have Eve close and the boy at a bit of a distance.

Sutton hovered, pouring wine. Marcus didn't usually require a footman when the earl was out of town, but one appeared bearing a tray with the first course.

"Poached salmon with mousseline sauce and cucumbers," Sutton announced as the footman began to serve.

"It seems we're to have an elegant meal," Marcus said. "Not the usual fare tonight, Mr. Sutton."

"No, sir," Sutton responded. "We have guests."

"Indeed we do," Marcus said, as Sutton and the footman left the room.

"You deign to address the servants?" Eve asked with mock disapproval. "No wonder you are ever at odds with your brother."

"Class distinction is starting to relax in most social circles, but perhaps Gabriel isn't quite ready for it at Thornbrook Park."

He watched her roll her eyes as if in bliss as she took a dainty nibble of the salmon and wished he could effect the same response in her. She looked up to see him watching her and he took a bite of his own fish, lest she accuse him of staring.

"I'm sorry," he said in a soft voice while leaning closer to her, "for taking liberties earlier. I hope I didn't offend you."

"You kissed me," she answered, equally quietly, then laughed out loud. "I was a little shocked at first, perhaps, but I'm over it."

"Over it?" His heart sank. Not the reaction he'd hoped. Perhaps he was out of practice.

"I rather enjoyed it, if you must know. It has been a long time since I've had such a kiss. Nothing like a bold and lingering kiss. How I've missed it. Ah, now you look shocked. Good. I've had my revenge." She continued eating as if she had just told him that she loved a good book or a musicale.

"Could I have some more of that fish?" Brandon asked Mr. Sutton suddenly, reminding Marcus of the boy's presence. "It's bloody fizzing."

"Watch your language, Brandon. We've a lady present." Marcus's voice deepened to a threatening low, reminding him suddenly of his own father's voice. "And where did you pick up such slang?"

Brandon shrugged. They both knew he'd heard it on the streets. "I'm sorry, Mrs. Kendal. I hope I didn't offend you."

Eve smiled and shook her head. Marcus nodded, satisfied.

"You ran away so fast." He lowered his voice again. Relieved that his technique was not in question, he leaned closer to her. "I thought I'd scared you off."

"I thought so, too, at first. I sat in my room and I wondered how I could possibly come down to dinner with you. But I knew Brandon would be joining us and Mr. Sutton would be nearby, if not listening to our every word, and I felt much better."

"I'm glad." He leaned in and placed his hand over hers.

Her bright eyes met his, but she didn't pull her hand away until Mr. Sutton reappeared with the footman bearing yet another tray. That's when he realized that perhaps their time away from Thornbrook Park had emboldened them both.

"Lamb with mint sauce," Sutton announced loudly. "Chateau potatoes, creamed carrots, and green peas."

"Oh my, Mr. Sutton. Delightful. Traveling has left me famished. You must have known."

Famished? Marcus had expected her to pick at her food, as he was accustomed to seeing women do. But she jumped right in with aplomb, taking healthy mouthfuls of sliced lamb and vegetables. His attention had been diverted, but he realized he was rather hungry himself.

"It's almost as good as Mum's," Brandon declared.

"Your mother must be a very good cook," Eve said.

Except for the occasional outburst of delight from Brandon, they ate in silence, devouring the meal.

After the plates were cleared, Sutton gave them time to linger over claret.

"Tomorrow then," Marcus said, turning his attention from how much he wanted to taste her for the next course, "you have your meeting with the solicitor. What have you found out?"

"My husband sunk our fortune into a diamond mine, it seems."

"A diamond mine? Did Mr. Strump seem to think it a wise course?"

She shrugged. "He said that he introduced Ben to the mine owner. I remember Ben visiting Golkonda, the location of the mine in India. I'm certain he wouldn't have invested our entire savings lightly. Mr. Strump seemed to think it might take some time to research the investment and retrieve the funds, but that it was entirely possible. I hope so. I hate to remain a charity case at Thornbrook Park for too much longer. Sophia has made sure that I feel welcome, of course, but one longs for a place of one's own."

"Good news, then? Dare to hope. To your security." He raised his glass.

"To our success." She raised hers. They drank. "You must have something you want at Thornbrook Park, Marcus, else I can't imagine you would return. It had to be more than a few words on a page to bring you back."

"You're right," he acknowledged. And she listened with rapt attention as he, with occasional help from Brandon, told her all about the Coopers and his hope to bring them to the farm.

❧

Eve thought they'd only been at the table for a short while when Sutton came in to replace the candles that had burned down to nubs.

"Have we been here that long talking?" she asked Marcus. "It hardly seems more than an hour."

Though Brandon had excused himself and gone off to explore the house some time ago, Eve realized.

Marcus flashed the wolfish smile, the one that warmed her down to her toes as if she'd taken a sip of brandy. "You're being kind. I've been boring you for hours now. It's time that I make sure young Brandon has made it to bed, I suppose. Sutton, old man, do you know what has become of the boy?"

"He went to his room finally, after making a thorough study of your father's sword collection in the gallery. I sent the footman to see that the young man had everything he needed before bed."

"Thank you. I suppose he's in capable hands." The crease in Marcus's brow belied his words. Clearly, his feelings of responsibility for Brandon went deep. "We've run you ragged, Sutton. I couldn't live with myself if I caused you to lose more sleep. As it is, you'll be up before dawn seeing to our breakfast. Please, to bed with you. We can manage capably on our own from here." Marcus issued the order gently, but Eve could tell it was more than a simple request. His tone held some urgency for them to be left alone.

"Dinner was lovely, Mr. Sutton. Thank you. An elegant affair. But now perhaps it's time we all went to bed." Eve felt the enchantment fading, like reaching the last few pages of a favorite book.

"Perhaps just one more glass of wine?" Marcus asked. "Then we'll make our own way up for the night, Mr. Sutton. I promise."

"If you're sure you won't be needing anything?" With no further requests from Marcus, Sutton excused himself.

"One more glass." She eased her chair closer to Marcus. "I hate for such a wonderful evening to end."

He moved closer, too, leaning over to pour the wine. "Sutton outdid himself."

"We have to give some credit to your cook. She's better than I'd realized, considering my previous meal here was a mediocre stew."

"Is that what they'd fed you? I had no idea. I assumed they'd treated you better than that, an esteemed guest of Lady Averford."

She giggled. "I'm not so certain about 'esteemed.' But it was my fault, really. I'd requested a tray to be sent up to my room, but I stayed too long in the bath."

"I love to hear you laugh." He eased his chair closer to hers. She found herself leaning more toward him as well. "It has been too long since these old walls have echoed sounds of joy."

"Instead of anger or sorrow?" She reached for his hand. "Life is too short for unrelenting gloom, Marcus. I think your coming to Thornbrook Park was a good idea, whatever happens with the farm. It's not healthy for you to be left here alone with dark thoughts."

"I don't believe I ever confessed to having dark thoughts." He arched a golden brow.

She caressed the rough calluses over his knuckles. "My apologies. I just assumed, with the prizefighting? A good prizefighter must have a fair amount of built-up tension to unleash in the ring. Ah, but you never *said* you were good." She smiled, her voice taking on a teasing tone. "From the way you looked on the first night I saw you…"

He threw back his head and howled laughter. "I'm good, Mrs. Kendal. I'm very good."

"I'll have to take your word for it."

"Instincts make a good fighter, the ability to read one's opponent." He eased his chair as close to hers as space would allow.

"What do you read in me?" she dared ask, her voice a sultry whisper.

"I would hope that you're not my opponent." He brushed a hand along the nape of her neck and trailed it around to cup her cheek. "But I do believe you're issuing a challenge."

"A challenge?" Her stomach tightened as his hand dropped lower to toy with the crystal beads along her décolletage. "What an idea. Show me."

"Show you?" His mouth dropped open.

She laughed, jumped to her feet, and took his hand. "How to read an opponent in the ring. Let's spar. Isn't that what you call it?"

He remained seated.

She stripped off her gloves, balled her hands into fists, and hopped from foot to foot. "Afraid? I promise I won't hurt you."

He laughed, a low chortle, and got to his feet. "Not with your hands curled like that you won't. Hit someone like that and you're more likely to break your thumbs."

Taking her fist, he urged her fingers open and tucked her thumb over them. "There, thumb outside the fingers, not curled into the palm."

"Oh." She studied her fist and swung it in the air. "Yes. Much better. I see."

He shook his head. "You would be hopeless in the ring."

"Ha! Come now, Marcus." She brushed him gently on the arm. "Let's go a round."

He sighed resignedly. "All right. If you're serious, let me go check on Brandon and I'll meet you in the library, where there's more open space."

❧

Eve took the opportunity of Marcus's brief absence to change out of her gown and into a simple blouse and her new skirt, the one with the shorter hemline, the better for bouncing around.

"That's better," she said to herself, taking a quick glance in the looking glass. She rolled up her sleeves and practiced a quick jab at her reflection. Satisfied with her effort, she went off in search of the library.

She found him waiting for her, in the act of sliding a sofa back against the wall, out of the way. He had removed his coat, tie, and waistcoat, and draped them over the back of a chair.

"Now then." He turned to greet her. "I see you've come prepared."

Her heart skipped a beat when his eyes lit with a smile of approval. "I mean business, Captain Thorne. I'm eager to learn."

"First, let's work on your stance," he said, studying her.

She dropped her hands to her sides. "What's wrong with my stance?"

"Absolutely nothing, if your intention is to ornament the room. I daresay it looks a damn bit brighter with you in it." He closed the distance between them and flashed the wolfish grin again.

"Men." She rolled her eyes and placed a finger under his chin, directing his gaze from her décolletage back to her face. "Impossibly easy to distract. Perhaps this is how you ended up with a bloody lip this afternoon."

"My opponent did not offer the slightest distraction. I simply looked away at the wrong time. Had you been my sparring partner, looking away would not have been an option."

"Then I have my work cut out for me." She jabbed him in the arm. "Or maybe not, if you're just going to stand there and be a target."

"We're working on your stance." He took her by the waist. "You need to bend a bit here. And your knees. Bend your knees. That's it. Now bob a little back and forth."

She held her breath, trying not to be the one distracted by the motion of their bodies swaying together, back, forth. "I think I'm catching on."

He shook his head. "No, still too stiff. A fighter needs to be flexible. Try shaking your arms out and finding your stance again."

"Like this?" She dropped her arms to her sides and waved them around a bit, then bounced from foot to foot and put her fists up again.

"Better. Much better. Now square your shoulders. You want to be flexible, but with a core of steel." He ran his hands along her collarbone and in a line straight down the center of her body, flattening his palm against her abdomen. "That's it, tighten up."

"Tighten up? I'm coiled like a spring." How could he be so serious when his slightest touch had sent her mind reeling?

"Indeed. You're in fine form now." He took a step back and mirrored her posture. Then he began to bounce from foot to foot in front of her, jabbing the air in her direction. "Ready?"

Without his coat and tie, he looked so much more imposing, as if to remind her that the bulk was all him, solid muscle, not the bunches of fabric that had covered him. Underneath the finery, he was a hulking specimen. As if she needed reminding. A lump rose in her throat. "I suppose."

She forgot to move. She forgot to breathe. He landed a light jab to her bare upper arm.

"Try to hit me," he urged.

She shook her head to clear it and bounced lightly on her toes. She swung a fist, aiming for his square jaw, and missed. He dodged it in time.

"You see? Instinct. Try again." He spun a circle around her, bouncing from foot to foot all the while.

She swung again. And missed. "Oh, for goodness sake."

He circled her again. And again. She kept up but began to feel a little dizzy. "You jab like a girl."

"I am a girl," she said, gritting her teeth. She began to sense a pattern in his movement. Left foot, sideways movement, left, right, back, left, moving a circle around her all the while.

"A fragile little—"

"Fragile?" That did it. She swung and knocked him right on the chin. "Ha!"

"Ow." He staggered back.

"Are you all right? I didn't mean to hurt you. I got carried away." She reached for him, eager to assess the damage.

He laughed, slipping an arm around her waist. "I'm well, thank you. Good left hook. You got me."

"I did." She smiled. "Taunt me, will you?"

"Never again," he promised, still holding her in his arms. "Any blood? I think you might have reopened my wound."

She studied his full lips, her breath slowing. "No blood."

"Are you sure?" She felt his heart hammering right up against her. "Look closely."

She ran a fingertip along the edge of his lips, her knees weakening. "Not a trace."

His gaze met hers, gold glistening in the amber depths. "Perhaps I'm not as good as I'd thought. I barely offered you a challenge."

"I nearly gave up when you started going in circles."

"Did I make you dizzy?" He leaned in, pressing his forehead to hers.

"You are good." She remained against him, fighting the urge to kiss the lips only inches from her own. "I didn't stand a chance."

His eyes widened, studying her. "I warned you."

"My downfall. I've never been much good at heeding warnings." They stayed there, each of them daring the other to make the move that neither would make, the need bubbling up in her until it nearly burst out, becoming impossible to contain. But contain it she would. She took a sudden step back. "We should go up to bed."

"We should." He shook his head as if to clear it, breaking the spell that had held them transfixed.

"Thank you for a wonderful evening," she said, restoring formality.

"Good night, Eve. Unlike your last stay at Averford House, I won't be disturbing you in the dead of night." He smiled.

She laughed to hide her disappointment and drifted away to the stairs.

Eleven

HE HADN'T SLEPT. NOT A WINK. HE'D PACED HIS room. He'd tried to read a book. He'd even gone down the hall to stare at the portraits of his father's dearly departed hunting dogs, hoping to restore his mind and body to peace. No use. His mind remained all too aware of her, of how she smelled like oranges and felt a perfect fit in his arms. And his body? His body remained at rigid attention.

He'd stood outside her door for God only knew how many minutes at a time hoping that she would sense him, take pity, and open the door. He hadn't dared to try the knob in case she had locked it against him. In the end, he'd resorted to the use of his own hand to try and ease the tension brewing inside him. But even that had brought him little satisfaction.

He wanted her. No one and nothing else would do. How long would he suffer in such a predicament? He hoped only as long as they were together at Averford House. He prayed that being back at Thornbrook Park would break the spell, this enchantment that had suddenly taken hold of them.

Eventually, he gave up on waiting for sleep to take him, got up again, washed, dressed, and made his way to the breakfast table. He hadn't even seen Paulson, the footman who acted as his valet at Averford House, until Paulson came to the breakfast room to greet him.

"You didn't need my services this morning, sir?"

"My traveling clothes were still decent and I managed on my own. But you can see to my evening clothes. I'm afraid I left them in sorry shape right where I removed them, in a pile on the floor by the bed."

Paulson nodded, as if unsurprised by this bit of news. "Good, sir. Ring if you need me."

Sutton appeared on cue as Paulson left him. "Cook is seeing to your eggs. The boy is still in bed. Shall I have Danvers wake him?"

"Let him sleep. We won't be setting off for London until this afternoon. And the lady? Any sign of her yet?"

"She rang for Lettie some time ago."

"Not all that long ago, Mr. Sutton." The sound of her voice preceded her entrance to the room and Marcus felt his pulse quicken. "I don't need more than an hour to pull myself together in the morning."

If the sound of her voice had sent his pulse racing, the sight of her made his heart beat time out of mind. Her cheeks had a vibrant glow. Her eyes, riveting blue, pierced his from across the room.

"Good morning, Mrs. Kendal. Please have a seat." Sutton got her settled and poured her tea. "I'll go back to see how Cook is coming along with your breakfast."

"Someone got some sleep." Marcus waited for Sutton to leave the room before addressing her. "I'm envious."

"Appearances can be deceiving. Big business to manage today. I felt it was important for me to appear rested, even if actual sleep proved elusive."

"How do you manage it?"

"A woman has her secrets, Sophia might answer. But I will tell you straight out that I'm pleased to find Lettie has a light touch with powder and rouge. She's a gem. It's a wonder she remains hidden away here instead of being put to proper use at Thornbrook Park."

"The answer to that mystery is as simple as the fact that my brother the earl and his countess spend so little time here in London. Perhaps you can give Lettie a good word with Sophia and spare her the purgatory of Averford House."

"I think not. I mean to snap her up for my own household, once established, and it will be so much easier to lure her if she remains unappreciated here."

"You're a crafty minx, Mrs. Kendal."

She smiled and brought her cup to her lips. "Too clever for my own good sometimes. May it serve me well at Mr. Strump's office."

❧

On arrival, Marcus reached out to ring the bell.

"They never answered last time," Eve informed him. "I ended up walking in."

After waiting a minute, they decided to do the same, but this time the office was in chaos. There were papers strewn everywhere, on every surface, and most of the furniture had been overturned. Two men completely ignored them as they toted boxes of retrieved papers back and forth through the tiny entry space. A third stopped in front of Eve when he dropped his armload. She recognized him as Gibbs, Mr. Strump's assistant. When he stooped to retrieve more of the scattered papers, she took advantage of the situation.

"Mr. Gibbs?" She stripped off her gloves, ready to get down to business. "Is Mr. Strump in? Today, he's expecting me."

"Oh." Gibbs looked up. "Oh dear. No."

"He's not here? Could you tell me where I might find him?"

The man straightened, tucked his papers under his arm, and faced her. "If only any of us knew."

"Knew where to find him?" she asked, confused.

"Yes. Mr. Strump seems to have gone missing."

"Missing? How can it be?" Her heart skipped a beat. It was a blow she wasn't expecting. "Someone must know what has become of him."

"When I came in this morning, I found the place ransacked." He gestured at the obvious disarray. "The other partners arrived promptly enough, but there was no sign of Mr. Strump at the usual time. We sent a boy over, and Strump's wife said that he packed a bag and boarded a steamer to India late last night."

"Last night? To India? But my husband's investment was in Golkonda. Perhaps he has gone to see to my affairs?" Hopeful, she turned to Marcus. He had been standing back to let her manage on her own, but he shook his head as if in doubt.

"Captain Marcus Thorne." He held his hand out to Mr. Gibbs. "You had no warning at all that the man was making off for India? And the office just happened to be robbed on the same night? What was taken? Have you contacted Scotland Yard?"

"We don't know that it was a robbery." Mr. Gibbs pushed his spectacles further up on the bridge of his nose. "We haven't discovered anything taken, as yet, but a detective has been in to investigate."

"Good. The office is torn to bits on the same night one of your partners goes missing. Or, makes a hasty departure for India. Damned suspicious, don't you think?"

"I agree, Captain Thorne. The whole matter has left us rather unsettled. If only we knew what motivated Mr. Strump to flee."

Eve's money might have provided the motivation. How much had Ben invested? Enough to tempt a man to claim it and disappear? She had her doubts.

"Perhaps he hasn't fled willingly," Marcus suggested.

Eve looked at Marcus, her mouth agape. "You suspect foul play?"

"Precisely what the detective conjectured, Captain. Indeed, it would be unlike Mr. Strump to simply run off without a word."

"Someone was looking for something, it seems," Eve said, unable to chase the suspicion that the "something" involved her request for information on her finances.

"Mrs. Kendal is a dear friend of the family." Marcus completely stepped in front of her to continue the conversation with Gibbs, nudging her aside and nearly making her cross with him until she realized that he was using a ploy to extract more information. "She's bound to be distraught at suggestions of, ahem, foul play. Perhaps she would feel better if she could call on Mrs. Strump?"

"Certainly," Mr. Gibbs agreed. "By all means, she should pay a call."

Marcus lowered his voice to a whisper. "If you might have the address? I don't wish to upset her further by asking her to recall it just now."

"Yes, of course. One minute." Mr. Gibbs ran to an office down the hall. Eve took the time to try to look upset, not a struggle considering how worried she was about her finances. Only yesterday, she'd been so hopeful for the best, and now she had no idea when, or if, she would ever recover her funds. "Here it is."

Gibbs pressed a slip of paper into Marcus's palm.

"Thank you, Mr. Gibbs. You've been most helpful. Here's my card. Should you recover any files regarding Captain Benjamin Kendal's affairs, send word immediately."

"I will. At once. Please give Mrs. Strump our regards."

Marcus escorted Eve from the office and back to the street. "I'm sorry, Eve. I know you were counting on better news."

As the bleakness of her prospects continued to sink in, Eve felt more like throwing herself into Marcus's arms and crying. But she refused to give in. Of all things, she would not be helpless. "We'll just have to go to the Strump residence and see what we can find out about Mr. Strump's hasty departure."

"I would like to share some details with a friend

of mine, a private detective, and see what he can uncover. He has some contacts at Scotland Yard who might be able to offer some information."

"Perhaps we should split up. Sophia is expecting us back in time for dinner. I'll go check in with Mrs. Strump. You see what you can find out from your friend and take care of Brandon. We should be able to meet back at the station in time to make the train."

"I hate to leave you alone. Yesterday you thought you were being followed."

She waved him off. "I'll be at the Strump residence, one woman calling on another. I don't think it should raise any alarms. Just in case, I'll keep an eye out for bowler hats in my midst." She took the slip with the address from him. "Bloomsbury, a lovely neighborhood. I know it well, just a short walk away."

"Eve." He stroked her cheek with the back of his hand. "If anything should happen to you…"

"Don't be ridiculous." She steeled herself against the wave of emotion, determined to remain capable of managing alone. "I'll be perfectly well. Working separately will allow us to cover more ground. One of us should be able to turn up something of use."

"If you're certain you'll be safe alone?"

"I'm certain. I'll meet you at the station for the afternoon train."

She walked off, suspecting he simply stood in place watching her until she was out of sight. The Strumps lived in a well-kept house across from a garden square. As she climbed the stone steps to the front door, she pondered what she might say.

The butler answered the door before she'd prepared

enough to reach for the bell. A butler? Given the address and a barrister's likely prospects, Eve never expected to find a butler in the couple's employ. A few maids, perhaps a footman. The Strumps had higher prospects than she had imagined.

"Oh." He seemed as surprised to find her standing at the door as she was to find a butler in a middle-class house. "How might I be of service?"

"I'm paying a call on Mrs. Strump," Eve said. "I imagined that she might get lonely during the absence of her husband."

"You've heard? So soon." He looked around, left to right, as if looking for someone else. Apparently satisfied, he stepped back inside and opened the door wider. "Please come in."

"Thank you. I haven't had the pleasure of making Mrs. Strump's acquaintance, but her husband is a friend of the family. A dear friend. I'd been hoping to meet with him today, but Mr. Gibbs at the office informed me of his hasty departure."

"Please have a seat, Miss…"

"Mrs. Kendal. Mrs. Strump may have been more familiar with my husband, Captain Benjamin Kendal. Our husbands had business together."

"Mrs. Kendal. I'll see if Mrs. Strump is in."

"Very well. I'll wait."

More directly, he would see if Mrs. Strump would agree to see her. She looked around. The place looked newly furnished and badly decorated. She decided to stand, as it looked as though no one had yet tried the ivory-cushioned sofa trimmed in gold braid. Mrs. Strump had a taste for things trimmed in gold, apparently. Gilded mirrors, candlesticks, even the walls had a gold leaf trim. The butler returned not a minute later with the news that Mrs. Strump would not see her. "I'm sorry. It appears that she's gone out for the afternoon. I will share your kind regards upon her return."

But Mrs. Strump, with golden hair that looked to be more of a wig, and slightly askew at that, appeared behind her butler. "No need, Gerald. I've returned. Please bring us some tea. Shall we have a seat, Mrs. Kindle?"

"Kendal. Thank you." Eve took a seat on the sofa, opposite Mrs. Strump in a high-backed chair. "I've heard that your husband has gone out of town. Rather suddenly. I hope nothing's wrong."

"Wrong?" Mrs. Strump patted her hair, as if to put it in place. Her cheeks were over-rouged and her lips were an unnatural shade of plum. Eve couldn't tell the woman's age, exactly, but she looked at least ten years Eve's senior. "Oh no, he'd been planning this trip for some time. India. On business."

"Odd that he didn't mention it yesterday. I went to see him. On business, coincidentally, involving India, and he didn't mention it. In fact, we had an appointment this morning. Imagine my surprise when he didn't show up and his office was in complete disarray."

"Oh?" Mrs. Strump quirked a brassy brow. "Those fellows at his office, useless without Edgar."

"It appeared to be more of a robbery," Eve said matter-of-factly.

"Gerald!" Mrs. Strump screamed for her servant

instead of ringing, the more usual method. "What's keeping the tea? I'm sorry." She turned back to Eve. "I'm parched. Aren't you?"

"I'm more curious than parched." Eve shifted forward in her seat. "Have you any idea what sort of business drew Mr. Strump away so suddenly?"

"We're women, Mrs. Kendal." Her gray gaze met Eve's, sending a shiver through her. Those eyes held an unmistakable shrewdness and malice that did not quite jibe with the woman's flibbertigibbet exterior. Eve knew at once that she was dealing with someone capable of deception, at the very least. "Certainly we don't involve ourselves with something as ponderous as business."

"While I would love to be at liberty to deny it, I've had no choice but to manage my own affairs since my husband's passing. We do what we must, Mrs. Strump. I sense that you're a woman who understands necessity. I ask you again, do you know what business occasioned your husband's abrupt departure?"

Gerald arrived with the tea tray, interrupting their conversation. He started to pour, but Mrs. Strump put her hand on his to stop him.

"Too late, Gerald. Mrs. Kendal will be leaving us. No, I do not know what business he had in India." The words came out through clenched teeth. "My husband was a peculiar man, Mrs. Kendal, given to flights of fancy."

"Ah, but you said the trip had been planned for some time." Eve rose. "And I can't help but notice that you speak of him in the past tense. I will be on my way, and I'll leave you my card. If Mr. Strump happens to write or return, I would appreciate you letting me know. And if not, well, I'm a widow. I know what it is to be a woman on her own in the world. One day soon, you might find you need a friend."

She placed a card with Sophia's Thornbrook Park address on the tea table in front of an apparently stunned Mrs. Strump, turned on her heel, and started for the door. She was nearly there when the sight of a black bowler hanging on the hat rack drew her up short.

She turned back, gesturing to the hat. "Does that belong to your husband, Mrs. Strump?"

"Oh, no," Gerald answered, probably following on her heels to make sure that she got to the door. "That's Mr. Law—"

"It belongs to my brother," Mrs. Strump interrupted, rushing down the corridor in time to place a hand on the butler's arm. "He's visiting. Go back to Yorkshire, Mrs. Kendal. The country must be so much lovelier than town this time of year."

"As it happens, I'm headed back there now." A shiver snaked down her spine, as if she had been distinctly threatened, though she couldn't say what could possibly be threatening about a woman with a bad wig and shoddy posture suggesting a country retreat. "Good day, Mrs. Strump."

Once she was back out in the street, she took a minute to collect her wits. She leaned against the railing, closed her eyes, breathed deep, and opened them again to see a man standing across the road at the edge of the garden, watching her.

Twelve

"MARCUS." SHE CALLED HIS NAME AND CROSSED THE street to join him. "What are you doing here? You couldn't possibly have had the time to conduct your inquiries."

"I have not," he allowed, taking her hand and placing it in the crook of his arm. "I never actually agreed to your suggestion that we should conduct our business separately. I simply gave you a head start and then followed you here."

"You should have told me. I would have argued, perhaps, but I'm guessing you would have insisted." They started off down the walk, away from the house.

"I didn't want to bully you into seeing it my way, but it does make the most sense to stick together. You'll have to accept my apology." He dreaded finding a look of disappointment on her face when he finally met her gaze, but was pleased instead to find a smile in her eyes. "Besides, I needed you to seem completely unaware of my presence so that I could watch for anyone following you. For the record, no one did, but at least I can be assured of your safety."

She shook her head. "But we've lost time. How will we manage it all and make the train?"

"There's a later train. If we miss the one, we'll catch the other, though we might incur Sophia's wrath if we turn up late for dinner. Now, what did you find out inside?"

She shuddered perceptibly, making him glad that he'd gone against her wishes this once. What if she'd needed him? "Mrs. Strump claims to have no idea what sort of business took her husband away so suddenly. She tried to say the trip had been planned for some time, and she referred to her husband in the past tense."

"Intriguing. Go on."

"There's not much else, I'm afraid. She's a peculiar woman, but that in itself is no crime."

"There's something else." He narrowed his gaze. "Something you're not telling me." Else why would she have appeared so shaken as she stepped away from the house?

She shrugged. "A small detail. It mightn't be cause for alarm."

"But it did strike a nerve. What was it?" He stopped walking and turned her to face him, stroking her arm all the while.

She sighed. "A bowler hat. A black bowler hanging on a rack by the door. She said it belonged to her brother. You see? It's probably nothing."

"But it could be something. Reilly says—my friend Tom, the detective, we're on our way to see him now—Reilly says that anything that draws your attention as out of the ordinary probably is. There's probably something to it. Trust your instincts. We'll see what he has to say."

"But first, I was hoping to stop in and inquire after a friend at the Langham," she said, as they resumed walking.

"A friend of yours? Here?" He was unaware that she had friends in London.

"Colonel Adams. He accompanied me to London and business was to keep him here for a fortnight. I'm hoping he stayed a bit longer so that I might ask him to conduct a search for Mr. Strump when he returns to India."

"Ah, a good idea." He tried to ignore the wave of jealousy he felt for this man, Colonel Adams. "Older gentlemen, this friend of yours?"

She nodded. "With a wife, Adela, back in Raipur. They took it upon themselves to check in on me after Ben's death. Grateful as I was, they did become a tad overzealous. I think they fancied me to be like a daughter. They lost their only child, a girl, to illness in her infancy."

"How awful for them. Losing a child is about the worst thing I could imagine." Losing a good friend had been hard enough. As if she could read his thoughts, she slipped her grip down his arm to his hand and squeezed. When he looked at her, her eyes were clouded with emotion. "Losing anyone is hard," he added.

"We've both suffered our losses. Brandon as well, losing a father. It can't be easy on the boy. You're very good with him."

"I do my best, but I'm never really sure it's enough.

I used to think…" He paused, fighting a wave of emotion. "I used to think it would have been best had I died in place of William Cooper. I wished to God he'd made it home to his family."

It was her turn to stop and urge him to face her. "Marcus, no. That line of thought can only lead back to darkness. War is brutal. Of course, you wish things had turned out differently, but—I'm so glad you made it home. There are people here who need you, too."

He laughed to lighten the mood. In truth, he was touched that she would be glad for him. "Yes, what would my brother do without me? He'd have no one to harass."

"Exactly. And I would have no one to escort me around London and teach me how to spar. Oh, look, we're already at the Langham. That's it up ahead, is it not?"

"It is. Perhaps we'll make our train in time after all."

"I liked your friend Mr. Reilly," she said, once they'd completed their business, retrieved Brandon, and found their seats on the train.

"I believe he liked you, too. Perhaps a little too much." Marcus sulked a little in his seat next to her. Brandon sat across from them, where he proceeded to fall asleep almost immediately for the journey. She wondered if a touch of jealousy accounted for Marcus's suddenly surly mood, and she found that she didn't mind the idea.

"He seemed eager to be of service. I can't wait to hear what he finds out. It's a shame about Colonel

Adams, though." At the Langham, they'd discovered that Colonel Adams had already departed for Raipur. "I'll write to him and ask for his help in locating Mr. Strump there. Perhaps it's best that we have a contact in India after all."

"If Strump took a late-night steamer, Tom might be able to track down some manifestos and get a name of the ship. If we're lucky, the colonel can catch up to Strump on arrival, the best time to find a man."

"And if not?" The possibility seemed all too strong that something had happened to the man and he'd never gone to India at all.

"If not, Tom will find that out, too. Tom has a knack for drumming up minute details. I'm sorry the day wasn't more productive for you."

She stifled a sigh. "Just when I had my hopes up. But I'm not giving in. We have Mr. Reilly on the case, and something's bound to turn up to direct us toward recovering at least some of Ben's investment in the mine."

He reached for her hand. "You're not the type to give up."

She felt like giving up, but his faith fed her determination. And his hand on hers, warm and solid, distracted her from dwelling on her misfortune.

They sat in silence for some moments. The comfort of being close to him and the rhythmic rocking of the train lulled her to sleep.

As they pulled into the station, he gently nudged her.

She lifted her head and realized she'd rested her head on his shoulder the entire ride. "I'm so sorry. I fell asleep on you."

"I nearly fell asleep myself," he said. "After last night and this morning, I guess we're both fairly exhausted."

"Last night," she echoed. Last night, when she'd been full of hope and in his arms. How she wished they could turn back time.

Without another word, he woke Brandon and escorted them off the train to where Dale was waiting with the car.

Something about pulling up to the door felt like a fairy tale ending prematurely, enchantment over before the happily-ever-after part could come around.

"And there's still time to freshen up before dinner," she said. "No risking Sophia's disappointment."

"A good thing for us all."

He helped her from the car and escorted her to the door, where Mr. Finch waited.

"Welcome back, Captain Thorne, Mrs. Kendal," he greeted them on entrance. "And a young man. It seems you've picked up a third in London."

"Surprised to see me?" Marcus asked playfully. "Were they placing bets on my return?"

"I'm not at liberty to say." Finch closed the door behind them.

"This is Brandon, my young charge. Brandon, Mr. Finch."

"You're the Thornbrook Park Mr. Sutton," Brandon said with some amusement.

"Oh, Brandon." Eve laughed. "That's no way to win Mr. Finch's favor. You would do better to say that Mr. Sutton is the Averford House Mr. Finch."

Brandon wrinkled his nose, betraying his confusion.

"Nothing to fret about." Marcus winked at him.

"You'll catch on. Mr. Finch, I'll explain about Brandon to the earl over dinner. If you could be so kind as to set Brandon up in a room near mine and bring him a tray for dinner?"

"That can be arranged. We'll be sure to make him comfortable. Will you be needing anything, Mrs. Kendal? Some tea or coffee?"

"Oh no, thank you. I have just enough time to prepare for dinner. I'll be headed straight up."

"Your trunks arrived this afternoon. I had them brought up to your chamber. I know you've been eager for them."

She'd asked about them nearly every day. There wasn't much left of material value, of course, but the memories every item in her trunks represented meant more to her than any amount of money could ever replace. She might be at Thornbrook Park longer than planned, but she could finally feel at home with her most precious possessions close. "Yes, thank you. I'm happy they're here at last."

"I'll be headed up, too, Mr. Finch, after I give Brandon a quick tour.

"I'll see you later then, Brandon. And I'll see you at dinner, Marcus," she said, then thought to correct herself. "Captain Thorne."

"Until then, Mrs. Kendal." He tipped his hat and turned to follow Brandon and Finch from the room. She watched him move, admiring the grace and authority in his posture, before turning to go up the stairs.

A minute after she got to her room and began to undress, she heard Lucy come in after her. "I think I'll wear the blue tonight, if you please, Lucy."

"Lady Averford is wearing blue, if you want to know."

"Hmm," Eve considered. "Black it is. The one with the draped sash and silver stitching around the hem."

If she was stuck in black, she might as well wear one of gowns that had been altered to be less severe. She wished she hadn't agreed to allow Lettie to repair some of the beading on her new gown and ship it later. A white dress would be such a welcome change.

"A perfect choice," Lucy agreed, drawing it out to prepare it while Eve undressed.

"But hurry. We haven't much time."

"And we still need to do something with your hair. It's looking a bit mussed from your hat." Lucy talked as she worked. "I feel I should warn you that the servants, especially, are not unaware of things that go on both in and out of the house."

"So I should expect." Eve nodded, adjusting her underclothes before slipping into the gown.

"One thing, if you don't mind the advice?"

"Advice? Go on." Eve was intrigued. Timid Lucy had advice for her?

"It hasn't escaped notice that you and Captain Thorne went to London together yesterday and came back together today. I'm sure it's no cause for alarm, but he's a handsome man and you're a widow. Some of the maids, the younger ones mostly, dream up possibilities. Everyone loves a good romance, if you know what I mean." Lucy nodded in the mirror.

"Goodness." Eve laughed. "No, Lucy. I believe I'm quite safe from Captain Thorne's seductions. Lady Averford means to make a match for Captain Thorne, but not with me."

"With Lady Alice, yes." Lucy blushed as if she'd revealed too much.

"As you said, Lucy. Servants are not unaware of what goes on at Thornbrook Park. I'll keep it in mind. If any rumors get started about scandalous behavior on my part, I hope you will be the first to let me know." Eve smiled and hoped she presented the picture of innocence.

"You look so well together, though, you and the captain. A few of us noticed from the upstairs windows when you were setting out."

"Oh dear, how stories get started. He's a handsome man, as you say. He might make even Mrs. Hoyle look like a blushing maiden."

Lucy laughed at the idea.

"My, you've made me a vision." Eve looked in the mirror, eager to change the subject. "Upswept hair complements the low neckline. Thank you. I'd best get to the drawing room before they all go in."

∽

A day away from Gabriel worked wonders, but was he ready to face his brother again? Marcus considered having a tray sent up to eat with Brandon. How could he explain Brandon to Gabriel? It had to be done, but he waited so long trying to find the words that he showed up late, after they had all given up on him and gone in. He took a deep breath, entered, and wordlessly settled in the empty chair to Eve's left.

"Oh, you decided to join us." His brother looked up as the footman spooned sauce over the trout on his plate. "That will be all, Bill. Fetch my errant brother his portion."

"I'm glad you made it back on time," Sophia said. "I would have begun to be concerned, except that Eve was just telling us about your train ride home."

"Was she?" He looked at Eve, a slight tingle rushing through his veins when she met his gaze. What was that? Familiarity? Nerves? "I hope she didn't bore you with the details. I believe I fell asleep."

"Are you accusing me of being a bore, Captain Thorne? I thought you were a gentleman." Eve smiled. "And we both know that you weren't the one to fall asleep."

"A gentleman's son." Gabriel couldn't help making a distinction.

"You were great company, not a bore at all." Bill sauced the fish on Marcus's plate, temporarily blocking his view. "On the contrary, my conversation might have been a little lacking, distracted as I was. My apologies for being a poor companion."

"Ah, you were no doubt distracted by the beauty of the woman beside you. And who could blame a man for that?" Alice's hazel eyes twinkled in a way that left Marcus no doubt that she meant to make mischief at the table.

Sophia looked up suddenly, her eyes darting to Marcus and back to Eve as if she'd only just considered that the two of them might have connected in a way that Marcus had yet to explain to her sister.

"I don't mind that you're late, of course." Sophia shrugged unconvincingly. Everyone seated knew that she minded. "But if not the train, what kept you?"

Marcus hesitated. The opportunity presented itself. He might as well jump in with both feet. "I was seeing my charge settled in the room next to mine."

"Your charge?" Gabriel's brow knit.

Eve reached for his hand under the table. How like her to know that he could use some support. "My ward. The young man in my care. I've brought him to Thornbrook Park."

"Why the devil would you do such a thing?" Gabriel demanded. "You couldn't leave your by-blows in town with a nursemaid?"

To his surprise, Marcus found himself more amused than angry, no sign of an impending rage. "Brandon Cooper is not my by-blow, Brother. And how indelicate of you to suggest such a thing in front of the ladies."

Gabriel had the sense to look discomfited.

"You were at war with his father." Waving her fork as if conducting a spell with a wand, Agatha suddenly joined the conversation. "I sense his spirit around you."

Marcus nodded. "Yes, I was. William Cooper, Brandon's father, had the grave misfortune of setting off a bomb that he was in the process of handing over to me to dismantle. He died bravely, with me at his side. How could I help but seek his widow out when I got home and take some responsibility for the family? Brandon has two sisters and a brother at home with his mother."

"And you mean to provide for them?" Gabriel leaned back in his chair. "The whole family?"

"I do what I can for them. When Brandon seemed to keep getting into trouble, falling in with a bad crowd, I decided it was time to get him out of London."

"And do what with the young ruffian? Bring him

here to rob us blind?" Gabriel's fist pounded the table, startling Sophia and nearly toppling his claret.

"Brandon's not a thief. He's a good lad in need of some responsibility. I was hoping to put him to work at Tilly Meadow Farm."

"Oh," Sophia mused. "Yes. It seems like a timely suggestion. There's plenty for a young man to do on the farm, and I'm certain Mrs. Dennehy could use the help. She's getting on in years. How old is the boy?"

"Fourteen," Marcus said. "Stout for his age, good with his hands. I hope to ride out and speak to Mrs. Dennehy about it tomorrow."

"Make it Thursday," Gabriel demanded. "The boy should be comfortable enough here at Thornbrook Park in the meantime. I'll ride out with you. She might be more receptive if the request comes from me. She hasn't seen you in years. My schedule is set for tomorrow, but I was planning on heading out there Thursday morning anyway."

"All right," Marcus agreed. "Thursday it is."

He could look forward to the pleasure of spending a morning with his brother on Thursday, but all things considered, his proposal to bring Brandon to Tilly Meadow had been accepted much more easily than he'd anticipated. He looked over to Eve as she raised her glass and had the distinct impression that she raised it specifically for him, a toast to his success. And again there was that odd tingle in his veins.

❦

Eve kept her seat, reluctant to take note when Sophia suggested they pass through to the drawing room and leave the men to their brandy. It seemed ill-advised to leave the brothers alone together when they were barely getting along.

Or maybe her tense nerves made it all seem worse than it was. Every time Marcus shifted in his seat, she jumped a little in her own. She couldn't even watch his hands move without remembering them stroking her cheek or wrapped around her waist, directing her body in how to move in the ring. Perhaps it was best she followed Sophia away from him. But as soon as they were all in the drawing room, she found herself staring at the dining room's double doors, willing them to open and for Marcus to come through and take a seat next to her.

Sophia took the seat instead. "So tell us about London. Was your business a success?"

"Not exactly." A dull ache throbbed between her temples. She didn't feel like talking about London, certainly not about business. She picked up a book from the table next to her, hoping that Sophia might think she intended to read instead of talk, but Sophia perched eagerly on the edge of her chair. "My husband's solicitor has gone missing," Eve offered.

"Missing?" Sophia would not be deterred, especially with the introduction of a mystery.

"His wife claims he ran off to India, which suits my needs, I suppose. Ben invested our money in a diamond mine there. Perhaps Mr. Strump simply went to investigate or withdraw my funds." She tried to pass it off as nothing, but the dull ache became a sharper pain. "Sutton took good care of us, though. We had a fine meal at Averford House."

"We? Of course. You and Marcus were there

together." Sophia's eyes flashed with something like concern. "Did you see much of him?"

"We talked a bit over dinner, and Brandon was with us."

"Yes, the boy. What a surprise. No wonder Marcus has been reluctant to leave London these past few years." Sophia smiled, clearly relieved to find that they were chaperoned. "I hope you spoke of Alice. A little nudge in the right direction?"

"We did speak of her," Eve said, feeling her face color a little. They'd spoken of her, but she would never be able to repeat what was said.

"And, let me guess, you spoke of books. You probably bored each other to tears exchanging quotes and reviews all night long."

"No tears, but I think he caught me yawning once."

"A wonder he didn't bring the boy to dinner tonight. The poor thing must be bored and hungry. I'm eager to meet him."

"I think he's acclimating. No need to rush things. Mr. Finch was instructed to bring him a tray."

"I must tell Marcus to bring him to dinner tomorrow. No need to keep him hidden away, now that we all know of him."

At the piano, Alice began to play, with Agatha seated beside her to turn pages. Eve was grateful for the interruption to their conversation, and even more grateful when Alice hit a series of bad notes, causing Sophia to flee to her sister's side.

"Dearest, no. Beethoven sets such a somber tone. Let's keep it light, shall we?" Sophia started leafing through the sheet music. "Here's one."

"'Bright Silver Star of Love'? A show tune?"

"Why not? We need a little fun. And if you feel like it, sing along."

"You want me to sing?" Alice paused, hands above the keys.

"It doesn't hurt to show off a little."

Alice rolled her eyes. "You sound like Mother."

Sophia ignored her and had started back across the room when the gentlemen made their appearance. "Marcus, thank goodness you're here. Alice was just about to sing for us, but she needs a male accompaniment."

"I believe Gabriel is your man when it comes to singing. I'm not quite in voice tonight." Marcus met Eve's gaze and headed in her direction.

"Nonsense. Gabriel doesn't have the spirit for show tunes. Do you, darling?"

"I believe I could pull it off." As if accepting a challenge, Gabriel approached the instrument, surprising Sophia and Eve as well. How dare anyone suggest that the earl couldn't manage something as well as his brother?

"May I sit, or will I distract you from your reading?" Marcus gestured at the book she held in her lap but had almost forgotten. "Romantic poets? A good choice. I like a little Byron before bed."

She hadn't even realized what book she held until he mentioned it. "Byron's suitable, but I'm more inclined to Shelley."

"Partial to rebels and upstarts, are you?" He arched a brow. "'She walks in beauty, like the night.' I don't think your man Shelley can top that for opening lines."

"'The golden gates of Sleep unbar where Strength and Beauty, met together.'" She smiled at him. "I think Byron has been topped. One man admires beauty. The other seeks to find his equal."

"Perhaps you're right. I can see how finding one's equal would appeal." He held her gaze.

Her heart raced. They couldn't pursue a flirtation in the drawing room, in front of everyone. Her mind flew back to what Lucy had said about the maids noticing how well they looked together. Would Sophia notice, too? Would she be cross with Eve for stealing Marcus's attentions? Alienating her one friend was not a risk that she could afford to take, not now that her financial stability seemed dubious at best.

"Byron could have been writing of Sophia, our raven-tressed beauty." She raised her voice to prove that they weren't having a private conversation. "Don't you think?"

"I have a preference for blondes," he said, leaning in.

"I heard my name," Sophia turned. "What's this you're saying about me?"

"'She Walks in Beauty,' the Byron poem?" Eve held up the book. "We think it could have been written about you."

"Flatterers!" She accused with a laugh. "What a silly suggestion."

"Enough of poems." Gabriel cleared his throat. "You've asked us to sing. Kindly pay attention to our performance."

"You're ready?" Sophia turned back to the piano. "Such a treat! I'm sure we're all looking forward to it. Agatha, come sit by me."

Agatha, who had been roaming the room since Gabriel sat down with Alice at the piano, did as instructed. Marcus took a seat in turn, right by Eve on the sofa.

The performance began. Only a few notes in, Marcus reached for Eve's hand and held it discreetly, barely hidden by the volume of her skirt.

Thirteen

THE TENSION BETWEEN BROTHERS HAD BEEN SIMMERING just beneath the surface ever since Marcus's arrival. He felt it, visceral, a pain throbbing just behind his eyes, threatening to build to explosion. But he couldn't let it. Gabriel had been surprisingly accepting about Brandon. It was a start. Marcus couldn't afford to lose his temper and alienate his brother now that Gabriel had offered to help him. Just as he'd started to feel his attitude soften a bit toward his brother, George, the footman acting as Marcus's valet, showed up with a summons to Gabriel's office on his breakfast tray.

"Important matter to discuss?" Marcus read the note and tossed it aside. "I hope he hasn't changed his mind about Brandon. George, you'd better pack a few things for me, just in case."

"In case of what, sir?"

"A hasty exit, of course." Marcus laughed. "A private meeting with my brother can only come to no good. I might have to make a run for it back to London."

"He seemed in good spirits this morning, if it helps any, sir. I happened to be delivering the freshly pressed newspaper to the breakfast table when he came in whistling a tune."

"Whistling a tune? I didn't think Gabriel knew how to whistle, unless it was just to call his dogs out for the hunt. For that matter, I hadn't imagined he knew any tunes until last night." Gabriel had given a capable performance with Alice, though Marcus had barely paid attention. He'd been too busy fighting off the urge to kiss Eve Kendal.

"I think it was 'Blow the Man Down,' sir. Though I could be mistaken."

"Huh. Perhaps the old man finally stayed a whole night in his wife's bed. Or she in his."

"Lady Averford came down to breakfast today as well. She doesn't very much of the time, preferring a tray in her room. She did look rosy-cheeked, if I may say. But then, she always does."

"Ah, yes, you're not immune to my sister-in-law's charms."

George blushed in response.

"Don't worry, man. I won't expose you as an admirer. She's a beautiful woman. Most men can't help but notice. I've noticed. Fortunately, she's not my type. Any word on Mrs. Kendal?"

"She wasn't at breakfast. I believe she had a tray sent up."

"Ah, well. I guess I can't put it off any longer. Fetch my coat, George. The black one. I've an appointment with the earl."

Once dressed, he took deep, soothing breaths as he walked, trying to picture the seaside or a sunset or any of a number of comforting images, but all that came to mind was the sight of himself stripped down in the ring, delivering a solid right jab to his opponent, an opponent who looked remarkably like his brother. Though, of course, Gabriel would never engage in any sport that put him on equal terms with the common man.

"Halloo, Brother," he said, entering the study without knocking, trying to keep a devil-may-care attitude, though he did care, dammit. When it came to his brother's opinion of him, he always cared, far too much.

"Marcus," Gabriel spun around in his chair like some kind of Machiavellian version of Satan on his throne. "Good to see you. Have a seat."

"And if I prefer to stand?"

"Do as you please. You will anyway." Gabriel shrugged. "But I don't mean to be quick."

"All right." Marcus took the seat. "What is it? Clearly, something's bothering you. Did I not bow and scrape enough upon arrival? Oh, that's right. You weren't there to greet me."

"I had pressing matters. Running an estate this size takes a fair amount of work, much more work than you'd imagine."

"I'm sure it does. I've never envied you the possession of it, or the responsibility."

Gabriel laughed. "No, I don't think you ever have. But here's the thing. The annuity that keeps you in fine style—"

"I wouldn't say my style is all that fine." He straightened his lapels. "I lead a fairly simple life at Averford House."

"You haven't exceeded your income, I'll give you that."

"Damn straight." Marcus sat up a little taller in the seat.

"But it could all go away, you know. Poof. Just as easily as it comes."

Marcus raised a brow. "The estate's not in any danger, is it?"

"It's not that, no. When you have a wife, Marcus, and your wife wants something very badly, you want to give her what she wants, her heart's desire. You might understand if you had a wife."

"Her heart's desire? A child? Sophia wants a child, and you can't quite perform your duties? I would be more than happy to step in for you, old man. We do look enough alike, I suppose, that there would be no question."

Gabriel fisted his hands and seemed like he would stand, then kept his seat after all. "Thank you for making this so much easier for me, Marcus. You always do. I do want something from you. And if you aren't willing to play along, it's going to cost you."

"Cost me? How? What could you possibly want?"

"As I was saying, it's what Sophia wants that matters. She wants you to marry her sister, Alice." He waved his hand dismissively. "Well, she's hoping you'll fall in love with Alice and decide you can't live without her, and all that romance business the women like."

"All that romance business? Gabriel, no wonder you were always such a favorite with the ladies."

"They do like me." Marcus's sarcasm went straight

over his brother's head, as usual. "But what I'm saying is, will you woo and when the time is right, propose to, Lady Alice?"

"I hardly know Lady Alice. I doubt it. Besides, she's not to my taste."

"Your taste runs more to Mrs. Kendal, I suppose? Don't think it escaped my notice that you were cozying up to her last night on the sofa. A dashed good thing Sophia didn't pick up on it."

"On what? My sitting next to her friend and engaged in a harmless discussion on books? I thought I was to think of Alice. Now we're back to Sophia."

"On the obvious attraction between you and Eve Kendal." His brother tossed a rumpled ball of paper at him. "Imbecile. You know what I mean. I want you to marry Alice to please Sophia. She wants to keep her sister close and—"

"That settles it. I'm not the best choice. I would only whisk her away to London and make her miserable."

"Where in London? Averford House? I don't think so. I might convince Mother to let you and your bride have the Dower House permanently, though it would mean taking Agatha on here."

"You expect me to marry and stay on the estate, close to you?" Marcus eased forward in his chair.

"Sophia wishes it. I wish for her to be happy."

"Why? Why would Sophia wish such a thing? She knows we don't get along, and I can guess that you haven't exactly given me a glowing recommendation as marriage material. She cares for her sister. Wouldn't she wish for Alice to be happy?"

Gabriel sighed and drummed his fingers on the

desk. "She wants Thornbrook Park to have a proper heir, as do I. She loves it here. Like me, she sees the need to have someone who loves the house as much as we do in line to inherit it. But we have different ideas of how best to go about it. We lost a child, did you know?"

"Good God, Gabriel." Marcus felt as though he'd been punched in the gut without warning. "I'm sorry. I had no idea. When?"

Gabriel stopped drumming and ran a hand through his hair. "Four years ago. You were away. The pregnancy went well. There were no problems. We had no reason to believe—" His voice broke.

"You don't have to go on. I know I'm the last person you would choose as a confidante." Marcus had never felt such a surge of pity for his brother. It was a new and uncomfortable sensation for him.

"No. You should know. It was a boy. My son. Born healthy, or so it seemed. But Sophia had a terrible time with the delivery. She lost a lot of blood and the doctor was concerned. Mother made herself useful and took turns along with the nurse tending Sophia and the baby. It was Sophia I was worried about. We all were.

"Meanwhile, this tiny baby, seemingly perfect in every way, died in his sleep on his very first night of life. We didn't tell Sophia until she seemed strong enough several days later. She was devastated, of course, and furious that no one had told her until after her son was buried. I was only trying to protect her." When he looked up, Gabriel's eyes glistened with gathering tears.

"She forgave you?"

Gabriel nodded. "But we haven't been the same, these past four years. She lets me get close only to push me away again. She's afraid for me to touch her, afraid to risk conceiving in case it should happen again. She couldn't bear it. I think she sees Alice and you together as our best hope, the two of you being so close a match, blood relatives to us both. Family. If you and Alice were to marry and have a child, it would be the next best thing to Sophia and me having another, with no further risk to her. Thornbrook Park would have an heir, and Sophia would always have her sister close."

"But there's no reason to think it would happen again. Sophia could have an easier time of it. And the baby? Did they ever find out what—"

"Edward. His name was Edward."

"After Father." Marcus nodded. It was exactly what Gabriel would name his firstborn, the obvious choice.

"And no, they never did find out what took him. The doctor said it simply happens sometimes with infants. You put them down to sleep and they never wake. There were no signs of suffering or pain, nothing at all wrong with him."

"I'm very sorry, Gabriel."

"Mother went off to Italy not long after. I think she felt that Sophia blamed her. Mother is the one who settled Edward in his cradle that first night."

"I wondered why she'd run off. When you and Sophia married, I thought she would stay around forever simply to make your lives an agony. She hated to think that Thornbrook Park had a new mistress."

"At first." Gabriel smiled at last. "I do believe she'd begun to get used to the idea and life in the Dower House. And then…"

"You can't give up, Gabriel. Sophia loves you. And I've never seen a man love the way you love Sophia. You fell hard and fast."

"Love at first sight. I don't plan to give up. In fact, I'm in the unusual position of attempting to court my own wife. I'm taking her out for a picnic today."

"That kind of love doesn't simply fade with time. She'll want you back, if not today, soon. You'll have an heir. You don't need me. And what good is it if Alice and I aren't willing?"

"Precautionary. It will take the pressure off Sophia to think she has to be the one to produce an heir. Once the pressure's off, she might have a change of heart. You will be willing, and I'm sure you can win Alice over."

Marcus steeled himself. He could feel the tide turning. Gabriel had been warm and forthcoming, but now he had the hard glint back in his sable eyes. "And if not?"

"As I was saying, about your annuity." Gabriel pulled a stack of papers from a drawer behind the desk and shoved them in front of Marcus, their father's will. "Apparently, I control it. I have approval of the entire estate budget from year to year, and your annuity is part of it."

"Father figured my annuity into the estate budget? But most of it comes from Grandfather's legacy."

"Which he controlled and added into the estate for ease of management, and which he handed over to me when he left me his heir. I control it all, Marcus, like it or not. And I can simply draw a line through your annuity and it's gone. Gone."

The ache throbbed behind Marcus's eyes, a steady pounding that went straight to the base of his brain. "You wouldn't."

"Tell me, is your army captain salary enough to support you? If you need to find a new place to live? Will it stretch to take care of that widow and children you've taken on as your own personal charity case?"

Marcus took a calming breath and sat back down. "Dammit, Gabriel, why? What if Alice doesn't care to play along?"

"You're a charming man when you want to be. I'm sure you can persuade her."

"We both know you're bluffing. My inheritance is secure. It's mine. Any court of law could see it plainly. If you choose to force the point, I could always respond in kind. But let's not go down that road. I'm your brother and I'm willing to be reasonable."

"Oh, a sudden change of heart?" Gabriel picked up the stack of papers and put them back in the drawer.

"Contrary to popular opinion, I don't like to find myself at odds with you. I have a proposal that could give us both what we want, no threats necessary."

Gabriel nodded. "I'm listening."

"I want the farm, Tilly Meadow, for the widow and children you mention. I brought Brandon here to see how he liked it and to help gradually win Mrs. Dennehy over to the idea of retiring and letting the Coopers take over the farm."

"I knew there had to be more to it than you getting the boy some work."

"I am responsible for the Coopers, and I don't like the idea of the impressionable youngsters growing up on the streets of London."

"Bad influences abound?"

"It's not the same when you grow up without a title and the security of a large estate."

"No, it wouldn't be. But Mrs. Dennehy is comfortably settled. I doubt she would be willing to step aside. Her husband died there. They made their whole lives there together. I won't ask her to leave."

"But if I could somehow convince her? I will woo Alice and do my best to win her heart as long as you promise me the farm for the Coopers."

"If you can convince Mrs. Dennehy to step aside and you can convince Alice to marry you, then you can do what you like with Tilly Meadow Farm."

"Challenges I'm ready to accept," he said, with a pang of regret for what he was about to lose with Eve—a promising friendship and possibly more. "For the Coopers."

When Lucy greeted her with a tray in the morning, Eve thought that Sophia was sleeping in instead of going down to breakfast.

"Thank you, Lucy." She accepted the tray. "Have you heard if the lady has plans for us today or is she still abed?"

"You're at your leisure today. The earl and countess had an early breakfast together and have plans for the afternoon."

"Plans?" This was new to her limited experience

at Thornbrook Park, the lord and lady having plans together. She thought it a positive development. A married couple should escape for some time alone now and then.

Nodding quickly, Lucy obviously shared her enthusiasm. "He's arranged a picnic lunch. They're to have a carriage ride through the countryside followed by lunch alfresco. They're not even bringing a footman. The earl himself will manage the horses."

"Is it unusual for them to proceed unaccompanied?" Lucy's excitement told Eve that it probably was.

"Very unusual, of late anyway. When they were first married, and I was just a kitchen girl, they used to go out alone all the time. Then, gradually less and less until it became a rare thing." Lucy held her hands in front of her apron and blushed as she spoke, probably embarrassed to be telling tales.

Eve was glad for the information. She hoped that if they had drifted apart, they could find their way back to each other. But perhaps there hadn't been a rift and it was simply a matter of them making more time for one another. It wasn't any of her business, of course, but she wanted Sophia to be happy.

"A day to myself? What a novelty." She hadn't had a day all on her own, without any pressing business, since she left India. "You're free to go, Lucy. I won't be needing you until it's time to get ready for the evening."

"Are you sure? You can ring for me later if you need me."

"I believe I can manage. But thank you."

Not long after Lucy left her and she'd eaten her breakfast, Eve got up to go through her trunk. She found her saris, each swath of bold color a reminder of the daring adventures she'd had. Prama, her maid, had showed her how to drape the fabric around her body. She'd worn the chartreuse on her first and only elephant ride through the village that ended when her ride stopped for a drink and almost tipped her into the stream.

Once, in the crimson, she'd surprised Ben with her willingness to hold a snake from one of the vendors in the marketplace. She hadn't even minded how it wrapped around her wrist and slithered up her arm. It was cool and smooth, not slimy and not poisonous, or so the vendor had insisted.

Next, she found her spices. Ah, how she wished she had packed more of them. She couldn't make more than a few dishes before running out, but perhaps she could write to Adela Adams to send her more. Some of them were probably more valuable than most of her remaining jewels: the amethysts that had belonged to Ben's mother, the jade bangles he had bought her at the market, the gold ring that Ben had placed on her finger when they'd wed. A year after his death, it had proven too painful a reminder of the fact that she'd been a wife and was no longer. She'd packed it long before leaving.

There was a bronze statue of Vishnu, a quilt from her childhood, the last of Ben's cigars, unsmoked. How she'd hated the smell that now held bittersweet nostalgia. Perhaps she would light one later to jog her memory. Her *Kama Sutra* that Prama had translated from Sanskrit to English. She opened the book to a racy illustration, a man and a woman kissing each other in private areas, but she did not blush. Some things needed no translation.

Most importantly, she found her photographs. There he was—Ben, his square jaw, his bold gaze looking straight into the camera, but not in the same way he'd looked at her. She would never see that look again. Tears came to her eyes, and for a half minute, she couldn't breathe. Ben.

She remembered the day he'd sat for the photograph, how she'd laughed at the faces he'd make, sticking his tongue out, crossing his eyes. In the end, he'd looked all too somber, seated upright, ramrod straight, no hint of a smile, not quite himself. But still, it was Ben, her Ben. Her husband. Her life. Her whole life, or so it had been not so very long ago.

Sometimes, it felt as though it had been so long since she had seen his face that he'd started to blur around the edges. Sometimes, she tried to imagine that Ben and his features would distort into Captain Thorne's. She felt ashamed that she could lose Ben so easily. But she would never lose him. Not really. He would always be a part of her. Staring at the photograph stirred a profound sadness that she didn't want to feel.

She closed the trunk, dusted her hands, washed, dressed, and decided to go in search of some writing materials. It was time she wrote to Colonel Adams, asking for his assistance in locating Mr. Strump. She could enclose a note for Adela, too. And then, perhaps, if time remained, she might get started on her novel at last. If she couldn't recover her fortune, she could try to make a new one with her writing, enough to get by, at least.

The library, she realized, was a room she hadn't taken the time to explore. She knew they had one at Thornbrook Park. She'd walked through it quickly on her first day before moving on to get through the rest of the house. It held an extensive collection of books, filling shelves tall enough to require a ladder, and a few shorter shelves in the middle of the large room with two writing desks, reading tables, and several seating areas.

It dwarfed the library at Averford House, not that she'd taken time to look through that one, either. She'd merely sparred with Marcus in the center of the room. She stroked her lips, remembering the feel of his kiss, then snapped from her reverie. Yes, it was time to investigate the library.

When she arrived, she stopped at a reading table behind the center shelves. Someone else had been enjoying the library, from the looks of it. A snifter remained on the table next to a book of Romantic poems, the same book she'd held last night. Marcus? Had he come here after dinner? There was still a little liquor in the bottom of the glass. Brandy, she deduced, swirling it around in the stream of sunlight stretching across the room from the far window.

On the other side of the table was a small leather-bound book, a pen tucked inside, ink neatly capped next to it. She picked up the journal and the pen rolled out. The pen had probably been marking a place. Eve didn't want the owner, possibly Marcus, to think she had been snooping. It appeared to be a notebook or a ledger. She picked up the pen from the floor and opened the book to replace it. At least, that was her intention.

31 May, 1898

   So lonely. I expected war would be brutal. Violent. Desolate. But I never counted on the loneliness. How can one be lonely when surrounded by a hundred other men?

   It's as if the walls are caving in. The feeling is more cramped and dark with every passing moment. I need laughter. I need light. I need... something. Something that feels so very far away.

Marcus's war journal, she realized. She knew she should stop reading, put it down immediately. These were obviously private thoughts, meant for him alone. But she wanted to know if his whole four years were so bleak and lonely, so awful. She had to know that he'd found some of the light and the laughter he craved. One more page. She skipped ahead.

19 June, 1898

   Cooper and I patrolled the edge of the field, searching the brush for potential dangers. He was the first to find one of the box bombs we'd practiced dismantling. I warned him to take his time. He rushes so that one would think it a race against time. And of course, there's always a danger, but more danger in making a mistake than not disabling a bomb fast enough.

   Only this morning, he shared the letter from his wife, Prudence, with a story of their son, youngest of the four children, getting a new tooth. No matter what happens, it remains imperative that Cooper gets back to his family. I couldn't ask for a better friend.

Eve smiled at the lightness of his tone, despite the obvious dangers he and his friend Cooper faced. She was glad he'd found a friend.

She skipped another few pages, read a bit, and then another, before she finally forced herself to put it down. When she read his comparison between his bond with Cooper and his lack of camaraderie with his own brother back home, her heart nearly broke for him.

"Oh, Marcus," she said out loud and then jumped at the sound of her own voice. She wasn't concerned that he had heard her, wherever he was, as much as she feared that speaking it aloud would make it true, that she was falling a little in love with Marcus. But it wasn't love, she corrected herself. It was infatuation, perhaps. Or lust, pure and simple.

Of course, it couldn't hurt for Eve to imagine herself in his arms, to think what she might do to watch those lush lips part to speak her name. She was entitled to her fantasies, as long as they stayed just that.

She imagined herself in costume as an exotic harem girl and Marcus as the sheik who'd purchased her. They'd look over a copy of *Scheherazade*, taking turns to read to each other aloud. She would perform her own version of the Dance of the Forty Veils, swiveling her hips and dropping veil after veil until finally Marcus couldn't bear it any longer.

Fourteen

"A LITTLE LIGHT READING?" A VOICE INTERRUPTED Eve's fantasy.

She startled and dropped the journal. The shelves had concealed her from the door, lending her a false sense of security. She hadn't counted on the thick Aubusson rug masking his steps until it was too late.

"Marcus." Her heart hammered. How to explain herself? "I just wanted to put the pen back in the journal. I didn't know it was a journal, of course, until I opened it." She swallowed guiltily. "I should have known you were here from the book of Romantic poems, of course."

"The same volume you held last night." He closed the distance between them one slow step at a time, stopping so close that their bodies nearly touched. She wondered if he held his hands behind his back to prevent his reaching out for her, as she longed to reach out for him. "I brought it over after dinner. My refuge, the library. Gabriel never comes here."

"It's an excellent library. I don't blame you. Your father's doing?"

"His great-grandfather. Some of these books are older than the house."

"Built in 1722? By the first Earl of Averford?" She struggled to remember what Finch had said when he'd recounted the history of the house while showing her around that first day.

"In 1724." Marcus smiled. "Very close. The first Averford was reportedly a favorite of George the First."

"Which is why your great-grandfather was named George? I'm guessing. I noticed his portrait in the gallery."

"You're probably correct. I never thought about it. Great-Grandfather's first son was George, too, but he met a nasty end at an early age. Drowned in a barrel of wine while trying to steal a taste. They say he haunts the wine cellar, but I've never seen him."

"Perhaps Finch invited Mrs. Hoyle down there to scare him off. We could always ask Agatha if she senses a presence."

"Gabriel wouldn't like that since one of Agatha's séances sent Sophia's first maid scampering, or so I've heard."

"I would have thought Bowles more loyal. She'd been with Sophia since our coming out. Mrs. Jenks is a vast improvement, though. I'm not sure Sophia could get on without her."

"I wouldn't underestimate Sophia. She's most likely made of steel to be able to put up with my brother."

"The sixth Earl of Averford, who, curiously, is not named George." She didn't wish to speak of her friends any longer. Perhaps because thinking of them was at odds with what she wanted to do with the man intended for Sophia's sister. "The tradition ended after the drowning?"

He nodded. "Grandfather was Edward, and so was Father. Mother wouldn't dream of using a family name. She went with Gabriel, the angel, because she admired his statue in the Pantheon. An angel's name for my brother, isn't that rich?"

He didn't laugh, so neither did she. "You should be Michael, then, shouldn't you? Gabriel and Michael, both angels?"

"Mother has a sense of humor. She named one of us for an angel, and the other for the god of war, Mars, practically assuring from my birth that we would never get along."

"Or perhaps she named you for Marcus Agrippa, the commissioner of the Pantheon? If she holds a fondness for the Pantheon, it would make sense."

"Marcus Agrippa?" He narrowed his eyes. "How do you know so much?"

She laughed at last, her spirit lightened, and gestured around them. Wouldn't Colonel Adams scold her for showing off? "I read, Marcus. Everything and anything. When you spend a lot of time alone, you begin to consider—"

"Books to be your friends." He finished for her, the crooked half smile spreading into a full one. "They were mine, too, growing up, my very best friends. I suspect that we're a lot alike."

"Perhaps too much alike," she said, meeting his gaze. "I should go."

He let his hands free to take one of hers, lacing their fingers together. "Stay. No one's at home to bother

us. Sophia and Gabriel went out. Brandon trotted off
with the groundskeeper to explore. The servants have
straightened up in here by now. We can be alone."

"Exactly why I should go. We can't torture ourselves. This can't go much further." Once she said
it, she realized her mistake. She should have said
that this couldn't go *any* further, putting an end to
all possibility.

He nodded in agreement. "I know. Gabriel cor-
nered me today about marrying Alice. He tried to
force me."

"Force you, how?"

"With idle threats. Ridiculous, really. He threatened to eliminate my inheritance."

"Can he do that? Would he?" She knew the brothers didn't get along, but she had no idea that Gabriel
could be so devious.

He shook his head. "Of course not. He can't. I'm
not sure he wouldn't try. But I made a deal with
him instead. I agreed to marry Alice in exchange for
the farm."

She dropped her hand as if scorched. "What about
Alice? How does she feel about all this? Did either of
you even consider her?"

"No one's going to force Alice into anything. I
think I can win her admiration, if not her love. It's
possible that we could be happy together. Tolerably
so, at least."

"What every girl dreams, to be tolerably happy in
life." She felt a little sick.

"Please, don't be cross with me." He reached out to
stroke her cheek with the back of his hand. She wished

she were numb to the low, rolling hum of desire skittering along her nerves. "You know I'm in a bind. I'm responsible for the Coopers. I will not deceive Alice. I'll be sure she knows how I feel about her."

"Which is?"

"That I hold her in very high esteem."

She exhaled, not even realizing that she'd been holding her breath awaiting an answer. "But you don't love her?"

"No. I don't love her. Not now, maybe eventually." He looped an arm around her waist. "People marry for reasons other than love all the time. You know it well."

She peeked up at him from under her lashes. "I do."

"Then please don't hold it against me. I feel like we're having a lovers' quarrel, and we're not even lovers."

Yet. She sensed that he'd been about to say "yet" and thought the better of it. But was he so far from wrong? Even now, she was prepared to return his embrace, to cradle his head against her bosom and tell him it would all work out somehow.

And that was precisely the problem. As impossible as it seemed that they could get together, she'd hoped it would all work out. Could she do that? Become a man's lover? She'd begun to believe it possible, even as she denied it could be. She knew it was wrong, but how right it felt between them.

"I don't hold it against you, Marcus," she said at last. "I wish you well. It's noble that you want to give the Coopers a better life. As long as Alice gets to know you as I do, I'm certain that she won't be able to resist you."

She turned away, toward the bookshelves behind them, to hide her forming tears.

"Eve." He placed himself in front of her again. "I'm not promised right now, at this moment. I'm free to give myself to anyone I choose. We can't have any more than today, but we can have today."

"What are you suggesting?" Her pulse raced, wild-fire in her veins.

He gripped her by the shoulders, his mouth open-ing ravenously on hers, and then he broke the kiss as suddenly as it had begun. "For today, at least, we could pretend we have each other, and no one else. No demands, no promises to keep."

Heat pooled at her core. For today. Truly, what harm would be done? "What would you think of me?"

"The same that I think of you now. You're a beau-tiful woman who deserves to be adored. Do you mean to shut yourself away and never love again?"

She didn't mean to remarry, but she'd enjoyed relations with her husband. Could she really imagine giving it up entirely?

"'Gather ye rosebuds while ye may,'" she quoted Herrick. This was her chance. She might never have another.

"That's it, yes." His eyes were heavy-lidded as he leaned in to kiss her again. "My suite or your room, which is closer?"

"No. Here. Now. Before I change my mind. You said we were safe from discovery?" Frantic, she pushed his coat from his shoulders.

He shrugged out of it. "No one will interrupt us."

She sought his mouth, nibbling gently on his lower

lip as he fumbled with the buttons on her dress. He managed one, two—she lost count—but suddenly his palm grazed her breast and she stilled, savoring the sensation of flesh on flesh. Two years of pent-up desire simmered in her veins, building toward an unstoppable release. His body pressed against hers, backing her up and lowering her to the table. She ran her hands over him, shifting beneath him so that she could feel more of him against her.

"Marcus." He found the hem of her skirt and pushed it up, allowing her to wrap her legs around him, to pull him tighter against her until she could feel his erection straining against his trousers and her linens. She gasped at the heat of his hand on her tender thighs and mewled softly when he slipped a finger inside her. "Yes."

"Yes," he echoed, sliding the finger in, out, and circling around her delicate nub until she quivered, biting her lip to keep from calling out. He leaned over her, blazing a trail of kisses down her neck to her breast, flicking his tongue across her nipple through the silk of her chemise that he couldn't quite remove. "I can't hold back. I need you now. Please."

Please. On top of everything else—his kissing, his caresses—that one word, "please." She came undone.

⤳

God help him, Marcus tried to stay in control. The beauty of the woman, her fallen hair like spun gold against the dark of her gown, challenged his resolve, but her softness beneath him drove him over the edge. He couldn't remember ever feeling so lost in a woman before Eve. At the moment, he could scarce remember his own name.

She moved a fraction, rubbing against him, and he hardened to the point of aching. He set his teeth on edge, struggling to hold back, to make it last, though he felt like a schoolboy, new to all sensation. She made him feel new again, filled with awe and reverence.

On a kiss, he entered her, the wave of ecstasy threatening to pull him under as she pulsed around him. He gasped for air, the feeling of being inside her nearly overwhelming him. She writhed and urged him deeper, faster, pulling him to her on a ragged whimper and burying her face in his shoulder as she climaxed with a violent shudder. He joined her there at the edge of heaven, dissolving like foam in their ocean of bliss.

For a moment, he stayed atop her, both of them struggling to steady their ragged breathing. Their gazes locked and held. Those gas-flame eyes led him right back to her through the gauzy haze, and he'd never felt more intensely alive and aware.

Suddenly, she sat up, adjusted her skirts, and began to button her dress. He did up his shirt and retrieved his coat from the floor. A hundred times would never be enough, a thousand, millions. How could he court Alice? How could he not?

But they still had today. All day. He reached for her. "Eve."

"They'll be coming back." She flashed a dazed smile. "They'll all be back, who knows when. I need to freshen up."

"Of course. I'll meet you back at your room, then. It's our day, our only chance. I'll take you for a picnic, how's that? Somewhere no one will find us, our own little paradise."

"A picnic? It sounds lovely, but—"

He placed his fingers to her lips. "A picnic. Why not? It seems to be the day for it. Unless you have any objection to sitting on a blanket over grass and eating cold chicken, cheese, and bread?

"No objection." She smiled. "I'll get my hat."

&

Filled with a sublime joy that she'd never thought to feel again, she rode beside Marcus in the front seat of the car.

"When did you learn to drive?" she asked, trying not to sound astonished by his unexpected accomplishment.

"Another thing I learned away at war."

"Lord Averford took his lady out in a carriage, so I assume your brother doesn't know how to drive."

Marcus nodded, never taking his gaze from the road. "Why would he? He employs a driver to make a position for someone in need."

"I see. Why learn to drive and risk putting a man out of work?" She knew Lord Averford well enough by now.

He raised a fist and deepened his voice to an authoritative tone. "It's our responsibility to provide."

They swerved slightly and she gave a shriek. "Both hands on the wheel, please, Captain Thorne."

"Don't be a ninny." He flashed her a smile. "Or I'll go faster."

"I think we're going quite fast enough." It was a much more thrilling ride than any she had taken with Dale. Her spirit felt as light and free as the breeze whipping through her hair with the glass down. She didn't even mind that her chignon had fallen loose. "Where are we headed?"

"I'm not sure, but I'll know when we get there. As long as we're headed in the opposite direction from the earl."

She agreed. "We can't afford to run into them. Do you know where they've gone?"

"Gabriel's favorite spot is the grassy banks of the creek just before it widens to the lake on the northwest side of the property. Good fishing. I'm guessing he's brought his pole."

"To fish? While they're picnicking?" She nibbled her lip. "Sophia won't like it."

"No?" He seemed surprised. "She objects to his manly pursuits?"

"When they take his attention from her, of course." She laughed.

"I see." His brows knit. "How do you think things are between them?"

"Between Sophia and Gabriel?" At once, she realized that he shared her concerns for them.

"It's hard to say. Is Sophia happy? Yes, I suppose. She has the life she has always imagined for herself."

"The life of a countess."

"In a fine house in the country. She detests London."

"I've noticed. They hardly spend any time there. Gabriel comes when he has business, of course, but Sophia usually stays behind at Thornbrook Park."

"I wasn't sure she loved him when she married him. It was a subject of disagreement between us."

"Her marrying my brother?" He sounded surprised.

As great a critic as he was of the Earl of Averford, he seemed to think any woman who landed him would have been a target of envy, which was honestly true. An earl was considered a fine catch.

"She started the arguments between us, for my eloping with Ben. How could I run off with an army captain?"

"Ouch."

"You're a Thorne, no ordinary army captain. But Sophia thought I should reconsider marrying when my family disapproved. Was it enough to be in love? I decided that it was, but she made a good point. It has never been easy for me to lose them."

"I understand." He reached out and placed a hand on her thigh.

She struggled to hold focus on other matters with the heat of his touch fogging her brain. So well she remembered his hands in intimate places, what he'd done to her. What they'd done. Just that morning. "But I couldn't imagine not marrying a man I loved. When she announced she had accepted your brother, I was shocked because she hadn't confessed to being in love with him. She did admire him, and she liked him well enough. But love? I wasn't sure."

"She liked the idea of being a countess well enough, though?"

"Not just a countess. Gabriel's countess. All of the girls were in love with him." She confirmed his obvious suspicions. "He was the greatest catch of the season next to the Duke of Rustledge, and Rustledge had nothing on your brother as far as looks."

He rolled his eyes. "I can't imagine it. He's such a…"

"Such a?"

"Well, he's Gabriel. What's there to like, let alone swoon over?"

"He's your brother. You see him differently than a swarm of marriage-minded debutantes all out to capture the season's prize."

"The booby prize." He laughed, took a turn down a short dirt road between some low-hanging trees, and pulled over. "We walk from here." He gestured at the trees.

"Into the forest? Should I be afraid?"

"You can hang on to me if we encounter wild beasts. We're actually just cutting through the outlying wilderness to a wide meadow filled with wildflowers. It used to be another farm, the McGintys' place. Old man McGinty passed away when I was a child. I would sometimes walk out here and bring home bouquets for Mother."

"Quite a long walk." They'd only been driving for a quarter hour, but the walk would take hours for short legs.

"On foot, it's faster if you go through Thornbrook's land, past the orchards, and cut through Mrs. Dennehy's grazing fields. Of course, you have to make sure Dennehy's not watching out the window with her shotgun."

"Lovely. I look forward to meeting her one day." They got out. He picked up the basket and she took his offered hand.

"She's friendly enough, just protective of her land."

"But it's Thornbrook Park land. She's a tenant?"

He lifted a branch to lead her through the trees.

"Technically, yes, but years have given her a sense of ownership."

"And McGinty? Was he also a tenant farmer?"

"His lands were his own, I think still for sale. The idea of repairing the old house and barns and restoring the fields to fertile land is daunting and expensive. Farms are disappearing across the country in favor of factories. It's all about industry now."

"But Mrs. Dennehy hangs on. I have to admire her tenacity, though she adds a crimp to your plan for the Coopers." She clung to his hand, allowing him to help her over a fallen log. "We won't get into any trouble for trespassing?"

"No one comes here any longer, as far as I know. I believe we're perfectly safe." They emerged through the trees and overgrown weeds to a clearing.

"It's beautiful." She looked over the breathtaking expanse of tall grass and flowers that gradually sloped down toward a dilapidated old barn. "Look at all the sunflowers and thimbleweed. Is that Thornbrook there, off in the distance?"

He shook his head. "It's Skipham, farther off than it looks."

"Picturesque. Do you think there might one day be a factory here?" She followed him to a patch of grass, where he set down the basket.

"One day, perhaps. What sort of factory do you think?" He opened the basket. She helped him spread the green plaid blanket over the grass. "Whizgigs? A whizgig factory?"

"Or whatsits." She smiled, reaching for a wrapped bundle. He shooed her hand away.

"Sit. I'll serve." He helped her to the ground, crouched down beside her, and began removing and uncovering things from the basket. "Perhaps whizgigs and whatsits together. A whizgigs and whatsits factory."

"A shame to lose all these gorgeous sunflowers. And Thornbrook Park might lose a few servants to new opportunities."

"Horrors. Are you suggesting they're not all loyal to the earl after he's taken such responsibility to provide for them all these years?" He withdrew two glasses and a bottle of wine. "Hoyle and Finch will stay on to the bitter end."

He opened the wine, poured, and handed her a glass. She raised it. "To loyalty!"

"To us!" His gaze stayed on her as he clinked his glass to hers. "Enough about my brother and his estate. The afternoon is ours."

Ours. She loved the sound. If only for the day.

"I'm famished," she confessed, though she did not add that she hungered for more than food. Their lovemaking had been everything she'd craved, urgent and uninhibited, but she still felt caught up in a dream. Had it all been real? She wanted him once more to be certain of it. Slower next time, lingering to savor each other properly with the overwhelming need to claim each other out of the way. "Mrs. Mallows has outdone herself. We have a feast. Chicken, cheese, bread. Are those strawberry tarts?"

"Not apple, alas. But all I really need is you here by my side." He handed her a plate.

They ate quietly, enjoying the food, the scenery,

easy companionship, and a most excellent chilled white wine. Their hunger sated, their attention turned to other needs. He gathered the food and plates, tucked them back into the basket, and eased onto his back, his head in her lap.

"Nap time?" She stroked his hair.

"No, I'm simply lulling you into a false sense of security." He reached up and guided her head down to meet his kiss. "Mmm, you taste of strawberries."

"You taste of wine." She slipped out from under him, removed her hat, and moved to stretch out next to him on the blanket. "A good combination, strawberries and wine."

The blue sky overhead had filled with a few clouds. They would have to leave soon if it started to storm, but it seemed they still had time. He propped up on an elbow and arched a golden brow. "You, Mrs. Kendal, are in quite a lot of danger."

"Danger?" She tried to appear unruffled by the idea, but a thrill snaked up her spine.

He reached for her bodice and tugged it low beneath her breasts, exposing her. She bit her lip to stifle a gasp as the light breeze grazed her nipples. "I mean to explore you thoroughly this time."

"Take heed, Captain." She trailed her hand down the length of him to his trousers, stopping to brush his growing erection. "I'm prepared to answer all threats measure for measure."

Fifteen

HIS STOMACH FLIPPED WHEN SHE SUGGESTED THAT she would respond to his exploration in kind. But when she freed him from his trousers and began to stroke his shaft, he thought perhaps he had died on the spot.

He closed his eyes against the rush of sensation. "Woman, you'll be my undoing."

"That is my intention," she said, flashing a wicked smile as she rolled onto her stomach and repositioned herself between his legs. "But slowly, and with excruciating detail."

Her mouth replaced her hand and he shuddered from the sheer pleasure of it, the light pressure of her lips sliding up and down, the exquisite laving of her tongue along the tip. When she took him all the way to the back of her throat, he couldn't stifle his moan. As she enthusiastically conducted her onslaught, he wasn't sure he could hold on.

"Oh no, sweetheart. Your turn." He sat up, twisting around to shift her underneath him, lifted her skirts, and parted her legs around him. Sliding his hands up her delicate legs, he paused at the juncture of her thighs. "You're beautiful, Eve. Every inch of you."

She moaned as he parted her to him and kissed her intimately, rolling his tongue around the pearl at her core before delving inside her and out again. He repeated his attentions, savoring her sweet taste, until she pulled his hair.

"Now. Please," she begged.

"Darling, not soon enough." He rose over her, steadying his weight on his arms and meeting her gaze. He wanted to watch her as they joined, cementing the memory of their connection into his mind.

He moved deliberately, urging her to move with him as he entered her, then pulled back and eased in again. With great restraint, he resisted the temptation to rush the pace, while her crystalline gaze held him enthralled. He failed to notice the darkening sky or increasing winds until the rain began to fall on them.

She gasped and clung to him, her slick legs tightening around his hips. He fell into rhythm with the raindrops until her silken heat gripped him as she found her bliss. He peaked with her and remained atop her, shielding her from the weather and looking into her eyes, holding on to their moment for as long as he possibly could.

"We're getting soaked," he said finally, after catching his breath.

She laughed. "It's only water. Hurrying off won't make us any less wet."

He helped her to her feet and pulled her into his arms, kissing her again as the drops fell more rapidly around them. She refused to be hurried along, drawing his tongue in.

He wished it never had to end, but he picked up their wet things while she adjusted her dress.

"I've ruined my hat." She picked it up by the sagging straw brim.

"I'll buy you another."

She smiled. "No thank you, Captain Thorne. I can buy my own hats."

A shame. He liked the idea of them shopping together. They sat in silence on the journey back, probably both wondering if Gabriel and Sophia would be waiting for them. He wouldn't be bullied, he decided. If Gabriel had an issue with him taking Eve out for a drive, so be it. He'd agreed to court Alice, but he'd never said when he would begin.

Dale came out for the car as they pulled into the drive, held an umbrella over Eve, and escorted her into the house.

"Thank you, Dale," Marcus said upon the man's return. "I'll manage without the umbrella." He made his entrance and hoped for the best.

Mr. Finch alone stood waiting to greet them with warm blankets that he wrapped around them as they came in. "A shame that you got caught in the downpour."

"It's only water." Marcus flashed Eve a grin. When he saw her return a smile, his heart gave a queer flutter. Bloody hell, he couldn't be falling in love. It was infatuation, nothing more. And it would fade as he set on course to woo Alice. Wouldn't it?

"And the earl and countess?" he asked, struggling to recover. "Did they get caught out, too?"

"No," Mr. Finch said. "They made it back well before you."

The grim set of the butler's mouth cued Marcus that it might not have been a happy homecoming.

"Dinner will be brought up on trays tonight. Lady Averford thought it best to leave everyone to leisure," he said, as if to confirm Marcus's suspicion.

"Just as well," Eve said. "I have correspondence to keep up with."

"There was a caller for you while you were out," Mr. Finch informed Eve. "A gentleman."

Her eyes widened with excitement. "From London? Was it a Mr. Strump? Or perhaps Mr. Gibbs? Or Gerald?"

Finch shook his head. "His name escapes me. He didn't leave a card. He said he was your cousin, long lost, eager to reconnect."

"My cousin?" Her nose wrinkled. "I don't believe I have any cousins. None that I'm aware. Perhaps on the American side? Did he sound American?"

"I'm not certain I know what American sounds like," Finch said. "But it's possible. He didn't leave word where he was staying, but he said he would come back."

"Until then, it's a mystery," Eve said, turning to Marcus. "I suppose everyone needs a little mystery now and again. A cousin? Imagine! I might have family."

"Imagine," he agreed, not wanting to disappoint her. A sour taste rose in the back of his throat. The timing seemed suspicious. "We'll find out when he returns. Why don't you run along and get some dry clothes? We can't have you catching your death."

"Good idea. Thank you for our ride, Captain Thorne." She blushed as she lifted her eyes to him and held out her hand for a friendly shake. "I had a lovely afternoon."

"As did I," he said, watching her go up the stairs. He waited until she was all the way up before he turned to Finch to confirm the dread growing in his mind. "By any chance, was this visitor wearing a black bowler hat?"

"In fact he was, Captain Thorne. Though I hardly found it worthy of note, black bowlers being so common. Do you know the fellow?"

"I can't imagine so." He shook his head. But he planned to make some inquiries to see what he could find out.

∽

When he'd agreed to go riding with his brother, Marcus had failed to imagine it would mean getting up at the ungodly hour of seven in the morning. His brother was a barbarian. But he'd always known it. Why should he expect anything had changed, that his brother would have been tamed by marriage?

The wonders of married life were lost on Marcus, and thank goodness. With the wonders of sleeping late, however, he was well acquainted. And he wished to stay well acquainted, snuggling deep into the down blankets. He had to hand it to Sophia; she had replaced the scratchy Averford linens with the softest cotton sheets. His bed felt like a cloud around him, and he did not want to leave it. But he felt George watching over him.

"On penalty of death, you said. By firing squad." George spoke from between clenched teeth. "'Make sure I'm out of bed by six in the morning, George,' you said."

"You're a good lad, George. Forget what I said about the firing squad. Give me another hour in bed, and I will whisk you away to Averford House when I return to London. I'll make you my permanent valet."

George's answer was to tear the covers clean off Marcus's body. "I don't want to go to London, sir. And I'm not sure whether to believe the threat of firing squad or the promise of promotion."

"The promotion, of course."

Normally, six wouldn't feel such a torture. The army got a man used to getting up early and sometimes functioning on very little sleep. He would have to rely on his training. But his army days were drifting to the past and he certainly hadn't gotten much sleep, staying out late to visit every inn and tavern within a wide radius in an attempt to find the mysterious stranger in the black bowler hat, to no avail. He wasn't as young as he used to be. He wished he had another hour to catch up on his sleep.

"I'm still not certain it wouldn't be the firing squad. For my next move, I plan to upend the pitcher of water all over your bed. How would you like sleeping then, sir?"

"You are a taskmaster, young George. Finch has taught you well. He had better watch out, for that matter. Are you aiming to take over as butler?"

"One day perhaps. But not until Finch is well and done with it. The place wouldn't be the same without Mr. Finch, sir."

"I quite agree. I wish I could lure him to Averford House. Sutton is quite the stoic. Have you met Mr. Sutton?"

"I haven't had the pleasure. I've never been to the London house."

"No loss, really. It's not as grand as Thornbrook Park. But it's home. Well, not really home. It's a place to stay. For now. One day, I suppose I will need a home of my own."

"One day, sir."

"One day," he echoed, getting out of bed to prepare for the day ahead. One day very soon if he managed to succeed with Alice, he thought with a pang of regret.

"Be sure you look after Brandon for me, George. Let him sleep as he long as likes and then keep an eye out for him. He took a shine to the new litter of pointers, so I assume he will be off to the kennel for the afternoon. He should only be with us for a few more days."

They had decided to ride out to the farm to see how Mrs. Dennehy felt about hiring new help before introducing Brandon. Marcus hurried through his bath and shave, and an hour later, was seated on the big brown stallion his brother had called Viking, but the stable lads referred to as "Crazy Legs." Marcus had not ridden since the war. It didn't bode well. His brother's horse, the gentlest and most obedient of mares, Wilmadene, cantered along. "Viking" was certainly a more respectable name for a mount than "Wilmadene," but "Crazy Legs" lurked ominously in the back of his mind.

"So, you've made some changes to the grounds, I take it?" Marcus opened conversation. "Any special alterations I should be aware of as we ride?"

"Nothing earth-shattering, I suppose," Gabriel said. "Winthrop's ordered a new fence to be built for the pasture past the cottage. The old one has rotted away."

"Winthrop, the estate manager? How's he working out?"

Gabriel shrugged. "He's no trouble at all compared to what one might expect with his reputation. He likes to be left alone, but it's not a surprise to find him pitching in with the groundskeepers. Perhaps hard work helps him forget his personal struggles."

Logan Winthrop had grown up the younger brother to a baron, much like Marcus taking second to his brother, the earl. There were some rumors of Winthrop murdering a rival, but he'd been acquitted of the crime. The former estate manager had recommended Winthrop to Gabriel upon his own retirement. A good man, he'd said, under unfortunate circumstances. *Give him a chance.* And Gabriel had.

"Strong fences make good neighbors. Must keep out the cows," Marcus said, getting back on the topic of the farm. "And sheep? Does Mrs. Dennehy still have sheep?"

"A few old girls and one or two rams. She hasn't been mating them. It would break her heart if the sheep outlived her, she says. She wouldn't leave the responsibility of their care to anyone else."

"Perhaps I can convince her otherwise. The Coopers have farming in their blood." That they had no actual experience with raising livestock or vegetation, Marcus left unsaid. He gently nudged his horse to keep up with Wilmadene.

As if sensing Marcus's struggle to control Viking, Gabriel nudged Wilmadene to a brisk trot.

"Curious way you have of wooing Alice," Gabriel looked back to Marcus. "By taking Eve Kendal out for a drive."

"I thought my paying attention to another woman might intrigue Alice."

"You believed you were making her jealous? Deuce it, man, have you courted a woman since Eton?"

Marcus almost made a retort about Gabriel having to court his own wife, but checked himself in time as it would have been needlessly cruel to point that out.

Instead, Marcus chose avoidance, urging his mount to step quicker, giving him an unintentional dig with his heel. Viking charged, full speed ahead. Worse even than being thrown from a wild horse would be needing his brother's help to control one. He urged himself to keep a cool head and regain dominance over the beast. Until then, there was no sense in letting Gabriel believe he'd made a foolish mistake.

"Race you!" He called over his shoulder, even as he held on for dear life while Viking plundered the land.

Fortunately, of its own accord, the horse decided to slow to a stop at the edge of the meadow near the stream. Marcus wasted no time in getting down as soon as it was safe to dismount.

"There, there, boy." He stroked the horse's flanks as it leaned over to drink.

"Are you insane?" Gabriel said, once he caught up. "Race me? We're not boys anymore, need I remind you. A gentleman doesn't go tearing up the land willy-nilly."

"A gentleman doesn't say 'willy-nilly,'" Marcus countered, feeling very childish indeed. "Shall we leave the horses to rest and walk the rest of the way to Tilly Meadow?"

Gabriel agreed. "We'll send a lad over from the farm to tend them."

They walked in silence until Marcus caught sight of the little barn, faded from red to brown from years in the rain and sun. "It looks as though it has seen better days, Gabriel. Are you sure Mrs. Dennehy is managing alone?"

Gabriel shrugged. "She says so. She's very insistent. Her husband died here, and I believe she intends to as well."

"But she's not ready for that, certainly. She was younger than old man Dennehy, if I recall. By about twenty years?"

"True," Gabriel nodded. "She's sixty, sixty-five, not a day older. But the years are showing. Without the farm, she would be dead, she says. It keeps her going."

"I can imagine, but working it alone might be taking a toll. A few hired hands can't replace what she used to have with her husband. What's become of her daughters?"

"They married. One of them moved to London with her husband, a railway man. The other is in Orkney. His family had land there. They come to visit now and again, but not often enough."

"Probably as often as we attempt to see Mother." Marcus laughed at that, and even Gabriel responded with a chuckle.

Even though Marcus had been Mother's favorite,

he'd never felt like more than a shiny toy to her, a temporary distraction from her endless social engagements, afternoon teas, formal dinners, and the glittering evening affairs she claimed to loathe but never canceled or turned down.

"Fair enough, I suppose. Shall we go and say hello?"

"Yes," Marcus said. No one answered their knock, but they heard a faint "Come in" and entered to find Mrs. Dennehy bent over a full, heavy pot, pouring a mixture from it into another by way of a sieve.

"Separating the whey from the curd," she said. "Be right with you."

Both men stepped forward to assist her with her load, but she shrugged them off.

"I may be old, boys, but I'm still strong as an ox." She finished and turned back to them, wiping her hands on her apron. "Now, what can I do for you?"

Marcus removed his hat. "I've come to say hello, Mrs. Dennehy. I've been home for a visit."

She squinted, then clearly recognized him. "Marcus Thorne! Here to steal my apples, are you? The barn's full of them. The lads are pressing cider, but I'm sure you might make off with a bushel. How are you, dear?"

"Very well, Mrs. Dennehy. Better after having some of your famous cheese last night, the taste of home."

She smiled with pride. "Ah, well, it takes some work, but I'm still making the cheddar, and some softer cheeses, too. A shame I have no one to pass the recipes on to with the girls so far away. It is good to see you all grown. I confess, I worried that you might not make it back."

"No need to fear for me. I made up for my lack of experience with my quick wits."

Gabriel rolled his eyes.

"Oh no." She laughed her hearty laugh. "I knew you would make it back from the war. I just wasn't sure to expect you would ever return to Thornbrook Park, once this one took charge of it all." She gestured at Gabriel. "Oh, the way you two fought as lads!"

"We may still come to blows. I wouldn't have come back to see him," Marcus confessed honestly. "But he has a lovely wife who had the sense to write to me about your apples. How could I stay away?"

"Is that how she lured you?" said Gabriel, who seemed not at all surprised by the conversation. "I had wondered about it. She wrote you so many times without success."

"I know you'll refuse any help." Marcus changed the subject back to Mrs. Dennehy's work. "So I'm just going to lift this heavy vat and hold on to it until you tell me where you want me to put it down."

With care not to spill the contents, he hoisted the pot from the floor, the one into which she had been draining her cheese mixture.

"Oh, very well," she clucked. "Place it back on the stove top, please. And have a care. You'll spoil me. Before you know it, I will put you to work harvesting the rest of my apples and chopping and stacking my wood."

"I would be delighted," Marcus said. "After being at war, leading the leisurely life of a landed gentleman holds very little appeal. I'm likely to be bored to death at Thornbrook Park if I lie about there much longer."

"I see that it's time I paid more attention to this place," Gabriel admitted. "The barn could use a stain and maybe a few repairs."

Traditionally, it was the landlord's responsibility to maintain the buildings, though the equipment, maintenance, and farming fell to the tenant.

"Don't trouble. We've always done for ourselves."

"Before your husband's passing, that might have been the case," Marcus said. "But we could certainly live up to our responsibilities now that you're on your own. In fact, I have a boy in mind who might help keep things in order…"

He launched into his proposal for Mrs. Dennehy to take Brandon on as a new hand around the farm and hoped that he would meet success in winning her over to the idea. And once Brandon proved himself indispensible on the farm, could the rest of the Coopers be far from acceptance?

Sixteen

THE NEXT MORNING, ANY HOPE EVE HAD OF RUNNING into Marcus was dashed by Mrs. Hoyle, who informed her that the men had gone out together early and that Sophia hadn't rung for her tray. It was just as well. Marcus had to start paying more attention to Alice, and Eve had best get back to her business of finding out what had become of her husband's investments.

She'd stayed up late writing to Colonel Adams and Adela, and then turned her attention to crafting a new outline for her novel, newly inspired by Marcus's war stories, a romance between a war widow and a soldier from the opposing side. With more time on her own that afternoon, she'd gotten a solid start on Chapter One when she was interrupted by a knock at her door.

"Get your coat," Sophia said, all impatience. "Let's go for a walk."

The idea of spending a beautiful day out of doors appealed, but Sophia's sudden determination to get out of the house seemed suspect.

"A walk would be welcome," Eve agreed. The fresh air might spur her creativity.

"Such a good idea," Sophia congratulated herself once they got outside. "Smell that autumn air."

"It's lovely." Eve inhaled. Not as lovely as it been yesterday when she was in Marcus's arms, even with the rain. Especially with the rain.

"I'm worried about how things are progressing between Marcus and Alice," Sophia confided as they crossed the dusty path through the garden. "I mean to stop at the Dower House and encourage Alice to spend more time at Thornbrook Park."

"More time? She's with us most of the time as it is." Having Alice around would no doubt aid Marcus in his quest to win her heart, so Eve couldn't say why she felt such a sharp tug of disappointment at the idea. "She and Agatha would have been there last night, had you not decided to take dinner in your room alone. Were you unwell?"

"Of course not," Sophia snapped, then softened her tone. "Gabriel and I were quarreling, to be honest. I wasn't ready to face him again last night."

"I'm so sorry, Sophia. Is there anything I can do?"

She shook her head. "We made up this morning. It's just that Gabriel is unusually tense with his brother around, and his idea of a relaxing afternoon alone together and mine didn't exactly mesh."

The fishing, Eve thought to herself. "I'm glad you've made up."

"Thank you for keeping Captain Thorne entertained. Mr. Finch said the two of you went out for a drive."

Color rushed to Eve's cheeks. "Yes, we did."

"A pity that it rained on you."

"I didn't mind the rain." The image of Marcus's wet shirt clinging to his chest as he made love to her filled her mind so that she almost veered off the path into the shrubs.

"Careful." Sophia took her arm. "Uneven ground."

"Thank you. Clumsy me." As they crested the hill, Eve caught sight of the Dower House at the edge of the green and the village beyond.

"I only wish you'd thought to include Alice on your adventure, to give her more time with Captain Thorne. It's such a comfort for me to have her close."

"But you said that Gabriel is tense with his brother around. Perhaps it's for the best if Alice marries someone else? There must be plenty of eligible bachelors in Yorkshire." Eve nibbled her lip.

"Someone else? No. Captain Thorne is perfect for her. And Gabriel's mother would certainly quit the Dower House in favor of them. It's the best of all worlds, my mother-in-law staying away and Alice close at hand. Gabriel and Marcus will get used to each other again in time."

"Sophia, please." Eve gripped her arm. "Stop a moment and tell me what's wrong. Why is it so important to keep Alice close? To have her marry Captain Thorne? What if they don't welcome the idea? Alice told me that she prefers not to marry, and Captain Thorne—"

"Yes?" Sophia arched a thin, dark brow. "What of Captain Thorne?"

It was her chance to confide in her friend, to tell her what had happened. But it wasn't her secret alone to give away. What if it ruined Marcus's chance to set up Brandon and bring the Coopers to the farm? She couldn't say anything, not now. "He hasn't singled Alice out for any particular favor yet. What if he doesn't fancy Alice?"

Sophia waved off the concern. "He's a man. He hasn't yet recognized the fact that he needs a wife. But I'm sure I've seen them flirting, don't you think? He must be lonely, all that time at war and then alone in London."

Eve shrugged. "He has the Coopers, Brandon's family. They've taken him in. And he has friends in London. He gets on rather well with Sutton." She smiled, thinking of the two of them. Stoic Sutton and Marcus always trying to get a reaction out of him. "He might not welcome the idea of moving back to Thornbrook Park for any length of time. And what then? If he marries Alice, she could end up going right back to London with him."

"Not that." Sophia's cornflower eyes flashed with concern, or was it fear? "I want them both to love Thornbrook Park as much as I do, to raise their children here. They have to!" She turned her head away suddenly and leaned against the trunk of a large maple at the edge of the lawn as if in need of physical support.

Children. The way Sophia said the word, with a hint of envy in her tone, struck a note with Eve. Suddenly, she realized that Sophia's need for Alice to marry Marcus and stay at Thornbrook Park might have more to do with the estate's future than it had to do with simply keeping Alice nearby.

"Sophia?" Eve approached, put a reassuring hand

on Sophia's back, and found that her friend was sobbing. "I've never told you that I'm afraid I can't have children, have I? Six years with Ben, and no pregnancies. Every month, I broke down in tears when I got my flow and knew it was another chance gone. It broke my heart at the time. Then I lost Ben and realized there were worse things."

Sophia turned abruptly. "There are worse things, I assure you. Devastating things. All those letters back and forth, and you never told me about your heartbreak and your fears. Just as I never told you."

"Never told me what, love?" Eve felt tears of sympathy in her own eyes, fearing what Sophia would reveal next.

"I had a baby. A son. Gabriel and I had a son, a beautiful boy with downy blond fuzz and the purest blue eyes you ever saw, like the midsummer sky. We named him Edward. He died on the very first night we had him, died sleeping in his own cradle. Delivering him wiped me out. The doctor said I'd nearly died myself. And when I was sleeping, trying to get my strength back so that I could be a good mother to my boy, I lost him. I didn't even know for days. Days! What kind of mother doesn't feel it when her child dies? I didn't deserve him, Eve. God took him away."

"You can't really think that! Oh, sweetheart." Eve hugged Sophia to her, both of them crying. "It wasn't your fault. I'm so sorry."

"These things happen." Sophia wiped her tears with her hands. "That's what my mother-in-law said by way of condolence. *These things happen.* They certainly didn't happen to her, she with her two strapping, beautiful sons. A month later, she left for Italy, and good riddance. I think Gabriel blames me for driving her away."

"I doubt he blames you for anything. He lost a child, too."

Sophia sighed. "I know. I still see him looking out in the direction of the grave. Edward is buried in the family plot across the field, next to Gabriel's father."

"Also named Edward." Eve nodded. Dear God. Her poor friends. All this time, she'd had no idea. "When did it happen?"

"Four years ago. He would have been four this past spring."

"We weren't writing much then." It began to make sense that Sophia hadn't shared her happy news when she'd found herself in the family way. "I was getting settled in India, and you were enjoying Yorkshire as a young bride."

"I won't go through it again, Eve. Never again."

"And so you think Alice and Marcus might produce an heir, most like you and Gabriel."

"An heir to grow up here at Thornbrook Park and love it as much as Gabriel. Don't you see? They have to get married, Eve. It has to be them. They're our best hope."

Eve didn't know what to say. She understood Sophia's need to pair Alice and Marcus together more than she cared to admit. It made sense, as odd as it seemed and as much as she hated that it did. "We'll see what happens. I'll do what I can to help."

"Thank you, Eve." She squeezed Eve's hands in her own. "I'm so glad you've come. I knew I could count on you."

Guilt heavy as a cannonball settled in the pit of Eve's stomach. Guilt and sadness. Sophia trusted her. She could never be with Marcus again.

They resumed their walk and reached the edge of the green, soft grass, giving way to cobbled street that made her glad she'd changed to sturdy boots instead of staying in her thin slippers.

"Here we are." With a new burst of cheer, probably forced, Sophia turned toward the Dower House. "Let's see if we can convince Alice to come along home with us so she can be there when the men return."

The maid, Mary, greeted them with the news that Alice and Agatha had a guest. Eve's heart lurched when she saw that it was Marcus.

"I thought you were out with the earl." Sophia seemed as surprised as Eve was to see him.

"My brother and I had a look around the farm together." He'd been perched at the edge of a chair near Alice, no doubt hanging on her every word, but he rose to greet them. "Gabriel was distracted by some potentially good birding on the way back."

"That man." Sophia threw her hands up in vexation. "Can he do anything without having to stop and catch or kill something?"

Eve met Marcus's gaze. He raised a brow.

"He is fond of chasing wild game. I'm sure he'll be home before long." He addressed Sophia, but his amber gaze remained on Eve. She felt the danger of being close to him even now, in a room full of people, people who couldn't know they'd shared any more intimate connection than passing acquaintance would allow.

"Join us," Alice encouraged. "We were discussing the merits of London being chosen to host the next Olympic Games."

"London? I thought the Games were being held in Rome. I'm certain the Dowager Countess wrote me about it." Sophia sat herself down to tea and took a seat on the sofa next to Agatha.

"That was before Vesuvius erupted," Marcus informed her. "With the ongoing effort to restore Naples, the games have been looking for a new home."

"And since London was under consideration in the first place, I think it's a natural choice." Alice nodded at the point on which she and Marcus apparently agreed.

"But London? Think of the expense. And it's crowded enough already. No. I hope they choose some other place." Sophia sipped her tea.

"You've never been interested in athletics. I think it a fine idea. They'll have to build a stadium, of course. Let the crowds come! It's all revenue for the crown."

"The way our good king reportedly spends, he needs all the help he can get," Marcus agreed with Alice.

"I would like to learn to play tennis," Alice declared. "Is that an Olympic sport?"

"It is." Marcus nodded.

"You like the idea of running on a lawn dressed all in white," Sophia called her out. "When we were children, nothing guaranteed you returning home covered in mud more than dressing you in clean, white clothes."

"I happened to be the best baker of mud pies in all of Delaney Square." Alice laughed.

"I can teach you to play tennis," Marcus offered.

Sophia cast a delighted glance at Eve. "The back lawn is perfect for it. We only have to set up the net."

"Perhaps I could help as well." Eve couldn't stop herself from joining an activity that offered the perfect chance for Alice and Marcus to get close. What was wrong with her? "I know how to play. Though, of course, three's a crowd."

"I'm sure it wouldn't hurt to add a second instructor. And what do you think of London hosting the Olympic Games, Mrs. Kendal?" Marcus's eyes lit with a mischievous glow.

"I haven't given it a thought. Perhaps Aunt Agatha could tell us if hosting the Games will lead to triumph or tragedy."

Agatha rubbed her temples. "I'm not seeing it clearly at this time, but then the scent of roses always seems to interfere with my visions."

"The scent of roses? Yes." Eve followed Sophia's gaze to the grand bouquet on a nearby table, pink roses and yellow alstroemeria. "Did the gardener bring them in for you? He hasn't cut any of the like for Thornbrook Park's arrangements. We seem to be getting all heather and chrysanthemums lately."

"Captain Thorne brought me the flowers." Alice flashed Marcus an appreciative smile, and Eve thought she detected a hint of triumph in her tone.

"What a surprise, Marcus. How considerate of you." Sophia beamed. "Pink roses mean admiration. Alice, I believe Captain Thorne might be trying to tell you something."

"Sophia," Alice chided. "It was simply a gallant gesture."

"There aren't roses enough to express my admiration for the lot of you. I'm a lucky man to be surrounded by such beauty and grace. My brother's a fool for not coming to tea with me. His loss."

Sophia nodded all too eagerly.

"Men generally don't pay attention to such things, but I believe I heard somewhere that sunflowers represent adoration." Marcus looked at Eve with the heavy-lidded gaze that made her heart beat faster. "We saw a whole field of them on our drive yesterday."

"Before the rain." Eve feared that they were giving themselves away, but she couldn't avert her gaze from his.

"I believe it's a Victorian notion to analyze flowers for meaning." Sophia dusted her hands as if done with the topic now that it had veered off a course that suited her. "We must embrace our new times. Perhaps there's no meaning other than to celebrate beauty."

"It is a glorious arrangement. Miss Puss likes them very much. In fact, she's trying to take a bite out them but her mouth keeps passing right through the petals. Poor dear." Agatha laughed at the sight apparent only to her, but they all squinted as if trying to catch Miss Puss in action.

"Naughty dear. Stay away from my flowers, Miss Puss." Alice shooed the air around the vase.

"Can I get you some more tea, Captain?" Alice asked.

Things seemed to be progressing well for Alice and Marcus. Alice seemed surprisingly receptive to the attention, and Marcus had seemed happily engaged in conversation when they'd arrived. As it should be. Eve suddenly felt like an intruder. She had to go.

Immediately. "If you'll all excuse me, I'm going to continue with my walk. I've been meaning to have a look at the shops in town."

"Oh, now, no need for us to rush off." Sophia probably thought her presence was needed to sow the seeds of romance. "Let's visit a little longer. One more cup."

"You stay. I need a new hat. We can meet up in town. Thank you for tea, Lady Alice." She hurried off before anyone could stop her. She walked in quick steps until she passed the hedges that lined the street along the edge of the property. Leaning against the front gate, she took a minute to catch her breath before continuing on.

❧

Marcus had felt vaguely unsettled since Eve had run off. Was it something he said? Or perhaps it was as awkward for her to watch him try to flirt with Alice as it was for him to court another woman with Eve in the room. He stifled the urge to go after her. *She can buy her own hats.* He smiled at the recollection from their conversation in the rain.

"How is Mrs. Dennehy?" Sophia asked, calling him back to the present. "Did you and Gabriel find her well?"

"Very well." Too well, perhaps, for an older woman on her own. "She had no complaints, though the farm could use some attention—a few coats of paint for the house, stain for the barn, and some repairs. She's happy to put Brandon to work in exchange for room and board and a salary, a meager one but more than

sufficient for a young man in his position. I'll be bringing him there tomorrow and then dropping in from
time to time to check on him, of course, at least until
he's settled." The one person he had wanted to tell of
his success had run off before he'd had a chance.

"That would be one less burden for Gabriel. I hope
he appreciates your enthusiasm. Alice, have you seen
the farm? I know you would adore the lambs, such
darlings." Sophia not so subtly dropped the hint that
he could bring Alice along.

"The lambs are all grown, but they add to the
bucolic setting. Perhaps you would take a ride out
with me and have a look, Alice." Marcus offered
the invitation.

"If we can go on horseback. I haven't ridden in the
longest time."

"You enjoy riding?" He sipped his tea for something to do with his hands. Eve's leaving had made
him want to run right after her, but he couldn't be
obvious about it.

"I do."

"She's quite the horsewoman." Sophia was all too
eager to list her sister's accomplishments.

"Thornbrook Park has fine stables and plenty of
land for riding. I can show you some of the paths I
enjoyed growing up. I've spent enough time in the
saddle today, I'm afraid. In fact, I should be getting
back to prepare Brandon for his new adventures and
perhaps fit in a rest before dinner." He rose. "Thank
you for the tea."

"Thank you again for the flowers." Alice got up to
see him out.

In hope of catching up to Eve, he set off toward Mrs. Carrigan's shop, the very place to buy a hat.

"Good day, Mrs. Carrigan." He entered, looked around, and was discouraged to find no sign of Eve. "I'm looking for a woman."

"I'm sorry, Captain Thorne," Mrs. Carrigan said with a slight smile. "You might have come to the wrong place. The tavern is still on the other side of town. But it's good to see you home again."

"Thank you, but I think she was headed here. She's about so tall." He held his hand up to the middle of his chest. "Blond, with the most radiant blue eyes."

"Mrs. Kendal." She nodded. "I just sold her a hat, nearly gave it away. She drove a hard bargain, but she's already gone off with her prize."

Relief gave way to panic once again. "Did she say where she intended to go next?"

"Perhaps back to Thornbrook Park. I wouldn't know."

In his haste to leave, he nearly knocked over a stand bearing a hat decorated with six taxidermied parakeets around the rim. He shuddered and hoped Eve hadn't chosen the likes of it. Back in the street, he looked right and left, desperate for any sign of her. Once he rounded the corner, he caught sight of her in the distance, in her dark coat and what was probably the new broad-brimmed hat. She walking briskly, dangling a hatbox from her arm.

"Eve!" He called out, but she was too far off to hear. He picked up his pace.

He was about to call out to her again when he saw a man emerge from the hedgerow along the walkway behind her. The man in the black bowler hat stepped out and fell into pace with Eve, closing the distance between them, his hand raised. Was that a glint of metal? A knife?

"Eve!" He hollered for her, his blood running cold through his veins. "Eve!"

He ran as fast as he could, but he feared he wouldn't make it in time. By some miracle, he managed to gain ground and reach out for the man just in time, before he made it to his prey.

Something, perhaps the knife, flew from the man's outstretched hand and into the bushes as Marcus took him by surprise and jerked him around.

"I've got you now, bloody bastard." He landed a left jab, followed by a right hook, before they tumbled together, Marcus landing atop him and pinning the man to the ground. "What do you want with Mrs. Kendal?"

Seventeen

HER SPIRITS RESTORED BY AN INVIGORATING BOUT OF haggling with the shopkeeper, Eve wore her new hat with some degree of pride that she'd obtained it for such a small price. Prama, her maid in India, had coached her on making deals in the marketplace, and she had learned her lessons well. On her way back to the Dower House, she debated if she should boast to Sophia about her bargain or simply let her friends admire her purchase. She was nearly there when a commotion started behind her and she turned to see Marcus wrestling a man to the ground.

"Captain Thorne?" The sight of them fighting astounded her, but her gaze was instantly drawn to the black bowler hat on the ground at their feet. A chill washed over her.

"Let me up!" The man continued to twist in Marcus's grip, but Marcus was obviously the stronger of the two.

"Not a chance." Marcus grunted with the effort of keeping him pinned. "Not until we're at the constable's office."

She walked over to them. "Let the man up to explain himself, Captain."

"Let him up? He was following you. I think he intended you harm. He held a knife. The constable, at once!" Marcus ordered one of the handful of lads who had gathered, drawn from their work by the fuss. "Run and get him."

Eve stepped around and leaned down to examine the man's face. "Why would you intend me harm?"

"I don't. He lies." The man could barely get the words out.

She stopped to retrieve the man's hat for him and steeled her spine. Her instinct told her that Marcus knew what he was doing. "I believe you've knocked the wind right out of him. I don't see any knife, though. Just this watch." She picked up a shiny, round, silver watch on a chain. "It glints in the light, perhaps like a knife?"

"He *had* a knife," Marcus insisted. "Look around. In the bushes."

Eve took a moment to rifle through the foliage but found nothing. "I don't see a knife."

She returned to look at her supposed aggressor. The man was much stouter than Marcus, but short and apparently not very fit. He had the kind of hair that was probably once carrot orange but had paled with a liberal dose of gray running through it, what little he had left of it. He reminded Eve of her landlord in India. She'd only met him once or twice, though, so it was hard to be certain until he moved just the right way. "But you are my landlord from India. Mr. Lawson, what are you doing here?"

The lad came back with the constable trailing after him.

"Let me up," Lawson said. "I'm not going to run. I wasn't going to hurt anyone, I swear."

"Let him up," the constable said.

Reluctantly, Marcus let go and stood up, adjusting his coat and cuffs as the constable helped Mr. Lawson to his feet.

"Now then." The constable turned to Eve. "What's the complaint, and who is our damsel in distress?"

Eve blushed, feeling all eyes in the crowd suddenly on her. "I'm Mrs. Eve Kendal, visiting at Thornbrook Park, but I don't believe I'm in any distress." Not from Mr. Lawson, surely. But how odd that he should be walking behind her unannounced and wearing a black bowler hat. Coincidence? She thought not.

"He had a knife, and he followed Mrs. Kendal in deliberate pursuit. I saw it all from up the way." Marcus gestured toward the row of shops in the distance.

"And you rushed over to play hero?" the constable asked in an accusatory tone, as if suggesting that Marcus went looking for the chance to stage a rescue.

Growing redder in the face, Marcus looked as if he might explode. Eve touched his arm lightly. His every muscle tensed.

"I'm sure it's a misunderstanding. Mr. Lawson was my landlord in India. We, my husband and I, rented his house."

"A misunderstanding, yes." Lawson straightened his waistcoat. "I came to town looking for Mrs. Kendal. I only want to settle a debt."

"A debt? With a knife?" Marcus lunged at him

again, only to be blocked by the constable stepping between them.

"Your husband has quite a temper, perhaps?" the constable suggested.

"He's not my husband," Eve clarified. "This is Captain Marcus Thorne. The war hero."

Marcus groaned. She'd learned that he didn't consider himself one, but he'd fought in a war and saved countless lives. Like it or not, a hero he was.

The constable looked suddenly sheepish. "Captain Thorne, didn't recognize you. Very sorry, sir."

"Jack Smith?" Marcus tilted his head and looked at the constable. "I didn't recognize you either, to be honest. It has been a few years, yes? This man needs to be held and questioned. I will come to the station with you. Mrs. Kendal, please go to the Dower House, where you can call Dale to come round with the car. I have the situation in hand."

"It involves me. I don't see why I shouldn't go to the station, too. Won't I need to make a statement?" She wouldn't be pushed aside to let the men handle her affairs.

"It *is* the usual procedure in such a case." The constable scratched his head, as if uncertain.

"Indeed not," Marcus said, taking charge. "Mrs. Kendal can make her statements here and go home where she is safe."

"It's Chief Constable Smith now, if you will, Captain Thorne. I will certainly make allowances for your family. The woman is free to go."

Eve rolled her eyes. Would they all discount her so easily? She, the supposed target of the alleged attack? She held her ground. "But first, Mr. Lawson, what is this debt you speak of? I don't believe I owe you anything."

"I owe you." Mr. Lawson shook his head. "A small amount, but fair is fair. Your husband overpaid. I only wanted to make it right."

"There, you see." Eve turned to Marcus and the constable. "No harm done. Why don't we let the man pay me and send him on his way? Thank you, Mr. Lawson. I appreciate the effort you must have gone to in order to track me down."

Mr. Lawson nodded. "Quite an effort."

Marcus shook his head, unsatisfied. "All that effort to pay a pittance? Why not rely on the mail? I don't believe it."

"I'm an honest man," Lawson said. "Do I look like a murderous ruffian?"

Constable Smith threw up his hands. "Who is to say? It seems a logical explanation. Why would he come all this way to make mischief, Captain Thorne? Let's allow the man to settle his affairs and be done with it here. No need for questioning. We have our answers."

"Perhaps I would like to press charges against this clod for attacking me." Mr. Lawson gestured at Marcus. "Yes, I believe I would."

The constable sighed. "To the station it is, then. Both of you. We'll settle this once and for all. Good day, Mrs. Kendal."

"But I should come along as a witness," Eve said.

"You will do no such thing. Go home, Eve. I'm asking, not commanding. I would prefer to know you are safe. Please."

The look of concern in Marcus's eyes made her knees turn to jelly.

"Very well, then. I will see you at Thornbrook Park."

Trying mightily to hold on to her composure, she walked off, grateful for each step that took her farther from Marcus when all she wanted to do was propel herself into his arms. Perhaps after slapping him for not letting her manage the business on her own.

It was time she faced the facts. She had a longing for Captain Marcus Thorne that she could not deny. To pursue him any further would mean alienating her best and only friend, and being left to fend for herself in the world—a very uncertain prospect considering her lost savings—as well as destroying Marcus's chance to help the Coopers. If she craved Marcus like an opium addict craved the tincture of the poppy, it didn't matter. It was entirely hopeless between them.

She had to fight her attraction, bury it deep, and pretend it didn't exist. She had no other choice.

For the first time since coming back from the war, hitting a man had not abated Marcus's rage. He'd wanted to pummel Oliver Lawson into a bloody, mashed-up pulp—and then keep going. Not even being in the presence of the chief constable, a boyhood rival and occasional friend, would have stopped him. It was looking into the depths of Eve Kendal's eyes that had calmed him, the striking blue washing over him like the foam of ocean waves, soothing him at once.

She didn't seem to realize the danger posed by a man following her with a knife clutched in his hand.

But then, she hadn't watched the scene unfold as he had.

Why would anyone wish to harm Eve Kendal? The charges against Marcus were dropped readily enough as soon as they arrived at the constable's office and Marcus began countering Lawson's accusations of brutality with questions regarding Lawson's intentions toward Eve. The connection of Lawson to her life in India troubled Marcus immensely. There was something more there, something sinister.

Marcus believed it had to do with money, but not as Oliver Lawson claimed. He'd established that Lawson hailed from London and claimed ownership of several properties in India, which he apparently rented to expatriates like the Kendals. According to Lawson, Captain Kendal had eschewed the usual arrangements made by the army in favor of renting privately to put his wife in a more familiar setting, a small country house such as one might find in England.

Marcus couldn't explain why he'd felt a twinge of something like envy at the thought of Eve and her husband living comfortably together in a house. Her husband had obviously been considerate and doting, and Marcus should be satisfied to hear it. Eve deserved happiness.

His feelings on the matter were all mixed up. He couldn't tell exactly what to make of them, the queer tugging in his lungs when he'd thought of her getting hurt, the sudden peace that had come over him when he'd looked deep into her eyes.

He had saved Eve from personal injury; he knew he had. Somehow it all tied back to her husband and

his investments. Marcus was certain of it. Her missing solicitor, and now this man Lawson coming after
her with a knife, there had to be a connection. He
would get a telegram to Tom Reilly and step up the
investigation into Eve's finances. God only knew why
he felt it his duty to solve Eve Kendal's difficulties, but
suddenly he had an overwhelming urge to protect her.

Of course, becoming personally involved with his
sister-in-law's friend instead of the intended Lady
Alice was in direct opposition to his goal of helping
the Coopers. He had to tread carefully. And perhaps
it wouldn't hurt if he avoided looking deep into Eve
Kendal's exquisite eyes.

He took Lawson's money to give to Eve, a few
pounds that wouldn't make much difference here or
there, and then he waited at the station to see that the
man boarded his train. He couldn't convince Chief
Constable Smith to keep Oliver Lawson locked up,
but he felt better seeing that the man had gone back
to London, out of Eve's way.

Eve remained safe for now, but Marcus would feel
uneasy until he could see her again, could reassure
himself that she had made it back to Thornbrook Park
safely. He walked as fast as possible up the hill and
beyond, only allowing himself to stop and breathe
once he rounded the corner and came across Eve,
perfectly well, with Alice and Mr. Winthrop out on
the lawn.

"Alice was eager to begin her tennis lessons,"
Eve explained. "She accompanied us home from the
Dower House."

So it seemed that Eve hadn't informed the others

of the attack. She didn't want to worry them, or didn't think it worth mentioning? Drat, if he couldn't manage to get her alone again soon.

"Tennis, Captain Thorne." Alice smiled. Her cheeks were flushed, but it seemed more from activity than from any delight in seeing him. "I found Mr. Winthrop and harassed him until he agreed to join us for doubles."

"I had to have a fellow fetch the net anyway. I might as well join in." Winthrop came over and shook his hand. "Good to see you again, Captain."

"And you." Marcus wondered what kind of magic Alice possessed over Mr. Winthrop to convince him to join in an afternoon's sport. "We're to have a game, then?"

"First, what are the rules?" Alice made her way to Marcus. "Perhaps you could show me how."

"Show you?" Marcus started. Was she flirting with him? He didn't mind Alice's company, but it would feel awkward taking her in his arms, even to demonstrate tennis, with Eve looking on.

Alice tossed the ball in the air and caught it. "Of course. Mrs. Kendal can play with Mr. Winthrop, and I will play with you. You can instruct me as we go."

Marcus would much rather have been on a side with Eve, to be close to her, but he was safer sticking close to Alice. "Are you game, Mr. Winthrop? Is the court ready for us?"

"You had better be good, Mrs. Kendal." Winthrop removed his coat and draped it on the porch railing. Marcus followed suit. "When I play, I don't like to lose."

"Very interesting confession, Mr. Winthrop."

Eve took up a racquet. "I might have guessed that about you."

She might have guessed? Marcus did not like the turn of events. At all. Eve found Mr. Winthrop interesting? He suddenly summed Winthrop up as a rival instead of merely his brother's estate manager, and he was strangely dissatisfied with the result.

Marcus had to admit that Winthrop was not a bad looking man. Dark hair, dark eyes. Though Winthrop had about five years on Marcus, he was in as good or better physical condition, undoubtedly from hauling soil and wood all hither and yon, since he insisted on laboring with the groundskeepers. If Marcus wasn't mistaken, the man stood an inch or two taller than he was. And finally, he had the undeniable advantage of being resident at Thornbrook Park, in the cottage at the edge of the estate, under employ, and in no danger of being cut off for preferring Eve to Alice.

Suddenly, and without thinking, Marcus whacked the ball in his rival's direction.

"Heads up," he shouted, thinking the better of it once he'd let it fly. "Sorry, that one got away from me."

"Quite all right, Captain Thorne." To his combined relief and disappointment, Winthrop leaped out of the way in time.

"How do you hold this properly?" Alice, who had seemed perfectly capable moments earlier, suddenly struggled to get a grip on her racquet.

Forgetting his earlier misgivings, Marcus wrapped his arms around Alice and pulled her close, showing her how to place her hands on the grip, all the while looking over to see if Eve took any notice. She did.

So much the better. It reminded him of holding Eve in his arms to teach her how to spar.

"Like so," Marcus said, whispering right into Alice's ear as he adjusted her fingers, then pulled her tighter so he could demonstrate the motion of the swing. Together, they leaned, moved their hips, and followed through. If he wasn't mistaken, Eve made a face from across the court. "There, you see? Smooth and easy."

"Yes, I see," Alice said. "One more time to be sure I have it right."

They repeated the procedure, but Eve had turned to say something to Mr. Winthrop. Winthrop laughed. Eve laughed. Both Alice and Marcus seemed to freeze in place, as if forgetting what they were doing.

"Should we try it with a ball now?" Marcus said, trying to get back to business. He dropped his arms and stepped away.

"No, I've got it." Alice made her way to the net. "Shall we all shake hands first and wish each other a good match? Isn't that the sporting thing to do?"

Marcus wasn't about to argue with a chance to get close to the net and take Eve's hand. He dared to look at her directly when he did so, and her eyes flashed a challenge. The minx. Did she think she could beat him?

"We'll go easy on you, Lady Alice. Since it's your first time." Mr. Winthrop seemed equally smug.

Alice snorted in response. "No need. I'm a fast learner. Shall we, Captain?"

He nodded. "I believe it's customary for the new-comers to serve first."

"I've never heard of such a custom," Eve said from across the court. "But we will allow it. She might even take a few practice shots before we start counting points."

Alice delivered a hard smack of a serve, sending the ball flying straight in Eve's direction before Eve had time to react.

"Whee! I believe that's a point for us." Alice jumped up and down.

"Yes. Fifteen-love," Winthrop said. "Again, Lady Alice. Just like that. You're doing well."

Eve laughed. "Whose side are you on, Mr. Winthrop?"

"Love? Who said anything about love?" Alice seemed bewildered until Eve explained the scorekeeping.

Apparently, Winthrop was on Eve's side after all. They went on to win the first set, with Marcus scoring the decisive point to tie them up on the next.

"One more," Winthrop said. "I've got some work to get back to before the sun goes down."

"Yes," Eve agreed. "It's getting late."

Marcus barely paid attention to the conversation because he was so busy watching Eve's breasts rise and fall as she lifted her arms to make the serve. How he wanted to see her in all her glory, without a single stitch to cover her! Intimate as they had been, they still hadn't been afforded an opportunity to strip down together. And he wouldn't have the chance, he reminded himself. It was Alice he should be imagining naked.

For her part, Alice seemed more taken with Mr. Winthrop than she was with Marcus. It seemed perhaps Alice and Marcus found themselves in a similar predicament, destined for disappointment.

They played the last match with a marked lack of enthusiasm, as if they had both completely given up and let their opponents win.

Game over, Eve put down her racquet and prepared to head back inside. She'd wanted to win, but it felt a hollow victory when she looked across the lawn to see Alice and Marcus together. Though she wanted to hear what had happened with the constable, she suddenly couldn't get away fast enough.

"Thank you, Mr. Winthrop. I must get back." She turned on her heel and fled before Marcus and Alice were done patting each other on the back for their efforts.

"Mrs. Kendal." Marcus caught up with her just inside the hall.

"Yes, Captain Thorne." Deliberately formal, she took a breath and turned to face him before he followed her all the way up the stairs.

"Eve." He gripped her hands. "That man meant to kill you. We both know it."

"I'm not so certain, Marcus. He is an odd bird, I'll grant you. I only met him a few times, but he seemed courteous enough, mild-mannered. He's not the type to strike fear in the heart, really, is he?"

He placed the pound notes in her palm. "He had these for you, or so he claims. Your refund for your remaining month's rent."

She tucked the notes in her pocket. "Well, that should come in handy. There, you see? He was true to his word. He dropped the charges, I presume?"

Marcus nodded, but remained steadfast in his effort to change her opinion of Lawson. "I think we both know it has to do with your money. He's wrapped up in it all somehow. That cousin who came looking for you? It was Lawson. He claims he didn't think you would have responded to his request to see you if he gave his name. I think he meant to lure you out of the house to kill you. It's a good thing that we were out when he called."

"It is curious that he turned up now, of all times." She nibbled her lip, considering. "I wonder if it was Mr. Strump who introduced Ben to Mr. Lawson."

"It will be easy enough to work out the connection once I fill Tom Reilly in. I made sure Lawson got on the London train. You're safe for now. For tonight." He pulled her close and embraced her. "Good God, Eve, if anything had happened to you."

The last thing she wanted was to push him away. She felt safe in his arms, treasured. It was a feeling that she'd never thought to have again. "Not here, Marcus. Anyone could walk in."

"To the library, then? Let's go." He urged her along. "No one will find us there. I need you to myself for just a little while."

"We're playing with fire," she said, even as she willingly went along, desperate to be scorched.

Eighteen

ONE OF THE MAIDS HAPPENED TO BE DUSTING THE library when they made their entrance.

Marcus dropped his hand from Eve's waist and took a discreet step away from her. "It's a page-turner, Mrs. Kendal. I believe it will hold your interest. Now where did I leave it?"

He began perusing a shelf for the supposed reading recommendation that had brought them to the library as Ginny, the maid, bowed and left the room.

"Oh, I remember where I left it." He spoke loudly in case Ginny remained at the door. "I'll bring it to you in the drawing room before dinner."

"Thank you, Captain Thorne."

He lowered his voice to a whisper. "In five minutes, make your way to my room. Don't knock, just enter. I'll go ahead first so we're not seen going together."

Such a risk, it seemed, but no less so than making love in the library. Once he left her, she picked up a book to look occupied in case Ginny returned. She would go to his room, and she would tell him that they couldn't possibly continue. It was madness to think they could carry off an affair at Thornbrook Park without drawing further notice. As the minutes ticked away, she wondered if perhaps she shouldn't meet him at all.

But as the time drew nearer, her feet followed the corridor straight to Marcus's bedchamber. She reached for the knob, but pulled her hand back, turned, and went to her own room. It was the right thing to do, she assured herself. Going to him now would only make it harder to leave him to Alice. She stepped inside, shut the door fast behind her, and leaned against it with her eyes closed.

How close she had come to a foolish decision!

She opened her eyes. Sunflowers. Sunflowers over every surface, draped on tables, scattered across her bed, in a vase on the dressing table, woven through the knobs on the drawers, a trail across the carpet. Sunflowers mean adoration, he'd said. He'd known then what she would find. He'd somehow made time to pick them before he'd gone to Lady Alice with roses. Pink roses, for mere admiration. He must have had a trusted footman waiting to scatter them while she was out. She picked up a handful and ran down the hall to his room. This time, without hesitation, she turned the knob and walked in.

"What do you mean by this?" she meant to say. "Where do we stand? Is it true? You adore me?" But the words died in her throat. She simply held the flowers out, the questions in her eyes.

"Eve." Even if she'd thought of turning to leave, she was in his arms as soon as the door closed behind her. Marcus ran the pad of his thumb across her lower lip, and she felt the heat pooling deep inside her, molten ore.

"Marcus." Eve dropped the flowers, rose on her toes, and cupped his face in her hands, the roughness of a half-day's growth of beard scratching her palms. She dropped a light kiss on his nose.

"I want to undress you." His voice was a velvet whisper as he returned her kisses, blazing a trail down her décolletage. "I need to see you. All of you. Just once."

"Just once." Just one more kiss, one more time. She dreaded the day that they finally kept their word, but that day was not upon them. She worked at the buttons of his shirt. "I want to feel your skin on mine."

He pulled her body against his and kissed her, his hot, open mouth covering hers, devouring her. She tangled her tongue with his, daring him to go deeper, molding her body against his so that she could feel the length of his erection. His longing, pressing against her, was as undeniable as her own need curled into a tight coil inside her.

She eased his shirt down off his shoulders, exposing his bare, muscular arms and chest. Her fingers traced his shrapnel scars and ran over his taut, rippled stomach and down to the trail of golden curling hairs that led under the waist of his trousers. His hand covered hers, encouraging her, helping her undo his clothes. Her breathing slowed as his trousers eased down his hips, tan skin giving way to white as he became exposed. She nearly gasped at the beauty of him standing before her like her own Roman god.

"You should have been named for the god of love," she said.

"But Cupid is a terrible name." He laughed. "Besides, Psyche couldn't look on Cupid, and you seem to be enjoying the sight of me."

She blushed. "I am. But Psyche is from Greek mythology, with Eros. There's no equivalent for the Roman."

And a good thing, she thought with a pang. Psyche's punishment for looking at Eros was to lose him, a situation that mirrored their reality all too closely. She had to give him up, sooner rather than later.

"Your turn, my lady. Let's get you out of these clothes." He embraced her and began to unfasten her gown.

"But it takes so long to get them on again. Perhaps you could just lift my skirts."

"Suddenly shy, Mrs. Kendal? Would you deny me my heart's desire? I don't think so." His breath was warm on her cheek, his lips so close.

"Sophia might come looking for me."

"Not here she wouldn't." He paused from unbuttoning her to trail a finger along her collarbone. "Besides, she's probably napping until dinner."

"Or Gabriel could come in search of you."

"Gabriel"—The gown undone, he gave a tug and it slipped down her shoulders—"is still shooting. I'm the last thing on his mind."

"We left Alice alone with Mr. Winthrop." Instinctively, she caught the fabric before it slipped to pool on the floor. He took her hands, dropping kisses on her palms, and the gown fell.

She heard his breath catch as he looked her over in her corset and petticoat. "My own good fortune is all I can think of at the moment. Come here."

He kissed her again as his skillful fingers toyed with her laces, loosening her stays and leaving her bare in his arms in a matter of minutes. He stood back to have a look.

Naked before him, she did not shy away or cover herself. She let her arms fall to her sides while he took her in, heat in his amber eyes.

"You're exquisite," he said. "Beyond my imagination."

The slow smile tugged at the corner of his lips. He urged her to the bed and fell atop her gently. Finding her mouth again, he parted her lips with his tongue. She reached for him, but he gripped her arms and pulled them back over her head, pinning them to the mattress with one hand, while his other hand quested. He stroked her neck and shoulders, and paused at her breasts before taking one nipple between his fingers and rolling gently. He followed with his mouth, laving, circling his scorching tongue around her swollen bud, and then he moved lower.

Her stomach tensed with anticipation and her desire coiled tighter. He let go of her arms and dipped his head to her navel and lower, causing her to tremble. His hand covered her mound, his fingers parting her slit to his touch, and he slipped them inside her one at a time, pushing deep and pulling back with a smooth, rhythmic motion. She moved against him.

"More."

"As intended." His voice was husky and thick with need, but she could hear the smile in his voice even with her eyes closed.

He parted her legs wide, dipped his head lower,

and blew on her, her delicate nub quivering against the sudden stream of air. He cupped her buttocks and pulled her into his mouth, feasting on her like a starving man. She arched against him and cried out, then prayed no one had heard her.

"Marcus," she said. She needed to feel him inside her, filling her. He took another moment to kiss her more intimately than she'd dared hope until her need spiraled out of control, snapping like a whip. Colored lights began to pop behind her eyes. Only then did he straighten up, grip her by the waist, and slide her to him, his hips meeting her own.

He laced his fingers with hers, lowered his hips, and entered her slowly, as if savoring every inch. Inside her at last, he began to move and she moved with him, the two of them in their own private dance. She savored the feeling of him against her, skin to skin, as she tangled her legs around his waist and shifted so slightly that she was in his lap, pulling him tighter against her, deeper inside her. He held her against him, one arm curled around her waist, as they found their release together again and again.

Spent, she settled snugly at his side and let the bliss wash over her.

It was then, as Marcus pulled the sheet up and tucked it around them, nudging her into his arms to rest her head on his chest, that the door opened and the footman, George, entered. He nearly tripped over the sunflowers and Eve's discarded gown, caught sight of them, and dropped his bundle of laundered shirts to the floor. They'd made love in the library and in the open outdoors, but they were finally discovered in a proper bedroom, of all places. Her stomach turned.

"One word of this to anyone, George, and I can no longer promise you that promotion."

"Captain Thorne, I wouldn't dream of—Mrs. Kendal?" George averted his gaze and backed toward the door. "No, I'm sorry. I won't speak of it. Of course. I'm sorry." He left the room as quickly as he'd come in.

"The servants will all know of it by dinner," Eve said. "What have we done?"

"I think George can be relied on for his discretion."

She shot Marcus a look, one eyebrow raised.

"Seriously. He's a good sort, and I believe willing to accept a bribe. Our secret is safe."

"But for how long?" She sat up. "I should go back to my room. Before word spreads. What if he comes back with Gabriel?"

He urged her to rest on him. "I'm telling you that George can be trusted. I know the servants well enough. Stay with me. Just a little while longer."

Resigned, she dropped her head to his chest. "Just a little while. Just one more kiss, one more… We have to stop. Once and for all."

He stroked the bare skin of her back. "I'm not convinced that I can."

With a sigh, she sat up and pulled away. "Then I will. For your sake and mine. You need to secure the farm and Alice's affections. It's not going to happen as long as you're angling to get me back to your bed."

"Eve." She feared an argument. Would he try to convince her to stay? But she turned around to look at him. All too relaxed, he rolled onto his stomach to face her, lying crosswise across the bed. He propped his chin on his hand and showed no concern for covering his stark, white backside. A slow smile tugged at the corner of his lush lips. "I'll see you at dinner, then?"

She sighed. How utterly adorable he looked, and how devastatingly sexy at the same time. She wanted to go back and roll between the sheets with him all afternoon.

"Yes. Later." Instead, she gathered her things and stepped into his adjoining room to dress as best she could and make her escape. There would be no avoiding him as long as they remained under the same roof.

⁓

Eve did not go to dinner.

Instead, she sent a note with her apologies and stayed at her writing desk, absorbed in her work for half the night. The other half, she spent pacing the floor, unable to sleep. And then she began to pack, just a few things in a black leather case so that she would be prepared to spend some nights at Averford House. She could not face Sophia, not after what she'd done with Marcus, not yet. She would have to confess eventually, but better that she took some time to get her affairs in order first. If she couldn't recover her money, she could see about finding a position somewhere. There was no shame in finding employment. Better to provide for herself than to rely on the charity of friends.

At first light, she made her way to Sophia's room and slipped a note under her door, explaining her temporary escape to London to investigate her finances. From there, she made her way to the train station, opting to walk instead of waking Dale at such an early hour to drive her. It was a pleasant walk, the air crisp and refreshing, the smells of autumn in the air. Only once did she fear the sound of footsteps behind her, following close, but she turned to discover that she trailed a branch that had somehow become attached to her skirts. She laughed, freed it, and walked on.

In London, she headed straight for the office of Marcus's detective friend, Tom Reilly, and hoped she would find him in.

"It seems fortune is smiling on me nearly as brightly as the morning sun," she said when he answered the door. "You are here, Mr. Reilly. And I hope that you have the time to help me."

"I've never turned down a pretty woman in need of my assistance," Mr. Reilly said, smiling in a way that enhanced the deep dimples in his cheeks. "And I'm not about to start now. Marcus has been keeping me up to date on your case, and I've made a few discoveries. Shall we abscond to an inn for some breakfast, and I'll fill you in?"

"That sounds delightful, Mr. Reilly. I haven't eaten."

He grabbed his coat and hat, and took her arm, but somehow she didn't feel that same familiar warmth she'd felt while walking arm in arm with Marcus. A pity. With his dimples and twinkling eyes, Mr. Reilly would have made a charming and available long-term companion for her future lonely nights in London.

Over breakfast, he grew more serious as he informed her of his findings. He waited until she'd nearly finished eating before he placed his hand over hers. "I feel you should know that they've found a body."

She pulled her hand away to stifle her gasp. "Mr. Strump's body?"

He nodded. "The wife identified him, though she seemed reluctant to do so. At first, she claimed it wasn't him, and then she blamed her misidentification on grief. Poor man's head was bashed in before he was dumped in the Serpentine."

"Did you tell Captain Thorne?"

He shook his head. "It's not the sort of news for telegram or telephone. I wanted to tell you in person. And here you are."

"Here I am." She smiled weakly.

"Curious, though, when Mrs. Strump came in to have a look at the body, she gave her name as Lawson, Mrs. Leona Lawson."

"Lawson?" Eve felt her mouth drop open, and there was no hope of concealing it this time. "But that's—"

"Yes, Captain Thorne informed me of your run-in with your former landlord. I've been investigating him as well. It struck me as odd when Mrs. Strump initially identified herself by the wrong name. It's the kind of thing to raise flags. After Marcus telephoned yesterday, I investigated further and turned up the most interesting connection between the two."

Eve thought back to her unusual visit at the Strumps' house and the hat on the hook. "He's her brother."

"So they say."

"What do you mean? He's not really her brother? They're only pretending to be blood relatives?" She gasped as she made the connection. "Is he really her *lover*?"

"Very good, Mrs. Kendal. But that's not the whole

of it. I did some more checking. It turns out that Mrs. Leona Strump was formerly Mrs. Leona Lawson, born Leona Gibson."

"But how could she be Leona Lawson? Unless—"

"Yes, they're married. Her marriage to Mr. Strump isn't on the records, not legal. But her marriage to Oliver Lawson is right there in ink, recorded for all time. Along with their arrest records, of course."

"Arrests? Lawson and his wife, both?"

Mr. Reilly nodded. "For fraud. They were caught selling interest in a supposed inn in Brighton, meant to attract vacationers to the seaside. One of the investors finally decided to go enjoy a stay at the inn he'd invested in, only to find nothing at the address but a pile of sand. He alerted authorities, and they used a deception to catch the Lawsons."

"A deception?"

"Detectives went in pretending to be potential investors and caught the Lawsons in the act. Oliver took the fall for both of them, claimed the wife was his innocent dupe in the affair. He served a few years in prison, and Leona was waiting for him when he got out. That's when he started buying land in India. I think he realized it would be harder for authorities to keep tabs on him there. We think that's where he hid half of their money in the first place. The investors were never paid back, due to Lawson's lack of funds upon his arrest. Probably unaware of Mr. Lawson's background, Mr. Strump was acting as his solicitor for the land purchases in India."

"I believe it is through Mr. Strump that my husband and Mr. Lawson met."

"At some point, they must have decided to defraud Mr. Strump and convince him to marry Leona in a bogus ceremony, with Lawson posing as her brother. Unless Strump was in on it all along, which seems unlikely."

"I see where you're heading with this. The diamond mine is a fraud. It doesn't exist. My money's all gone." She didn't feel as empty inside as she'd believed she would. Deep down, she'd probably known it all along.

"I'm sorry. Yes."

"I might have gotten the poor man killed." Eve's heart sank. "When I went in asking questions, stirring Mr. Strump to action. If he didn't realize the mine was a fraud, he might have discovered it that night when he started looking into Ben's investments."

"Don't blame yourself." Mr. Reilly placed a hand on hers. "With those two, it was probably inevitable. Nasty characters. They'll get theirs eventually."

"Eventually?" She raised a brow. "Why not now?"

"There's nothing to tie them to the murder so far. I'll keep investigating, of course, and I have some of Scotland Yard's finest on the case with me. We do have a potential murder weapon, a bookend found wrapped with the body in a rug. As for the fraud, it's even harder to prove, considering the supposed mine is in India and the fraud most likely took place there."

"Let me guess. The bookend is gilded?"

"How did you know? It's a gilded monkey."

Eve shuddered. "If you'd been in the Strumps' house, you would know. The Lawsons killed him. I'm certain. Can't your investigators get in and have a look around?"

"We're working on it."

"Tell me more about this deception that nailed them the last time they committed fraud. I think I might have some ideas of how we could get them again."

"Mrs. Kendal, I must say, you're quite a surprise." His gray eyes sparkled with mirth. "I like the way you think."

"It shouldn't be too surprising, Mr. Reilly. They took my husband's money, *my* money. If I can't get it back, I should at least have the pleasure of seeing them imprisoned for the rest of their God-given days."

⟡

"What's the news?" Marcus asked as he came to the breakfast table, meaning both around the world and in their household. He expected that George could be trusted, but what if he were wrong?

"Finland has given women the right to vote." Gabriel shook his head disapprovingly. "They expect some of them will now run for office."

"Women? Running for office? Lady Alice will celebrate the news. We're sure to follow suit eventually. The world is changing."

Gabriel rolled his eyes over the top of his paper. "I won't be the one to tell her."

Marcus sifted through the fruit bowl in search of a shiny, red apple. "I'm sure she follows the reports."

"Are you sure from intimate conversations? How are you faring with Lady Alice?"

"Well enough." Marcus shrugged, giving up on the fruit. He would find plenty of apples at Tilly Meadow. He had made a weak attempt to flirt with Lady Alice at last night's dinner, but his heart wasn't in it. He'd been preoccupied with thoughts of Eve and their phenomenal afternoon lovemaking. Her absence at the table signified that it wouldn't happen again. She'd cut him off. One of them had to do it. Clearly, she was stronger than he. She was extraordinary...

"Marcus? Would you care to answer, or have you taken to ignoring me?"

"Sorry. I was mentally making plans for my day with Brandon at the farm."

Gabriel shook his head. "That's exactly what I asked you: 'Are you headed to the farm with the boy today?' And your answer could have been, 'Yes, Brother, I am.'"

"I sent George to wake him, get him ready, and gather up his things. He should be down at any moment and we're off. Bill, have we any coffee?" Marcus asked the footman, eager to discourage more conversation with his brother. He felt his mood darken with every word between them.

"Of course, sir. I will bring some immediately."

His brother favored tea, a pot of which remained on the table in front of Gabriel. Sophia floated in wearing a black frock with white sleeves, a high white neck, and a wide red sash.

"You look lovely, as always." Marcus pulled out her chair and helped her get settled. Gabriel remained seated.

"Thank you, Marcus. I'm glad someone notices such things."

"I notice you, my darling. I always notice," Gabriel said somewhat defensively.

"It doesn't hurt to say so."

"Well, do *you* notice *me*?" Gabriel put down the paper and leaned across the table. "I don't recall your complimenting me on my attire. If women are going to be demanding equal rights, there are going to be some role reversals to contend with along the way."

"Role reversals?" Marcus returned to his seat with his breakfast as Bill brought out his coffee and poured. "What an interesting assertion. I'm sure Lady Alice would have lots to say on that, too."

"On that, too?" He'd piqued Sophia's interest. "Have we been discussing my sister this morning?"

"Only that Finland has adopted universal suffrage. Perhaps she might consider relocating."

"Goodness, no. I couldn't stand for Alice to be that far away. But she would like the idea, wouldn't she? I wish she had come to breakfast."

"And Mrs. Kendal?" Marcus tried to stop his pulse from quickening as he dared speak her name. "Where is she this morning?"

Sophia sighed. "I found a note under my door. She's run off to London to tend her business affairs. Can you imagine anything more tedious? It's not like her to be so—spontaneous. Well, perhaps it is. I've no idea what habits she picked up in India. And a bad habit it is, dashing off without a word, leaving a note. I had plans for us today."

"London?" Marcus felt a pang in his chest. She didn't leave a note for him. "She just ran off?"

"Mmm. Just like that." Sophia snapped the fingers of her left hand while pouring tea with the right.

The pang in his chest turned to an icy stab of fear. Lawson was back in London. But of course, she would go straight to Tom Reilly, and Reilly would look out for her, wouldn't he? Marcus would have to try to telephone to be sure. "I still have some business in London. I might head out tomorrow myself, once I get Brandon settled."

At once, Sophia's and Gabriel's heads shot up, and their eyes narrowed with suspicion.

"To London?" Sophia said, a chill in her tone. "Both of you at Averford House again? How cozy."

Brandon came bounding into the room, saving Marcus from a response.

"Oh." He stopped short. "Lord and Lady Averford, how do you do?" He gave a short bow.

Despite spending time with them the other afternoon, a day after his arrival, Brandon still seemed intimidated by them. It annoyed Marcus to no end. They were only people, for goodness sake. A title didn't make them superior by nature, even if it gave them privileges denied the common man.

"Very well, this morning, thank you." Sophia beamed, charmed.

Even Gabriel smiled, apparently taken by the boy. At least, Marcus could be grateful for that. "On your way out, stop by the kennel, would you? I've arranged for you to choose your favorite pointer puppy to bring with you to the farm."

Brandon's mouth fell open. "A dog? For my very own?"

"I have more than I can handle," Gabriel said, puffing out his chest as if quite pleased with himself. "And you've taken such a shine to them. A boy should have a companion, don't you think?"

"He has me," Marcus said, between gritted teeth. "I'm not sure he'll have much time to be caring for a dog of his own with all Mrs. Dennehy has planned for him. You should have checked with me. Deuce it, Gabriel, did you even think to check with her?"

"He has *you*?" Gabriel had the nerve to laugh. "I'm not sure you'll prove as loyal or as constant as a dog for a companion, Marcus. Yes, I checked with Mrs. Dennehy. She thought it a fine idea, as long as the boy trains the pup on his own. You can do that, can't you, lad?"

"Yes." Brandon could hardly contain his excitement. "I know exactly how to manage him. Mr. Parsons told me everything I need to know."

"Mr. Parsons?" Marcus cocked a brow.

"The kennel master." Gabriel shook his head. "You might want to take some time to get to know the place again, Brother. You're going to be spending a lot of time here from now on."

Marcus met his brother's gaze. Both of their eyes flashed in warning, one to the other. Of course, Gabriel was right. If Marcus married Alice and was forced to take up residence in the Dower House, he would be spending too much time at Thornbrook Park.

"Brandon, get some breakfast. It's time we went off to the farm."

Nineteen

"OF COURSE IT WILL WORK." EVE WENT OVER THE plan with Mr. Reilly one more time. "They're greedy. If they see the chance to get their hands on more money, they're sure to incriminate themselves."

"You have a point there, but it's risky. Dangerous. We know the Lawsons are capable of murder. If anything happens to you, Marcus will have my hide."

"Nonsense, Mr. Reilly. I take full responsibility for my actions." Her heart fluttered. Would Marcus really go after Mr. Reilly in the event that something happened to her? Would he mourn her? Even as he prepared to marry Alice?

"Try telling him that if…" He gestured, drawing a finger like a knife across his throat and lolling his tongue out.

"Stop." She delivered a playful slap to Mr. Reilly's arm. "Nothing will happen."

"I still don't like the idea of you going in there alone."

"It's the only way to set it up. You'll be outside, should anything happen. I'm certain you can get inside in time to prevent the worst, in any event." Her stomach churned. She was not so certain at all, but there was no help for it. With her money gone and her heart hopelessly devoted to a man she could not have, she had nothing left to lose. It was worth the risk to think of the Lawsons paying for their crimes.

"I'm going to give you a knife, precautionary, to strap under your skirts or up a sleeve, somewhere accessible. I won't send you in without a weapon, just in case. I wish there was time to teach you to shoot."

"I'm not exactly skilled with a knife, either. I could always pick up a blunt object, something gilded, and defend myself with it. But it won't come to that. Leona Lawson won't hurt me. And you said yourself that your Scotland Yard man never saw Mr. Lawson come off the train."

"We've had no sight of him at all. Marcus saw him get on the train in Thornbrook, but no one saw him get off. We have no idea where he is. He could be in the Strumps' house."

"He could have gone back to Thornbrook. If he was that determined to injure me, as Marcus insisted and it seems that he was right, it's most likely he would have gone back to try again. But he could be anywhere. I'll be on guard."

Reilly sighed. "If you're ready, then."

"I am." She adjusted her hat, pulled on her coat, and they were off.

They took a cab most of the way from Mr. Reilly's office, then she walked the short distance from the corner with Mr. Reilly trailing a safe distance behind her. She went up the few stone steps and rang the bell.

"Mr. Gerald, so good to see you again. You

remember me, don't you?" She greeted the butler familiarly when he answered the door.

"Yes. I'll just see if the lady is in." He started to close the door but she swept in past him.

"I know she will want to see me, the poor dear. She must be so lonely with her husband gone. Or has he come back?"

The butler shook his head. "I'm afraid we've had a bit of bad news. Mr. Strump was found dead."

"Dead?" She mocked horror. "You don't say! How awful for poor Mrs. Strump. Perhaps this is a bad time. Though, nothing like a distraction to get through the grief. I know from having gone through it myself. Run and get her, would you? I'll have a seat and wait."

The butler stood still a moment, either over-whelmed or trying to decide how to proceed. Eve held her breath until he turned on his heel and went off to fetch his mistress. She took the time to make a sweeping assessment of the room. There were plenty of gilded objects on the end tables—a chess set with gilded pieces, a statuette of a unicorn—but no monkey in sight, and no bookshelves, for that matter. Maybe in another room?

A moment later, Leona Strump appeared, all in black and dabbing at her eyes with a kerchief, all for effect. Eve didn't see any actual tears. "I'm surprised to see you in London. I thought you were—well, in the country somewhere. I don't recall."

An honest reaction, perhaps, if Leona's husband had gone to murder Eve in Thornbrook. Eve decided she had best keep to some grain of truth. "I've only just arrived. Yesterday. I'm embarrassed to admit that my friend tossed me out. I had nowhere else to go."

"Tossed you out?"

"Oh, Mrs. Strump. I shouldn't share the news, but it's spreading fast enough as it is and I feel that I can trust you. I felt a connection to you on my very first visit. I was caught in flagrante with another of Thornbrook Park's guests."

Despite her grieving widow act, Leona Lawson's painted lips curved into a smile. "I see. You've hit bottom. But I'm sure Gerald has told you I'm not much for company. If you're looking for information, I've nothing to give."

"Oh no, I'm done with looking into the past." Eve waved her hand. "Please, sit and talk with me. I think we can be useful to each other and I hope you will hear me out."

"Useful?" Leona arched a penciled brow. "How would you be any use to me?"

"I've come into some money," Eve blurted out, pushing further into the room and taking a seat on the sofa. She'd been planning to make more conversation first, but she had a feeling Mrs. Strump was ready to throw her out. "Recently."

"Gerald, make some tea." Leona Strump made her way to the sitting area and took the chair across from Eve. "Why on earth do I want to hear about your good fortune when I'm lamenting a change in my own? My husband's gone."

"Come, Mrs. Strump. I'm very sorry for your loss. But I remember our last conversation. You pointed out that we've no heads for business, being women, and I retorted that I had no choice but to start managing my own affairs following my husband's demise."

Leona dabbed at her eyes again. "I remember."

"Here you are, in the same spot. I've thought of you every day since our visit, how awful it is to suddenly find yourself alone. And now that I find out your husband is dead—"

"Don't think to soften me with your attempt at pity." Leona dropped the handkerchief as if a symbol of her dropping the act. "I know nothing about your affairs, as I said. I can't help you recover your husband's investments."

"I've given it up as lost, but I no longer have a need for my husband's money now that I've taken up with the Comte."

"The Comte?" Leona perched on the edge of her chair. The butler brought the tea.

"Comte Louis Lestrange, from France. You must have seen him mentioned in the society pages?" Eve took the liberty of pouring herself tea and picked up her cup. She counted on Leona being the type not to read the papers. "You know our king's interest in foreign affairs? Bertie and Louis became fast friends at court in France."

"Perhaps I've seen him mentioned." Leona took a sip of tea.

"I wouldn't go around talking about it, certainly, but Lord knows, I need a friend. The Comte and I have fallen in love. He has a wife in Paris, of course, so it's quite a scandal. *Une scandale astronomique*, as Louis says. He vows to leave his wife for me."

Mrs. Strump reached out and patted Eve's leg. "They all say that, dear."

"But it's true. I have to believe it. I have nothing else. Alas, he's afraid that his comtesse will take everything he has in the divorce. They have five children. She can destroy his reputation."

Mrs. Strump nodded, clearly becoming caught up in Eve's tale.

"That's why I've come to you. After all my time in India, I know so few people in England, and most of them refuse to see me now that the scandal has broken. You're my last hope. Louis wants to invest a large sum of money in something fast, before his wife hears the news of our affair and gets her hands on his fortune. She can only take what she can find, after all. I know you've no records of my late husband's investments, but I'm praying that you still have information on the diamond mine."

"The mine?" Her eyes narrowed.

"Diamonds, such a sound investment, don't you think? I was telling Louis the sad story of my lost money, and he jumped up and said so. A diamond mine! It's the perfect investment. How could you not make money investing in diamonds?"

"That's what my late husband used to say." Mrs. Strump nodded eagerly. "Diamonds are always increasing in value. He invested some of our money in the mine, I must confess, and we did quite well. The yields were high, Mrs. Kendal. It was the investment in the mine that enabled us to buy this house and improve our station. We live well. Alas, he's no longer here to enjoy it."

"So you do know a bit about it, the mine?" Eve pretended to be surprised.

"Not about any of the other investors, sadly. I don't know what happened to my husband's records. But I do know how to get in touch with the owner of the mine to discuss making an investment. He happens to be a friend of my brother."

"Your brother? Oh, I think you mentioned him the other day." Eve noticed that Leona did not mention her brother by name, probably eager to keep Eve from making a connection.

Mrs. Strump nodded. "I might have. Come to think of it, he might have an idea of what money your husband had coming to him, too. He must have the records. Why didn't I think of it before? You probably have a small sum coming to you, and here I thought I could be no help to you. He would know. There's your answer."

"It makes no difference now. Perhaps I'll reinvest it, if you think it's a lucrative prospect." Suddenly Leona was singing a new tune, probably trying to appear more reliable with a new potential fortune on the line.

"I do. Why don't I put together a meeting between Mr. Royce, the mine owner, and your comte?"

"You would be willing? The solution to all of our problems! Louis will be so happy. He can leave his wife without losing his entire fortune, and I can be the next Comtesse Lestrange."

"Comtesse?" Leona smiled. "It does have a nice ring to it. Why don't you give me your address in town so I can keep in touch?"

Eve recoiled. "I'm afraid I must keep it a secret. Louis wouldn't want the press to catch wind that we were sharing lodgings."

"I see, yes. I'm certain I can arrange for Mr. Royce to meet with you here. Let's say a week from now? Same time?"

"So sudden. Louis will be overjoyed. Time is of the essence. Thank you, Mrs. Strump." Eve rose, ready to make a swift exit in case Oliver Lawson was hiding and ready to pounce. "Or, as Louis would say, *merci beaucoup*! You're a savior. Again, my condolences. See you next week."

Mr. Reilly leaned against a light post just down the street. In case she was still being watched, he waited until Eve walked by and fell in behind her. "About time. I was about to charge in and rescue you."

She did not turn to speak until they were around the corner. "Sorry. It took a little longer than I thought. I had to make sure Leona was falling for the setup."

"And she did?"

"We're meeting her and the owner of the diamond mine at this time next week. Oh, but some small details. You need to work on your French accent, and is there any way we can plant some items in the society pages?"

Mr. Reilly shook his head. "French? That wasn't part of the plan. Let's get some tea and you can explain."

⤳

By the time Marcus returned from the farm, it was late, and he was exhausted down to his bones. Every muscle ached. As soon as George helped him pull off his boots, he dismissed him in favor of simply stripping off his clothes and getting right into bed.

Outside, he was a wreck. On the inside, though,

he felt better than he had in years. A hard day's work had done him a world of good. It had been even better for Brandon, who truly took a shine to each task and looked forward to the next. The boy delighted in the sight of the cows and sheep, and hadn't even minded cleaning the pens. To Brandon, it was all an adventure. Together, they repaired the barn's loose planks, patched the roof, fixed the fence, and split some wood for Mrs. Dennehy's fire. In return, she'd fed them a hearty meal.

Over dinner, Brandon talked about his mother and siblings, and Mrs. Dennehy smiled through it all. Brandon would be good company, she'd concluded. And an even better farmhand. She wouldn't mind taking on more of his sort, she'd said, once his brother and sisters were old enough for rough work. But when Marcus mentioned that Prudence might also be a good fit on the farm, a capable cook and someone to take over making the Dennehy cheese, Mrs. Dennehy shook her head.

"There's only one cheese maker at Tilly Meadow Farm," she'd insisted. "And those recipes are sacred, for Dennehy eyes only."

Still, the way she'd taken to Brandon, Marcus felt encouraged. Maybe in a year or two, once she got used to having more help around the farm, she would bring the whole family on. In the meantime, Marcus would have to make sure the Coopers fit in plenty of visits with Brandon.

The sight of the boy with red in his cheeks, radiating happiness and good health, raised Marcus's spirits. He thought about spending the night to make sure

Brandon was settled, but Mrs. Dennehy talked him out of it.

"Better the boy gets used to it," she'd said.

Besides, Brandon had his dog, the pointer he'd chosen from the litter and named Scout. With Brandon settled, Marcus was free to head off to London to catch up with Eve. He didn't care what his brother had to say about it. Eve could be in danger, and he wasn't about to leave her out there alone. Or alone with Tom Reilly, anyway. Reilly was a man, after all, and Eve was a beautiful woman...

Marcus had just stripped off his shirt when a knock on the door interrupted his musings.

"Yes?" He opened it without thinking, hoping to find Eve, expecting it might only be George, and startled when he saw one of the maids on the other side instead.

She took advantage of his stupefaction to ease by him and into his room.

"I'm sorry. I'm about to go to bed. Is there something you need, miss?" A footman, specifically George, would be sent with important news or to tend him late at night. This one was up to something, and he wanted her gone.

"Ginny. My name is Ginny." She reached out and stroked a hand down his chest. "Going to bed sounds just right to me."

He blinked, stunned, then gestured to the door. "Please leave. I'm tired and I would like to sleep. Alone."

She placed her hand on the door and closed it. "That's not what I think."

"You apparently have the wrong idea."

"I don't think so. I think you like to have company in bed. I'm offering my services, Captain Thorne."

"Your services are quite unnecessary. You have a lot of nerve, Jenny. Do you have any idea how improper—"

"Ginny. And it will serve you well to remember it." She sat on the bed. "Plush. It will do. Look, Captain Thorne. I'm making it easy for you. We can do what you like right here, in the privacy of your own chamber. No one needs to know."

His patience ran out. "And I'm telling you one last time, leave now and I won't inform the earl of my recommendation that you be dismissed for this serious lack of judgment. I don't want what you're offering."

"Yet you had no qualms with Mrs. Kendal. What is it? Am I not your type?" She stood and unbuttoned the top buttons of her black frock, revealing a red corset underneath. "Some say I'm pretty."

"Stop. Leave."

"Come now. I saw everything. In the library?"

"Everything?" His heart lurched. Had she witnessed their lovemaking?

"I was cleaning when you and Mrs. Kendal came in the other day, pretending to look for a book. All too obvious. The attraction between you was unmistakable. And then I happened to see her go into your room. And she didn't come out with any speed, either. It would take a fool not to see it. But perhaps I'm working for fools, if they haven't deduced your feelings yet. I'd be happy to inform them."

"Unless I make it worth your while?"

She put her hands to her ample bosom. "I love a man who understands me. We could be a great team."

"We're no team. You'll be lucky to have a job tomorrow."

"I will hold my position. You wouldn't dare say anything, lest I tell Lord Averford what I know about you and Mrs. Kendal. I have a feeling that you don't want that."

"I don't. But I refuse to be held prey by a scheming seductress."

She threw back her pretty blond head and laughed. "Paint me in the role of seductress? Yes, I like the sound of it."

"You're lucky that I was being kind. How much?"

"I'm sorry?" She blinked.

"How much will it take to get you to leave here and keep your mouth shut? I don't care what my brother thinks of me, but I won't have you tarnishing Mrs. Kendal's reputation. Name your price."

"Twenty pounds? But I planned to make it worth your while." She dropped to her knees.

He pulled her up again. "Get up. You'll take your money and get out. I'll give you ten pounds now and the rest in a week, as long as you don't breathe a word to harm Eve Kendal." A week should be enough time to figure out how he was going to tell Gabriel, but he would be paying this woman to keep quiet for as long as it took. "It's the best deal you'll get."

"I'll accept." She took the notes, stuffed them in her corset, and buttoned up. "Pleasure doing business with you, Captain Thorne."

"I don't care for your sort of business. Take care not to be seen going away from here. Someone might get the wrong impression and blackmail you."

He closed the door behind her. It would be his pleasure to get Ginny sacked, but it would have to wait. One week. It was essential that he hasten to London to help Eve figure out her situation. Gabriel would probably remove the promise of the farm, but Marcus would figure something out for the Coopers. Eve was his primary concern now. If she had her own money back, she could pursue her dream of writing without any interference. The thought of her being threatened set his teeth on edge, and he couldn't easily forget that he'd put her in such a position. It was time he set matters right, even if it meant losing her for good.

Twenty

"MR. SUTTON?" EVE ASKED OVER BREAKFAST AT AVERFORD House the next morning. "Have we a morning paper?"

"The paper, Mrs. Kendal? Why, of course. My apologies. Lady Averford never reads the paper when she is here. But then, you're not quite the same as Lady Averford. I should have thought to inquire."

"Don't take yourself to task, Mr. Sutton. I'm not all that much unlike her. We're friends, after all. I only want to glance at the society pages before I leave for my train."

"A few moments, please." Sutton bowed, left the room, and returned a short time later with the freshly pressed pages. "Here you are."

"Thank you." Eagerly, she glanced through the articles until she found the one she sought, a few lines at the top of the gossip section. As promised, Reilly had avoided dragging Lord and Lady Averford through the mud. Thornbrook Park wasn't referred to by name.

Scandal at a Country Estate!

A certain visiting Comte seemed to have forgot-
ten his manners as the guest of a well-respected

Countess this past week. Imagine her surprise when the proper and esteemed Lady A walked in on Le "strange" Comte and her dear friend mistaking her beloved estate for a Yorkshire pleasure palace! Bertie, have a care and keep a better eye on your foreign friends.

"Oh, it's perfect." Eve clapped in delight. "It says just enough without saying too much. I like the way they fit in Lestrange. And the suggestion that our comte is a special friend of the king? It will confirm my story for Mrs. Lawson, who is sure to be checking the papers for validation. She will have no reason to suspect foul play. Mr. Reilly is an absolute gem. "

"I beg your pardon, Mrs. Kendal? Mrs. Lawson? Mr. Reilly?"

She waved him off. "Never mind, Mr. Sutton. I was talking to myself. I'm afraid I must get ready to leave you now, but I will be back within the week. Possibly sooner."

Depending on how Sophia reacted when she confessed to her weakness for Captain Thorne. But first, she had to find Marcus and convince him that they needed to make an honest start with Gabriel and Sophia. Gabriel seemed a reasonable man. Certainly he wouldn't take his disappointment with Marcus out on Brandon and Mrs. Dennehy by removing the boy from the farm. And Sophia had to forgive her. They were friends. Besides, no one had consulted Lady Alice as yet, and Alice's feelings toward Marcus, or lack thereof, might make all the difference in the world.

At the station, Eve waited patiently for the incoming

passengers to disembark before she could board. She dropped her overnight case in astonishment when she saw Marcus step off the train.

"What are you doing here?" she asked, as his eyes lit up at sight of her.

"Coming to save you from imminent danger. What are you doing here? I thought you were tending to your affairs." He closed the distance, picked up her case, and held on to it.

"I've tended them, at least as much as I can for now. I have an appointment to wrap things up next week, but there's nothing to be done for now."

"What do you mean?" His eyes narrowed. "Wrap things up? Have you recovered your money?"

"I would love to tell you, but we need to talk and I hate to miss this train. Do you have any other business to keep you here?"

"Checking in with the Coopers, but it can wait. Come on." He took her arm and escorted her to the train.

"But you just got here." She hesitated.

"And I've found you safe. I have no other pressing concerns. We can hold our discussion on the way back to Thornbrook Park."

"All right." They boarded and settled into seats before they resumed their conversation. She felt herself becoming annoyed with him. Coming to save her? "Before we begin, I feel the need to point out that I do not need you to save me. I've been handling matters rather well on my own."

"On your own with Tom Reilly?" He cocked a brow.

"Of course. Thank you for keeping him informed. Perhaps I do need a little assistance here and there, but it hardly means I'm a helpless female in need of saving."

"You're right." He toyed with his collar. "Poor choice of words."

"Hmm. I hope so. If you think I'm in need of a man to guide me through life, you're sadly mistaken."

"Eve." He reached for her hand. "I know you're capable of managing on your own. You're remarkable. But you're dealing with an unsavory lot. I know you don't believe me, but that man had a knife."

"I believe you." She had to confess as much. "Scotland Yard turned up Mr. Strump's body, confirming that he had been murdered. And Mr. Reilly turned up much more on the connection between the Lawsons and Mr. Strump."

He listened patiently while she told him the whole story. When she was done, he shook his head. "I can't believe Tom let you go in there alone."

"Oh, that's all you take from this?" She scooted a bit away from him on the seat, crossing her arms. "I've unfolded a whole sordid tale, not to mention my brilliant plan to catch the villains in a confession, and all you can say is that I should have been more closely supervised?"

"Eve, that's not it. I—I was worried sick about you all night long. You have to understand." His eyes darkened with the recollection of fear.

She softened. "I suppose I understand. Tom didn't want me to visit Mrs. Lawson on my own, either. And I was a bit nervous, to tell the truth. But all is well. We're on the verge of tripping them up."

He entwined his fingers with hers. "But Oliver Lawson is still unaccounted for. He could be any-where, lying in wait." They both looked around them on the train. Plenty of men in black bowler hats, but none of them looked like Lawson.

"Not for much longer. I'm sure his wife will be in contact and get him to attend our meeting."

"Perhaps," he agreed, finally easing back in his seat. "Now, then, we have other matters to discuss."

"We do." She took a breath, unsure of how he would react. "I want to tell Sophia of our affair. I feel terrible hiding things from her, Marcus. She's my best friend, and she has been so kind."

"I agree." To her surprise, he nodded along. "As soon as we get back to Thornbrook Park, I'll find Gabriel and confess, while you have your talk with Sophia. We can't go on as we have been, hiding and sneaking." He told her of the maid, Ginny, and her blackmail.

"We're confessing none too soon, then. She'll have no power over us after today. It was lovely, though, while it lasted." She hated to end it, but it had to be so. She would find a small flat and something to do in London. He would marry Alice and make an heir for Thornbrook Park. "Thank you for reminding me of how restorative love can be."

"Was lovely? What do you mean?" He turned to her, alarm flashing gold in his amber gaze.

"We can't continue, Marcus. You know we can't. You have your Coopers and the farm and Lady Alice. I think you still have a chance with her. Thornbrook Park needs an heir."

"No one says it has to be with Lady Alice. Well,

besides Gabriel and Sophia, but I think we can change their minds. And if not…"

She couldn't let him give up on everything he'd worked to set up with Brandon and the Coopers at the farm, all the while destroying Sophia and Gabriel's hopes for an heir. Marcus was a noble soul. She knew he would offer, and she loved him for it. *She loved him.* It was why she had to set him free. She forced a smile.

"I'm flattered, but we can't fool ourselves into thinking we have any sort of future together. I'm not planning to marry again. Your brother has plans for you. I don't think our brief indiscretion will put him off, or even change Sophia's mind. If you can win Lady Alice's affections, there's no reason not to go on as planned."

He dropped her hand. "Just like that? You don't plan to marry? You don't intend even to give us a chance?"

"Marcus," she placed her hand on his cheek, savoring the warmth and roughness of his slight growth of beard. He must have run off without shaving this morning in his haste to get to her. It made what she needed to say that much harder. Her heart ached. She felt a scorching emptiness in the pit of her soul that she didn't remember feeling even after losing Ben. But it had to be done. "I care about you a great deal. And I know you care for me. We've made memories that I will treasure for the rest of my life. But I think we both know that our affair has run its course."

"I didn't know." He pulled away. "I didn't know until just now, but it's all becoming clear. I think we've said all we need to say."

They rode together in silence for the rest of the journey back.

⤨

On arrival back at Thornbrook Park, Marcus didn't feel anger as he stomped off in search of his brother. He felt sadness and loss, a pain deep in his gut not unlike the grief that had overwhelmed him upon losing William Cooper. Had their affair been a mere diversion for Eve? Something to restore her after losing her husband? A lark? He'd nearly lost his heart to the woman. Nearly. Now he only felt like a fool.

Nonetheless, he would confess his foolishness to his brother, who would no doubt use it like a club to beat the wayward Marcus back into submission. *That will teach you for attaching yourself to willing widows! Marry Alice. Produce an heir. Or else!*

The black rage edged in, overcoming his sadness. His brother, the high and mighty earl, making the rest of them dance like puppets to do his bidding. How dare he? Perhaps Marcus couldn't have his heart's desire, Eve, but it didn't mean he had to accept what his brother wanted for him. He didn't need Gabriel. He didn't need Thornbrook Park or his inheritance. He could find something else for the Coopers, some other way to make a living without his annuity. He didn't need Eve Kendal. Dash it all!

He stormed into Gabriel's study. "Brother, I'll have a word with you."

Gabriel looked up from his desk, one golden brow arched in annoyance, or was it amusement? "Yes, have a seat."

"I'll stand."

"As you wish." With his elbows on the desk, Gabriel tented his fingers and waited for Marcus to go on.

"I've been having an affair with Eve Kendal. Did you know?"

"An affair?" Gabriel dropped his hands. "Do you mean the two of you have actually been carrying on? I knew you were flirting. Any idiot could tell you had an interest in each other. But a full-blown affair? I had no idea. I wouldn't have expected it of her."

"Of course. You expect it of me, but she's a lady. A fine, upstanding, remarkable woman, if we're being honest. 'Lady' doesn't do her justice. It seems weak somehow. And she's anything but. She's—" Marcus paused, desperate to gather his thoughts. He was rambling, he knew. Making a mess of this discussion when he'd meant to be the one in control. But there was no hope for it. Not an hour earlier, on the train, his heart had been smashed to bits, and what he really wanted was to run to a dark corner and have a good cry. Like a child. A wounded little boy. No, he was stronger than that. "She's exquisite, Gabriel. I've never known anyone like her."

"You love her." Gabriel stood, seemingly astounded by the news. "You mean to tell me you've fallen in love with Sophia's friend?"

He shook his head. "No. Yes. I—I do love her, but she doesn't return the feeling. She *cares* for me a 'great deal.' But that's not love. It's hopeless between us. She said so. Our affair has run its course. But I wanted you to know."

"Thank you for your candor." Gabriel nodded. "Now that you've got all that out of your system, I suppose you're ready to step it up with Lady Alice?"

Marcus, who found that he'd been pacing though he'd hardly realized what he'd been doing, stopped in his tracks. "Step it up?"

"You know, make more of an effort to court her properly? To win her over instead of taking all your time chasing Eve Kendal's tail. Lovely as it is."

"Do you care to repeat that?" Marcus stepped closer to Gabriel, who stood behind his desk.

"Repeat what?" Gabriel came around to the other side of the desk, standing at full height, keeping his dark eyes trained on his brother's. "That Eve Kendal has a lovely backside? I'm married, Brother, not dead. And she's apparently willing to show it off."

Marcus didn't hear his brother's last words for the sudden pounding in his head, like a train running off the rails, the rage in full force, clouding his vision and dulling the rest of his senses, all except one, the sense of touch. He balled his hands into fists. His brother stood in front of him, growing fuzzy around the edges perhaps, but Marcus could still see that smug, self-satisfied grin, his brother's look of triumph.

He felt an overwhelming sense of satisfaction at last, the rage ebbing, as he smashed his fist squarely into Gabriel's jaw. Gabriel recoiled, falling back, but it only took a second for him to right himself and hit back, delivering a sound punch to the side of Marcus's head. *Good.* This Marcus knew, fighting. This he could best his brother in at last, after all the years of taking Gabriel's beatings when they were young. He bounced on the balls of his feet, just as he'd shown Eve how to do in the Averford House library.

"Come on, then," he goaded his brother. "Take another shot. I'll give you one more before I pound you to the bloody carpet."

"Ha, you can't win against me. You never could." Gabriel swung at him again and missed. "Give up now before it's too late."

"Not before—" Gabriel got in one more good smash, Marcus had to hand it to him, a left hook right across his jaw that sent him crashing into the floor lamp. He shook it off and bobbed right back into action. "Not before I teach you not to interfere in my life, Gabriel. Ever again."

He rained his wrath upon his brother, blow after blow, until Gabriel, bloodied, fell to the floor. The rage was gone, at last. Spent. But oddly, Marcus didn't feel much better. The overwhelming sadness remained. He realized he'd been wrong about one thing.

He needed Eve Kendal. If only she needed him, too.

❧

It was a banner day for Eve. She'd just lost her lover, the one man she cared about in a way that rivaled the great love she had for Ben, something she'd never thought she'd feel again, and now she risked losing her best friend. She steeled herself, trying to bury the pain of letting go of Marcus as she prepared to face Sophia.

"Eve, you've returned just in time!" Sophia greeted her from the drawing room as Eve headed for the stairs.

"In time for what?" Eve thought Sophia would be

in her room, giving her a few more minutes to prepare what she would say, but better to face her immediately.

"The Dovedales are coming. Lizzy! You remember Lizzy Westwick."

"Oh yes, dear Lizzy. How is she?" Lizzy was a friend of theirs from their girlhood in Delaney Square.

"She is quite the woman of fashion these days, a Londoner. Her husband is a publisher. They have three little girls."

"Oh, how sweet." Eve felt a hitch in her lungs at the news. Three girls. At least one of them had been blessed with children. Eve wanted to hug Sophia. Instead, she was about to break her heart. Or her trust. Maybe both. "Sophia, I've something to tell you."

"Can it wait? I have to ring for Mrs. Hoyle and make sure she has arranged Lizzy's room exactly as I requested. Mr. Dovedale isn't coming for a few days. I've put them in separate rooms just down the hall from you. Do you think it will suffice?"

Eve shrugged. "Are they adjoining rooms? Married people do like to be together. Usually." She didn't mean for it to be a cut about the distance between Gabriel and Sophia, and she hoped it hadn't come out that way.

"I suppose." Sophia nibbled her lip, considering.

"What I have to say can't really wait, so if you could put Mrs. Hoyle off for just a bit?"

"But Lizzy will be arriving within the hour. Are you sure? Oh, you do look serious. Very well." Sophia took a seat on the sofa across from the portrait of her mother-in-law, looked up, and moved to the chair in the corner. "Come. Sit by me. Tell me what's troubling you. Quickly. I still have to ring for Hoyle and send for Alice."

Eve hated to rush such a conversation but she took a seat. Maybe it was for the best that Sophia had so much to occupy her mind. "I've been having an affair."

"What?" Sophia's cornflower eyes widened. Eve had her rapt attention at last. "What kind of affair? What do you mean?"

Eve shook her head. "You know what I mean. An *affair*. I hate keeping secrets from you, Sophia. It has been so hard to live with myself, knowing I've been deceiving you."

"You and Gabriel? Oh my word. Eve! How could you?" Sophia stood up, enraged.

Eve stood as well. "No, Sophia. Lord, no. Not Gabriel. *Marcus*. Marcus and I have been carrying on, if you will."

"Carrying on? You and Marcus?"

"Having intimate relations, the two of us. Yes."

"I'm astonished." Sophia paced. "I shouldn't say astonished. When I think of it, I'm not all that surprised. No one could miss the way the two of you look at each other. But I thought you'd never act on it, either one of you. I thought it a mere flirtation. And that in the end, you were only thinking of me and of Alice."

"I didn't give you enough thought, I'm afraid. I'm not ashamed of my actions, exactly. I needed to know love again. But I am regretful that I betrayed your trust. And I'm sorry that I fell for the one man you intended for your sister. It was"—she caught her breath, her heart fluttering—"disloyal. I've been disloyal, and I'm so sorry. I hope you can forgive me."

Sophia crossed her arms and stared straight at Eve, fire in her eyes. "Do you love him?"

"I... no," she lied, but felt it justified this time. She had no intention of being with Marcus again. "It's over between us. It will never happen again. I know you want him for Alice, and I believe he is ready to settle down and court her."

"Oh? Are you sure? You're all done now, so Alice can have him?" Sophia spat the words, an attempt at sarcasm.

"Sophia, it's not like that. I'm so sorry."

A loud crashing interrupted them, followed shortly by a maid running breathlessly to the drawing room door. "Oh hurry, it's chaos. They're killing each other!"

Both Sophia and Eve ran after the maid. "Who?" Sophia asked. "Who is killing whom?"

"Lord Averford and his brother! They're fighting."

By the time Eve and Sophia got to Gabriel's study, they found Gabriel sprawled on the floor, blood all over his face, his valet leaning over him.

"Dear God, Gabriel!" Sophia ran to her husband's side. "Gabriel, darling."

"Don't worry, love," Gabriel said, starting to sit up. "I'm not dying. Minor injuries."

The valet stopped him, applying a kerchief to his face. "The blood, sir. Stay down until your nose stops bleeding."

"Where's Marcus?" Eve looked around. There was no sign of him.

"He stormed off after he knocked Lord Averford out," the valet said. "No idea where he has gone."

The bell rang.

"Mrs. Dovedale's arrived." Another maid ducked in to inform them. "Mrs. Hoyle is out greeting her in the drive."

"Eve, please go and greet Lizzy for me. Make my apologies and say there has been an accident, no specifics. I'll be down as soon as I've seen to Gabriel." For a moment, Eve had hope that Sophia had forgiven her. Until she added, in icy tones, "It's the least that you could do."

Twenty-one

FORTUNATELY, ALICE AND AGATHA HAD COME OVER from the Dower House and were seated with Lizzy in the drawing room when Eve entered to join them.

"Lizzy," Eve held her hands out as she approached. "So good to see you again."

"Eve." Lizzy stood to greet her. "I was thrilled when Sophia mentioned you were here, too. Imagine, I get to catch up with you both. Just like old times."

"Just like old times," Eve said. If only Lizzy knew. "I'm afraid there's been a bit of an accident in Lord Averford's study. Sophia was called away, but she will join us shortly. Has Mrs. Hoyle gone to see to tea, Alice?"

Alice nodded. "Mr. Finch is arranging it. He'll be along any moment, I believe."

Lizzy had changed a bit since Eve had last seen her, but she had the same eager green eyes, welcoming, full-lipped smile, and abundant chestnut curls barely tamed in a chignon. She had become curvier with age and perhaps motherhood, with a fuller bosom and hips but still a trim waist. She wore a lovely cream-colored lace blouse with a burgundy organza overlay tucked into a black skirt with a wide satin sash, very fashionable for a publisher's wife. For all Eve knew, all publishers' wives were fashionable women.

A moment later, Sophia swept in, a picture of elegance in her lavender silk with black chiffon draped across the shoulders. Finch brought the tea cart in while they were catching up. "Lizzy! There you are. I'm sorry to keep you waiting."

"Not a problem at all." Lizzy took it in stride. "I'm happy to be here. Thornbrook Park is lovely as always. And you, breathtaking as always. I hope it was nothing serious, the accident?"

"Oh, no. Thank goodness. A light fixture broke free of its foundation and fell on Lord Averford, can you imagine? He's perfectly well now, just a bit of a bloody nose and maybe a blackened eye."

"Really?" Lizzy's eyes widened. "How unusual. It must have hit just right."

"I guess he tipped his head to look up as it fell," Alice asked. "Or how would it get his nose and eye? Falling from the ceiling?"

Sophia shot her a glare.

"As long as he's well. Wouldn't want to think it was anything serious," Eve said, relieved that Marcus hadn't done any significant damage. But where had he gone? What must he be thinking? She had a longing to comfort him that she knew was better left unsatisfied.

"Tell us about London," Sophia urged Lizzy. "The latest fashion? Gossip?"

"Shorter skirts are making a splash. Apparently,

they make it so much easier for modern women to get around."

"Oh, I like that," Alice said. "About time."

"We're also seeing a lot more sleevelessness in daytime as well as evening wear. Not with winter coming, of course, but come spring we'll all be baring our arms."

"Not all of us, dear." Agatha chuckled. "This old bird will stay covered up."

They all laughed.

"The Olympic Games are to be held in London," Lizzy said. "It has been decided."

"We were just discussing it with Captain Thorne." Alice nodded. "I think it's delightful. But some of us are not in agreement."

"London is crowded enough. Why would we want to attract more foreigners?" Sophia wrinkled up her nose in disgust.

"Oh, why not?" Lizzy waved her hand. "As long as they're interesting. London is always going to attract visitors. Might as well have a good reason for it. Is Gabriel's brother visiting, too? I don't think I've seen him since your wedding, though he stays at your house in town, does he not?"

"Usually." Sophia cast a cool glance in Eve's direction. "He has been visiting, but I think he might be headed back to London. One never knows with Marcus. He's unpredictable."

"She has been trying to make a match for him with me." Alice shook her head. "You know my sister. Incorrigible."

"I take it you object to the match then, Alice? What's he like? Not your type?" Lizzy dug for gossip.

Alice shrugged. "He's handsome enough, if you like that golden god sort. He looks a lot like his brother, really. Too much like, if you ask me. Though, I will admit that I almost changed my mind about him the other day when he brought me flowers and stayed to talk. He's a charmer."

Sophia smiled. "All you really need is a chance to get to know him without any distractions getting in the way."

Eve took the hint. Sophia tolerated her presence because they had a guest. Once Lizzy was gone, Eve had better prepare to head out as well. She would have to find a place of her own.

"Tedious business, matchmaking," Lizzy said. "Not as tedious as searching for a new governess, which I wouldn't have to care about, had I not proven so successful a matchmaker. I fixed up our governess with the music master, and now they're married and gone off to Vienna, where he's from. I'm interviewing for a replacement."

"I would think there are plenty of capable young women in London," Sophia said.

"You would be surprised. The truly accomplished girls, few as they are, all seem to dream of marrying instead of going into service. And those with less to offer, well, they have all kinds of options these days."

"Options besides marriage?" Sophia seemed surprised.

"Of course," Eve said. "They can be secretaries or nurses."

"Shopgirls." Lizzy nodded along. "Journalists. One of them wanted to be an actress on the stage."

"An actress, oh my. Not suitable company for impressionable young girls." Sophia shuddered.

"I don't think there's anything wrong with actresses. You would have been a wonder at it, Sophia." Eve enjoyed making light of Sophia as only friends who truly care can manage. Though, considering they were at odds, perhaps she had better not lapse into familiarity. "Who knows? If things had worked out differently."

Sophia shook her head. "Heavens."

Eve's life had turned out differently than she'd planned. With her savings perhaps lost forever, she pondered what she might do to support herself. Even if she finished her novel, there was no guarantee of success. An idea struck her.

"I could be a governess," Eve said suddenly. "I love little girls. I need to earn a living. Actually, more than need, I think I would enjoy earning a living. There's something satisfying about putting in a day's work. And being a governess is a fairly respectable profession."

"Certainly, your widow's pension provides enough to live on. Your situation can't be as dire as all that." Lizzy paused as if considering, her pretty green eyes flashing with concern.

"I have some money," Eve said. "Enough to live within very modest means, but not to be truly comfortable."

"Are you honestly interested?" Lizzy turned to face her. "Truly?"

"I am." Was she? London was the best place for her, a single woman on her own. And it wouldn't hurt to have established herself with an actual publisher, should she ever complete a manuscript. The perfect situation had fallen into her lap, but she would have expected to be more excited by the possibility.

"A governess, Eve? You can't mean it." Sophia seemed aghast at the idea, driving Eve to like it all the more.

"I'll talk it over with Geoffrey, my husband." Lizzy smiled at the idea. "You'll meet him in a few days. I think he will like the idea of taking you on as governess as much as I do."

"That would be lovely. Thank you," Eve said, although her stomach gave a little flip as if something didn't feel quite right about it. But her choices were limited. A happily-ever-after with the man of her dreams was not quite in the cards for her. At least with the Dovedales, she would be with friends and not completely alone as she established a new life for herself in London.

❦

Beating his brother bloody hadn't been as satisfying as he'd expected. Marcus's fists throbbed in a way that made him begin to appreciate Queensbury rules, with gloves, but it was no comparison to the ache he felt down to his core, the pain of rejection.

Eve didn't love him. Or, for some reason, she was pretending not to. He couldn't decide which. And did it matter? She didn't want to be with him one way or the other. After fighting with his brother, he stopped to check on Brandon at the farm and extracted a promise from Mrs. Dennehy that she wouldn't agree with Lord Averford to toss the boy out before Marcus returned from London, though he doubted that even his brother could be so heartless. After that, there was no point in waiting. He headed to the station for his third train ride of the day.

He decided to visit the Coopers first to give Prudence an update on how Brandon fared, and then he would look for Tom to see if there was anything Eve had left out or had not considered in her attempt to urge a confession from the Lawsons. After stopping for flowers and tea cakes, he made his way up to the Coopers' flat. To his surprise, Tom Reilly opened the door.

"Tom? What are you doing here?"

"Marcus, lovely to see you." Prudence came to greet him. "Mr. Reilly has become quite a friend to us since you introduced him to us. I guess you could say we look out for each other."

"I make sure the neighborhood stays safe for the children, and Prudence returns the favor by making me home-cooked meals. I think I've put on weight, but it's worth it."

"Glad to hear it." Marcus had hoped that Tom would be able to look out for the Coopers in his absence, but he never expected him to become so companionable with them. It added a bright spot to his otherwise dreary day.

Anna and Emily descended on Marcus for cakes, stealing his attention temporarily. Once all the young Coopers had their treats, he turned back to Prudence.

"You've nothing to worry about with Brandon. He's happy as a lark on the farm and a good worker. I'll bring him back home for a visit soon, and then maybe one day I can take you all out there to have a look around." One day. If he wasn't persona non grata on the grounds of Thornbrook Park and thereabouts.

When Marcus prepared to leave at last, Tom left with him so they could go to the pub and talk.

"Let me catch you up on my progress," Tom said, over a pint.

"Eve caught me up. You really let her go back to the Strumps' house alone?"

"She was determined. And her plan made sense. Plus, it worked, Marcus. We have them right where we want them. She's a clever one, your girl Eve."

"She's not my girl. She's a capable, independent woman. But I want you to keep a close eye on her nonetheless. I don't like the fact that you've been unable to locate Oliver Lawson."

"Believe me, we're still investigating it. If he turns up anywhere near his house, we've got him. So far, though, no sight of him."

"I wish we had such capable surveillance at Thornbrook Park." He hadn't given Lawson much thought all afternoon. Now that he had a clearer head, he worried about Eve in Yorkshire. How could he have left her there alone? But she wasn't alone, he reminded himself. Thornbrook Park was large and safe, and she had the sense not to go running about on her own. Didn't she? He would feel better if they were together, or at least under the same roof.

When Eve heard that Marcus had gone to London, she realized that she might not ever get the chance to say good-bye. She wasn't going back to Averford House, not with Sophia holding a grudge. She had to make a clean break. But if she had the chance to see him again, could she manage to leave him? Would he still want her? She had her doubts.

"I want you to know that you've upset me very much," Sophia told her after dinner once Lizzy had gone to bed. "And you've certainly made it harder for Marcus and Alice to come together."

"But you heard her, Sophia. Alice isn't interested in Marcus." If Eve had thought for one moment that she was, would she still have made love with him in the library? In the field? In his room? She couldn't be sure. Heat rose to her cheeks.

"That's not what I heard at all. She said she found him charming, and she'd begun to change her mind. If not for you, they might already be together."

"I want you to be happy, Sophia. I love you like a sister. I would never have hurt you on purpose and I hope you know how very sorry I am."

"Then go away," Sophia said coldly. "Not now. I don't want to give Lizzy any reason to be suspicious or to spread gossip in London. But once the Dovedales leave, go away and give Marcus and Alice a chance."

"I'll go away, and I hope things turn out in the way that you want. But you can't make them fall in love, Sophia. No matter how much you wish them to be together." Eve wasn't sure Marcus planned on coming back. To Tilly Meadow to visit Brandon, perhaps, but only as long as Brandon stayed there. He might be in London searching for a new situation for the Coopers even now. "I have an appointment in London in a few days, and then I'll be taking the position with the Dovedales. I'll be out of your way."

The next day, the rain came and they were stuck inside. They played games, charades, backgammon. Sophia seemed to forget sometimes that they were at odds, and other times she treated Eve with false cheer. But Lizzy had no reason to suspect that they weren't getting along. By the third day, Eve decided to share her treasures from India after Lizzy began asking questions about it, a place where her husband, Geoffrey, had spent time away on business without her.

They looked through Eve's picture books and dressed up in Eve's saris for a laugh. Eve chose a deep green sari and went behind the screen to change. She emerged wrapped in a length of hand-dyed and embroidered silk that bared one shoulder and showed a flash of skin along her midriff.

"*Namaste*," she said, coming out and bowing with her hands pressed together in front of her, as she had seen Prama and so many others do.

"Nama—what?" the others asked.

"*Namaste*," Eve pronounced the word slowly. "It's a traditional greeting. It's like wishing someone well. It means simply hello or more reverently, 'I recognize the holiness within you.' *Namaste*." She bowed again.

They all repeated the word.

"Turn around." Sophia stood to feel the silk. "Eve, this is extraordinary. You look beautiful. It suits you."

"Go ahead, try one on," Eve urged.

"Is it comfortable?" Alice asked.

"Very," Eve answered. "You'll feel like an exotic princess.

"I want to try one." Lizzy jumped up. "The gold."

"It would go very nicely with your chestnut hair. Shall I show you how to drape it?"

"Please. I'll never figure it out on my own."

Eve helped them into saris, the peacock blue for

Sophia, which made her eyes all the more striking, and a crimson for Alice, which did not clash with her red-brown hair at all, as Sophia had feared. When they were all done changing, they admired each other in the unfamiliar garb.

"Something's not quite right. Our hair. It's all wrong. Look." Sophia held up a page from Eve's book of photographs. "It should be parted in the middle and smoothed, perhaps loosely gathered in the back. I'll call Jenks."

In the end, they looked like Englishwomen pretending to be exotic beauties, but they were admiring each other delightedly when Lucy came up with a message.

"My lady," Lucy said, clearly working to control any response to their surprising new looks, "Mr. Dovedale is arriving from the train station. Lord Averford suggests you join him to greet the car."

"Of course. Thank you, Lucy."

"Wouldn't it be fun if we went down like this?" Alice suggested with a laugh.

"I would like to see the look on Lord Averford's face," Sophia said.

Lizzy nodded. "And on Geoffrey's. He will wonder what you have done to his wife. Let's do it."

"Do let's." They all giggled conspiratorially.

Eve, though, felt no urgency to run out with the others. Her spirits were beginning to flag. She would meet Geoffrey Dovedale soon enough. She had been eager to share some spices with Mrs. Mallows, and she took the opportunity to go down to the kitchen instead of out to greet the new arrival. Mrs. Mallows labored over preparations for the evening meal, making Eve hesitant to interrupt.

"Yes, what is it?" The cook turned to her, surprise at Eve's costume etched clearly on her face.

"I've brought some of my Indian spices. I wanted to share one of my recipes with you, but I can come back another time."

"Oh no, dear. It's a good time. And you've treated us to a look at traditional Indian costume, I suppose. Very daring, Mrs. Kendal. Look at that embroidery." She leaned over to study the fabric. "Mrs. Hoyle would be envious of the stitch work."

"Perhaps I will show her before I change."

Mrs. Mallows handed Eve a spoon. "Stir the sauce while you tell me about these spices and what we can do with them."

Eve stirred and shared recipe ideas while Mrs. Mallows tasted all the spices, some familiar, some not. Turmeric, pomegranate seeds, coriander, star anise, saffron, fenugreek, green and black cardamom, and more. In the end, they agreed on an apple squash curry with stewed chicken, something that combined the familiar ingredients they had in abundance with exotic new flavors. Mrs. Mallows thought they could add the dish to the evening's menu.

The kitchen was hot and Mrs. Mallows was a strict taskmaster, but Eve enjoyed cooking with her for the rest of the afternoon until it was time for her to change for dinner and join the others, especially since it took her mind off having to leave Sophia, Thornbrook Park, and Marcus behind forever.

⌒⌒

When Eve returned to her room to prepare for dinner, she decided on a pale orange gown, silk with a fine filigree of cream lace draped over it. It was older, true, but too pretty to ignore. The neckline was edged in black with a flourish of purple ribbon on the left side. It wasn't cut too low, though it swept the tops of her breasts. In it, she felt every inch a lady. She wished Marcus were there to see her under different circumstances, should things have worked out between them.

Lucy came to help with her hair and admired her without reserve.

"Mrs. Kendal, you're like a princess from a fairy story."

"Thank you, Lucy. I feel a tad old to play the princess, but maybe I won't once we've done something with my hair."

"You're not so old as all that, are you? Twenty-four? Maybe twenty-five? So young yet."

"Nearly twenty-six," Eve said, sitting down in front of the mirror. "But let's not speak of it."

Lucy arranged Eve's wavy curls into a softly romantic cascade.

"Perhaps I should bob my hair. The way they show in the magazines, have you seen it? Such a bold new style."

"I think it would suit," Lucy said, meeting Eve's gaze in the mirror. "It would lend your delicate features some pixie-like charm."

"Perhaps once I'm back in London with the Dovedales," Eve said. "Thank you, Lucy. New hair for a new start."

Before she made her way down to dinner, she

stopped for one last thing. Among her treasures, she still had a few necklaces, the ones that couldn't fetch a high enough price to be worth selling. Ben's mother's amethyst beads would go best, but she chose the melo pearl she'd had on when she'd first encountered Marcus at Thornbrook Park.

She had bought it after haggling in a marketplace in Calcutta, or as Prama had taught her, Kolkata. She'd been so proud of her purchase, especially after Prama had told her that she had driven a hard bargain and ended up with a very fair price. Wearing the necklace reminded her of that feeling, of being the strong, proud, independent woman she meant to be for the rest of her life.

As Eve approached Sophia's suite, Sophia was just stepping out. They greeted each other coldly, and Eve felt another pang of loss. What a mess she'd made of things.

Sophia wore a stunning ivory satin with pearl gray embroidery and pale blue beading.

Wordlessly, they went down to dinner together. Gabriel and the Dovedales waited in the parlor. Gabriel managed the introductions.

Geoffrey Dovedale took her hand. He was a tall man, standing an inch or two over six feet, and thin, as if he possibly skipped meals due to a busy schedule. His dark hair was slicked back but just starting to recede at the temples, and he had a dark, thin mustache.

"I'm so pleased to meet a dear friend of my Elizabeth." He peered down at her through his spectacles. "I look forward to getting to know you."

"The honor is all mine. I'm a great reader. I would like to hear more about your work."

Once Agatha joined them, they went in, Gabriel taking his seat at the head of the table with Sophia to his right, and Agatha to his left. The Dovedales sat together next to Sophia, with Geoffrey directly next to Sophia and Eve across from Lizzy. Alice filled the seat next to Eve that was normally filled by Marcus. It seemed off somehow. She wished they could have left his chair empty, but perhaps that would have made it all the harder to bear his absence.

"Elizabeth said that you have three girls, Mr. Dovedale," Sophia said. "You are outnumbered by females, poor man."

Eve forced herself to pay attention to the conversation. She was going to be the Dovedales' governess, but all she could think about was Marcus.

"I consider myself very fortunate. Daughters are wonderful things. Though I do mean to teach Margaret, our youngest, to play cricket. She has quite an arm."

"Now, Geoffrey, you will do no such thing." Lizzy turned to Sophia and Alice. "Can you imagine?"

"I think, given the right opportunities, girls can do anything as well as boys," Alice said, as the footman made the rounds with a well-done roast and gravy. "You're wise to start her young. Margaret Dovedale, first female cricket champion. I quite like the sound of it."

"Not if her mother can help it," Dovedale said. "But we'll see. Also, I'm not quite as outnumbered as you might think, Lady Averford. I have recently acquired my most devoted companion, Drake. He's a pug. I love my daughters, but I must confess that I haven't had one moment of concern since leaving them at home with their nurse for the weekend. I do, however, worry about my Drake. What will he do without me?" Dovedale asked.

"Make a shambles of your study, that's what," Lizzy said with a knowing nod. "I hope you didn't leave any valuable manuscripts lying around."

"Only one from Mr. Forster. I told him it was completely unbelievable and I needed a rewrite. And he told me it was all based on true events and I might consider stuffing it in a place, well, it's not polite conversation. But, at any rate, he informed me that I was not the only publisher in town. I informed him that I was perhaps the only publisher offering a chance to improve his story, but that he was free to make up his own mind."

"Is Mr. Forster a talented writer?" Eve asked. "I haven't read anything of his yet, that I am aware of."

"You will." Mr. Dovedale paused, fork in the air as he prepared to taste the next course. "Most assuredly. He's brilliant. Especially if he learns to take some good advice. E. M. Forster, yes, you would do well to look him up. His debut garnered some strong reviews and high praise. What do you like to read?"

"Lately, I'm enjoying Edith Wharton, but I also like Henry James, Thomas Hardy, and always Jane Austen," Eve answered with a smile.

"Jane Austen, of course. You're a romantic. Most women are."

"She also likes Kipling," Alice teased.

"And Brontë," Agatha added. She'd been so quiet that Eve had almost forgotten she was there. "We had a conversation about Brontë just a short time ago at this table, in fact."

With the exception of the Dovedales, no doubt they all remembered the last conversation about Brontë and the man who inspired it, Marcus. Everyone grew quiet for a moment as if the ghost of Marcus had joined them at the table, channeled by Agatha. Sophia shared a glance with Gabriel and moved the conversation along.

"When we were girls," Sophia said wistfully, "Eve and I had a pact involving *Jane Eyre*. Do you remember, Eve?"

She liked Sophia remembering their past. It helped her believe they could yet have a future. "Of course. You were determined to marry a Mr. Rochester of your own. But I think perhaps you ended up with a Mr. Darcy."

"What's that you're calling me, Mrs. Kendal?"

"It's a compliment, Lord Averford," Lizzy said. "Rochester was bombastic and cruel. Darcy may be proud, but he was honorable."

"Rochester was deceptive, perhaps," Alice defended. "I don't think he meant to be cruel. He didn't have much choice."

"He had every choice. He could have said, 'Jane, I love you, but my mad wife is in the attic.'" Lizzy speared her broccoli with a passionate flair. "But did he say a word? No!"

"But Rochester was cruelly forced into a terrible first marriage by his father. And brother," Eve observed, looking directly at Gabriel. Would it be lost on him, the trouble that occurred when marriages were forced? "Given his choice, he might never have married Bertha."

"And once she took ill, he did the best he could for her. He kept her out of institutions," Alice said. "And who could fault him for trying to hold on to love when it finally found him?"

"Well, Mr. Darcy is a bit tame by comparison," Eve said, eager to move the conversation to safer territory. Arguing the merits or failings of Rochester could only make tensions rise. Readers were passionate in defense of beloved characters.

"Come with us to shoot birds in the morning. I will show you tame," Gabriel boasted.

"I would love to," Alice said, miming taking aim with a rifle. "I think I could be a crack shot."

Gabriel laughed, not taking her seriously. "Gentlemen only, I'm afraid."

"I need to return to London in the morning," Eve said. "Wrapping up some business with my solicitor." She hadn't mentioned that her solicitor was dead and that the business was locking away his murderous "wife" and her "brother."

"What is it you're writing, Mrs. Kendal?" Mr. Dovedale paused to push his spectacles further up on his nose. "Elizabeth tells me you're working on a novel."

"I am. A love story between a South African widow and an English soldier."

"A tragedy? These things never end well for the women. Madame Bovary, Anna Karenina." Dovedale nodded authoritatively.

"Absolutely not." Eve shook her head. "For once, I would like to see a woman in a love affair have a proper ending. A happy ending. Why not? What's wrong with wanting to be loved? She's no innocent, but she's not hurting anyone by following her heart."

For the second time of the evening, conversation halted at the table. Sophia and Gabriel looked at her. Let them glare. She couldn't take back what had happened and she didn't want to, though she wished for all the world that she and Marcus had proceeded differently. But she was getting to be a bit annoyed with Sophia. So it wasn't the future Sophia had planned, but why wouldn't her friend want *her* to be happy? They were like sisters, biology aside, so why wasn't she good enough for Marcus? True, she feared she couldn't have children and Sophia wanted an heir for Gabriel, but was an heir more important than two people one cared about finding love?

"The readers generally think it's immoral for a woman to carry on with a man who is not her husband," Dovedale observed. "It's the readers we aim to please, and they like to see a moral lesson. Bad behavior can't be rewarded."

"I think it's time we acknowledged that a number of novel readers, perhaps a vast number, are women, Mr. Dovedale," Eve said. "I doubt that women want to read about other women being stoned or thrown into the path of a train or swallowing poison, merely because they've fallen in love without the benefit of a marriage certificate. It might be time to try something new."

"That's not the kind of book *I* want to read," Sophia said, averting her gaze.

"Oh, Sophia, you're so old-fashioned." Alice rolled her eyes. "It's exactly what I would like to see. Eve, write it and you will be my hero."

The footmen started serving the curry that Eve had prepared with Mrs. Mallows, and conversation turned to the unusual new dish. Eve was grateful for the distraction. The last thing she wanted was to stir up more trouble between herself and her friends.

Twenty-two

"I SHOULD HAVE TAKEN THE TRAIN TO MEET HER."
Marcus paced, unable to settle his mind or body while
Eve was out there and Lawson remained unaccounted
for. "What if he went looking for her? What if he
found her?"

"She's due here any minute. You need to relax,"
Tom Reilly, seated calmly at his desk, urged his friend.
"If he wanted to hurt her, he would have done so by
now. There's been no sign of him at the Strumps'
house. Perhaps he fled the country to get away from
his wife. She sounds like an odious woman, by Mrs.
Kendal's account."

"Is that all supposed to sound comforting?" Marcus
cocked a brow. The bell rang, interrupting them, and
a minute later, Eve was standing right in front of him,
perfectly safe. He wanted to enfold her in his arms and
keep her there. Instead, he simply said hello.

"Marcus," she said. "I wasn't expecting you."

"You didn't expect me to let you conduct your
operation without me? My French accent is much
better than Reilly's. I actually know some French."

"But—there's no need. Tom and I have gone over everything."

"And Tom has gone over everything with me. If someone is going to be next to you coaxing a confession from cold-blooded killers, I want it to be me. Please, Eve. Let me help you."

She looked to Tom first, as if she needed his permission.

"He'll be good in the role. You two are more natural together." Tom shrugged.

"You're not staying at Averford House?" he asked her.

She shook her head. "I mean to get a room at the Langham. It's expensive, but I can manage for a day or two. Things didn't exactly go well with Sophia. She has been tolerating me while her friends, the Dovedales, are visiting, but we've agreed that I will be leaving Thornbrook Park in a matter of days."

"Leaving?" He closed the distance and reached out to her, unable to help himself. Even the feel of her sleeve under his hand was nearly too much to bear. How he wanted her in his arms! "Eve, I'm so sorry."

"It's for the best." She smiled. "I didn't plan to stay there forever. I've taken a position as the Dovedales' governess, provided I survive today."

"You'll survive. I'll see to it myself. A governess? Not what I expected. Does this mean you will be in London?" He tried not to look too hopeful.

"Yes. In time, maybe Sophia will forgive me. Have you spoken to your brother?"

"Ha." Marcus shook his head. "Does Gabriel have the power of speech? I hope I didn't hurt him too badly."

"His nose wasn't broken, no loose teeth. Thank goodness. Can you imagine how that might have affected his self-esteem?"

They laughed. It felt wonderful to laugh with her again. It was a start.

"I'm glad. I didn't stay around to see how he fared. I felt the need to depart immediately. I went to see Brandon, and then I came straight here to London. Brandon's thriving, at least. I'm not sure I'll be able to get the rest of the Coopers settled, but there's time to work something out."

"You're brothers. He will have to forgive you. I guess we really made a muddle of things." Eve's eyes were full of compassion. She really did care for him, if nothing else.

"I did. I should have told my brother from the start that I had no intention of marrying Lady Alice. It was about time I set him straight. Unfortunately, you had to pay the price for my bad judgment."

"We both made bad decisions. Do you mean it? That you won't marry Alice? Sophia is still counting on you."

"She'll give up eventually. I couldn't possibly marry Alice. Not while my heart is engaged elsewhere."

"I hate to interrupt, but we're running late." Tom Reilly had sneaked out of the office at some point during Marcus's conversation with Eve and now ducked his head back in. "We'll have to iron out the rest of the details in the car on the way over."

⁂

Eve struggled to listen while they finalized their plans.

She was to act her part as she'd established it with Leona Lawson, with Marcus playing along as her Comte Lestrange. Detective Brian Davis, an officer from Scotland Yard, would be going in with them, posing as the Comte's solicitor. And if he could manage it, Tom planned to sneak in the back while they had Leona Lawson distracted and search the place to see if he could find anything incriminating.

All she could think about were Marcus's words—that he couldn't possibly marry Alice while his heart was engaged elsewhere. With her? He had to mean that his heart was with her. He loved her? Truly? She couldn't wait to get him alone. They had so much to discuss.

"Comte Louis Lestrange," Marcus said. "A ridiculous name. It sounds too made up."

"I *did* make it up. I had to think of something fast, and it just came to me while I was in conversation with Leona. I figured she would be less likely to know a foreign visitor, and he had to sound wealthy. My French is a little out of practice."

"We'll have to remedy that." Marcus flashed her a grin that sent a tingle through her veins from top to toes. Paris? With Marcus? What a beautiful dream.

"We slipped some items in the paper, gossip section, to make it more believable. I don't think we'll have any problems," Tom said. "We checked out this Mr. Royce she mentions. He does not exist. At least, as far as we can tell. Our best guess is that she's bringing in an actor or a cohort to pose as this Mr. Royce to complete the con."

"We just need her, or Royce, to confirm that they

are selling you shares of the mine. We might be able to catch her on fraud with that."

"Don't we need to prove that she doesn't actually own the mine?" Eve asked.

"It should be easy enough to track that down once we get her to seal the deal. Overall, it would be best if we could somehow link her to the murder or catch her in a confession that she killed her husband, but that's not as likely," Detective Davis said. "The more solid our case, the better chance we have of her being convicted and imprisoned. And of course, we need to find her partner in crime."

"Oliver Lawson is still out there somewhere." Eve tried not to sound too concerned. Perhaps he had given up on trying to kill her.

"Once we have the wife in custody, he's sure to come around," Tom said, either to comfort her or to keep Marcus calm. "There has still been no sign of him. If he has managed to sneak into the house, we'll have to deal with that surprise as it unfolds."

"But there won't be much point in him trying to keep you quiet once their scheme has been revealed," Detective Davis said. "I believe you will be quite safe after today, provided all goes well."

Eve liked the sound of that, and so did Marcus, it seemed, from the way he laced fingers with hers.

"Here we are. Are you ready to be my paramour, *ma chérie*?" he asked, a tender look in his eyes.

"I'm ready," she said, though she knew he referred only to their playacting for Mrs. Lawson. "Let's go, Comte Lestrange."

"*Allons!*" Marcus assumed character. He'd donned

a cloak over his formal wear and added a silk top hat. Eve wasn't sure he looked French, but the cloak and hat did add a touch of extravagance.

They stepped out in front of the Strumps' house, and he surprised her by turning her in his arms and delivering a slow, lingering kiss, taking her breath away.

"For effect," he whispered in her ear before releasing her. "In case anyone is watching."

"Of course." Eve took a minute to find her footing and head to the front door.

Tom stayed with the driver in the car but Detective Davis got out and followed along, trying to look the dutiful servant to his comte.

Eve rang the bell. Mr. Gerald, the butler, answered. "I hope you've been expecting us," she said.

"Yes. Mrs. Strump is in the drawing room. I will show you in."

He led them past the parlor where Eve had been seated before and down a short corridor to a drawing room adorned with even more gilded furnishings, knickknacks, and figurines. Right inside the door stood a miniature statue of a naked cherub—gilded, of course.

"Mrs. Strump," Eve said. "How are you? Better, I hope, than the last time we met?"

Leona sat alone on the rococo sofa, the cherub motif repeated in carvings on the legs of the end tables and even smaller gilded cherubs on the tabletops. No sign of Mr. Royce.

"One day at a time," Leona said, rising for introductions. "You know how it is, unfortunately."

"Ah, but past misfortune has given way to new

happiness," Eve said, a little too gaily perhaps. "Now I have my comte. Might I present Comte Louis Lestrange?"

Gerald had taken Marcus's cloak and hat, but Marcus looked every bit as suave without the trappings. Had he darkened his hair? Eve was surprised she hadn't noticed it earlier, but she'd been so overwhelmed simply to see him again.

"*Enchanté, ma jolie.*" Marcus took Leona's hand and kissed it. "*Et,* may I present, *mon avocat,* Monsieur Bolange." His accent *was* impeccable, Eve noted. Perhaps they would pull this off.

Detective Davis stepped forward and gave a curt bow.

"Oh, your *avocat*? I didn't know we were expecting a third. Mr. Royce couldn't make it, but he has left me his power of attorney. Would you like to see the papers? I'm free to act on his behalf."

"Louis won't go anywhere without his solicitor these days," Eve stage-whispered. "The divorce, you know. Can't be too careful, though he barely speaks a word of English. And your brother? Will he be joining us?"

Leona shook her head. "Sadly, no. He has also been detained."

Eve felt relieved not to have to see Mr. Lawson again, particularly since he could have recognized Marcus, but it would have been better if they'd been able to catch the Lawsons together.

"Shall we talk business, then?" Eve said, eager to move things along.

"*Non.*" Marcus clapped his hands, surprising her. "No business wizout ze pleasure first, eh? Bolange, *le vin, s'il vous plait.*"

Eve guessed he was giving Tom time to try to find a way in through the back, and keeping the butler in the room with them wasn't a bad idea, either. Detective Davis stepped forward with the case he held and extracted a bottle of Bordeaux. Eve wondered what else he had in there—handcuffs, a weapon? She could hope.

"What a lovely idea." Leona nodded in agreement. "It's a little early for wine, perhaps, but why not? A toast to our new venture. Gerald, open the wine and bring the glasses."

While Gerald poured, Marcus pulled Eve closer to him, a possessive hand around her waist, and dropped a kiss on her cheek. "*Ma petite chou-fleur.* You will have to excuse me, Madame Strump. I haven't seen enough of *ma chérie* these past few days. *Nous parlon de diamants?*"

"We've been together all morning, darling," Eve said, shaking her head. "Not in front of Mrs. Strump. We're doing business. I'm sorry, Mrs. Strump. Frenchmen."

"Oh, I understand. I don't mind at all."

"He wants to know more about the diamond mine," Eve translated, taking her best guess.

"Certainly, shall we sit?" Leona gestured at the sofa and settled in a chair next to them. Detective Davis remained standing, causing Leona to look at him.

"Oh, Monsieur Bolange never sits in the Comte's presence without permission." Eve made it up as she went along. "And he won't have any wine."

The butler passed around the glasses to the rest of them.

"*A votre santé!*" Marcus said, raising his glass. They all followed suit. Eve took a small sip, eager to keep her wits about her.

Leona showed no such inclination, taking a hearty gulp. Perhaps she needed fortification to con a fortune out of supposedly unsuspecting fools. "Mmm. Very nice vintage."

"*Maintenant, de retour aux affaires. Les diamants?*"

"Ah, now he is ready to talk business," Eve translated.

"Excellent." Leona downed her wine, put down the glass, picked up her own case of papers, and pulled out a map. "Here's the mine."

She pointed to a spot, circled in ink, in central India. "Golkonda. I know it." Eve nodded. "I've never been, but I remember Ben embarking on a trip there once. Perhaps it was with your Mr. Royce."

"He does spend time there to check on operations. Maintenance costs are low, and workers come cheap. Yields are high, though, and so are profits." Next she presented some papers that Marcus pretended to look over carefully before handing them to Detective Davis.

Davis nodded at Marcus, and Marcus looked back to Leona. "Impressive."

"You'll get a twenty percent return on investment in the worst of times, Comte Lestrange. And in the best? I've seen as much as forty percent."

Davis leaned over and whispered in Marcus's ear. Marcus pretended to be annoyed and waved him off. "He says zis is unheard of, ze forty percent."

Leona nodded. "I know it's hard to believe, but we're talking diamonds, Comte. And you know the value of diamonds, I'm sure. With such yields as this."

For the pièce de résistance, Leona pulled out a small, blue velvet pouch and dumped the contents on the table. Diamonds. A fortune's worth, if they were real. Davis produced a jeweler's loupe and examined one of the larger stones, then nodded at Marcus.

"I am, how do you say, windblown by zese results, Madame Strump."

"I think he means blown away," Eve offered, smiling at Marcus. He was quite the charlatan. She would have to keep that in mind.

"Yes, of course. So was I, at first. But as I was telling your… um, Mrs. Kendal, we bought this house with our profits from the mine. A lowly solicitor can't afford such splendor, as you can imagine." She gestured around her. "No offense to Monsieur Bolange."

Eve's gaze followed Leona's waving arms around the room and noticed the bookshelf across the way. It was only a quarter of the way filled, which was no surprise. But at the end of one shelf, holding up a few volumes of law manuals, was a lone gilded bookend. A monkey. Eve knew then that they could tie Leona Lawson to the murder of Edgar Strump.

She breathed deeply to calm her nerves as her heartbeat sped to double time. She nudged Marcus and tried to gesture, but he was engaging Leona in conversation about yields and ratios, and how much he could possibly invest at once without a report being filed to draw attention.

Eve got up to stretch. "Oh, that wine is making me sleepy. Forgive me, darling, I think I need to take a turn about the room."

"Go on." Leona waved her off. "Your comte and I will talk business while you walk."

Eve strolled over and casually lifted the gilded

monkey off the shelf, taking care that the books didn't topple behind it. Yes, it had considerable weight.

"What a strange bookend," Eve said, interrupting the conversation to show the others. "Have you a pair? Louis collects curiosities, do you not, *mon ange*? He would be interested in purchasing them, perhaps."

She brought the bookend over to show him, and Leona bristled uncomfortably in her chair.

"What do you think, Monsieur Bolange?" Marcus handed Detective Davis the monkey bookend. "Should we offer a fair price?"

They never even had to complete the mine transaction. In a flash, Detective Davis drew a pistol and dropped his bag.

Leona's eyes went wide. Oh yes, she knew. Eve had found proof that the murder weapon had come from the Strumps' house. Leona's reaction confirmed all suspicion. She bolted from the room toward the back of the house, but Tom Reilly brought her back into the room not a minute later, holding her arms pinned behind her back. He must have been lying in wait after getting a look around the place. Davis shackled her and sat her back down in the overstuffed white chair trimmed in gold braid.

"I didn't kill anyone, especially not my husband," she blurted out.

"Because your husband is still alive. Isn't that right, Mrs. Lawson?" Tom asked.

"I–I don't know what you mean." Her face registered alarm as she realized that he called her Mrs. Lawson instead of Mrs. Strump.

"Your marriage to Edgar Strump was never legal,"

Davis observed. "We have fraud charges stemming from that, at the very least, but a little more investigation into this diamond-mine fiasco should net more charges. And then we have murder…"

"I got lucky sneaking in the back way," Tom added. "I found what must have been Mr. Strump's study. The murder certainly occurred there. There's a pool of dried blood on a carpet hidden under another rug. In the desk, I found papers to connect the Lawsons and Mr. Strump to a con operation involving the mine, plus lists of investors. Oh, we have a solid case, Mrs. Lawson. A very solid case, I assure you."

Mrs. Lawson's eyes widened with the sudden realization that she was facing prison. "But I didn't kill him. It was Oliver. All of it was Oliver's idea. Once that woman came asking questions, she made Edgar suspicious. When Edgar confronted Oliver… And now Oliver's left me here to take the blame, just like he did ten years ago."

"And where is Mr. Lawson now?" Marcus asked.

"I don't know. I swear! He left ages ago, after killing Edgar, to take care of her." She pointed at Eve. "With all those questions she asked, he feared she would go to the authorities and ruin our lives with another investigation. But clearly, she's still alive and he never came back. Maybe you should ask her what she has done with my Oliver. Did you kill him, Mrs. Kendal? Before he could get you? Is that it?"

"I have no idea where your husband went after he tried to attack me," Eve said, smiling at Marcus. "Lucky for me, I had someone to look out for me."

"It was my pleasure, my little cauliflower." Marcus

wrapped a protective arm around her waist and Eve didn't mind it at all.

"Ah, *petite chou-fleur*. I was wondering what that particular term of endearment meant. I couldn't come up with the translation."

"It's the only French endearment I could remember on the spot."

"You're not even French!" Leona gasped, insult added to injury.

After that, it didn't take much to get the whole story out of Leona Lawson. How Edgar Strump had kept watch for potential investors. How Oliver Lawson would explain the operation and show off a real working mine in India, claiming ownership, and then display the diamonds they supposedly mined out, actually purchased at a deep discount from a past associate, a London fence.

"Oliver masterminded the whole idea of the mine and everything from using Edgar Strump to lure potential investors to insisting I marry Edgar to keep him complacent. But it wasn't enough. When Edgar found out that we really didn't own the mine, after Mrs. Kendal came around, he threatened to put an end to the scam and tell all the investors. That's when Oliver did it."

"Did what? Where, exactly? How did it happen?"

"In Edgar's study. Edgar demanded a list of all the investors so he could tell them the truth. Then he realized that he had a list—of the people he had referred to rent from Oliver. That's when Oliver came up behind him and whacked him on the back of the head."

"With the monkey bookend," Detective Davis confirmed.

Leona nodded.

"Then he ordered me to clean up while he took the body to the river. I didn't realize the bloody oaf had taken the one bookend but not the other."

"Thank you, Mrs. Lawson. You've been very helpful," Tom said.

"You're not French either, are you?" She flashed what must have been her come-hither stare in Tom's direction. "But you're adorable. I shouldn't be in jail very long, and once they hang Oliver for murder, I'll be single. Look me up in two to four years."

"I'll see you at the trial, where I will testify against you from the witness stand," Tom said. "That's as close as we're going to get."

Twenty-three

"CONGRATULATIONS, YOU'VE DONE IT." MARCUS leaned to kiss Eve on the cheek gently, as if fearing a rebuff. "Your plan worked. We have Mrs. Lawson, and she and her husband will be locked away where they belong as soon as we find him."

"We did it." She smiled at him as they stood outside the Strump house and watched Leona being carted away by Scotland Yard. "I couldn't have done it without you."

"And your fabulous French accent. I couldn't have mastered it in time." Reilly shook his head. "No, you two are great together. And in better news, we've recovered a listing of all their accounts and frozen them, the ones in England anyway. The ones in other countries will take some time to shut down. The money will be used to repay their victims. Like the next of kin for one Captain Benjamin Kendal, who entrusted the Lawsons with eight thousand pounds, according to their records, which are now in our hands."

"Thanks to you, snooping around in Strump's

study. Well done, Tom." Marcus clapped Tom on the back.

"Eight thousand pounds?" Eve couldn't hide her astonishment. "It's more than I dreamed we had. I'm going to get back all eight thousand pounds?"

"It might take some time to clear through the courts and whatnot," Tom said. "But yes, by this time next year, you should be very comfortable. Probably much sooner."

"It's wonderful." Eve couldn't believe her good fortune. She would get her money back after all. She had everything she would need. "I have enough to live on fairly well until I get my money. I don't need to rely on the charity of friends any longer."

She felt free, freer than she'd felt in years. She hugged Tom and then hugged Marcus. She wanted to hug the world and shout at the top of her lungs. *Free!* But she managed to contain herself.

"The person I want most to share this with is here by my side." She turned to Marcus.

"You mean me?"

"Of course I do, my Comte Lestrange. You've been so supportive and kind. And…" She couldn't really say much more with Tom standing right next to them. "And wonderful. Thank you."

"I'm really glad you feel that way." He pulled her closer to him, an arm around her waist.

"Well, that's all wrapped up," Tom said, staring off as the car containing Leona Strump drove toward Scotland Yard. "We should go celebrate."

"I hate to say it, but the only place I want to be is Thornbrook Park," Eve said, peeking up through her lashes, a little afraid to see Marcus's reaction. "I feel that I can meet my friends on more equal terms now, no longer a charity case. I need to tell the Dovedales that I no longer wish to work for them."

"You don't want to be a governess?" Marcus had the consideration to mock surprise, at least.

"No, I want to be a writer, and now I have the means to find a place of my own, take my time, and finish my novel."

"It's going to be splendid," Marcus said.

"I hope so. I'll never know until I finish." She leaned her head against his shoulder, savoring the feel of his solidity beside her. It didn't escape her notice that they were more equal now, too. She was no longer an impoverished widow. She was a woman who had the means to choose any life she wanted.

At some point, she would have to screw up her courage and confess that she wanted him. But first, they had relationships to repair. "I need to patch things up with Sophia. As soon as possible. I hate the way things are between us, and I need to go back and try to work things out with her one more time."

"I understand." Marcus nodded. "But don't think I'll let you ride the train alone again with that lunatic Lawson still out there unaccounted for."

"You heard Detective Davis. I'm probably safe now. But you would come back to Thornbrook Park with me? I would be so happy if you and Gabriel could reach accord."

"We will, eventually. I'm not sure I'm ready to see him again just now. But I will go to Tilly Meadow Farm and check on Brandon. At the end of the week,

I want to bring him back to visit with his mother and show her that he's truly thriving."

"Speaking of Prudence, I'm headed over to the Coopers' place now," Tom said. "They'll be up for a celebration if you two insist on leaving me right away."

"We do," Marcus affirmed. "We're going straight to Thornbrook Park. Give my regards to Prudence and the family. Tell them I'll visit again soon."

The ride on the train was a much more pleasant one than their previous ride, though Eve was full of nerves. "I'm more nervous to face my own dear friend again than I was to face Leona Lawson."

"Take a deep breath." Marcus rubbed her shoulders. "You will find the words."

"But what if she still refuses to forgive me? And the Dovedales? They will be so disappointed to have to continue their search for a governess."

"They will manage. You have a novel to write. You'll be far too busy to be looking after someone else's children."

"I was looking forward to being with children, though." She hazarded a look at him as she approached the topic. It might make all the difference in the world to him, if he planned on resuming their romance. She thought it only fair she let him know. "I'm not sure I can have my own. Six years with Ben, and no pregnancies. Our doctor never found anything wrong with me, but I suspect I could be barren."

She feared he might push her away at the news, but he only hugged her closer. "Without a proper diagnosis, I'm not sure you can come to that conclusion. Perhaps the time was never right. Perhaps it had something to do with Ben. Perhaps all kinds of things. But I'm sure it's something that a man who loves you could accept without hesitation."

"You think so?" She turned to him, hopeful. This was turning out to be a much better day than the previous days of her week. "I'm glad to hear another opinion on it."

They rode in silence for the rest of the journey back, but this time it was a comfortable, companionable silence instead of a cold and lonely one.

❧

Marcus had insisted on seeing her all the way to Thornbrook Park before taking the cab back to Tilly Meadow Farm.

"Stay safe. Don't go out alone. Stay in after dark," he warned, opening her door and helping her out.

She laughed. "I believe we have nothing to worry about now."

"Good luck, Eve. I hope everything goes well for you with Sophia." He bowed his head to hers solemnly. "I have so much more I want to say to you, but it's going to have to wait. You need to straighten things out here first. And then maybe there will be time for us. We'll do things more properly this time. In London? I'm headed back there in a few days with Brandon. We could meet at Averford House. I'll be looking for my own place soon, but Averford House is still home for now. As long as I'm there, you will be my honored guest, no matter what happens with Sophia."

"Averford House," Eve agreed. "I will meet you there."

It seemed odd to be standing with him there on the driveway outside Thornbrook Park. So much had changed between them, but still so much was the same. They would have a chance to do things right, perhaps. A second chance. Her heart soared with hope for their future. He enfolded her in his embrace and held her tightly for more than a minute. But he did not kiss her. Without another word, he turned and got back in the car.

"Give my love to Brandon," she said. "I hope you find him well."

Mr. Finch opened the door. "Welcome back, Mrs. Kendal. A pleasure to have you with us again."

"Thank you, Mr. Finch." He took her coat.

"Lady Averford is in the drawing room with Mrs. Dovedale and Lady Alice."

"Oh." She needed to get Sophia alone to say what she had to say. "I'm going to head up to her sitting room. If you could discreetly manage to alert her and send her to me there? I have something I need to say to her. Privately."

"Of course. You can count on me." He winked conspiratorially, an unexpected touch from the normally staid butler. "She will be with you shortly."

Eve paced as she waited, trying to form the words. She would start with another apology, mention what Sophia has meant to her all through the years, perhaps refer to their girlhood and hope that nostalgia might tug at Sophia's heartstrings, and end with a promise to be loyal and devoted and honest with her friend for the rest of their lives. It could work. She hoped so. How she missed her friend, especially after all that had happened! The one thing she wouldn't do was promise to give up Marcus. It wouldn't be fair to either of them. He had no future with Alice.

A minute later, the door flew open and Sophia swept in. "Eve!"

"Sophia?"

"Eve." Sophia hugged her. "I'm so glad you've come back. You left me bereft. I could hardly pass a moment without thinking about how horribly I've behaved and wishing you back so I could apologize."

"So you could apologize? But I'm the one who is so very sorry."

"No. No, no." Sophia shook her head vehemently. "It is I. To think that you had to keep your love a secret because you feared what I would think. It should never have come to that. Never. You're my best friend."

"And you're mine."

"Still? You'll forgive me?"

Eve felt tears welling. Sophia's tears were already running. "Of course I forgive you. If you can forgive me."

"I do. I'm happy for you, Eve. You should have love in your life. To love again! It doesn't come easily, does it? And here you had it, and I wouldn't let you enjoy it. Marcus is a good man. Though, you won't hear me say it around Gabriel just now." She placed a finger to her lips. "But of course you're good together."

"We're not together, exactly. Not now. Perhaps one day. I'm certainly not giving up."

"I'm glad. He loves you, Eve. I know he does."

"How do you know?"

"Once Gabriel and I finally got to talking about what happened between him and Marcus, it was oh so clear that the man loves you. He was defending your honor and refusing to give you up."

"Oh? Was that it?" What had Gabriel said about her that Marcus had to defend her honor, she wondered, but wouldn't ask. They were friends. Better that she didn't know. "Refusing to give me up?"

"Even under threat of losing his inheritance. That's love."

"We certainly care for one another, but—so much has happened. I want to tell you all about it."

"And I want to hear. Should we go down? Is it a story you can share with the others?"

"I suppose I had better, since I no longer care to be the Dovedales' governess."

"Thank goodness." Sophia laughed. "I was hoping you would give up such a scheme. Even when I was angry with you, I wanted to stop you. I wouldn't wish working for Lizzy on my worst enemy."

"She's not so bad," Eve said.

"In small doses," Sophia allowed. "I'm enjoying her visit but I can't imagine living with her all the time. Let alone taking orders from her. Come along. Let's share the good news."

Downstairs, Eve told them all about her solicitor's murder—taking part in the deception that trapped Leona Lewis, getting her to confess, recovering Eve's fortune, and even Marcus's fantastic French accent.

"He loves you," Alice said, obviously pleased with the turn of events. "I knew it. I could tell. What man would go to such trouble and care for a woman he didn't love? And you were so intent to pair me with Captain Thorne, Sophia. It would never have worked. The last man I would marry is one who looks so much like your husband."

He loves me? Eve thought, trying it on. *He loves me.* She liked the sound of it. She hoped it were true.

"What's wrong with my husband?"

"Nothing, but he's a brother to me. So his brother feels like my brother. And besides all that, he's yours."

"That he is," Sophia smiled, a tad uneasily. "All mine."

"But it's wonderful that you will have your fortune back," Lizzy Dovedale said. "I couldn't be happier for you. We'll find another governess."

"I hope you will. Thank you." Eve was so happy to be back at Thornbrook Park. How sad she would have been without Sophia's friendship. "Now if you'll excuse me, I need to go in search of Lord Averford."

"Gabriel? What do you want with him?" Sophia seemed surprised.

"A word about his brother. Someone has to convince them to work out their differences. I thought I would give it a try."

"Well, good luck," Sophia said. "It will be a miracle if you can manage where I have failed, but all things are possible, as you've proven by recovering your fortune. The men got back from birding a short while ago. He's most likely to be in his study."

⁓

Eve knocked and waited. Maybe he wasn't there.

"Come in," he said a second later in his authoritative

tones. She almost changed her mind, but she thought of Marcus.

"Good day, Lord Averford." She entered and walked up to his desk. "I would like a word with you."

He cocked a brow, so like his brother. "Have a seat. I see you're back. Did you come alone?"

"I had an escort. Your brother is a gentleman and insisted on escorting me here, though he wouldn't come in."

"Of course not." Gabriel smirked and pointed to his eye. "Too bad. He will miss the chance to get a look at his handiwork before it fades."

"I'm afraid you have the wrong idea about me, Lord Averford, after all that has happened with Captain Thorne."

He shook his head. "No. You're lovely, Mrs. Kendal. No one could fault you for falling under the spell of a lothario. It happens sometimes."

"A lothario? Marcus?" She laughed. "What an unfair characterization. It couldn't be further from the truth. No wonder he hit you."

"Excuse me?"

"You deserved it, bossing him around, expecting him to fall into line. Threatening to take away his inheritance? You are a bully, Lord Averford. I forgive you for it. I know you're a good man, and I know you were only trying to help Sophia get over her pain. She told me about your son."

"Edward." He nodded. "Our son, Edward. I haven't spoken of him in years, and suddenly I've said his name several times in the past month. It feels good, you know, to speak of him. I hate feeling like he's some sort of secret that needs to be buried because it pains Sophia to think of him."

"Perhaps you need to tell her that. It might not hurt her to speak of him, too. She finally told me about him. I had no idea. She's still grieving the loss."

"She blames me. I buried him before I told her that he'd died. I only wanted her to be strong enough to bear the news."

"She thinks you blame her, too. You two really need to talk about him. But I leave that to you. I came to talk about Marcus. You can hardly blame him for how he behaved, as wrong as his methods might have been."

"Beating me? And you call me the bully."

"We both know who the bully is between the two of you, Lord Averford. You're older and in control of the estate, and you used your power to try to intimidate him. But Marcus isn't that same boy who used to fear you. I hope you can handle that. And you only goaded him into hitting you because you mistakenly believed yourself to still be the physically dominant one of the two of you."

"Goaded him, did I? You weren't here."

"Marcus wouldn't have hit you without provocation, Lord Averford. We both know it. I'm not here to rehash your argument. I simply wanted you to know what you're missing in not repairing your relationship with your brother. He's a good man, Lord Averford. Kind and tenderhearted, but strong and fiercely protective of the ones he loves."

"You don't say." Averford rubbed his jaw where there was still some light bruising.

"I have a feeling he gets that from you, actually. I don't know what he was like when you were boys, regretfully. But I know the man he is now, and he takes my breath away. You should see him with Brandon, the way he cares for the boy. He takes his responsibility toward the Coopers very seriously."

"I know," Averford agreed. "It's commendable."

"And he's the only brother you've got. The way I see it, you would be fools not to make up with one another. I don't have my family anymore and I miss them all the time. What I wouldn't give for my brother to contact me."

"I'm sorry for your situation, Mrs. Kendal. It's a damn shame for your family to be missing out on you. I'll take what you have said under consideration. That's as much as you're going to get out of me for now."

"Fair enough. I'll take it. Thank you for listening to what I had to say."

"Mrs. Kendal?"

"Yes?"

"For the record, I think my brother is a very lucky man to have your love. I hope things work out for the two of you."

"Thank you." Eve smiled to herself as she closed the door and walked off down the hall to rejoin her friends.

Twenty-four

THE NEXT DAY WITHOUT MARCUS PASSED SLOWLY, though Eve had a wonderful time catching up with her friends. She felt his absence acutely, and Thornbrook Park wasn't the same without him. At dinner, she informed Sophia that she would be headed to London, to Averford House, sooner than planned.

"I wish you all the best, my dear," Sophia said. "I hope you find what you need."

In the morning, she overslept and arrived in London later in the day than she'd planned. By the time she got to Averford House, she heard from Sutton that Marcus had already come and gone.

"Do you know where I can find him? Or when he might be back?"

"I believe he was spending the day with the Coopers, but I don't have their address. Brandon was with him."

"Good." She nodded. "His mother will be happy to see him."

Not in the mood to shop or walk around London,

she settled in the library with a book, hoping Marcus would return home soon.

Hours later, Sutton found her still with the book to share the news that they had a guest, a friend who had been with Marcus, Mr. Tom Reilly.

"Mrs. Kendal? What a lovely surprise." Tom smiled in a way that set her at ease, his gray eyes twinkling. He held his hat in his hands. "I came to meet Marcus. I had afternoon appointments and I thought we were to meet back here, but it seems he went ahead without me. Or perhaps he left straight from the Coopers and assumed I would figure it out."

"Figure what out? Where do you think he's gone?"

"He made arrangements for one final fight at the Hog and Hound before he heads into retirement from prizefighting."

"Retirement? It's his last fight?"

"Yes. I don't think he was expecting you until tomorrow."

She shook her head. "He wasn't. I came early."

"So you did. I wouldn't wait up. These things go late. I hate to run off, but he's expecting me."

"Mr. Reilly." She crossed her arms. "If you think I mean to sit here tapping my foot until he comes home, you're mistaken. I want to watch him fight."

"At the Hog and Hound? It's not quite a suitable venue for a lady, Mrs. Kendal. He'll have my head."

"Wouldn't he prefer to know that you escorted me safely rather than that I set out on my own just as soon you left?"

Tom sighed. "It seems I'm doomed one way or the other. Get your coat. I'll hail us a cab."

∼⌒∽

Marcus had planned to meet Tom at Averford House, but he had a change of plans when Prudence gave Brandon her blessing to attend the match.

"This one last night," Prudence said. "He's obviously getting on so well at the farm, and he loves it so. Thank you, Marcus, for taking care of my boy. Bring him home in one piece. I mean to have him sleep under his own roof tonight, late as it is, and tomorrow, too. I miss him. You can bring him back to the farm another day."

"A few days," Marcus agreed. "Mrs. Dennehy said she could spare him and that she would take care of Scout while he's gone."

"I can't wait to meet her," Prudence said, and they were off.

Marcus figured that Tom would know to meet them at the Hog and Hound when he didn't find Marcus at Averford House. But Tom would have to settle for being a spectator. For tonight's match, Brandon was going to be Marcus's second.

Thanks to Eve, there was no rage left in him, only a demand for satisfaction. He was no longer the same man who needed to beat something senseless or to take punches just to ease his troubled mind. Being at Thornbrook Park had helped to heal him. *Being with Eve*.

Unfortunately, possessing all of his mental faculties made it nearly impossible to stare across the ring at Smithy Harris and not be more intimidated than usual. The man was enormous. Marcus reminded himself that he had beaten Harris in the past, and he could best him again.

"Brains over brawn, eh, Brandon?" He had taught young Brandon that one didn't back down from a challenge, and he meant to prove himself triumphant.

Tom finally appeared at the side of the ring, holding out Marcus's gloves. He took them. American rules weren't quite as appealing with his knuckles still bruised from Gabriel's stony jaw. "Thank you. Aren't you going to come on up? Have a seat in my corner?"

Tom shook his head. "Not today. I don't want Brandon to feel I'm supervising. You're in good hands. I'll be in the crowd."

Before Marcus could protest, Tom was off like a shot. Marcus supposed Brandon was all the support he needed. He stripped down as the crowd cheered and whistled, took his corner, and waited for Jameson to call the crowd to order. Jameson called for seconds and young Brandon stepped up in the ring. He shook hands with the troll Augustus Hantz, haggled with Jameson, and came back with a look of triumph on his face.

"American rules." Brandon crossed his arms over his chest.

"Really?" Damned impressive for the kid to win Jameson over to American rules, after all the times Tom had failed. Why did it have to be now? "Isn't that the way of it, then?"

"No. I'm joking with you." Brandon laughed. "I tried, but they were having none of it. Queensbury rules. Get your gloves on."

Marcus tried not to sigh with relief. "Queensbury it is."

"Well," Brandon said, once Marcus was ready.

"What are you just standing there for? Dance around. Warm up. Just like you're always telling me. Do you want to be an easy target?"

Marcus bounced from foot to foot, trying to get worked up, trying to get angry remembering Oliver Lawson poised behind Eve, knife raised. At last, he began to feel it, not the black, mind-numbing rage, but a good solid wave of righteous anger. Anger would serve. He jumped around taking swings at the air.

"Good," said Brandon. "Stay solid."

The crowd began to chant, some calling out for Thorne, some for Harris. For once, Marcus was minutely aware of every little thing that went on outside the ring. The whips came down to drive the crowd from the ring's edges and Jameson called his name, an introduction. He held up his hands to the crowd. A few of them applauded. Next, Jameson called out Harris, and the crowd erupted with cheers and exclamations. They loved Smithy Harris. For the first time, Marcus realized that the crowds were there not to support him, but to see him beat.

"You're going down, Harris." He pointed at his opponent. If he couldn't win them over with size or power, he would have to rely on bravado. He pumped his gloves together. He could hear his name now from the crowd, their chants a little louder. Perhaps he had won over a few of them.

Harris merely laughed, a deep throaty rumble that swayed any few Marcus had inspired back to Harris's corner. Doubt him, did they? He would fight harder to win them over. He simply wasn't going to be taken down.

As soon as the bell rang, he pounced with a right jab that took Harris by surprise but only seemed to fuel the blacksmith's lust for Marcus's blood. Harris lunged. Marcus sprung backward. Harris delivered a solid hook, but Marcus ducked and came up behind him. Marcus rained some light punches on the giant's chest, but weaved and dodged a one-two solid return. The bell rang. Marcus went back to his corner.

"Some nimble footwork out there," Brandon encouraged him as he handed him his water. "Keep it up."

Back in the ring, Marcus faced Harris with a jab-hook-jab combination that sent the giant staggering for all of a second before he steamed forward with retribution blows headed for Marcus's jaw. Marcus bobbed, ducked, danced, and ended up back in front of Harris with a square blow to the chest and one that landed straight between the giant's eyes. Harris wobbled on his feet but then seemed to get his bearings. He landed a crooked punch to Marcus's chin as the bell rang to end the round.

"Just keep wearing him down." Brandon sponged at the blood dotting the corner of Marcus's lips. "Remember to keep moving. Don't let him get you next time."

"Sure, boss." Marcus tried to smile but his mouth was tight with swelling. "I'll try."

"He's been favoring his left side. You might try coming at him from the right."

"Thanks." Marcus felt warmth spreading in his chest and knew it was his pride in Brandon. The lad made a capable second.

The bell rang again. Marcus had never been so aware of the crowd, the noise, and his opponent. He was used to looking at everything through a black haze, but it was all so clear to him suddenly.

He didn't run at Harris directly this time. He came at him from the right, as Brandon recommended, and he noticed the bruising under Harris's right eye, where he knew he had not laid a glove. Someone else had landed a blow there recently. It was a weakness that Marcus could manipulate, and he needed all the help he could get. He jabbed, ducked, danced to the left, and came at Harris from the right with a sound left hook. Harris never saw it coming. Marcus slammed his gloved fist directly into Harris's jaw and Harris swayed, steadied, swayed again, and went down.

Jameson leaned over him, counting, "Ten, nine, eight, seven, six." Marcus breathed heavily from exertion as Harris managed to lift his head and groan, then drop his head back to the mat. "Five, four, three, two, one." Jameson lifted Marcus's arm, his win confirmed. "Knockout! Thorne wins the match!"

Brandon couldn't manage to stay in his corner as Marcus was pronounced the champion. He ran at Marcus and hugged him around the waist, unconcerned with the film of perspiration Marcus had worked up.

"You won! I knew you would."

"I'm sorry, Brandon," Marcus said, meeting Brandon's gaze. "I appreciate your support, but I know you probably would have liked filling your pockets more."

"What do you mean? You won!"

"Yes, but—"

"I bet on you, you dolt. This time, I took my chances on you."

"Oh." Marcus smiled. That Brandon believed in him enough to bet on him, even after Marcus went down to Harris last time, meant the world to him. "Now what did I tell you about placing wagers? I believe I've warned you against it, young man."

"Pfft." Brandon rolled his eyes. "I'll stop when you stop."

Marcus nodded. "Good answer. We've both just retired from boxing and betting."

After the thrill of the fight and the win, he didn't need it any more. In his mind, he knew what he wanted. He wanted Eve. And he meant to have his chance. Eve was worth any risk.

❧

Tom Reilly hadn't wanted to bring Eve to a rough place like the Hog and Hound, but she had insisted. How could she stay away?

Seeing Marcus in the ring, stripped down to his bare chest, she felt overcome by a sudden wave of longing. That man, the mass of muscle and sinew before her eyes, was the man she'd given herself to time and again. The memories gave her a secret thrill.

It was too late to say anything to Marcus before the match, and Tom Reilly kept her a safe distance from the ring, insisting that Marcus would personally hold him responsible, should anything happen to her. No matter. She could see well enough from their seats at the back of the room. She watched Marcus jab at the air, bouncing from foot to foot, as he waited for his opponent to climb into the ring with him.

A young man in shirtsleeves and tweed trousers, his brown hair falling into his eyes, offered Marcus a pair of gloves. When Marcus smiled and took the gloves, she could see the pride shining in his eyes from across the room.

"He let Brandon Cooper in the ring with him? Is it safe?" she whispered to Tom.

"He wouldn't let any harm come to the boy. He loves him like his own."

"I see." She could tell that they'd grown very comfortable with one another, young Cooper and Marcus Thorne. And then, her gaze caught on another man just climbing over the ropes. More like stepping. He was tall enough that he didn't really need to climb, exactly, and so thick with muscle that he made Marcus look like a schoolboy. A cold bolt of fear shot down her spine. She reached for Tom's arm.

"Tell me that's not his opponent."

"Smithy Harris, that's him all right."

"Marcus means to fight him? The man's a giant, like something out of a story book." She stood and called out. "No, stop! Stop the match!"

Tom tugged at the hem of her coat, encouraging her to sit back down. "Hush."

"Mr. Reilly, this can't go on. He'll—he'll be killed." And before she even had a chance to tell Marcus that she loved him.

"He has faced Smithy Harris before, don't you fret."

"And won?"

Tom laughed. "Well, not exactly. Once, it was

a sort of a draw. Marcus managed to tire Harris out before he could land a solid punch. And the next time, Harris laid Marcus flat. I think he felt that one for a week afterward, maybe more."

"Oh, but Tom." The two fighters walked toward each other in the ring. She bit her lip nervously. She didn't want to look, but she couldn't look away. "Marcus!"

"It hasn't even started yet," Tom explained. "Just introductions. It doesn't start until after the bell rings."

"Then, there's still time to stop them." Her heart raced, frantic.

"Not a chance." Tom put his arm around her to keep her calm, or to keep her seated. She wasn't sure which.

Then the bell did ring, and she felt helpless, cringing with every jab at the man she—oh yes, she knew now for certain—the man she loved. As soon as this was over, if he lived, then she would tell him. There was no use wasting another moment.

The bell rang again, and Marcus remained on his feet. She applauded. "That's it, then? It's over? He's survived."

"That's just the first round," Tom said. "I never should have brought you here. I should have known that you couldn't bear it. Let me take you home."

She straightened up, determined. "No. I'll contain my nerves. I'm sorry. I can bear it. I will."

When the bell rang again, she almost changed her mind. And then, Marcus started to get some hits in and duck and weave and practically dance around the ring, away from Harris, and she was transfixed. She focused on his movements, on his body.

"He's magnificent," she said, with awe, unaware she'd even said it out loud.

"Yes, he is." Tom laughed. "He's doing a remarkable job."

"He is, isn't he?" The bell rang again and she watched him with Brandon, how well they interacted, how they even seemed to share the same gestures. They were so completely together in the fight. Brandon wasn't throwing punches, but he seemed as invested in the outcome as the fighter himself.

The bell rang again, and the fighting commenced. Marcus had a look of deadly focus in his eyes, and suddenly Eve thought Smithy Harris should be the one to be afraid. Not a few seconds later, Marcus landed an incredible smash to Harris's jaw and the giant fell to the mat. The countdown began.

"Knockout! Thorne wins the match!"

Eve and Tom jumped to their feet. They hugged. They cheered.

"That was nothing short of amazing," Eve said, in a mix of pride and wonder as she struggled to catch her breath.

"We can go and see him as soon as the crowd dies down," Tom said. "They all swarm at the end, eager to collect their winnings."

They sat back down and watched for another minute, remaining out of the fray. Eve watched Brandon run to Marcus, and Marcus hug the boy and muss his hair. *He's a natural father*, she thought. And Tom's words stayed with her. *He loves him like one of his own.* And that's when she knew that they could never be together. There was no hope for them. None at all.

Despite what he'd said about accepting her inability

to bear children without hesitation, he really did want children of his own, she suspected. What if he began to resent her as the years went by and they remained childless? She couldn't do that to him. Would the Coopers be enough for him, or would he watch them grow and begin to wish that Eve had been able to give him a child of their own?

"I'm sorry, Tom," she said. "I shouldn't have come. You're right. This has been a terrible mistake. Please, take me home."

"But it's over now. We can go congratulate him."

"I know. It's not that. I need to leave. Please, don't tell him that I've been here. I don't want him to know that I was in London. I can't explain, but I need to go."

Twenty-five

Eve had kept to herself as much as she could since returning to Thornbrook Park. Sophia had asked her what had happened in London, and she hadn't wanted to discuss it. What was there to say? She'd discovered how much she loved Marcus and then realized it was precisely why she couldn't be with him. It made her unspeakably sad to be leaving Thornbrook Park, but it was for the best.

"Lizzy and I are going over to the Dower House. Aunt Agatha is holding a séance." Sophia found Eve staring out the drawing-room windows, deep in thought.

"Are you certain a séance is a good idea after what happened last time?" Eve recalled that a séance had scared away Sophia's previous lady's maid, Mrs. Bowles.

"Lizzy wants to see if she can contact her dearly departed grandmother. I remember Lizzy's grandmother as a fairly gentle woman, so I'm hoping she's a very tame spirit. Join us?"

"No, thank you. I'm more interested in the living these days." Eve smiled. "I think I'm going to have a walk around the grounds. I haven't yet been to the legendary orchards or had a glimpse of the farm. I will be back in time for tea."

"I would like that, too," Sophia said. "Until later, then."

Eve dressed warmly in her dark coat paired with a purple scarf, gloves, her black wool dress, stockings, and walking boots. She started off along the path that crossed the gardens. She inhaled deeply of the fresh woodsy scent and the crisp fall day.

Her mind was on Marcus as she walked along, trying to see the grounds as he might have seen them, growing up on such a grand estate. Had he raced his brother across this very green? Stumbled and skinned his knees on those very rocks? Climbed the big oak tree at the edge of the meadow? Through the years, he might have struggled to get away from it all, but it remained a part of him.

She loved Marcus, she knew beyond any doubt. His laugh. His sensitivity. She loved how he ached for the people he'd had to hurt in South Africa. She loved that he didn't stop being who he was simply because his brother disapproved of him. She loved the way he said "please," when another man might have just taken what he needed without asking.

Because she loved him, she didn't think about staying more than the next few days. It seemed more important than ever that he should have everything he wanted in the world, even if it couldn't be with her.

She spied the orchards ahead, neat rows of apple trees stretching back for acres. And then beyond, there were empty fields, probably too much for Mrs. Dennehy to keep up with planting on her own.

As she approached, she saw some sheep out on the green munching grass. There was a faded red barn, a dirt road leading to a wire-fenced pen currently full of scratching chickens, and an old brown house with a porch that looked as though it had been recently repaired, the new wood yet unpainted and brighter than the old. Tilly Meadow Farm, she supposed. Perhaps she would have a look around and say hello.

She found Mrs. Dennehy in the barn milking cows.

"I'm sorry to interrupt," she said, standing in the doorway. "My name is Eve Kendal. I've come from Thornbrook Park, and I was hoping to have a word with you."

"Just give me a minute to finish. I assume you know I'm Mrs. Dennehy, since you've come to see me, and I'm glad to meet you, I'm sure. Forgive me for not offering you my hand." The woman laughed at her own comment until she snorted.

"I can wait," Eve said. "If there's anything I could do to help?"

"You ever milked a cow?"

"No."

"You wearing fine clothes?"

Eve shrugged. "Not my finest."

"Fine enough, I would guess. Then you're fairly worthless on a farm, although I mean no offense in saying so."

"None taken." Mrs. Dennehy was a bit abrupt, but Eve liked her. She felt it was promising that the woman seemed overworked and in need of help. "You seem a bit shorthanded."

"I have some boys who come around and help now

and then, and another I just took on more permanently. The one has gone for a few days, but he'll be
back. Another one of 'em's sick, and the other stole
some of my equipment. Little devil. I told him I'd
shoot him if he ever came back."

"I'm sorry," Eve said. "How dreadful."

"At least he left the sheep. If he'd taken one of my
favorite ewes, I would have had to track him down
and kill him. They're dear to me, the old girls."

"I saw them in the pasture as we approached."

"Only five of them left. They don't give me quality
milk anymore. Used to make some fine Wensleydale
with them. Those were the days."

"I've had your cheddar," Eve said, edging closer,
careful not to step in anything that might ruin her
shoes. "It's delicious."

"Award-winning." Eve couldn't see Mrs. Dennehy's
head, as she leaned over a bucket between the cows,
but she thought perhaps Mrs. Dennehy was nodding
from the way her back moved up and down. Or perhaps that was just the milking motion. "I don't make
as much as I used to, but I still get on all right. Are
you a fine lady out to steal my recipes for your own
tenant farmers?"

"Of course not," Eve said. It was only after a
second that she realized Mrs. Dennehy had said it with
a laugh. "I'm a friend of Lady Averford's, visiting."

"There, there now, Miss Betty." Mrs. Dennehy
stroked the side of the cow and stood up. "You can
rest. I'm all done with you."

She came out from between the cows holding what
looked like a very heavy bucket of milk. An identical

one stood near Eve by the door. Eve picked it up.
"Now, where are we taking these?"

"Follow me," Mrs. Dennehy said. Eve trailed
behind her right into the kitchen of the house. They
set the buckets down beside the stove. "They'll be fine
here for a bit. Let me wash and then we can talk. I like
you. You didn't give me a chance to say no. You just
picked that bucket up and followed me in. Reminds
me of someone else from Thornbrook Park."

"Who would that be?" Eve asked.

"Thorne," Mrs. Dennehy said. "Captain Marcus
Thorne. Go on out and have a seat in my parlor, if you
please." She gestured to the door across the room. "I'll
be right with you."

"Very well," Eve said, and she found her way out to
the other room. It was a large room, open, clean, with
furniture that had possibly seen better days, but nothing
some slipcovers couldn't dress up a bit. She wondered
if Marcus's Mrs. Cooper was any good with a needle
and thread. There was a large, round handwoven rug
over polished wooden floors. The wood posts that
were either decorative or instrumental in holding up
the house were marked here and there with pocks and
dents. Eve took a seat on the plaid sofa, across from a
flowered chair near the hearth. She folded her hands in
her lap and waited.

"Here we are, then." Mrs. Dennehy came out carrying a tray with tea, toast, and what looked like a pot
of soft cheese, and a plate with some chunks of a harder
cheese. Eve stood. Mrs. Dennehy placed the tray on a
low wooden table in front of the couch and took a seat in
the flowered chair, which she pulled closer. "Please, sit."

"It's a big house for a woman on her own," Eve said, taking up a cup of just-poured tea and looking around. "A lot of upkeep. And that's just the house. You must be exhausted at the end of every day."

Mrs. Dennehy had tucked up the few stray gray hairs around her face and had removed her apron. She was a good-looking woman, hale and strong, with clear skin dotted by a few freckles. Considering her age, her face was surprisingly unlined, but one could tell she had lived through some hardship by the tightness around her eyes. When she offered the cheese, her fingers curled awkwardly on the knife.

"A touch of arthritis?" Eve asked. "My grandfather's hands used to do the same. He was an American, in textiles. He moved here with my mother when she was just a girl."

Mrs. Dennehy nodded. "Getting old. It's not so bad. My fingers are just a little tired from milking the cows. You're close to Captain Thorne, then?"

Eve straightened in her chair. "I'm a friend of all the family."

"It's just that your face lit up a certain way when I mentioned him out in the yard."

Eve blushed. "My, you're observant."

"Young Marcus was always my favorite of the boys, I have to say. I shouldn't have favorites and I would never tell him so, you understand."

"Your secret is safe with me."

"Good. I hope so. When he was about eight or nine, he used to hide out in my loft with a stack of books and a bushel of my apples. Said his brother was going to beat him if he was caught reading around the house, that Gabriel thought he was trying to show him up in front of their father."

"It sounds like Gabriel, a bit. I'm not sure he would have hit him actually or if he was all talk."

"They got into it now and then, as boys do, but you're right that Gabriel has always been more bluster than action when it comes to his brother. But I would let Marcus stay up there with his books. He never bothered anyone. Sometimes, he would even come down and help my daughters with their chores. I have two girls, one about five years older than Marcus and the other just a few months older. They grew up and moved away, as children do."

As she had. Eve wondered if her mother ever got that sad, wistful look in her eyes when she thought of her, like Mrs. Dennehy did for her girls.

"My youngest girl, Junie, she had an attraction to Marcus. Her father heard her up in the loft with him one day trying to convince Marcus to kiss her. Robert nearly grabbed a pitchfork and climbed up there after them, until he heard Marcus saying no, that he wouldn't kiss June. He let her down gently, said he would love to kiss her but he didn't feel they were ready to take such a step. He would have to court her properly and face her father with his intentions, because that's how a gentleman did things, he said. Isn't that the sweetest thing?"

"Very sweet," Eve agreed. She took a bite of cheese and felt her stomach lurch. She tried to hide it. It certainly wasn't the cheese. The cheese was delicious, but—there it was again, a wave of nausea. Eve realized suddenly, horrifyingly, that she was going to be sick.

"Honey, are you unwell?" Mrs. Dennehy noticed.

Eve shook her head. She couldn't speak for fear of losing her composure.

"Oh, dear. I've seen that look, too. There's a water closet around the corner." She directed Eve right to the door and stood outside ready to help as Eve tried, and barely managed, to contain her nausea.

Fortunately, the wave passed. Eve splashed a little water on her face and rejoined Mrs. Dennehy. "I'm sorry," she said. "I don't know what came over me. It certainly wasn't the cheese. I love cheese."

"How far are you along?" Mrs. Dennehy asked with a knowing grin.

"I'm sorry?" Eve said.

"How far?" She patted her stomach. "I couldn't stomach cheese during either of my two pregnancies."

"Oh," Eve laughed. "I'm not pregnant."

But then she paused, and she considered. She hadn't had her flow in over a month, but she'd never been irregular. What could it mean? Had she been wrong about her ability to have children? Her heart beat faster with the possibility.

Mrs. Dennehy shrugged. "You would know best."

Would I? she wondered. Suddenly, she felt certain that Mrs. Dennehy could be right. She'd been such an idiot to run away from Marcus, especially after he'd said that a man would accept the woman he loved without hesitation. She'd told him that she feared she couldn't have children, and he didn't seem bothered by it. Not a bit. So why had she run out without giving him a chance? He was the man she loved. And she knew he loved her, too. How could she have just run away?

"Thank you, Mrs. Dennehy. It was lovely meeting you. I'm glad Brandon is working out for you. He's a good boy. I have to get back to Thornbrook Park. To London, actually. I left something in London."

Her heart. Marcus hadn't been expecting her until today and she hoped she could get there in time to keep their plans to talk. It wasn't too late to catch the afternoon train.

"My advice to you, Mrs. Kendal? See a doctor soon."

"I will," Eve said, managing to contain her blush. "Thank you for the visit."

"Brief as it was. Come back soon." Mrs. Dennehy walked her to the door. "You're always welcome."

Eve had to go back to London right away. It had been a big mistake to run off without seeing Marcus. She practically bounded down the green, eager to get home as fast as her legs could carry her, but she became winded and the last mile was slow going.

Ginny, the maid, was in the drawing room when she returned.

"Ginny, how are you today?"

"I'm well, thank you," she said. "I've got a message for you. I'm not supposed to let anyone else hear."

"Oh?" Eve cocked a brow.

"He wants you to meet him. He said you would know where."

"Meet him? Who?" She couldn't fathom that Marcus would have risked sending a message through a maid, but maybe he came back from London early. Maybe he couldn't wait to see her. Or had Tom told him about her visit?

Ginny nodded knowingly. "He said to meet him where the sunflowers grow."

So it *was* Marcus. "He's back? When?"

"Not long ago. He will be there. Waiting." Ginny turned to leave.

Marcus. Her heart surged. He'd come back early. He'd come back for her. But perhaps he wasn't ready yet to talk to his brother. He wanted some time alone with her? As much as she dreaded the thought of another walk, she felt energized by the idea of being alone with him. She didn't dare risk asking Dale to drive her.

"Thank you." Eve called after Ginny but the maid had gone. She took a deep breath and set off again in the direction of the farm, hoping she could find her way to the old McGinty fields.

She was just nearing the orchard when she heard heavy breathing from behind her. She turned and saw the weapon.

The scream died in her throat.

Twenty-six

THE TRAIN FINALLY ARRIVED AT THORNBROOK Station. As soon as Tom slipped up and told him that Eve had been there last night, Marcus knew something had happened to scare her off. He wouldn't stand for it, not this time. Whether it be Sophia or Gabriel or her own misgivings getting in the way, whatever it was, they could overcome it. He loved her. He refused to accept that she didn't return his affection. They had been too close for him to doubt it. His only hope was to rush back to Thornbrook Park and let her know how he felt, once and for all.

He wanted to push the slow-moving commuters out of his way and run from the train, run all the way to Thornbrook Park, to Eve. He didn't even want to wait for his bag to be unloaded from the train. He would send Dale to the station for it later. He would walk back, which suited him. No one expected his arrival. As he got close to the Dower House, he realized that the woman pacing back and forth in front of the gate was Sophia.

"What's wrong, Sophia? You look like you're seeing one of Aunt Agatha's ghost friends."

"Marcus. Oh." She laughed without much humor behind it. "Of course not. It's just that Eve was supposed to be home in time for tea, and she wasn't. She went for a walk this morning, and she should have been back hours ago. At wit's end, I thought maybe she'd come here, but..."

"She's not at Thornbrook Park? You've looked all around?" Every muscle in his abdomen tensed.

"We shouldn't be worried, of course, but I'm growing concerned."

"She's missing? Eve?" The panic deepened, slicing like a knife down his body.

Sophia took his hand. "Marcus, dearest. You care about her. You should have told me, both of you. I wouldn't have stood in your way."

He tried to stay calm. "Eve, missing? It can't be. Let's walk back to the house. She's probably there. What were your plans, exactly?"

"She had planned to go for a look around the grounds and then come back home in time for tea. She went out early. I was certain she would be back by now. Dale is already searching the grounds in case she got lost or confused somehow."

"Only Dale? What about the others? Gabriel? Mr. Winthrop?"

"Mr. Winthrop is out with Gabriel and Geoffrey Dovedale. They're shooting."

"A good thing, I suppose. If she's lost, they might come across her. There are not a lot of places to get lost. It's mostly open fields, and then the woods. Do you think she went exploring in the woods?"

"It's possible."

"All right, the plan is that we go home, and we look again. We look everywhere."

He tried to ignore the icy spike of fear that ran through his veins. They had to find her. She had to be safe and well, waiting for him where no one had thought to look. He couldn't accept the alternative.

⁓

As far as they could tell, Eve wasn't in the house. No one had seen her return. No one seemed to know where she had gone.

"Someone fetch Agatha. Let's see if she has any inkling where Eve is." Marcus was surprised that Agatha hadn't already appeared at the house, wringing her hands and proclaiming someone to be in great danger.

His sense of unease was overwhelming. Eve was in danger; he was sure of it. He felt a wave of nausea, bitter bile rising. Invisible fists pounded into his chest and lungs. He couldn't stop the pain, couldn't take a breath.

Agatha and Alice arrived. Agatha crossed the room to take his hands. "Have no fear, Captain Thorne. You will succeed."

"Do you see anything else? Where she might be?"

"The spirits are quiet today. I see trees. Lots of trees. It could mean something, or it could simply mean my vision is blocked."

Of all days.

"I can't just sit around," he said. "I'm going to start looking."

On the way out, he ran into Gabriel, Winthrop, and another man he took to be Dovedale.

"Marcus, what's wrong?" Gabriel had a look of genuine concern on his face. Marcus had left his hat behind, and he'd been running his fingers through his hair. He must look as frightful as he felt.

"Eve is missing, and Mr. Lawson is after her. I have to find her."

"The whole household cares for Mrs. Kendal," Winthrop said. "We'll find her."

"Lawson," he explained to Gabriel as quickly as he could, "is Eve's former landlord, and the man who defrauded Captain Ben Kendal out of his savings. He once came after Eve with a knife. And now Eve's missing."

"We're all at your service, sir." Gabriel's friend stepped forward.

"Has anyone checked the farm?" Gabriel asked. "Maybe she got talking with Mrs. Dennehy and lost track of time. Winthrop, fetch Dale to drive my brother out there to check on her, will you?"

"Dale is already out searching," Marcus said. "Sophia's orders."

"The horses." Marcus looked off to the stable, from where Gabriel, Winthrop, and Dovedale had just come. "They're probably still saddled."

But as Marcus entered the stable, he could see that the groom was rubbing the horses down. Catching up to his brother, Gabriel placed a hand on Marcus's shoulder. The others trailed in after Gabriel. "They're exhausted, Marcus. We'll have to go on foot."

"We?" He turned to Gabriel. "You'll help me?"

"I know the land better than you do. We'll go over

every inch if we have to, and we'll find her." That meant more to Marcus than he could say.

"I'll go look in town and check at the train station," Dovedale said. "Maybe they have some record of tickets sold or a note of departing passengers."

"Good idea," Marcus said. "And Mr. Winthrop will be here if she turns up at home."

"I'll take a few of the dogs and look for her myself in the opposite direction of whichever way you head," Mr. Winthrop said. "There are plenty of people here if she comes back. They can try to send word out to us if she's found."

Sophia approached, striding with purpose. Marcus hoped she had good news, but her grim expression said otherwise.

"Lucy has just told me something. From an upstairs window, she saw Eve come home from her walk. When she came down, she heard her talking to Ginny, one of the maids, in the drawing room."

"Did she hear what they were saying? Where's Ginny?" Ginny. It had to be Ginny, the blackmailer. No good could come of this. His head began to throb. "I want to see her at once."

"Ginny's gone." Sophia wrung her hands. "According to Mrs. Hoyle, she gave notice this afternoon and she's already cleared out her things. She said she had a better offer. Lucy said Ginny has been going out to the tavern after hours and was there nearly half the night last night."

Marcus put his head in his hand. Lawson. He was sure Ginny had run into him somehow these past two nights and started working with the man. What did she have against Thornbrook Park? Against Eve? He looked up again. "We'll head to the farm. Maybe Mrs. Dennehy knows something, or maybe we'll catch sight of Eve along the way."

"I'm with you," Gabriel said, appearing at the stable door with rifles and ammunition. "Let's go."

They would find her. And he prayed that they would find her safe and well.

Twenty-seven

FURIOUS, EVE STUMBLED OVER THE UNEVEN TERRAIN, driven by Oliver Lawson at her side who nudged her along and barked orders. Subtly, she tried to loosen the ropes that bound her wrists behind her back as she formed a plan of escape. Intense pain and throbbing behind her eyes made it hard to focus. She'd been hit on the head with something. When she'd regained consciousness, she'd found that her hands were tied securely. He threatened her with a knife, his only weapon.

"You listen to me carefully," he said, his face only inches from hers, his breath hot and rancid. "I need you. I'm in no mood for contradiction. You'll be quiet and you'll follow me out of here, away, and you won't scream out. I can kill you before anyone gets close enough to save you."

"I don't understand. What do you hope to accomplish?" Why hadn't he killed her already, if that was his intention?

"I stayed around here biding my time, trying to get rid of you. I finally gave up and made it all the

SHERRI BROWNING

way back to London in time to see my wife carted out of the house by Scotland Yard. I came back here for you. You owe me." He wore the same suit he'd worn when he first accosted her, dark frock coat over a jacket and waistcoat, but he'd lost the bowler hat.

"How? What have I ever done to you?"

"You came around asking questions, raising suspicion. I didn't want to kill Strump, but your coming around made him question our whole operation. Once he was out of the way, Leona and I needed to make sure you wouldn't come back to stir it all up again. I came to manage that, but you had an unexpected protector." He rubbed his head as if it still smarted from where Marcus had clocked him.

"Scotland Yard's on to you, watching for you. It's only a matter of time. I don't see what I can do for you now."

"You can be Leona Strump. We have accounts in India, set up by Edgar Strump. With Leona gone, I need someone to pretend to be Leona to access those accounts."

"You don't say." She couldn't resist adding the comment, but she paid for it with a sharp jerk on the rope that bound her and then a push.

"Faster. We've a lot of terrain to cover."

He slowed his pace when she kept him talking, so she continued the conversation. "Leona is beneficiary on her husband's accounts, I take it? Though, of course, he wasn't really her husband. You're counting on reaching India before the news of your wife's arrest?"

"Easily. We'll book passage tonight. We're taking

the train at Skipham. Don't want to risk being apprehended at Thornbrook. Though I suppose no one even knows you're missing yet."

"I had an appointment for tea. I assure you they're all out looking for me by now." She dared to hope. "I'm a dear friend to the Countess of Averford. The earl's a great hunter, you know."

"I'm shaking in my boots." He laughed. "We've got at least an hour on anyone looking for you."

"And how do you know Ginny?" She assumed he'd put Ginny up to luring her.

"There's no worse enemy to a house than a mistreated maid. I went to the tavern to ponder how I might nab you. There she was, with an axe to grind about Thornbrook Park. We came to talking and she had some very helpful suggestions."

"But why? What can anyone have ever done to Ginny?"

"Take it up with the earl, I suppose. 'Cept you probably won't ever see him again. You're going to come with me to drain our accounts as Leona Strump. I'll need money to live on if I'm going to be on the run again."

"You'll keep on running. It will get exhausting. Wouldn't it be easier just to turn yourself in?"

"And face a murder charge? I'll hang. No thank you." He loosened his collar as if loosening an invisible noose from his neck.

She might never see Marcus again. Her heart lurched, but her stomach followed.

"Come on, faster." He nudged her.

"I think I'm going to be sick," she warned.

"Nice try." Lawson gave her a shove that was slightly harder than previous nudges. "Keep moving. We'll get there if it takes all night."

"It just might," she said. "My head hurts. I feel ill."

"Boo-hoo," he said. "Move."

By now, Sophia must have realized something was wrong. Eve guessed that Lawson planned to kill her once he was done with her, sooner if he got frustrated with her delay tactics.

"Really, I wish you well," she said, beginning to ramble out of desperation. "I always thought you were a good man. You found a way to make a fortune, good for you. My grandfather was American. I appreciate industrious types. It's a wonder we didn't cross paths coming or going from London. I was there yesterday, too."

He groaned. "Would have made my life easier."

Carefully she moved, every step an agony. She had no idea how much time had passed between the hit on the head and their movement through the forest. Were they still on Lord Averford's land? "If you cut the rope binding my hands, I'll be better able to maintain my balance and move faster. I'm still a little hazy. Maybe it's the head wound."

He shoved her sharply from behind and she fell facedown to the forest floor, a carpet of pine needles barely cushioning the blow. She hated having her back to him, so she struggled to roll over as soon as she could move.

"I'm sorry," she said. "I lost my balance. Please. I can't go on."

He leaned over her, pointing with the knife once

again. "You will. Get up, or I'll really make walking miserable for you."

"I'll try," she said, growing more terrified as he pulled her back to her feet.

She moved a little faster now to satisfy him, afraid to say much more. She had to think. And suddenly, the nausea welled up again. She feared she would be sick.

She heard a sound. Perhaps Gabriel was in the area hunting? She kept her ears trained for the sound of rifles, dogs, anything. But she didn't hear it again. She kept walking.

❧

They'd searched the path to the farm without any sign of her. Marcus's heart sank when Mrs. Dennehy told them Eve was no longer there. His last hope was that Gabriel had been right, that she was simply visiting with Mrs. Dennehy. Now, they headed into the woods.

Marcus kept his head down, looking for any trace of a struggle.

"But why would anyone want to kill Eve?" Gabriel asked.

"Lawson probably feared that she knew more than she did. He'd stolen thousands from her husband that had been entrusted to him as investments. When Eve went looking into her affairs, I think she made Strump, her solicitor, start to question everything. Lawson killed Strump, and he was going to kill her, too." If he hadn't already, but Marcus couldn't allow such thoughts. She had to be alive.

"Look, the forest floor has been disturbed." Gabriel swept a hand out.

"You're right." Marcus noticed the pattern of scattered pine needles among the leaves and rocks. "Footsteps. And someone passed through here."

Marcus gestured at a broken twig.

"And here." Gabriel stepped through the branches and crouched down, looking right to left.

"Definitely," Marcus agreed.

Gabriel looked up at him. "When did you learn to track?"

Marcus sighed, exasperated, but he was too worried about Eve to let his brother get to him. "In the war. I defused bombs. We had to know where to look."

"Right," Gabriel said, straightening up. His eyes held a look of awe when he glanced back at Marcus, as if he'd never imagined that Marcus had really been at war until now. "Good God, little brother, you could have been killed out there."

Gabriel's sudden embrace shocked Marcus. Did his brother really care for him? He patted his brother's back before pulling away.

"Yes, well, I wasn't, and I learned a few things. Now Eve's the one in danger."

"We'll find her," Gabriel assured him. "I don't know when things started up between you two, but you could have said something. I wouldn't have kept pushing you at Alice."

"Now you tell me?" They both knew it wasn't entirely true.

"If I knew you truly cared for her." Gabriel shook his head. "I'm not a monster. We'll find her."

They'd gone a few miles into the woods, tracing an uneven but walkable path, when they heard a rustling up ahead. Marcus nudged Gabriel's arm and motioned through the trees. Eve's dark coat stood out starkly among the drab forest greens and browns. Lawson's back was to them as he pressed Eve against the trunk of a tree, holding a knife at the edge of her throat.

Marcus's breath caught. One wrong move and Lawson could drive the knife home, killing Eve instantly.

At the distance, it was impossible to hear conversation, but Eve appeared to be bargaining with the man.

Gabriel raised his rifle but, at Marcus's gesture of caution, merely held it at the ready, not looking to get off a shot while Lawson stood so close to Eve. As the brothers watched, Lawson removed the knife from her neck and stepped away, nudging Eve in front of him. Still brandishing the knife, he urged her along the path. Marcus was thankful that the man only had a knife and not a gun. A knife could kill, too, but he'd have to be close enough to use it. They would have to wait for their opportunity until Lawson allowed enough distance between himself and Eve for Gabriel to get off his shot. Marcus had complete faith in his brother for few things in life, but his ability to shoot straight was one of them.

Now that the man had become Gabriel's prey, Lawson didn't stand a chance.

Twenty-eight

LAWSON STAYED SO CLOSE TO HER THAT EVE COULD feel him breathing down her neck. He held on to the binding between her wrists and used it to push her along, sometimes to steady her when she bobbled.

"Just a few more miles," he said.

Her head throbbed. Her stomach churned. She wanted so badly to stop.

"Are we even going the right way? It looks like we've traveled in circles," she lied, desperate to add to his confusion and make him stop for a minute to think. She weighed her options. Once they emerged from the trees into civilization, he would have to release her wrists, wouldn't he? She could try to slip away then. Or would she even make it that far?

"We're going the right way." He didn't give her the satisfaction of stopping to look around. "There's still plenty of daylight."

She contemplated pointing out that they might miss the last train, but that would only make him push her harder and she was barely hanging on as it was. After walking all day, she was near exhaustion and wavering between fear and anger. It was useless to consider getting the weapon from Lawson.

What could she do with her hands bound behind her back? But oh, how she would love to get in a few jabs. She thought of Marcus in the ring, his magnificence. If only he would come bounding through the woods to save her, throwing punches, right, left, right, until Oliver Lawson fell to the ground bloody and knocked out. What a wonderful fantasy.

She thought perhaps it would be more satisfying to go down fighting rather than allowing herself to be pushed along to a slow death. If she dropped to the ground, a dead weight, could she manage to kick him down, too, and keep kicking, connecting soundly again and again until he finally overcame her and shoved the knife between her ribs?

Maybe they would never find her body, never know that she carried a child. Marcus would never know how much she loved him. The sudden ache of it all overwhelmed her, and she sobbed aloud.

"No sniveling." Lawson continued to push at her.

Her stomach gave a heave. She stopped to steady it. He pushed again.

"No, I'm serious," she said. "Give me a minute. I'm going to be sick."

With the threat of nausea imminent, she didn't care what he might threaten her with—death or dismembering. Nothing mattered but to calm the overwhelming urge welling up inside her.

He nudged. She ignored him, spreading her feet to lend stability as she tried to take a deep breath. He pushed. And that was it. She fell to her knees and nearly lost control, but she remembered to breathe deeply and hum, a trick Ben had taught her to ward off nausea on their passage to India. Breathe deeply and hum. It helped.

"If I could just lean against the tree a moment, no more than a moment, to catch my breath," she said, getting back to her feet.

He let her lean. That was it. She knew she wasn't going down without at least trying to fight. She rubbed her binding against the tree trunk. Subtle. She couldn't let him see her moving. It worked; the rope loosened. She held it with her fingers so that it wouldn't slip and give her away.

"Thank you. I think I'll be able to move much faster now."

"At last," he said. "Move along then."

"Mr. Lawson?" she said, beginning to bob on her feet as Marcus had taught her, left to right, left to right.

"Is that some kind of dance? Move on."

"No." She dropped her ropes and showed her hands, free at last. "It's from boxing."

And before he could react, she threw a left hook and hit him clean across the jaw. He staggered back, stunned.

And then, she heard the report of a rifle and shouts, and she tried to look up but another wave rocked her frame. She kept humming and focusing on each breath, in and out. Just as she thought she'd managed to contain herself, chaos in the form of Marcus Thorne descended.

In a flash, she saw him bounding through the trees at Oliver Lawson. Ignoring the knife, he grabbed the man by the collar and pounded him, a right hook, a left jab, and the knife dropped right out of Lawson's hand. One more jab, and Lawson himself fell backward into the leaves.

Apparently satisfied that there would be no more trouble from Lawson, Marcus rose, brushing the dust from his hands, and took her in his arms. "Damned good left hook you have there."

"Marcus." She fell into his arms. "I'm so glad to see you. Apparently, mine wasn't quite good enough. I needed a little help. You found me just in time." Not caring if his brother was watching, she kissed Marcus full on the lips.

She shook her hands, trying to restore the circulation. Marcus gripped her wrists, gently massaging her raw, tender skin. "He hurt you. He's lucky I didn't kill him. I'm so glad we found you. I don't know what I would have done." His voice broke, choked with raw emotion. "I love you, Eve. I've loved you all along."

"I love you, too," she said. "I thought you would never find me, that I would never have the chance to tell you."

She could have stood forever in his arms.

⁂

Later, after the doctor had looked Eve over and declared her in sound condition, Lucy helped her to her room where she'd drawn a bath and laid out the glorious silver-beaded evening dress Eve had bought in London.

"It arrived at last. I've been eager to wear it again." She remembered the first night she'd worn it, sparring with Marcus in the library. She didn't bother to suppress her smile.

The dress fit her perfectly, for now. There would be a lot of alterations in her future once she confirmed her pregnancy. She hadn't mentioned it to Doctor Pederson, preferring to wait for a more private appointment at a later date. Once ready, she went downstairs to meet with all of her friends.

She was early, she supposed, as she found herself alone in the drawing room. Everyone had been so happy to see her safe return that she expected they would all be waiting for her. Marcus had carried Eve all the way home while Gabriel had taken Lawson to the authorities. It made her smile to see the brothers getting along, working together.

"You look exquisite." The voice came from behind her. She turned and nearly gasped. The sight of Marcus always somehow managed to take her breath away, whether in his fine evening clothes, as now, or wearing absolutely nothing. Especially wearing nothing.

She beamed. "And so do you."

"No lasting ill-effects, then? The doctor gave you the all clear?" He closed the distance between them and placed his hand to her forehead as if feeling for a fever.

"I'm fine. If you think I feel a bit hot, I assure you that it's all you. Your proximity has that effect on me. Did you and Gabriel make up? You seemed to be getting along pretty well once he returned from the constable's."

"We've made our peace, yes. I think I made it obvious that I have no intention of marrying Lady Alice." He took her hands in his.

"Marry me," she blurted out. She felt they had no

need to wait or be polite. "Marcus, why not? I love you with all my heart."

"Mercy, woman, won't you give me a chance to say what I've come to say? I'm supposed to be the one to make the proposals. Why do you think we're alone in the drawing room so close to dinner time?"

"You arranged for us to be alone?" She couldn't hide her astonishment.

"Of course. They've all gone in to the dining room. They're waiting for us there. I shooed them in early so that I could have you to myself for a moment to do this." He dropped to one knee, her hand still in his. "Eve Kendal, would you do me the honor of becoming my wife?"

She sighed, for the drama of it and because she needed a moment to collect herself. The sight of him on his knee in front of her was enough to make her heart burst right out of her chest. They were going to be so happy. For always. Just the two of them. Or maybe three. She needed to find the right time to tell him about her suspicions. Now was not that time.

He pulled something out of his pocket and presented a shiny ring. With her still-blurry vision, it looked to be at least two carats, an enormous diamond. She knew she must be seeing it wrong, but it was beautiful no matter what. She looked at the ring and looked at him, stunned.

Then, he said the one word that she could never resist when it came from his lips.

He said, "Please."

Twenty-nine

January 1908

"IT'S A SHAME LORD MARKHAM GAVE UP HIS YORKSHIRE estate," Marcus said, adjusting his tie in the mirror.

He preferred to do without George's services when he had a chance to be alone with Eve. George had left the Earl of Averford's employ and come to work as Marcus's valet. Eve had hired Lettie away from Averford House to be her lady's maid, but the maid was also not needed at the moment. Sutton refused to leave London to become their butler, but he'd sent them Mr. Paulson with a stunning recommendation.

"Lady Markham never liked it here. She prefers London." Eve checked her hair in the dressing table mirror, her gaze drawn to the brilliant flash on her left hand.

Once her vision had cleared, she had seen that the diamond was even larger than she'd first thought. It must have been difficult to find a wedding band to match its magnificence, but Marcus had. Somehow. At their wedding, she'd been afraid to lift her hand and blind all of their guests once she'd said "I do" and he'd slid it on her finger.

"Alice said there were too many reminders of Lord Markham's first wife for the new Lady Markham to bear." Finished with his adjustments, Marcus approached her at the dressing table to massage her shoulders. "We might have a ghost. Perhaps the original Lady Markham is yet in residence."

"Mmm, that feels wonderful." She leaned into the warmth of his hands. He didn't even have to move her hair out of the way since she'd had it bobbed. She loved the new style. She felt so modern and free. Plus, having shorter hair was easier with the baby and her ever-questing hands. They called her Mina, short for Wilhelmina, named after William Cooper.

"Perhaps we can ask Agatha over to have a look for ghosts. For now, we'd best get going. Mina is settled with her nurse, and your sister-in-law is expecting us at Thornbrook Park for dinner at eight. I would hate to disappoint her. You know how she and Gabriel feel about punctuality."

"I do." Marcus reached up, undid his tie, and leaned down to kiss the back of her neck as his hands slid around to her breasts. "And I don't give a hang."

"Marcus, you're incorrigible." She playfully batted his hand away, and then pulled it back and slipped it inside the low neck of her dress. "That's better. We're the most unreliable couple in the neighborhood, but I can't say that I mind our reputation."

He gestured toward the bed with his head. She nodded her complicity.

"I'll be quick," he said.

"You'd better not be." She stood and kissed him full on the lips.

"Oh, before I forget." Just as she fully engaged in the kiss, feeling the heat begin to spread through her core, he pulled away. "A package came for you today. I think you should open it."

"I will. Later." She took his hand and tried to urge him to the bed, but he was insistent. He went to the closet, picked up a box, and put it on the bed.

"Open it," he said. "You won't be disappointed."

"Very well." She took the letter opener he offered and sliced the packing tape along the edge. "Oh!"

"It's what I think it is?" he asked.

She held up the first copy, a scarlet leather-bound book embossed in gold with the title and her name. "My author copies. *The Lieutenant's Bride* by Eve Thorne. I have to admit, it gives me goose bumps."

He took the book and flipped to the dedication, beaming with delight at the sight of his own name. "For my husband, Marcus, my light, my world, my everything. Thank you for sharing your stories and your life."

She peeked up at him from under her lashes to gauge his reaction. She'd told him she'd acknowledged him, but he had no idea what she'd said until now. "Do you like it?"

He nodded his approval. "Of course. I'd better get some thanks, considering I practically gave you the whole story."

"Your journal was very helpful, but you know I changed details to make it my own. You were my inspiration."

"I know. I'm proud of you, Eve. My wife, the famous author." He flashed a devastating smile.

"Not famous yet," she said. "But maybe soon. Geoffrey Dovedale said he'd like to discuss a second book tonight at dinner."

"Ah." He began to retie his tie. "We'd best get going, then. Your future is at stake. No time for making love."

"There's always time for that." She took hold of his hands and placed them on her stomach, the heat of him burning through the thin layer of silk. "Besides, I have a package for you, too."

A spark of gold shot through his amber eyes. "You're expecting? We're going to have another baby?"

She nodded. "Right around the middle of September."

"We have all the luck, don't we?" His hands slid around her waist and he pulled her to him. "I never dreamed I could be so happy. There's only one thing I want to do now, and it isn't head off to my brother's party. It involves you, me, and that bed."

She looked into his eyes and she said, "Please."

An Affair Downstairs

SHERRI BROWNING

AVAILABLE JANUARY 2015
FROM SOURCEBOOKS CASABLANCA

One

LADY ALICE EMERSON KNEW EXACTLY WHAT SHE wanted, and it wasn't a husband. She had a whole list of things she longed to accomplish in life, all on her own, with no one to tie her down.

Her plan had been years in the making. The first step had been to get out from under her parents' control. As Alice's father and her maiden aunt Agatha found themselves more frequently at odds, it had been child's play to convince Mother that accompanying Agatha on an extended visit to Thornbrook Park would be best for everyone. Indeed, it could save Father's health before being around Agatha made him apoplectic. Had it been anywhere else, Mother might have hesitated, but she had full confidence in placing Agatha and Alice in the capable hands of Alice's older sister Sophia, the Countess of Averford.

Alice knew that her mother expected Sophia to find her a husband, and her sister had been more than up to the task. In her nearly two years at Thornbrook Park,

Alice had dissuaded two of her sister's candidates from proposing, and she had faith that she could survive a few more attempts before Agatha was comfortably settled and she could announce her intention to depart. Who could stop her once she turned five-and-twenty, when she would come into the money her grandmother had left her? Just two more years.

Alice's great list of things to accomplish included lofty dreams: to travel the world, to climb a mountain, to ride a camel, to captain a pirate ship. And she had simpler goals that she could start on right away, like cornering the fox in a hunt, getting drunk on whiskey, and having a wild affair. She should know love at least once, even if she never planned on marrying. And she had just the man in mind, the same man who could teach her to hunt and to shoot, and who enjoyed a good whiskey—her brother-in-law's estate manager, Mr. Logan Winthrop.

Mr. Winthrop would be no easy conquest. For starters, he didn't seem to really *like* people, choosing to keep to himself as much as possible. When he did find himself in company, he maintained a cool, all-business demeanor. *Most of the time*. Alice had managed to break through his icy exterior once or twice, enough to fuel her hope that she could manage a seduction.

There were rumors that he'd killed a man, a rival for a woman's affections, and had come to Thornbrook Park to escape his dangerous past. Rumors didn't deter Alice. All men had pasts, and rumors were often far from fact. What made him the perfect candidate—besides his soulful eyes and god-like physique—was precisely that he was not the sort to form emotional attachments. There would be no pining after her or rushing into commitment. An estate manager's income wouldn't come close to supporting an earl's daughter in the style to which she'd become accustomed, or so he would believe. He would never expect her to marry him, even if she managed to seduce him. Once she could convince Logan Winthrop to let his guard down again, she would take her opportunity to kiss him.

She'd hoped to run into him that morning when she left the Dower House to breakfast with her sister at Thornbrook Park. The gardeners were preparing the grounds for winter, and she expected Winthrop to be out with the groundskeeper overseeing their efforts. Unfortunately, Winthrop hadn't been in sight. She stood outside the breakfast room, hand poised to turn the knob, when she heard his voice inside.

"Lemon trees?" His voice had that raspy edge that signaled his displeasure. Alice knew it from the many times he had asked her to stop asking questions and leave him to his work. She smiled. "I don't know much about the care of exotic fruit trees, but I will make a study of it."

"Four trees. I can't imagine what the woman was thinking, as usual." Her sister wasn't delighted by the prospect either, apparently. "It's practically an orchard."

Sophia had a tendency toward exaggeration.

"Mother means well. Likely she feared a few might not make the journey safely. She wants you to have lemonade, not exactly a sinister sentiment behind the gift. You could try to be more grateful." The rumpling of newspaper followed Lord Averford's explanation. Typical. He tended to hide behind the news once he'd had his fill of morning pleasantries, or unpleasantries, as it were.

"It's not that I'm ungrateful. I'll send her a letter as soon as they arrive, of course."

The old Dowager Countess was sending lemon trees to Thornbrook Park from Italy, where she had taken up residence these last few years? Alice, thinking of the hours she could spend in the warm conservatory with Mr. Winthrop, couldn't muster any disappointment. There were roses, sweet peas, and lemon trees on the way. What an ideal setting for a kiss!

"You know who has some experience with lemon trees?" Lord Averford asked, not really expecting an answer. "The Marquess of Brumley. I remember his wife had several trees, oranges and lemons. Perhaps I should invite him to come offer you a hand, Winthrop."

"I wouldn't mind some advice." Winthrop seemed to be none too sure. He might have meant the opposite, that he would mind very much indeed.

"Brumley?" The sound of her sister's teacup clinking in the saucer made Alice jump. "The *widower* Brumley? Your brother's former classmate, the one with the ancient wife who recently passed away?"

"The very one. Marguerite died last year, though, not so recent. He's—"

"Out of mourning." Alice could picture her sister clasping her hands in glee. "And a marquess. I'm sure he's lonely. We should invite him for an extended stay."

Alice felt the sinking feeling in the pit of her stomach. A widower. Her sister's next candidate to win over Alice to the idea of marriage. Not again. If the aroma of cinnamon toast tempted her to enter the room, the idea of a marquess being pushed at her changed her mind. She backed slowly away from the door. Perhaps she would break her fast with Aunt Agatha in the Dower House after all. She turned and began to walk quietly down the hall when the housekeeper, Mrs. Hoyle, sprang on her from out of nowhere.

"Good morning, Lady Alice. Have you come for breakfast?"

"I thought I left a pair of gloves behind last night. I just had a quick look in the drawing room. No gloves. I'll be on my way."

"But I've just come from the drawing room. I didn't see you come in." The infernal woman cocked an accusing brow. "Perhaps one of the maids picked them up. Come along to the kitchen and we'll have a look."

Alice couldn't imagine a way to decline gracefully, and at least the kitchen wasn't the breakfast room. She would manage to avoid her sister's attempts to make the Marquess of Brumley, undoubtedly a toad, out to be a charming fairy-tale prince. "Thank you, Mrs. Hoyle."

She followed the old hen to the kitchen, where the few maids at the table jumped to attention to greet her, causing Alice to blush and mutter an apology for interrupting them. The three maids all ran off to tend to duties elsewhere in the house despite Alice's protestations to stay put, and Mrs. Hoyle excused herself to ask Mr. Finch about the gloves, leaving Alice to stand alone next to the great table where the servants took their meals.

Off in the adjoining room, she could see Mrs. Mallows covered in flour as she rolled out dough and occasionally cursed at Sally, the kitchen maid. A footman rushed right by Alice with a tray, not even noticing her in his haste to fetch what he was after and get back to the breakfast room. Alice, glad to go unnoticed, stepped into a shadowy corner to wait for Hoyle's inevitable return with the news that her gloves were not to be found.

"Looking for your next victim, Lady Alice?"

"Mr. Winthrop." He hadn't failed to notice her. His voice caressed her like one of the velvet gloves she claimed to be missing, causing her heart to beat faster. She turned and stepped back into the light. "I'm not sure I know what you mean. I'm waiting for Mrs. Hoyle to confirm if she could find something I've lost."

"Oh, is that the ruse? You've *lost* something. Meanwhile, you're deciding which of the servants to trail after all day asking questions to the point of vexation." He laughed. Laughed! What a rare occasion. Never mind that he was laughing at her. She was entranced by the way his eyes lightened ever so slightly from black to cobalt with his mirth. So dark were his eyes, so normally inscrutable, that she'd had no idea that they were actually a very deep blue and not brown at all. Or maybe they simply appeared cobalt in the light, drawing from the dark blue of his coat.

Forgetting herself, she took a step closer to examine

them. He seemed to hesitate an extra second, staring back at her, but he didn't move away. "Naturally, Mrs. Hoyle will come along any moment now to report that she was unable to find the item, for you've lost nothing at all. What really brings you to Thornbrook Park?"

"*Why, you, Logan. I've come to deliver this, just for you,*" was what she said in her mind, as she imagined placing a hand to the silk plum waistcoat covering his solid chest and leaning in. In actuality, she stammered like a fool and clenched her hands at her sides. "Wh-why on earth would you suspect me of having an ulterior motive?"

She *had* lost something after all. She'd lost her nerve. She'd had the perfect opportunity to completely surprise him with a kiss, and she hadn't been able to manage it.

"Why do you do anything, my lady? Because you can. Forgive my impertinence." He cleared his throat. "I've come to fetch a set of keys from Mr. Finch. I'll leave you to your search."

He stepped back, obviously deciding that whatever course he'd been taking with her was the wrong one to follow. Flirting? Could she conclude that he'd been flirting with her? And if so, what had she done to frighten him away? He turned on his heel.

Quickly, she had to say something to bring him back. "Mr. Winthrop?"

"Yes?" He turned to face her again. She released the breath that she'd been holding.

"Do I really vex you?" She didn't attempt to hide the concern in her voice.

He sighed. "No, Lady Alice. You do not. I'm sorry to have upset you."

"Oh, I'm not upset." She hazarded a step closer to him, and another one. "I was simply making sure before I tell you that I actually know quite a bit about the care of citrus trees. Mother kept oranges in our conservatory back home. I might be of some assistance to you when they arrive, if you'll allow me."

He quirked a dark brow. "Oranges? Lady Averford didn't mention it."

Alice nibbled her lip, desperate not to be exposed as a fraud. Certainly she would have time to read up on the subject and try to appear knowledgeable. "She wouldn't. She didn't notice. My sister is so often in her own world."

"I see." He stroked his jaw as if considering. "And how do you know about the fruit trees, seeing as the news only came at breakfast and I don't recall you at the table when Lord Averford opened the letter in front of me?"

"You've got me there." Alice wasn't well-versed in the art of lying, but she guessed that a bit of candor might help when nearly being caught in a complete fabrication. "I was listening at the door. Eavesdropping, can you imagine? What a terrible habit. I didn't mean to, of course. I was about to join my sister for breakfast and then I heard—"

"The mention of Lord Brumley?" He nodded, and his lips curved up in a smile. "The countess enjoys a bit of matchmaking. Before you came along, she tried to pair me with her maid."

"Mrs. Jenks?" She wrinkled her nose at the idea.

Jenks was a mousy slip of a woman, no match for a robust, vigorous man like Winthrop.

"No, the one before her. Mrs. Bowles."

"Dear me, no." Worse than Jenks, Bowles was a snip-nosed shrew and certainly far too old for Mr. Winthrop. "I'm sorry. Despite her penchant for it, Sophia clearly has no talent for making matches."

"Perhaps not. You were wise to run away instead of sitting through another conversation about yet another bachelor. I don't blame you a bit."

"You—you don't?" Ah, a man of sense. She knew she could rely on his sound judgment, at least. And she appreciated it, though it would make seducing him more of a challenge.

"Any pretty girl in her right mind dreams of a dashing suitor to sweep her away, doesn't she? Alas, Lady Averford's only suitable choice for you so far had eyes for another."

"Captain Thorne." Alice rolled her eyes. "He's better off with Eve Kendal. They're perfectly suited. I didn't care for him much myself, if you must know."

"I mustn't." He shrugged. "It's none of my affair."

Alice bit the inside of her cheek. How she *wanted* it to be his affair. "There *isn't* a suitable choice. I'll never marry."

"Don't despair, Lady Alice. There's someone out there for you. Your sister simply hasn't found him yet."

"It's not despair." Defensive, she crossed her arms. "I've no interest in marriage. None."

His eyes narrowed as if he were trying to peer inside her soul. "I shouldn't have said anything. You might like Lord Brumley. I must go."

"No." She reached out, eager to stop him, and ended up with her hand on his sleeve, over the thick muscles of his upper arm that she had seen in full daylight, bared to the sun, when he'd removed his coat and shirt while out raking the early autumn leaves. "Please, tell me about Brumley. You know him?"

His gaze went to her hand, and trailed back to her face. "We were at Harrow together. I believe he made Lord Averford's acquaintance later, at Oxford. He might have changed considerably in so many years."

"Fourteen years?" She did the math. "If you're the same age as the earl, then it has been fourteen years since you were at Harrow."

"In fourteen years, a man can go through remarkable changes in his life." His full lips drew to a grim line. "In our youth, Brumley was a bit of an oaf. To be fair, I've no idea what kind of man he has become."

"I suppose we're about to find out. Sophia is probably already making out the invitation. But just in case, our mission should be to see the lemon trees replanted and thriving as soon as possible to send him on his way." *Our* mission. She liked the idea of them sharing in something. It was a start.

"Agreed, Lady Alice, on that point. I'm not looking forward to seeing the man any more than you are, I suspect. Perhaps much less."

"No sign of gloves, I'm afraid," Mrs. Hoyle interrupted. Alice had no idea how long the woman had been standing there watching them together. Not long, most likely. Mrs. Hoyle wasn't the sort to wait to be heard. "Will that be all, Lady Alice? There's still time to join your sister at breakfast, I believe."

"I suppose I will take a moment to say hello. Thank you, Mrs. Hoyle. Mr. Winthrop." As much as she hated to pull herself away from him, it wouldn't do to stand in conversation with the estate manager now that Mrs. Hoyle had reappeared. "I look forward to the arrival of the lemon trees. Good day." She delivered a brief nod in parting and willed her feet to walk away.

He'd made a new life for himself at Thornbrook Park. No longer was he a gentleman's son, free to court gentlemen's daughters. Lady Alice made him want to forget, but it wouldn't do to allow himself the liberties he wanted to take with her, a breath of fresh air in his otherwise dreary life. He'd failed to grasp happiness when fate might have allowed it, and now it was beyond his reach.

Alice deserved a young man of fortune and good standing, someone who could give her the kind of life befitting her station, not an estate manager with a tarnished past. But sometimes, when she stood close and studied him with that look of awe in her eyes, he wanted to take her in his arms and remember what it was to be young and in love. He was entirely wrong for her, and he dreaded the day he would have to make it clear to her by behaving in a manner that would frighten her away from him for good.

For now, he sensed she needed a friend, and it didn't hurt to lend an ear. How she did prattle on sometimes, drifting from one topic to the next. It made his work go by faster when she was around, like a symphony playing on the wind. And when he had a chance to stop and really listen to her, she had some remarkable things to say. The girl had good sense. Perhaps he needn't have worried that she seemed to be developing an inadvisable interest in him.

It was entirely possible that he flattered himself, imagining that a strong-willed young beauty could be falling in love with him. Likely, her real interest was horticulture, just as she'd often claimed when she appeared at his side as he supervised the trimming of roses, the planting of seedlings, or tilling of the soil. An estate manager needn't dirty his hands, but working the land helped Logan feel some little bit of hope restored, that he could control what grew from the earth, what flourished, and what faded, after so much time spent out of control in his own world. *His old world*. The life that came before, which he'd struggled to put behind him.

"Are you all right, Mr. Winthrop? You look a little pale." Mrs. Hoyle appeared with a cup and saucer in her hand. He'd been standing in the kitchen where Alice had left him, frozen in place after watching her walk away. "Something to refresh you?"

"Thank you, Mrs. Hoyle. I am a little tired." He didn't want the tea, but he accepted it, drank it down in one gulp, and handed her the empty cup. That he'd been up since dawn without stopping for a meal might have been the real reason for his mental ramblings. "You're very kind to think of me."

"Nonsense, Mr. Winthrop." A blush? From Mrs. Hoyle? "We must look out for one another. If one of us falls ill, who is to look after our family?"

"Our family? Oh yes." She meant Lord and Lady

Averford of Thornbrook Park. Their "family." "Must keep up our strength. I'm off to get some keys from Mr. Finch. Good morning, Mrs. Hoyle."

"And a good one to you, Mr. Winthrop." She turned to bring his cup to the sink.

With family on his mind, he set off to find the butler, Finch. Logan had a family, and they were not the Averfords. Logan's father had been the Baron Emsbury, as his older brother had become upon their father's death. Logan hadn't seen his brother since what they all referred to as "the incident," but he exchanged letters with him and his wife Ellen, and with Mrs. Lenders, Grace's governess, who assured him that the girl was happy and thriving in the care of Logan's brother and his wife. Grace would be nearly a young woman now, twelve years old, the same age her mother had been when Logan had first kissed her.

"Mr. Finch." He turned the corner, glad to find the butler at his desk going over an inventory list so that Logan could put thoughts of family behind him and delve back into his work.

Acknowledgments

My thanks to everyone on the Sourcebooks team for making me feel welcome and helping me to be at my best, especially Deb Werksman and Eliza Smith for their brilliant suggestions, Susie Benton for her patience, and Danielle Dresser for her enthusiasm. As always, I'm grateful to Stephany Evans for believing in me. And to my friends Julia London, Dee Davis, and Julie Kenner for always telling me what I need to hear and for the peach vodka; I love you, man.

About the Author

Sherri Browning writes historical and contemporary romance fiction, sometimes with a paranormal twist. A graduate of Mount Holyoke College, Sherri has lived in western Massachusetts and greater Detroit, Michigan, but is now settled with her family in Simsbury, Connecticut. www.sherribrowningerwin.com.